Praise for

T.M. LOGAN

'Logan belongs in the top echelons of British thriller writers'
Sunday Express

'Logan is the master of the everyman thriller . . . be prepared to sacrifice sleep'
Gillian McAllister

'Thriller of the year? This is the thriller of the decade'
My Weekly

'Clever, taut and twisty . . . full of tension and gasp-out-loud moments'
Claire Douglas

'An irresistible premise, a nerve-shredding nightmare . . . T.M. Logan has done it again'
Chris Whitaker

'Absorbing and tense, fuelled by a very real sense of jeopardy'
Adele Parks

'Assured, compelling, and hypnotically readable – with a twist at the end I guarantee you won't see coming'
Lee Child

'A truly addictive thriller'
Louise Candlish

'Logan is undoubtedly the master of the all-too-believable, it-could-happen-to-me story'
B.A. Paris

'Darkly gripping and addictive . . . T.M. Logan at his absolute best'
Sarah Pearse

'Even the cleverest second-guesser is unlikely to arrive at the truth until it's much, much too late'
The Times

T.M. Logan is a *Sunday Times* bestseller whose thrillers have sold more than three million copies in the UK and are published in 22 countries around the world. *The Holiday* was a Richard and Judy Book Club pick and was adapted into a four-part TV drama, as was *The Catch*. Formerly a national newspaper journalist, he writes full time and lives in Nottinghamshire with his wife and two children.

Also by T.M. Logan

Lies
29 Seconds
The Holiday
The Catch
Trust Me
The Curfew
The Mother
The Dream Home
The Daughter

THE
WEEKEND
T.M. LOGAN

ZAFFRE

First published in the UK in 2026 by
ZAFFRE
An imprint of Bonnier Books UK
5th Floor, HYLO, 105 Bunhill Row,
London, EC1Y 8LZ

Copyright © T.M. Logan, 2026

All rights reserved.
No part of this publication may be reproduced,
stored or transmitted in any form by any means, electronic,
mechanical, photocopying or otherwise, without the
prior written permission of the publisher.

The right of T.M. Logan to be identified as Author of this
work has been asserted by him in accordance with the
Copyright, Designs and Patents Act, 1988.

This is a work of fiction. Names, places, events and
incidents are either the products of the author's
imagination or used fictitiously. Any resemblance to
actual persons, living or dead, or actual
events is purely coincidental.

A CIP catalogue record for this book is
available from the British Library.

Hardback ISBN: 978-1-80418-521-6
Trade paperback ISBN: 978-1-80418-522-3

Also available as an ebook and an audiobook

1 3 5 7 9 10 8 6 4 2

Typeset by IDSUK (Data Connection) Ltd
Printed and bound by CPI (UK) Ltd, Croydon CR0 4YY

The authorised representative in the EEA is
Bonnier Books UK (Ireland) Limited.
Registered office address:
Block B, The Crescent Building
Northwood, Santry
Dublin 9, D09 C6X8
Ireland
compliance@bonnierbooks.ie
www.bonnierbooks.co.uk

For the Coffeys, the Lloyds, the Harmers and the Cruickshanks, with whom we have shared many adventures in Yorkshire and Derbyshire

Money doesn't change men, it merely unmasks them.

—Henry Ford

It's the hardest thing in the world. To hold a person's hand as they die.

The helpless agony as their grip slackens to nothing in that final surrender, to watch through your tears as the light fades from their eyes, as they draw their last rattling breath. To tell them it will all be OK, that help is on its way, even though you know there is nothing that can be done to save them.

Even though you know, with stone-cold certainty, that you've played a part in bringing them here.

PART I
THE CAVE

1

We're lost.

Jason won't admit it but I can always tell by the way he walks: striding ahead, full of confidence as if he *absolutely* knows where he's going.

Somewhere up on the last ridge, we should have followed the trail back down across the valley. I'm sure of it. But my husband insisted there was another great viewpoint above Scar House Reservoir before we looped back towards Pateley Bridge. Then the clouds had closed in and before we knew it we were in the middle of a December downpour, hard, cold rain driven by the lashing wind. The path all but vanishing beneath our feet. For an hour after leaving the pub, the six of us had been chatting as we walked along, but now the rainstorm has forced us into a trudging single file, heads down, gloved hands in pockets.

Jason is up front, Christian close behind him. The other three are strung out along the ridge behind me.

I check my watch. Alfie should be home by now, assuming his bus was on time. He'd promised to send a message as soon as he got back but of course when I pull out my phone there is no signal up here in the Dales. Raindrops spatter the screen and I push it back into my pocket. I tell myself again what I'd thought earlier, waving my son off as the bus pulled away. *It's normal that a seventeen-year-old wants to go home and spend New Year's*

Eve with his mates. He doesn't want to be stuck here in the middle of nowhere with his mum and dad and their boring friends. He'll be fine.

We walk on through the rain.

My trousers are soaked, sticking to my thighs, and the rain is starting to leak through the shoulders of my jacket too, the collar damp against the back of my neck. I think about the warm cottage, the log fire, a hot shower and change of clothes. A gin and tonic. A couple of hours from now we'll be back, warm and dry, getting dinner ready and preparing to celebrate New Year's Eve.

Ahead, Jason abruptly turns off the ridge and starts to scramble down a track to the right. It's barely a track at all really, more like an indentation made by sheep, a narrow gouge in the rough grass that winds through rocky outcrops on its way down into the valley below.

'Careful,' he calls over his shoulder, most of his face hidden by his hood, his voice half swallowed by the wind. 'It's a bit treacherous.'

'Are you sure this is the way?'

He gives me a thumbs-up and continues to pick his way down the hillside. Christian follows him and I do the same, sliding on wet grass and almost losing my balance. I turn again to check the other three are following us before gingerly making my way after my husband. There are no signs, no way markers, no wooden posts telling us where the path leads. No other people either. Just sheep that scatter when we come near. I make my way slowly, carefully, feeling the old twinge in my knee that always comes back on a steep downward slope. In places, the path widens into a stretch of deep mud and I almost get stuck a couple of times trying to make my way through. Jason and Christian are already way ahead of me.

After a few hundred metres, the track levels out a little and turns rocky, until it reaches a stream rushing through the bottom of the valley. On the far side, the thin gravelly path turns to run alongside the water, curving up and around into a stand of trees.

My husband is on the other side of the stream. It's only a couple of metres wide but it's moving fast, icy storm run-off rushing over the rocks. He gestures to a handful of flat stones standing proud of the water, holding out his hand so I can reach for it as I make my way across.

'You OK?' he says.

I give him a nod. 'Where's my brother?'

He indicates a dark opening in the rocks ahead, where jutting slabs of limestone form the opening to some kind of cave. Christian is sheltering just inside, perched on a large rock, drinking from his water bottle. I follow Jason in, grateful for the respite from the downpour. He reaches into his jacket and pulls out a map.

The mouth of the cave is dark and cold but mercifully dry. I move further back, the roof lowering as I go, until I find a rock that's flat enough to sit on. My flask is still half full and I take a long drink, the water ice-cold against the back of my throat, wishing I'd filled it with hot coffee instead.

Kat comes to sit down next to me, pushing her hood back to reveal her dark blonde hair, wet strands stuck to her forehead.

'Are we properly lost, Helen, or what?'

'I think that depends.'

'On what?'

I indicate Jason and Christian poring over a map at the mouth of the cave, talking in low voices about a way back to where the cars are parked.

'On how you define "lost".'

She studies them for a moment, pulling out her own water bottle. 'So, basically we haven't got a bloody clue where we are?'

'Sounds about right. I suppose the weather hasn't helped.'

My best friend shivers. 'I'm *soaking*. Yuk. I seriously need some new hiking stuff.'

'Me too,' I say. 'At least we've walked off a few mince pies, I suppose.'

We sit in silence for a moment, staring out at the valley floor. Outside the daylight is already failing, dimming towards dusk.

'Have you got any signal?' She takes out her iPhone as I shake my head, checking the screen. 'I've not got a single bloody bar.'

'Have to wait for Wi-Fi back at the cottage.'

She snorts, stands up. 'Assuming we don't spend all night out *here*, roaming the moors. Better go and see if the boys have figured out the way back.'

Miranda finally appears at the mouth of the cave, her bright orange Lululemon coat blazing like a beacon in the murk. She takes out her phone and starts to film a selfie video with the curtain of rain as a backdrop. Dev trudges in last, producing a vape from his pocket and taking a deep puff. He goes to stand with Jason and Christian.

I reach for my flask again, but in the gloom of the cave my fingertips brush the metal and then it's toppling backwards, rolling away down the back of the rock I'm sitting on with a *ting-ting* of bouncing metal. I grab for it but my hand only scrapes against rough stone and then it's gone, disappeared into the dark at the back of the cave where the sloping ceiling meets the floor. *Shit*. I can't see anything down there. I stretch forward over the boulder and reach down as far as I can, hard rock digging into my ribs. Nothing. Damp stone. Pebbles, then something softer, plant-like.

The flask can't just be *gone*. That's ridiculous. And it's the brand new one Jason got me for Christmas, I only took it out of the box a week ago. I reach again, touching blindly in the dark, hoping to feel smooth metal. Still nothing.

From outside, a crack of thunder.

The air in here is musty and damp, wet stone and freezing earth. As my eyes start to adjust, I can make out a deeper darkness between the back of this rock and the wall of the cave. I shift forward, taking my phone from my pocket and flicking on the torch. Light floods the space and shadows dance against a gap, a fissure in the limestone, maybe a foot wide. Big enough for a bottle to roll inside. I stretch forward again, my head almost in the fissure now, my arm inside the gap up to the shoulder, blindly reaching into the hole.

I'm about to give up when my fingertips brush against something.

But not metal. Not my water bottle. This is thick material, man-made, something solid beneath it.

My mind instantly forms a picture: *a sleeve, a jacket, a hiker dead beneath these rocks. A caving trip gone wrong.*

I flinch back.

'Guys?' I say it over my shoulder but my voice is drowned out by another rumble of thunder rolling across the valley.

No one responds.

Get a grip, I tell myself. *The gap is too narrow for a person to be stuck in there.* I reach in again, more slowly, and feel a surge of relief as my fingers close around the neck of the Chilly's bottle. I drag it out and drop it down behind me.

For a second I think about leaving the other thing behind. Whatever it is, it's nothing to do with me. But if it *is* a person, their family needs to know. I need to do the right thing. Can't just leave them. *Oh God, maybe a child could have crawled in here?* I take a deep breath and reach in again, my hand finding a strap, pulling on it, trying to ease it free.

It doesn't move.

Kneeling down so I can brace myself against the overhang, I try again. This time it starts to shift but it's heavy and bulky as I drag it towards me, my knuckles scraping on stone.

It's not a jacket, not a sleeve. Not a child or a mummified caving enthusiast.

It's a backpack. Much bigger than my own little hiking pack; two or three times the size. It only just fits through the fissure in the cave wall. With a grunt of effort I heave it all the way out, onto the slab of rock next to me.

'Guys?' I say it louder this time, but it's lost again in the white noise of the rain. The three men are still intent on their map, Jason holding his own phone torch up now to illuminate the folded paper. Miranda is perched on a rock, compact mirror in hand, checking her mascara hasn't run.

Only Kat turns towards me, a half-eaten banana in her hand.

'You OK, Helen?'

'I found something.'

She comes over, taking another bite of the banana.

'What the hell?'

'It was down there.' I nod towards the gap. 'Shoved all the way in.'

The bag is black, expensive-looking, but mildewed slightly around the edges. I pull the zip all the way open, from one side to the other, and fold down the front to reveal the contents.

The breath freezes in my throat. For a moment my brain won't register it, refusing to process what I'm looking at.

Inside the bag is more money than I've ever seen in my life.

2

The stacks of banknotes are packed neatly together, laid side by side in a solid slab and bound together with bands of white paper. All of them wrapped tightly in thick clear plastic and sealed like a huge cut of prime steak.

The thick plastic wrapping is smooth and dry to the touch, like a sheet of polythene. Some kind of heat seal has been applied to the end and it feels completely airtight, watertight, protected from the elements. My phone torch throws a bright white light onto the contents beneath the plastic, on familiar images of the monarch repeated in columns and rows, familiar symbols and shiny silver holograms, familiar text that says 'Bank of England' in a swirling old-fashioned font.

Only the colour is unfamiliar: a shade of pinky-red. Cerise, or maybe fuchsia.

I'm not sure when I last saw a fifty-pound note – on the rare occasions I use a cashpoint now I only ever get tens and twenties. Thinking about it, I'm not sure if I've *ever* seen a fifty, up close, let alone the neat stacks bundled together in this package. There must be hundreds upon hundreds of notes. *Thousands*. The notes in my purse mostly sit there for weeks on end, untouched, while I pay for everything on my card.

Kat comes closer, taking a last bite of the banana before shoving the skin into a pocket of her purple waterproof.

'Holy shit,' she says, through a mouthful of banana. 'Holy *shit*, Helen! What? How did you . . .'

'It was down there.' I flash my phone torch towards the narrow fissure behind the rock. 'My water bottle rolled into the gap, I was reaching for it and my hand brushed against the rucksack.'

She gives a hoot of hysterical laughter. 'Seriously? That is mad. Jesus, are they . . . fifty-pound notes?'

I grip the end of the plastic and haul the slab of banknotes up and out, laying it on top of the backpack. It's surprisingly heavy, a few kilos at least, like several reams of A4 paper stacked together. I lift it, hold it in both hands and turn it over. The other side is made up of stacks of slightly smaller twenty-pound notes, similarly bound.

'It looks like thousands,' I murmur. 'See how thick the whole thing is?'

Kat bends over to study the slab of money more closely, her hand running over the plastic and a broad grin on her face. 'Looks like drinks are on you tonight.'

The shadows around us deepen. I look up to find the other four have joined Kat and are standing around me in a semicircle, blocking almost all the natural light from the mouth of the cave.

Jason speaks first. 'What the hell?'

I repeat what I've just told my best friend, showing them the gap that is all but invisible unless torchlight is shone directly onto it. Jason studies the package as I talk, turning it over in his hands, an expression on his face somewhere between awe and disbelief.

Dev produces a heavy black torch from his backpack, switching on a piercing white light. I stand to make space for him as he lies down and flattens himself against the rock, inching downwards and twisting his body until his face is at the entrance to the fissure. He shines the torchlight inside.

Kat crouches down beside her husband. 'Anything else in there, love?'

'Not that I can see.' His voice is muffled, distorted by a flat echo. 'The gap goes back four or five metres then it looks like there might be a drop-off at the end.'

'No dead bodies? Wild animals?' She looks up with a grin. 'Michael MacIntyre not waiting to jump out on us, is he?'

Dev says something to his wife in reply but it's lost to the void inside the fissure.

Jason has been checking the empty backpack, feeling inside the other pockets, opening three other zips including one that is tucked into the lining at the back.

'There's no ID, nothing except this.' He hands me a slim curl of crumpled paper, yellowed with damp. 'Can you read that?'

I hold my phone torch up to the strip of paper. It's a till receipt from a shop called Hike!, an NE postcode that I'd guess might be Newcastle. A single item that looks like 'Bpack 45L Hawk Outdoors'. The wash of light from my phone is not strong enough to make out much else.

'Probably a receipt for the bag.' I tuck it into my pocket. 'Need to look at it under a proper light.'

Christian edges closer, holding a hand out. 'May I?'

I shrug. 'Be my guest. It's not mine.'

My brother lifts the package up, cradling it in the crook of his arm like a new father on the maternity ward. Examining it, turning it over, peering at the tightly wrapped bundles inside.

'It's got a heck of a weight to it.'

'Do you think it's real?'

'Hard to be sure,' he says. 'In this light.'

'It *looks* so real though, the holograms and—'

Movement flashes across the front of the cave. We all flinch as one, turning to see who has joined us in taking shelter from the storm. Christian, I notice, pulls the package quickly against his stomach, shielding it from view.

But it's just a pair of sheep, coats sodden with rain, their hooves clattering on the rocky path outside.

'Jesus.' Jason blows out a heavy breath. 'Thought we had company.'

Christian lowers the money, squinting after the retreating animals. 'No one else is out walking this afternoon. They all checked the weather forecast.'

Miranda takes the package from her husband and turns it over.

'I feel like I've robbed a bank,' she says with mock seriousness. 'Should really be in one of those black briefcases though, like in a movie.'

Dev hauls himself backwards away from the fissure and scrambles to his feet, brushing dust and dirt from his jacket. Miranda holds out the plastic-wrapped money to him as if it's his turn in a game of pass-the-parcel. But he holds his hands up as if in surrender.

'I don't want to touch it.'

'Why not? It's only money.'

'I just don't.' He runs a hand over his bald head. 'In fact, I reckon we should put it back.'

Jason looks up at his friend, a half-smile on his face.

'You're joking, right?'

'No. We should put it back in the bag, zip it up, shove it back in that hole where you found it. Forget this ever happened.'

'Are you *mad*?' Jason is frowning hard. 'We can't just put it back.'

Kat is nodding. 'Agreed,' she says. 'Dev, we can't leave it here, darling.'

'Why not?'

'Because . . .' Jason gestures at the package in Miranda's arms. 'I don't know. Because we know it's there, now. We can't just pretend Helen didn't find it. Could be evidence of a crime, or something, it could help the police crack an unsolved case.'

'Whatever it is, it's nothing to do with us. Nothing good can come of it.'

'But . . . mate, we can't just *leave* it here. We need to report it, do the right thing. We can't just pretend we never found it.'

'There's no police station within twenty miles.' Dev checks the heavy Garmin on his wrist. 'And it's going to be dark in less than an hour.'

'Then we take it back to the cottage for tonight and hand it in tomorrow. Count it, at least. Aren't you even curious to know how much it is? There might even be some ID tucked inside there, something to say who it belongs to.'

'Whatever,' Dev says. 'I'm not carrying it.'

He pulls up his hood and heads back out into the rain.

3

Jason flicks through another bound stack of fifty-pound notes and puts it on top of a growing pile on the heavy oak table, scribbling a number on the envelope beside him.

We're back in the cottage, a fire starting to take hold in the hearth, logs crackling and popping and yielding a pleasant warmth to the air. A faint, dry hint of woodsmoke is a welcome contrast to the dampness of the day outside. It's almost fully dark out there now, the big bay windows a black reflection of the six of us gathered in the oak-beamed kitchen-diner. We stand, or sit, watching my husband do the count. Mugs of coffee or hot chocolate to warm us up, except for Jason and Christian who have already started on bottles of Black Sheep ale. No one has said anything for a few minutes – no one, it seems, wants to break Jason's concentration. A strange, loaded silence has settled on the room as if we're waiting for news of a birth, a death, a diagnosis.

Our boots are in the porch but all of us are still in our hiking clothes, no one wanting to shower and change just yet. Not until we know exactly what we've found.

My phone beeps with a WhatsApp message, the sudden vibration making me flinch. A text from Alfie, finally checking in after we'd put him on the bus earlier.

Home ok can you send £ in case I need to get Uber later pls?

I put my mug down on the worktop and type a message back.

Will do. Make sure you eat before you go out, pizza in the freezer. Don't be too late and stay with Isaac and Alex. Have fun. Text me when you get back home later, we'll see you teatime tomorrow. xxx

As soon as I've sent it, I remember something else.

And don't forget your front door key! xxx

A moment later, the beep of a reply.

K

Which I had learned, bringing up teenagers, was an abbreviation of OK. When typing even two letters took too long.

I open my banking app and send him £15 to cover an Uber in case he needs one to get back from the New Year's Eve party at Grace's house later. We've agreed that Isaac and Alex can sleep over at ours tonight, which feels like safety in numbers rather than Alfie going back to an empty house. I switch back to WhatsApp, hoping he might send another message. But there is nothing more from my younger son. Nothing from my older one either, although he's spending New Year with friends in London and is even worse at communicating than his sibling. I slip the phone back into my pocket. It will be our first New Year's Eve without any of the children here and it feels strange, bittersweet, another of life's milestones quietly passing us by. Christian's teenage daughter from his first marriage had opted to spend the holiday with her mum in Harrogate instead; Kat and Dev's daughter is older and had flown the nest a couple of years ago, moving down south for work.

'All right,' Jason says finally, putting the last stack of notes on top of the pile. 'OK. I think I've got it.'

'So?' Kat says. 'How much?'

He takes a deep breath, blows it out. 'One point six million.'

'Shut up!' She's shaking her head, but smiling at the same time. 'No way.'

Christian has watched the count intently from the other end of the long wooden table.

'Say that again.' He gestures with his bottle of beer. 'Are you sure?'

'Counted it twice,' Jason says. 'One million six hundred thousand pounds. Exactly one point three million in fifties, three hundred K in twenties.' He holds up a neatly bound wad of notes about three inches thick. 'The fifties are bound up four hundred to a stack, so each one of these little bundles is twenty grand.'

He raises an eyebrow, throws the bundle to me in a gentle underhand. I catch the money awkwardly, the solid density of it heavy in my palm.

'There you go, Helen,' he says with a grin. 'Early birthday present.'

'Haha.' I run a thumb over the top note, the hologram, the crown, the indentations of the image. There is a real weight to it, a heft, a promise of something. It was ridiculous, really – this little bundle of polymer paper was enough to cover two years of university tuition fees for Alfie, halve the debt he'd be saddled with when he finished. Enough for the deposit on a flat for Noah, our eldest. Enough to pay for the private care at home that my mum so desperately needs. And there were dozens of stacks like this sitting on the table in front of me. I turn it over in my hand, the shiny polymer smooth against my fingertips. 'Alfie messaged me, by the way.'

He returns his attention to the money on the table. 'Huh?'

'He got the bus home earlier, remember? Going out with his friends tonight?'

'Oh.' He nods, distractedly. 'Yeah, right. Good. Good.'

He picks up two more stacks, tosses one to Kat and one to Miranda.

'There you go, ladies, get yourselves something nice!' He laughs. 'God, I feel like Al Capone.'

Kat's smile is broad, her eyes dancing with light. 'It's just mad,' she says. 'It's so crazy. None of the guys at work are going to believe this.'

Miranda holds the money flat in the palm of her hand, as if weighing it. 'So is it real then, or not?' She turns it so the hologram catches the light, a shiny rainbow of reflected colour. 'It feels real.'

Christian leans across the table and picks up a stack for himself, sniffs it, riffles the end of the stack like a deck of cards.

'You notice something?' He pulls out a single note and rubs it between his thumb and forefinger. 'None of these notes are new, you can tell they've been in circulation for a while. All of them have the Queen Elizabeth design.' His voice is slow, serious. Deliberate. 'Which means they were all minted pre-June 2024, when they switched over.'

Kat looks up at him, thoughtful. 'So?'

He shrugs. 'Just an observation, that's all. A fair amount of hard currency used in my business – the building trade still likes cash.'

Dev, I notice, has not moved from his position near the kitchen door. Arms crossed, leaning against the worktop, studying his phone with a deepening frown.

'And what if it's fake?'

Christian swigs his beer. 'What if it isn't?'

'Well according to this,' Dev says, 'it's an offence to have custody of fake currency, under the Forgery and Counterfeiting Act 1981. Punishable by up to ten years in jail.'

'OK,' Jason says slowly. 'But we haven't got *custody* of it. We just *found* it and we're looking after it until we can hand it over to the relevant authorities, or whatever. And the police stations around here are all shut this evening.'

I put the stack of fifties down on the pile with the rest, and pick up the black backpack lying discarded on the floor.

'Maybe we should check the bag again.' I pull the main zip all the way open then check all the other pockets. Even though it's been stuck in a cave for however long, it's not in bad condition. 'See if there's anything we missed.'

The receipt is in my jacket pocket, where I'd left it earlier. Under the bright light of a table lamp I study the crumpled strip of paper again. The ink is fading but I can make out the shop name and a postcode – 'Hike! NE1 5DN' – and one item, which had been bought with cash for £54.99: 'Bpack 45L Hawk Outdoors'. Which matched the label inside this bag. According to the Maps app on my phone, it's an outdoor activity shop in the middle of Newcastle close to the train station. Which didn't really tell us anything, apart from the fact that the backpack had been purchased there. Maybe the bag was only used once, and that's why the receipt was still inside? Perhaps it was bought solely for this. Whatever *this* was.

I relay the information to the others, handing the receipt to Kat. 'Can you read that date at the bottom?'

She pushes her glasses up onto her forehead, holding the paper up close.

'It's too faded. Looks like, maybe, third of June? Or is that a five? An eight? Can't make out the year at all.'

She holds it out to Dev who takes it from her reluctantly, as if it's some kind of unexploded device.

At the big kitchen table, Miranda is leaning in with her phone to line up a picture of the money until Jason holds a hand to block the camera.

'What are you doing?'

'Just a quick pic for the grid,' she says. 'This is *so* crazy.'

'No pictures.'

'Don't be such a grump.' Miranda grins. 'It's like we're bank robbers or something.'

'We shouldn't post any pictures of it. Not to socials, and not sent to anyone else.'

She frowns. 'What? Why not?'

'Handling it, touching it, is one thing – we can tell the police we were just checking what we'd found, so we don't waste their time. But I don't think it's a good idea to broadcast it to anyone else.'

She gives him a good-humoured shake of her head, but slides the phone into her pocket. 'You're getting awfully paranoid in your old age, Jason.'

My husband doesn't reply. Instead, he takes a long drink from his bottle of beer and gets up to pull the big floral curtains closed, shutting out the night. Even though we're in a cottage at the end of a long lane, on the edge of a tiny village in the north Yorkshire Dales, and nothing bigger than a fox is likely to pass by.

Dev is still by the kitchen door and has returned to looking at his phone.

'This is all academic though, right? It doesn't matter whether we take one picture, or a hundred, or none. Because we're going to hand it in tomorrow.'

Miranda reaches up to the cupboard and starts taking out tall champagne flutes, lining them up on the counter side by side.

'Whatever you say, Dev. Personally I think we should *stop* talking about money now and get our New Year's Eve celebrations back on track.'

Dev continues as if he's not heard her. 'The nearest police station is Skipton but that doesn't look like it's manned on bank holidays. Then there's one in Catterick, which is a bit of a detour from our route home. Or we wait until we get back to York.'

No one says anything. He looks around the room, first at his wife, then at Jason.

'We *are* going to hand it in, right?'

'Yes,' I say. 'Of course.'

Miranda extracts a bottle of Prosecco from the fridge, brandishing it by the neck. 'Who's for bubbly?'

There are murmurs of agreement from around the room, a general rumble that sounds like consensus. Either for a stop-off at the police station, or Prosecco – or perhaps both.

'Good,' Dev says. 'That's settled then. We hand it in on our way home tomorrow.'

'Fair enough,' Christian says, cracking open another beer. 'But how about we have some fun with it first?'

4

Jason studies his cards again, cupped tightly beneath his hand. He looks suddenly younger than fifty-three, alive and energised by the game. His dark hair is peppered with white and there are frown lines, worry lines too, the strain of work and money and life in general, the toll taken by his job over the years. But in this moment his features are lit with youthful enthusiasm – the man I had first met all those years ago.

'Raise.' He pushes two stacks of banknotes forward onto the dining table, drawing my attention back to our group of friends. 'Another forty thousand.'

The box of cheap plastic poker chips that we normally use lies untouched, unopened, on the windowsill. Instead, we're using the money I found in the cave. It had felt wrong when Christian first suggested it, none of us quite sure whether he was serious or not. Then a second bottle of Prosecco was opened, followed by a bottle of wine with dinner, and before long Kat was nodding and laughing in agreement at the idea of using cash instead of chips for our annual card game. Their enthusiasm was infectious – or perhaps it was the alcohol – but either way we let it happen.

They divided the money into six equal shares and gave us two hundred and seventy thousand pounds each, leaving the stacks wrapped in their tight paper bindings. Dev had been reluctant to even handle the money at first, worried about leaving fingerprints and telling us about the number of people he'd seen convicted on fingerprint evidence in his role at the magistrates' court. Kat rolled her eyes and gave her husband a playful hug, until eventually he had hunted out a box of blue nitrile gloves from the cupboard under the sink, where all the cleaning stuff was kept, and insisted we all pull on a pair before playing the game, like surgeons at the operating table. His objections had slowly quietened as the flow of beer and wine and Prosecco drew us closer to midnight; Miranda had already peeled her gloves off, telling us she had an allergy.

Most of the cash now sits in a messy pile in front of Jason.

My husband has always been a good poker player, able to tread the fine line between confidence and caution, able to read people. He knew when to bluff, when to be aggressive and when to back off. It was fun watching him – everything about our traditional New Year's Eve game was for fun. We never used real money, but the overall winner would get a free lunch at the pub tomorrow when the rest of us would cover their bill.

It was a tradition that went back almost as far as our New Year trips together, when our children were small and we realised that finding a babysitter on the last night of the year was nigh on impossible. So why not go away together instead? Three couples plus kids, an Airbnb in Grassington or Hawes, Hebden or Bainbridge, bracing winter walks, country pubs and a big meal altogether to see in the New Year.

After finding somewhere different each year for the first few years, we had settled on this place as our favourite when Alfie was still in primary school and couldn't believe we'd find anywhere better. It was an extended cottage that retained all of its original charm, with oak beams, a lovely open fireplace and a stone-walled courtyard big enough for three cars. It also had en suite bedrooms for all the couples, a games room for the kids and a modern kitchen that was much better than our own cramped kitchen-diner back in York. There was a traditional village pub within walking distance and beautiful walks around Nidderdale and Wharfedale were only a short drive away.

It was a home from home, and we'd grown to love it.

A round of poker had become our tradition too, a game just for the grown-ups once all the children had finally gone to bed. I return my attention to my own cards and my fast-dwindling stack of cash.

We've always played a version of the game called Texas Hold 'Em, where instead of having five cards in your hand you only have two – but you can combine them with five common cards that are laid face-up in the middle of the table. We knew each other's tics and tendencies, from the most carefree and reckless player – Miranda – to the conservative, middle-lane-of-the-motorway style that Dev had adopted years ago and never seemed to alter. I was somewhere in the middle, I supposed.

True to form, Miranda had been the first to be knocked out, throwing all of her money into an escalating and ultimately hopeless bluff against Jason. In the half-hour since, she has busied herself by taking over the party playlist of eighties and nineties music and topping up everyone's drinks. Dev had been the next to go broke before Kat was knocked out soon after.

I drag my attention back to the poker game. I'm down to my last three stacks of the dark-pink notes, my last sixty thousand.

Which sounds ridiculous.

My last sixty thousand.

Because it *is* ridiculous.

Not for the first time, I catch myself smiling at just how surreal this whole day has become. A New Year's Eve celebration we have held a dozen times before, friends and family I know better than anyone in the world, a game we have played more times than I can possibly count – all of it given a surreal, fantastical sheen by the 1.6 million pounds spread across this weathered oak dining table.

Jools Holland is on mute on the TV in the corner, playing piano surrounded by a big band as the clock counts down towards midnight. But no one is paying much attention to him.

Christian matches Jason's bet, turning over his cards to reveal a pair of queens.

Jason turns over a pair of kings with an apologetic shrug. 'Sorry,' he says.

Christian grins and pushes three bundles of fifties towards my husband. 'No you're not, you jammy bugger.'

Jason pulls the money in, adding it to the piles already in front of him. He holds one of the stacks in his hand, tracing a thumb over the hologram on the top note. 'How confident are you,' he asks, 'that this stuff isn't fake? That it's the real deal?'

All eyes at the table turn to my brother, waiting for him to answer. My tall, outgoing, generous younger sibling, who has the kind of casual confidence with money that makes people assume he was born into it. Rather than the reality: which was that he had worked harder than anyone else I know, six or seven days a week for years, decades, grafting through the wreckage of his first marriage to make his way in the world and build his air-conditioning company from the ground up.

'Actually,' Christian says, 'it's incredibly difficult to make counterfeit currency now. The amount of detail on each note, the number of anti-fraud measures built in by the Bank of England. Holograms, unique patterns and special inks. It's virtually impossible. Back in the day, when I was starting out in the building trade, you'd occasionally see fakes being passed off as the real thing, or a half-dozen real notes on top of a stack of bogus ones. But even then they were fairly easy to tell apart if you could sit down and look at them closely for a minute – and that was before all the extra security measures they've added.'

Jason's eyes drop to the mound of cash piled in front of him. Over the course of an hour of poker, he has accumulated most of it: well over a million pounds.

Kat circles the table, refilling glasses from a newly opened bottle of Malbec.

'Shit,' she says. 'And there was me hanging onto the idea that this cash was fake. This is well and truly bonkers.'

To hear it spoken aloud, that we were very probably playing with real money suddenly feels irresponsible, inexplicable, maybe even illegal. If a stranger were to walk in through the door now, what would we say? How would we justify it?

It is as if Christian's announcement has cast a spell over everyone in the room, a momentary glimpse behind the curtain of everyday life.

Jason is the first to snap out of it. 'Guys?' His voice is soft, as if he's talking to someone who's just woken up. 'Real or not, shall we crack on and get this game finished? It's not long till midnight. Helen, I think it's your turn to bet.'

I return my attention to the poker game, check my cards briefly – a three and an eight – before pushing them back to the dealer with a sigh.

'Fold.'

I'm almost broke, close to being knocked out, with enough to play two or maybe three more hands at the most.

Once again, I'm hit by the surreal details of this evening's game. The sums on the table seem to have changed the definition of *almost broke*. I remind myself that I still have *sixty thousand pounds sterling* on the table in front of me, nearly twice my annual salary. How quickly we have become used to handling this cash, this windfall, this ridiculous amount of money.

Jason and Christian continue betting on this latest hand of poker and my attention drifts to the coffee table where Miranda has produced her own set of cards, insisting on giving Kat a Tarot reading. My sister-in-law has been drawn to the mystical, holistic side of life as long as I've known her – reiki healing and crystals, Tarot and mindful meditation – and liked to give at least one of us a reading when we got together at New Year. In truth, she always seems much more engaged in this deck of cards, with its colourful painted images and Roman numerals, than with our traditional poker game.

For a few minutes, as I'm dealt one dud poker hand after another, I tune into the Tarot reading instead. Miranda makes a display of the oversized cards, explaining each one as she lays them out.

'The Tower,' she says. 'Harbinger of distress and ruinous change. Something coming which will alter the trajectory of your life.'

Kat pulls a face, the faint wrinkles around her eyes deepening. 'Maybe . . . tomorrow's hangover?'

Miranda takes no notice, relating details of the Tower's wider significance and all the different meanings attached to it. I hadn't realised how knowledgeable she is, and it's weirdly fascinating to hear her describe all the links to astrology, the elements, the zodiac. After a moment she reaches for a second card and lays it face up with a flourish. It's a picture of a man in medieval garb with a pack on his back, striding forward, head up, a cliff edge right by his feet.

'The Fool.' She taps it with a delicate forefinger. 'His appearance can mean a risk, a new beginning, a new cycle in your life – *or* that you're about to embark on an unwise journey. Can also signify extravagance, delirium, intoxication.'

Kat takes a generous sip of her red wine. 'He sounds like my kind of guy.'

My brother gives me a gentle nudge to bring me back to the poker game. I take a peek at my newly dealt cards and find the ace of diamonds and the five of spades. An ace gives me a fighting chance, at least, unless one of the other two also has an ace with a higher second card. A glance at my husband yields nothing, no hint of confidence or fear, his face the smooth calm of a lake on a still summer's day. He's always been unreadable, playing this game, his expression as blank as a sphinx at the other end of the table. He could have anything, literally any two cards and I'd be none the wiser.

Although it doesn't really matter. I already know what I have to do: as soon as I saw my ace, I knew that folding this hand was not an option. At this point in the game, it's all or nothing. Death or glory.

I just need to keep pretending I'm betting with paper, or pennies, or battered plastic chips.

Instead of two years' wages. Instead of private nursing care for my mum, or enough to cover all of Alfie's tuition fees and living costs at university. Instead of a way for his older brother to climb that first impossible step onto the property ladder, rather than spending the next decade saving for a deposit.

Just keep telling yourself: it's not real. And even if it is, it doesn't belong to me. It's just our usual New Year's Eve game, same as always.

On the coffee table, Miranda lays the last of the three Tarot cards face up next to the Tower and the Fool.

'The Devil,' Kat says, studying the image of a horned god of the underworld, complete with bat wings and cloven hooves. 'That can't be good.'

Miranda touches the image with the fingertips of her left hand, a chunky diamond on her ring finger catching the light. 'Negative energy,' she says. 'Seduction by the material world and all its pleasures. Obsessive, secretive, addictive behaviours. A life lived in fear.'

Kat sits back in her chair, blowing her fringe off her forehead. 'Blimey,' she says with a snort. 'Well, there you have it: Happy New Year, everyone.'

I return my attention to the poker, taking another peek at my ace to make sure I haven't imagined it.

Heart drumming in my chest, I push all my remaining cash forward in one final bet.

'All in.'

5

Christian doesn't hesitate.

'Call,' he says, matching my bet.

Jason calls as well, tossing more money onto the table in front of his cards. I notice, with a jolt, that he's no longer wearing the disposable nitrile gloves. His hands are bare, the thin blue rubberised gloves dumped in a deflated heap next to his growing pile of cash. I catch his eye, holding up my own gloved hand. But he simply picks up his discarded pair with a shrug, showing me a long gaping hole torn open along the index finger, before returning his attention to the poker.

Dev has already offered to shuffle and deal for the three of us left after being knocked out earlier. Kat comes over from the coffee table, resting one hand on her husband's shoulder as he deals in his typical methodical, deliberate way, laying out the first common cards face up in the middle of the table. The ten of clubs, queen of hearts, ace of spades. Each of us can use them, in addition to the two cards we've been dealt.

'All right then,' Dev says. 'This could be the decider, we've got a hundred-plus grand in the pot.'

Without hesitation, Christian pushes the last of his money forward.

'All in,' he says quickly. 'Another seventy-six thousand.'

Jason considers him for a moment and then calls again, matching the bet.

With Christian and I already fully committed, there is no more betting to be done. Time for the three of us to turn over our cards and hope for the best.

Kat claps her hands together.

'Looks like we have a showdown! Come on then, let's see what you've all got. Don't be shy now.'

With a rueful grin, Christian turns over a two and a six. Almost the worst two-card combination you can get in this game.

'God knows what I was doing.' He shrugs, reaching for his whisky. 'Hoping you'd throw in the towel, I suppose. Good luck, you two.'

I feel a bubble of hope as my husband turns over an eight – only for it to pop as he turns over his second card. An ace.

As the dealer, Dev surveys our cards, all of them now face up on the table.

'Christian,' he says, 'I'm afraid you need a miracle at this point, mate. But Helen is still in it, still alive. Her and Jason both have a pair of aces, plus a queen and ten from the common cards. If one of the last cards is a high one, it's a split pot.'

Which means my husband and I will share the winnings and I will live to fight another day – or another hand at least.

Dev lays the fourth common card in the centre. A jack. It means my brother is dead in the water, but my husband and I now have the same hand: a pair of aces plus three high cards. The only card that can win it for Jason now is one of the remaining eights, to give him a second pair. A five, on the other hand, would give *me* a second pair – as well as the money in the pot. My galloping heartbeat kicks up another notch.

Dev plucks the final card from the deck, taking his time to maintain the suspense before laying it with a flourish alongside the others. And sure enough, as if it was always destined to be, as if I've cursed my own luck just by thinking it, the last card is—

The eight of spades.

Which gives my husband a winning hand.

'Oh, *crap*,' Kat says, looking at my cards again. 'Bad luck, love.'

'It's OK,' I say with a shrug. 'Well done, Jason.'

As is our custom, he extends a hand and I reach over to shake it. Then he and Christian shake, the winner acknowledging both runners-up. Dev starts to shovel all the stacks of notes down the table towards my husband.

Christian reaches for his glass again, holding it up in a salute.

'We have a winner. Cheers, mate, well played as ever.'

Jason sits back in his chair, a slow smile spreading across his face. 'Cheers. Good game, everyone. Wow. All this in front of me is pretty intense.'

With the rest of us watching, he piles it up into a foot-high mound of notes in front of him. Then encircles the stack in his arms as if he's giving it a hug, grinning like he's just won the World Series of Poker in Las Vegas.

'So,' Christian says, 'how does it feel to be a millionaire?'

Jason's smile broadens. 'Pretty good,' he says. 'Pretty bloody good, Christian, actually. It's a definite rush, for sure.'

'Just imagine taking all that to the bank on Monday morning.' My brother chuckles, reaching for the bottle of red wine to refill Jason's glass. 'Ha! The teller would probably have a heart attack.'

'And then call the manager,' Dev mutters into his beer. 'Who would probably call the police.'

Kat leans over and takes one of the stacks from Jason's pile, fanning herself with the wedge of tightly bound notes.

'Imagine it though,' she says. 'How crazy would that be? Imagine looking at your banking app and seeing all that in your account. That big number.'

'Crazy,' Jason says, still smiling. 'Definitely.'

'It would be a pretty good start to a week though, wouldn't it? Or a New Year.'

My best friend is turned towards Jason but she's actually talking to all of us, I realise. All except Miranda, who has disappeared back into the kitchen.

Dev is shaking his head. 'We've discussed this already, babe,' he says. 'We've agreed what we're going to do tomorrow.'

Kat lays the brick of money back onto Jason's stack of notes.

'I know,' she says. 'I know. Just thinking aloud, that's all. Just a teeny-weeny thought experiment as we say goodbye and good riddance to this crappy year. Your wife's allowed to think out loud, isn't she?'

'Depends what you're going to say.'

I look between the two of them. Husband and wife. There had always been a balance there, a ying and yang, Dev's solid reliability steadying the scales against Kat's spontaneous, fun-loving side. They were the very definition of *opposites attract* but they were still together, still married after more than twenty-five years. It shouldn't work, but it did. Sort of. It was only occasionally that the balance got out of whack, normally when alcohol was involved.

In a way, it was the same with our friendship, Kat and me. She always wanted to be the last one to leave every party, while I had always made sure we had a taxi home. She brought me out of myself – and I kept her from flying too close to the sun. We were good for each other, always had been.

I glance up at the old wooden-framed clock on the wall. 'Only ten minutes of the year left, K. You'd better be quick with your thought experiment otherwise we're going to miss the fireworks on TV.'

'Right,' Kat says. 'So, you know the best two words in the English language, don't you?'

Miranda emerges from the kitchen with a bottle of champagne held aloft in each hand. 'I know this one!' She holds the bottles out, dark green glass still beaded with a chill from the fridge. 'The best two words are *Moët* and *Chandon*!'

Christian takes one of them from her and begins to peel the foil off the cork. 'Technically that's French, darling.'

Dev shrugs. 'Stay honest?'

'Good guess, love,' Kat says. 'But the best two words are actually: *What if.*'

Jason leans forward, placing a palm over the bound stacks on the table in front of him. 'As in ... what if it hadn't rained this afternoon, and we'd never taken shelter in that cave?'

'Not ... exactly.'

'So tell us.'

Kat gestures towards the money with her glass of wine. 'What if we have another think, a *proper* think, about all of this before we do something we might regret.'

'Such as?' Dev crosses his arms. 'What is it you think we might regret?'

Kat looks at each of us in turn, her eyes shining with excitement. My brilliant best friend, as close to a sister as I've ever had, this girl I'd first met when I was eleven years old, the two of us a pair of misfits starting at a school we'd both hated.

'What if ... ' she says. 'We *don't* hand it in tomorrow. What if we just keep it instead?'

6

There is an uneasy silence.

'Keep it?' Dev says, his tone heavy with disbelief. 'You're not serious, babe?'

'Just for a few days at first,' Kat says. 'See if we can find out anything about what the money was doing there. Give us time to do some proper Google searching – see if we can find information online about how it got there, maybe a news story. For all we know, it might have only been there a week or two, it could relate to something still happening now. *Or* it could have been there years. Forgotten about.'

'This is a bad idea.' Dev's face is flushed beneath his beard, the redness already creeping up to the tips of his ears. 'I keep saying it but no one's bloody listening to me. I'm a magistrate, for Christ's sake. A city councillor, I've got a reputation.'

'Hear me out, love,' his wife says. 'Just for a minute, OK? First thing we can do is double-check if Christian is right, if this stuff is real. And there's an easy way to do that.'

'How?' I say. 'Surely you're not going to ask a bank to test them?'

'Don't need to. At the shop, we've got UV lights next to all the tills, detector pens as well to use when someone pays with a twenty-pound note or bigger.' To the rest of us, she says: 'You stick it under the UV light and if it's real, it shows up the security features embedded in the note.'

I still hadn't really got used to the idea of my best friend as the manager of a shop, even a high-end boutique in one of the city's trendiest areas. She had spent so long working a corporate job, heading up the compliance department of a financial services company, that it seemed part of who she was. Until one day, not long after her fiftieth birthday, she had simply announced that she'd had enough. Enough of the rat race. Enough of targets and strategy meetings and key performance indicators, enough of the corporate grind and office politics and all the bullshit that went with it. That she didn't want to die in harness, slogging on for another decade towards retirement in a job that had already consumed the best part of her adult life.

She had mentioned it once or twice over the years but it had always been vague, a Friday night pipe dream after a crap week at work. I'd never believed she'd actually make the jump – until she did. She'd shifted from job to job for a year before retraining and landing a job at Bliss, getting promoted to manager earlier this year. She was good at it too, business savvy and popular with customers and staff alike.

Dev had supported her decision, had sat down with her to look at their finances, figured out how they could economise to take account of her salary drop.

But now he's shaking his head. 'And then what?' he says. 'Just for the sake of argument, Kat, say they look legit under the UV. How does that change anything?'

Christian jumps in before she can answer. 'Then,' he says, 'we can decide what to do based on *facts* rather than guesswork. If we're absolutely sure it's real, then at least we know what we're dealing with.'

'Ten minutes ago you were assuring us it *was* real.'

'But that's just my opinion, Dev. What we need is something more solid than that, more definite, rather than making a knee-jerk decision here, tonight, when we're all a bit drunk and we don't have the first idea what we're actually dealing with. So we can make a fully informed decision.'

'We know enough,' Dev says. 'We know it doesn't belong to us, that it's someone else's money. It could belong to *anyone*, and the odds are it belongs to someone you don't want to get on the wrong side of. And we know what the right thing to do is – we all agreed we were going to hand it in, didn't we?' He looks around the room, his voice taking on a harsher tone. 'Didn't we? Or did I imagine that? Did I just dream it?'

'No,' I say quietly. 'You didn't imagine it, Dev.'

'What if they're dangerous?' he says. 'The people who stashed that money? What if they come looking for it?'

Christian grips the champagne cork, turning the bottle gently with his other hand. 'How?' he says. 'How could they possibly connect it to us?'

Dev raises his hands. 'I don't know – and I'd rather not find out, if it's all the same to you.'

'Look,' Christian says. 'The genie's out of this particular bottle now, ladies and gentlemen, whether we like it or not. We can't put it back in. And three wishes from the genie makes one per couple. By my maths, each of those wishes is worth a shade over five hundred and thirty grand.'

Miranda puts a manicured hand on his shoulder. 'Ignore my husband, Dev, he's had too much to drink. You know what he's like, always gets a bit silly on New Year's Eve. Always pushes things too far, but he knows ultimately, when all is said and done, we need to give it back. Don't you, darling?'

With a percussive *thwup*, Christian eases the cork out of the Moët and begins to fill half a dozen tall flutes lined up on the side table.

Kat leans forward in her chair, firelight dancing across her features. 'The thing is, who would we even be giving it back to?'

I shrug. Of all the questions we have, this seems like one with an obvious answer. 'The police. Right?'

'But they're not going to give it back to its original owner, are they? They'll just put it in some evidence box in a dusty warehouse. It will never get used, no one will ever benefit, it will just sit there on a shelf until it's shredded or forgotten or no longer legal tender. And it's not *their* money, it doesn't belong to them.'

'It's not ours either.'

'Look,' she says. 'The way I see it, Helen, this is like buried treasure. Like a chest of gold that we've found on a desert island, or something. It's finders keepers, isn't it?' She looks around the room, until her eyes find her husband. 'Like, if we'd been out with our metal detectors and one of us had found a hoard of old gold coins buried under a tree, that would be ours, wouldn't it? We wouldn't be thinking we had to give it up straightaway.'

'That's *completely* different,' Dev says. 'If it's an archaeological site, then all kinds of different rules apply. The 1996 Treasure Act, for starters.'

Kat shrugs. 'I don't see how it's any different. It's just a matter of timing, that's all. Whether it was put there ten years ago or a thousand, it's the same principle. We found it, why shouldn't we keep it? What's that saying ... possession is nine-tenths of the law?'

Dev is still shaking his head. 'I'm talking about what's *right*,' he says. 'Can't believe we're even having this conversation.'

I'm about to agree with him when Miranda interrupts.

'Guys,' she says, her cut-glass accent softened by alcohol. 'Listen, we shouldn't fall out about this on New Year's Eve, it's bad luck. It's not even as if it's a lottery win, is it? We're not talking *life-changing sums*, are we? Fifty years ago it might have been, but not now. And anyway, life's too short to care about money.'

Jason's voice is low. 'Easy for you to say.'

Miranda turns to him, her face caught between a smile and a frown. Unsure whether he's just teasing or if there is something darker behind his comment. 'What's that supposed to mean?'

'You don't care about money,' he says quietly. 'Because you've always had it.'

'I *beg* your pardon?'

'From your folks, your family, from Christian, you've never had to worry about it, never had to think about it because it's always been there. The rest of us do, though. Paying the bills, the mortgage, keeping a car on the road, paying for your kids, your parents, trying to make some headway and never really getting anywhere. You might not have noticed but there's been a cost-of-living crisis for the last God-knows-how-many years.'

She glowers at him, her face twisting with anger. 'Piss off! You think I'm some bloody trust-fund princess, do you? It's all coming out tonight, isn't it? Just because you're a social worker, you think you know it all, that I live in some ivory tower?'

He holds her gaze. 'No,' he says calmly. 'But I see things every day at work that you have no idea about. The way some people have to live. And I think a share of this money might not be much in the grand scheme of things to you, with your dad being a lord or a baronet or whatever he is. But it would be to me and Helen, to our family. To the rest of us.'

Miranda sways unsteadily towards him and for a moment I think she might throw her drink in his face. I move to intercept, like a parent trying to keep two warring siblings apart. Under normal circumstances, Jason wouldn't have made a comment like that, a barb so likely to wind her up – he might have *thought* it, or aired it with me later when we were alone, rather than saying it in front of everyone.

But these were not normal circumstances. Too much alcohol had been consumed, empty bottles already clustered several ranks deep around the bin. And if we weren't careful, tempers were going to boil over.

'Hey,' I say. 'Listen. Let's not fall out, OK? Like Miranda says, we should be celebrating tonight, looking forward to a new year, right? All that good stuff.' I look around for inspiration, for a way to settle this fairly, properly, and get it over with. 'Why don't we . . . I don't know, shall we vote on it? Go with the majority?'

Dev gives an angry shake of his head. My husband shrugs, while Miranda returns her attention to the wire-wrapped cork of the champagne bottle.

'Let's just see,' I say. 'Let's have a show of hands. Who thinks we should hand the money over to the police tomorrow?'

Dev immediately raises his hand high, as if he's trying to hail a black cab on a busy street.

'And who thinks we should hold onto it for a few days instead?'

For a moment no one moves.

Then Kat tentatively raises her hand.

A moment later, Christian follows suit.

Miranda is struggling with the other bottle of champagne, while Jason's eyes flick from one person to the next.

Dev is shaking his head. 'This isn't going to work. Everyone has to vote one way or the other, otherwise it's not fair.' He points at me. 'Helen, you agree we should take it back? You already said—'

'Hang on,' says Jason. 'There's a better way of doing this.'

'What do you mean?'

'A fairer way.' He clears his throat. 'So everyone can say what they *really* think.'

7

'A secret ballot,' Jason says. 'That's what we should do. So none of us are influenced by the others.'

'Seriously?' Dev says. 'Why? It doesn't need to be secret, we all know each other, we've been friends forever. I don't mind who knows how I vote.'

'But the point is we all make our *own* decision, rather than being influenced by partners or anyone else. This has to be an individual decision. For all of us.'

Dev looks confused. 'We agreed earlier what we were going to do, so what difference does it make?'

An awkward silence settles on the room.

After a moment, Dev breaks the spell. 'This is mad.' He turns to his wife. 'Kat? Don't tell me you agree with this?'

She shrugs. 'A vote seems like a fair way to do it.'

'But we already *decided* this afternoon that we were going to the police station to hand it in.'

'When?' Jason says. 'When exactly did we decide that, mate? Did everyone genuinely have a say?'

My husband's voice is quiet but determined, a definite edge to it now. His clash with Miranda a few moments ago still hangs in the air like smoke; I don't like it when he gets combative like this.

Dev raises his hands with his palms up.

'So, you want to do this now?' His voice is taut with exasperation. 'After we've been drinking all evening, no one's even sober enough to drive, are they? Let alone make a sensible decision.'

'Why not?' Christian says. He's finished filling the six tall glasses with champagne, and now hands one to each of us in readiness for the midnight toast. '*In vino veritas*, and all that.'

Jason pulls open drawers on the old Welsh dresser to look for pens while I go into the kitchen to fetch the old wire-bound notebook pinned to the noticeboard. The pages are short and narrow, like a till receipt, bearing the masthead of a local steam railway attraction for tourists. I tear three of the small pages out and rip each page in half to make six pieces about equal in size, then drop them all into one of the large clay-fired mugs from the rack on the kitchen side.

Back in the lounge, the rest of them are already waiting expectantly, each clutching a pen or pencil from the motley collection Jason has found in the Welsh dresser.

I put the mug down in the middle of the dining table. 'One piece of paper each,' I say. 'Just write "Hand in" if you want to do that, or . . . I don't know . . .'

'"Keep",' Kat adds, 'if you think we should hang onto it for a bit.'

Dev is the first to reach into the mug for a slip of paper. Everyone else duly follows suit and I take the last one, holding it close and testing the old blue felt-tip pen that was handed to me. I glance up at others, four of them either writing or already folding their pieces of paper.

All except my husband, whose biro still hovers over the paper held close to his chest.

He sees me watching and we lock eyes for a moment. He raises an eyebrow just a fraction, his mouth forming a silent word. *What?* Under normal circumstances I think I'm pretty good at reading my husband, but in this moment it's as if we are back playing poker, his face unreadable again.

I shrug and write two words quickly on my slip of paper. *Hand in.* Then fold it three times and drop it into the mug.

Jason is the last of us to add his vote to the rest. 'Helen found the money,' he says. 'She should be the official returning officer.'

He pushes the mug across the table towards me. No one else makes a move or contradicts him, so I reach over and pick out the first piece of folded paper from the mug, opening it out to reveal two words in heavy capital letters.

I hold it up. 'Hand in.'

The next vote says the same but in flowing lower case handwriting, a little heart drawn over the 'I' instead of a dot.

I fish a third vote out of the mug. It's been folded incredibly small and tight, into a pea-shaped ball.

'Keep,' I say, showing the rest of them the unfolded paper.

On the fourth slip I recognise my own handwriting, turning it for all to see and dropping it onto the right-hand pile: three votes now for handing the money in. Only a single solitary vote on the other side to keep the money.

Dev, leaning on a chair back, takes a long swig of his champagne.

'Three minutes to midnight,' he says. 'And it looks like sanity has finally returned. Thank Christ for that.'

A glance at the muted TV in the corner shows crowds of people on Victoria Embankment in London, two hundred miles south of here, a countdown clock in the corner showing 11.57 p.m. But no one in the room is watching the TV screen. They're all watching me.

I pull out one of the two remaining slips.

Keep.

Only one vote left.

'Three against two,' I say. 'It's down to the last vote, then.'

I reach in and take the last piece of paper, suddenly unsure of what I want it to say. A few moments ago there had been certainty, as I wrote those two words on the paper, that we should hand over the money. But now, at the point of deciding to do just that, I can feel my resolve wavering. The piles of cash are still stacked haphazardly at Jason's end of the table. Far more than I've ever seen in my life – or ever will see again. Had I made a mistake?

My hands feel suddenly clumsy, fingers fumbling to unwrap the last slip of paper. I drop it to the table, pick it up, unfold the last crease and look at what is written inside: heavy, confident capital letters in handwriting that I recognise instantly.

'Well?' Christian says. 'Don't keep us in suspense, sis.'

I turn it around, hold it up for them all to see.

Keep.

For a moment there is silence around the table. The only one to react is Dev, who shakes his head and mouths something under his breath. Frankie Goes to Hollywood plays softly on the Bluetooth speaker: 'Two Tribes', which seems weirdly appropriate in this moment.

I add the last vote onto the left-hand pile.

'So it's a draw,' I say. 'Three votes each way. Now what?'

'There has to be a casting vote,' Dev says, rubbing a hand over his bald head. 'We need a tiebreaker.'

'Who?' Christian says.

'Helen.' Dev points at me. 'She found the bag. It should be her call what we do with it.'

'*Me?*' I put a hand on my chest. 'God no. I'm not deciding.'

'Then what do you suggest?'

Jason sits forward in his chair, arms crossed on the table. 'There's a simple answer,' he says, waiting as all eyes turn towards him. 'We just toss a coin. Heads we keep it, tails we hand it in.'

Dev stares at him. 'Are you actually insane? How much have you had to drink? You want to toss a coin for one and a half million quid?'

'It's no more crazy than scribbling on slips of paper. And no one can argue with the result.' He sips his champagne. 'Have you got a better idea?'

'Yes,' Dev says. 'We vote again in the morning, in the cold light of day. When everyone's sober.'

'So we vote again, and keep voting, until you get the outcome you want? Is *that* what you mean?'

'This is nuts, mate, and you know it. If you're going to toss a coin we might as well use bloody Tarot cards or read the tea leaves left in the pot this morning.'

Miranda frowns at him. 'Actually, Tarot is an ancient practice that goes back hundreds of years. And if any of you had listened to my reading, I can guarantee we wouldn't be in this mess now.'

Dev's eyes rove around the room, looking for an ally, until they land on me.

'Helen,' he says. 'What do you think?'

'It's a pretty arbitrary way to decide,' I say. 'Isn't there an alternative?'

Christian sighs. 'Let's just make a damn decision, for God's sake. Get it over with.'

'Ditto,' Kat says.

Jason produces a handful of change from the pocket of his jeans, plucking out a fifty-pence piece and holding it up between a thumb and forefinger.

'Heads we keep the money for . . . let's say, a fortnight, see what we can find out? Tails we hand it into the police on our way home tomorrow, and that's the end of it. OK? Agreed?'

No one says anything more. My husband seems to have found a solution to this impasse that nobody actually wants.

'Agreed?' he says again.

'Sure,' Kat says.

On the big TV in the corner, the countdown to midnight hits zero as the hands of Big Ben's clock align and the first fireworks arc up into the sky over London.

Jason flicks the fifty-pence coin up with his thumb. It rises high, the silver catching a glint of light from the fire, before falling back into his palm. He slaps it quickly down onto the back of his left hand and stands there, the coin still covered, looking at each of us in turn.

No one speaks. All of us leaning slightly forward to get a better look in the soft, shadowy light of the cottage.

Jason lifts his right hand to reveal the coin.

The queen's head stares back at us.

8

Sunday, New Year's Day

The other side of the bed is empty when I wake up.

Steam rises from a mug of tea on the bedside table, sunlight glowing golden around the edge of the curtain. From somewhere out in the fields, higher up the hill, comes the faint bleating of sheep. Apart from that – silence. No traffic noise. No neighbours. No barking dogs. Even though we'd been visiting the North Yorkshire moors for years, the blissful quiet struck me every time after the bustle of city life. More than once, Jason and I had talked about what it would be like to have a place of our own out here, somewhere we could come whenever we wanted to, a little bolthole in the Dales that we could share with friends and family. Although it had only ever been a pipe dream, because we'd never be able to afford to—

Memories of last night crowd in.

The money. The vote. The toss of a coin.

I reach over for the mug and take a first tentative sip of tea. For a moment I wonder if perhaps I've dreamed the whole thing, if it was all some kind of delirious fiction, one of those incredibly detailed dreams that feels so authentic, so visceral, that you wake up in tears or ecstatic or terrified before the real world reasserts its grip.

One point six million pounds.

It wasn't a dream.

Reality settles in as I sit up, the dull pounding of a New Year's Day hangover at the back of my head. I swallow a couple of paracetamol with another sip of tea and unplug my phone, which has been charging overnight on the side table. Switching it out of silent mode, I squint at the screen to check for messages from the boys on WhatsApp, Snapchat, Instagram or text. For any small scrap of evidence that they had survived the night unscathed and were not in a hospital bed, not in a cell or slumped in a shop doorway somewhere. Jason always told me I worried too much about our boys when they were growing up and he was right, I supposed. It had eased a little as they got older and bigger and more independent, but I knew it would never leave me. Not entirely – and I didn't want it to.

There are no messages from my sons. So I fire off a quick 'are-you-alive?' text on our family WhatsApp group.

Happy New Year @Alfie @Noah! How was your night? xx

It's still early for the weekend, not even eight o'clock, and I don't expect they'll be back in touch for a few hours yet. A little light stalking of Noah's Instagram doesn't reveal anything from last night either. I send a happy New Year message to my mum too, telling her I'll phone her later and come round to see her tomorrow. Even though I know that she probably won't reply and even if she does, she won't remember it when I speak to her this evening.

I leave the Messenger app until last. There is a single notification but I already know who it will be from before I even click on it: a variation on the same message that arrives on 1 January and my birthday every year.

Hey Helen, Happy New Year to you and yours, I hope you are really well ☺ Wishing you a peaceful, prosperous and healthy year and all good things, it would be lovely to catch up at some point. Take care, A xx

Reflexively, I glance up at the door in case Jason is coming in, wondering if this might be the year when I just ignore Alexander's message, unfriend him, block and move on. Knowing that I won't *actually* do any of that. Instead, I go through the usual delicate balancing act of being polite to a long-ago ex-boyfriend without saying anything he might take as encouragement. To be civil while keeping him at arm's length, trying to draw a line under it rather than get into a conversation.

Happy New Year to you too, Alexander! Hope you're well. H

I hesitate before adding one kiss after my initial. Then delete it, add it, and delete it again before pressing *Send*, a weird flush of guilt warming my neck. I put the phone face down on the bedside table and run a hand through my tangled hair.

More memories of last night return as I pull on my dressing gown and go into the en suite to splash water on my face. The tension in the living room, a loaded silence after Jason had revealed the coin on the back of his hand. Dev refusing to talk about it anymore, stalking off to bed muttering, 'This is bullshit. It's absolute bullshit.'

It had been a quarter past midnight before I realised we hadn't even joined hands for the traditional rendition of 'Auld Lang Syne', but by then it felt too late and it didn't seem right anyway, with only five of us left in the lounge. Kat had followed her husband up with a rueful smile and I'd gone to bed not long after, with Miranda already snoring lightly on the sofa. Jason and Christian in the two big armchairs by the fire, tucking into the single malt, talking in low voices so as not to wake her.

It had been a strange end to a strange day.

We spend the morning tidying the cottage and packing the cars up before a short drive takes us to Wharfedale, for a final six-mile hike over the top of Hebden Moor and down into Grassington for lunch at the Black Swan. Yesterday's thunderstorm is a distant memory and the weather is glorious: perfect blue skies over the Dales, pale green hillsides still glittering with fresh dew.

At the top of the last hill there is a collection of rocks, a jumble of mammoth-sized slabs dumped there by some long-gone glacier and weathered smooth in the millennia since.

My mobile buzzes in the pocket of my waterproof jacket as the others start heading down the hill. There's a message in the family WhatsApp group from Noah in London, just the letters *HNYx* and a kissing-face emoji. Nothing from his younger brother yet. I take a selfie with the view in the background and send it in reply – both boys regard my 'mum selfies' as *the ultimate in cringe* and I like to lean into that every so often.

'Stunning, isn't it?' Dev has also hung back and is standing close beside me, taking in the view. 'I could look at this all day.'

'It never gets old.' I glance at the others, who are already making their way down the hillside. 'Always wish we could stay a few more days, really.'

'It's not too late, you know.'

I snap another picture, capturing a pair of shaggy-coated sheep in the foreground.

'Not too late for what?'

'To talk some sense into them. Your husband, your brother, convince them that we need to do the right thing.'

I turn to look at him properly for the first time today, at the tension etched into his features. The bags under his eyes, the greyish tinge to his pale brown skin.

'Dev . . . you might be overestimating my powers of persuasion.' I tuck the phone into my pocket. 'My brother doesn't listen to anyone. Never has.'

'With Jason, then. You have to try.'

I return my attention to the sweep of moorland on the other side of the valley, where a flock of sheep are being expertly corralled by an energetic black-and-white collie.

'The thing is,' I say, 'I think Jason's already convinced himself that he *is* doing the right thing. The smart thing. Or that they're one and the same.'

'Look—' Dev's voice takes on a more urgent tone '—in my job, I can't say to students, *It's OK for you to ignore* that *part of the Highway Code as long as you follow* this *other part*. They have to follow *all* the rules of the road, same as everyone else. That's what I told your Noah when I was teaching him. And the law's the same – we don't get to pick and choose which laws we obey and which we ignore.'

'So tell the rest of them that,' I say. 'At lunch, before we head home.'

'I already tried last night and they won't listen to me. Miranda's away with the fairies half the time. But they'll listen to you.'

'Have you tried talking to Kat about it?'

He snorts. 'You know what she's like better than anyone. The more you push, the more she digs her heels in.'

I couldn't disagree with him on that. It was one of the things I had always loved about Kat because it translated into a fierce loyalty to her friends too – no matter what.

'Maybe once we're home,' I say. 'And it's just the two of you, she'll see sense.'

As if she's heard us – even though we're way out of earshot – Kat turns and waves us forward.

'Come on you two!' Her shout echoes, rolling across the valley. 'Last one to the pub buys the first round!'

Dev raises a hand to acknowledge her, before facing me again.

'We have to do something,' he says. 'Before it's too late.'

He turns and heads down the path, walking quickly to catch up with the others.

9

The Black Swan is warm and busy when we arrive, hikers and tourists mingling with a handful of locals, a hubbub of chatter contained by an oak-beamed ceiling and foot-thick stone walls. There are menus but none of us need to look at them because the pub only ever does roasts on New Year's Day – chicken, beef or lamb – plus a single grudging vegetarian option.

'Right,' Christian says after we're settled into a windowed alcove and shrugged off our coats. 'So after last night, we thought it would be good to set a few ground rules.'

Whether by chance or design, Jason, Christian and Kat have sat down together on the same side of the rectangular table, on the padded bench seat in the window. My husband, my brother, my best friend: almost certainly, the three who had voted to keep the money. Facing the rest of us in high-backed wooden chairs on the other side. Dev on my right, his arms crossed in front of a pint of zero per cent pale ale, and Miranda on my left, checking her makeup in a small compact mirror.

'*We?*' I say.

Christian indicates my husband. 'Jason and I just had a bit of a chat on the walk. About what to do next.'

With the waitress busy at the bar, my brother dives in as if he's chairing a board meeting at his company, talking quietly so as not to be overheard. The first of his ground rules is that we were not to mention the money to *anyone*. Not to children or parents, not to other friends, not to colleagues. Neither were we to text or email anyone about it, or leave any kind of electronic trail. We would pool our online research efforts to see if anyone could find a clue as to how the money had got there, and he shows us how to switch to private browsing so none of it would be saved in the search history. We would see what we could discover, and reconvene in person in twelve days' time – Friday week – to compare notes and make a decision.

I sip my lime and soda as Jason takes over, encouraging us to download a messaging app called Signal. It's more secure than other apps, he says, and it's better to separate it from all the day-to-day messaging stuff – less chance of a misdirected message landing in the neighbourhood chat, the Thursday book club thread or the choir group by mistake. But even on Signal, he suggests, we shouldn't use the words 'money' or 'cash' or talk about amounts – a code word would be better. His eyes wander over to the bar, a row of taps for the draught beers. The nearest one has the image of a handsome white dog. *Timber Wolf*.

'Timber,' he says. 'So if you have an update, you say, "I've found something out about the timber."'

Beside me, Dev snorts.

'Of *course*.' His tone is heavy with quiet sarcasm. 'Code words and private browsing and end-to-end encryption – it all sounds *completely* legit.'

Kat puts her hand over his. 'Nothing wrong with being careful, D.'

'No offence,' Miranda says. 'But this is all a bit cloak and dagger, isn't it? A bit ridiculous? Considering we haven't actually—'

'Hi!' Christian's tone is strident, cutting his wife off. 'We're all ready to order I think.' He's smiling broadly and I turn to see the waiter has arrived, a white-shirted twenty-something with a blond mullet and a nose ring.

After taking our order – three chicken, two veggie, one beef – there is a long moment of silence as the young waiter retreats towards the bar, weaving between tables and a pair of black Labradors sprawled by the open fire.

'As I was saying,' Miranda continues in a stage whisper. 'Before I was interrupted. This is all a lot of fuss considering we haven't actually done anything wrong?'

'*Yet*,' Dev says under his breath.

Christian holds a hand up. 'Sorry, darling. You're quite right, but it doesn't hurt to exercise a little caution from time to time. We're just covering ourselves, that's all.'

Dev, with the look of a man who senses this might be his last chance, seems to take the question as the cue he's been waiting for. He launches into a terse, hushed monologue arguing that while we're still here within a few miles of the cave we can just about justify what we've done. But taking the money home will be crossing a line – even though it's only fifty miles back to York, it's a big step away from 'concerned citizens doing the right thing'. He insists it's not too late to return the backpack to the place we found it and walk away clean.

'Walk away?' Jason says quietly. 'From a once-in-a-lifetime payday? Without even taking the time to think about it?'

'A payday is earned. You work for it.'

'Then this is even better, isn't it?'

Dev slumps back in his chair, throwing me a pointed look that says, *I told you so*.

I lean forward onto the table. 'I suppose there's still one other big thing,' I say. 'That we haven't really discussed.'

'*Obviously*,' Dev snorts. 'The fact that it belongs to someone else.'

'Well, yes,' I say. 'There is that, too. But what I mean is, I still don't see how the money can even be used. Even if we wanted to. It's just . . . too much. Too obvious. If it was some mysterious bank transfer that would be one thing. But this is bundles of actual cash.'

I realise, as I say it, that *this* is the thing that has kept me from getting as wound up about the situation as Dev clearly is. Because when it comes down to cold, hard reality, I don't really see how we could even make use of such a large amount of cash. Not anymore. Not when most transactions now are cashless and the idea of walking into the bank with a bag full of fifty-pound notes seems so . . . ridiculous.

Kat raises an eyebrow. 'There are ways, Helen,' she says. 'You just have to know what they are. Trust me.'

She exchanges a brief glance with my brother and I wonder if Christian has had 'a little chat' with her too, as he'd done with my husband on this morning's walk. Christian had trained as an accountant before starting his own company and he has a familiarity with tax and banking and regulations that are far beyond my grasp. Kat knows that language too, having spent time working in financial services and dealing with government watchdogs and financial regulators on a regular basis, before she packed in the corporate life for a change of direction.

In terms of her old job, I still have only a fuzzy idea of what it had actually entailed, but she has always been smart and had climbed a long way up the ladder before deciding to jump off.

'Ways?' I say. 'Like what?'

Christian holds a hand up. 'Let's cross that bridge when we come to it, shall we? *If* we come to it?' He finishes the last of his Guinness. 'Right, another round?'

We hug our goodbyes in the car park of the Black Swan and head back to York in a three-car convoy. I drive, while Jason scrolls on his phone as we pass by Fellbeck and Brimham, on our way east and south towards home. My thoughts turn to the boys, to my mum, to the Bank Holiday jobs that will need doing tomorrow before we both go back to work on Tuesday.

Jason's phone beeps and he reads out a couple of short messages from Noah, our eldest, who seems to have spent the night on a friend's couch after some kind of falling-out with the landlady of his own flat.

'That doesn't sound good,' I say. 'Is he OK?'

'Says he's fine, just a bit tired.' Jason taps out a response as he talks. 'He'll fill us in later.'

'Anything else from Alfie?'

'Nope,' he says. 'Probably gone back to bed.'

I call my mum on the hands-free but it goes to voicemail. She's not replied to the message I'd sent this morning either, although she'd always been a bit hit-and-miss with replies even before things got bad. We drive on in silence for another few minutes, the road now a single narrow ribbon through an expanse of rolling moorland that stretches away on both sides as far as the eye can see.

Jason puts his phone back into his jacket. 'He was going to take it back, you know.' He stares out of the window. 'This morning, before anyone got up.'

'What?' I say. 'Who?'

'Dev,' he says. 'I was up early because I couldn't sleep, thinking about the money. Came down to the kitchen and he was already there, boots on, map out, shoving the money into the rucksack like he was ready to take it back to the cave.'

It had ended up, instead, in the boot of our old Nissan, after another series of coin tosses over breakfast. Now it was wedged in between the cool box and the suitcases in the back, with an old picnic blanket laid over the top.

'What did he say?'

'Nothing much,' Jason says. 'Just put his jacket on and said he was going out for some fresh air.'

'He wants me to talk to you about it. Talk you around.'

'He's a lovely bloke but he's very set in his ways,' Jason says. 'Needs to loosen up a little bit.'

'Is that what you think about me, too?'

'No,' he says slowly, as if he's choosing his words carefully. 'I think you've always been too hard on yourself, Helen, always made out like you don't deserve the good things, or a bit of good luck, or a little bit of help now and again. But you do, love. You *do* deserve all those things, and more. Much more. I'm sorry I haven't been able to give you that, or at least not yet.' He breaks off abruptly, looking out at the rolling moorland scenery. 'Something like this just takes a bit of getting used to, that's all.'

I keep my eyes on the road as we lapse back into a tense, uncomfortable silence.

The house has a stale, sickly smell of spilled beer, overflowing bins and teenage boys.

When I flick on the light in the kitchen I see why: the table is a mess of cans and McDonald's wrappers, a collection of plastic pint glasses arranged in a triangular shape for an abandoned game of beer pong. Unwashed glasses clog the kitchen side and the sink is stacked full of ketchup-smeared plates. There is something sticky on the tile floor beneath my feet and some kind of wet stain on the white-painted ceiling.

Both cat bowls are empty. As if on cue, Katniss trots into the kitchen with a loud meow that is half greeting, half demand, winding her way around my legs. She pushes up against my hand as I stroke her head, the black fur smooth beneath my fingers. Her sister, Prim, stations herself next to the empty food bowls, blinking up at me with soft green eyes. I open the cupboard and put some dry food down, both of them tucking in immediately, purring as they eat.

Alfie appears at the bottom of the stairs, dark brown hair flattened to one side of his head and his face still creased with sleep even though it's late afternoon.

'Hi, Mum.' He clears his throat, taking a bag from his dad on the doorstep. 'Thought you weren't back till tomorrow?'

'Happy New Year, love.' I pull him in for a quick hug before he can escape. 'Did you have a few people back last night?'

He tolerates the embrace for a few seconds then wriggles out of my grasp like a cat that doesn't want to be handled. My younger son has his dad's height, tall and skinny, his hair short at the sides and long on the top and back in an aspiring mullet, a phase that I can't wait for him to grow out of.

'A few.' He clears his throat again. 'Got kicked out of Grace's early so some of us went to Maccies and then came back here.'

'Did you have a good time?'

'Yeah.' His T-shirt, I notice, is on inside out and back to front. 'It was all right.'

'Have you heard from Granny?' He shakes his head. 'And did you feed the cats this morning?'

'Er, yeah,' he says vaguely. 'Like . . . earlier?'

I go out to help Jason unload the car. Despite only being away for three nights, somehow we had managed to fill the boot and most of the back seat with bags of food, clothes, boots, games, hiking gear and bottles for the recycling bin. We go back and forth, stacking it all in the hall, and it's only as I'm heading back out for a second time that I join Alfie at the boot of the car. He's always been good like that, willing to pitch in and help with the fetching and carrying.

With a sick plunge in my stomach I see that he's picked up the black backpack and is reaching for the zip.

10

I move to grab it out of his hands.

'Let me carry that one, Alfie.'

'This one's mad heavy, Mum.' He shifts to hold it awkwardly in both hands, his thin arms clearly straining with the effort. 'What have you got in here, is it full of the books you took with you and didn't get around to reading? God, how many did you *take*?'

I reach out to pull the main zip shut again. 'I can carry that one.'

'It's OK, Mum. I've got it.' He shifts his grip on the backpack and makes a face as if he's deadlifting a hundred kilos at the gym. 'So did you?'

'Did I what?' I grab the cool box one-handed and hurry after him, adrenaline spiking.

'Read any of them? I was going to borrow that new one you got for Christmas, the Robert Harris one?'

He lowers the bag down among the rest of our luggage with a grunt of effort, and begins to reach around the side for the zip.

'Leave it.' I half drop the cool box onto the parquet floor with a *smack* of plastic on wood, putting my hand on his arm with more force than I'd intended. 'It's not in there.'

'What?' He flinches back. 'What's the matter?'

'It's full of dirty washing. Had to double-bag some of it because there was this field full of cowpats and I slipped over . . . It's all still wet and it stinks.'

He wrinkles his nose, moving his hand away. I reach into my day bag instead, rummaging around until I find the paperback he's asking for. But he gives me a strange look when I offer it to him, nodding towards the bookmark.

'It's OK, Mum. I'll borrow it when you're finished.'

Once the car is unloaded, I lead him into the kitchen and hand him a black bin liner to clear all of the cans, bottles and fast food detritus of his gathering last night. But he looks so tired, so pale from lack of sleep, that I take over after he's dealt with the worst of it. He gives me his best little-boy smile and asks what time dinner will be, before disappearing into the lounge in search of a New Year's Day football game on TV.

I watch him go, feeling a pinch of unease at my deceit. How easily I'd lied to my teenage son to divert his attention from the backpack – and how close he'd come to discovering what was really inside. Jason takes down two mugs from the cupboard and fills the kettle. As it boils, filling the kitchen with noise, we stand close together and talk in low voices about the best hiding place for the money. The garage is not secure enough, the shed likewise even though I do like the idea of it being out of the house. Wardrobes seem a bit obvious and the spare room is out because it's sometimes used by Alfie's friends after a night out, and we can't risk one of them stumbling on the suspiciously heavy bag. The attic seems a good option to me but it's only accessible by stepladder, and Jason says he wants to be able to reach the backpack in a hurry.

'Why?' I say. 'Why would you be in a hurry?'

He shrugs. 'Just like to be able to get it out of the house quickly, if I have to.'

In the end we decide on the king-sized ottoman bed that takes up most of our bedroom. Jason heaves up the heavy frame to reveal the storage space underneath and we shift around some of our summer clothes, making a space for the backpack among the stacks of T-shirts and shorts, sandals and summer dresses. Jason slides the bag in and for a moment we just stare at it, a new addition, an interloper, tucked into a corner of this slightly dusty rectangular space. All that money, under our bed. Someone *else's* money. The whole £1.6 million, minus £140 – two fifty-pound notes and two twenties – that we'd agreed Kat could take away for testing with the UV light at her shop.

Seeing it here in our house, in our bedroom, feels like crossing another line. Another Rubicon, already receding in the rear-view mirror.

Jason sees my expression. 'You want to hear something weird?'

'You don't think we've had enough weirdness for one day?'

He checks the bedroom door is firmly shut. 'Remember that TV show *Breaking Bad*? Walter White, Saul the lawyer, all that lot?'

I shrug. It had been one of Jason's favourite shows but it felt like a long time ago. 'Vaguely.' I gesture at the backpack. 'What's that got to do with this?'

'Remember when he gets his terminal diagnosis, Walter calculates how much his family will need to get by after he's gone? He does the sums and works out how much money he needs to scrape together: seven hundred and thirty-seven thousand dollars.'

'And?'

'In sterling, that's just under five hundred and forty grand.' He can't hide his grin. 'Which is almost *exactly* what our split of this money is. Don't you think that's weird?'

I look from him to the bag, and back again. 'My memory's hazy but I don't remember *Breaking Bad* having a very happy ending.'

'But it's a crazy coincidence, isn't it?'

'I suppose.'

His smile fades. 'You still think this is a mistake, Helen?'

I glance at the door, listening for any movement on the landing outside, any teenage eavesdroppers.

'This is not the sort of thing people get away with in the real world, Jason. They just . . . don't.'

'Is that the main thing you're worried about?' His voice softens. 'If we could be one hundred per cent sure there was no risk, how would you feel then?'

I wonder, even as he's saying it, which of my concerns is now the dominant factor. That it was morally wrong, dishonest, a form of stealing? Or, that we would be found out? Back at the cottage, it had seemed clear-cut, obvious. But now these two strands have become hopelessly jumbled, tangled around each other like creepers twisting around a vine. Now the money was installed in our house, under our bed, I wasn't sure if I knew how to separate them anymore.

'There's always risk,' I say. 'There's risk in crossing the street, nothing is ever one hundred per cent. And with this kind of thing . . . people always end up getting caught, don't they?'

'We're not people,' he says. 'We're *us*. We're smart. And besides, you only *hear* about the ones who get caught. So there's a built-in negativity bias.'

I shrug. 'Meaning what?'

'You never hear about the ones like us, the smart people, because they fly under the radar. It's like . . . when you hear about the so-called "lottery curse", right? All those people whose lives were ruined by winning millions of pounds, who blew it all on drink and drugs or saw their families disintegrate in feuds over the money?'

'If you think we're going to do that, we should *definitely* hand it in.'

'No.' He gives an emphatic shake of his head. 'No, that's my whole point. Because in reality, those "lottery curse" people only make up a tiny proportion of winners. Less than one per cent. But *those* are the stories that sell papers, so they're the ones we hear about – and the press loves them because they make people feel better about not winning – that money can't buy happiness, that it will only ruin your life anyway, and so on. The truth is more than ninety-nine per cent of winners *are* happier after they win – they buy houses for their kids and look after their parents and go travelling around the world, and their lives are better, not worse. It's just that's not a very interesting news story.'

'This is not a lottery win, Jason.'

'But it kind of *is*, though. A modest one.'

I point at the backpack.' And you think *that* will make us happier? Make our lives better?'

'It will give us more options, at least,' he says. 'Give us more ways to be happy, if we want to be. If we're smart about it. You can quit your job, take the time you need to find a better one. We could pay off Noah's student loans, pay off the rest of the mortgage, get your mum the help she needs. We can do some *good* with it, for people who deserve it. And God knows there's little enough of that in the world at the moment.' He takes my hand, gives it a gentle squeeze. 'And besides, Helen, it's not as if we've done anything *wrong* yet. We've not done anything that can't be undone.'

I'm not sure about that. Even the sight of the backpack makes me nervous and I fetch a blanket from the cupboard, draping it over the bag before Jason lowers the frame of the bed, concealing its hiding place.

Downstairs, I put a first load of washing in the machine and slide a frozen pizza into the oven for Alfie's tea, while Jason fills the sink and gets stuck into the washing-up. While waiting for the pizza to cook, I take out my phone and make the mistake of logging into my work emails. My heart sinks as the unread email counter spins up and up until it reaches a grand total of 296 since I logged off and walked out of the office on Christmas Eve. At a quick glance, it looks like maybe half of them are from my boss, Nigel, including a dozen or so sent on Boxing Day and a lengthy back-and-forth trail from New Year's Eve in which he seems to have copied in half the division, red-flagged as *high importance.*

I suppress a curse and click into the latest one, scan down the string of emails and am reminded of Nigel's two key characteristics:

micro-management and a broad-based incompetence. He's a forthright, well-spoken man of a certain age who has somehow fallen upwards, promoted well beyond his ability, adept at scooping up credit that he doesn't deserve while shifting the blame for his own failures. Behind his back he's known by his nickname, The Pigeon, because of his management style: to flap around and crap everywhere, then lose interest while others are left to clear up his mess. Jason has urged me to quit more than once. But the truth is, his job is constantly under threat from council budget cuts and we need at least one of us to have a guaranteed salary. I would struggle to get a PA role that paid as well elsewhere, and to be honest, I don't relish the idea of being back out in the job market at the age of fifty-four.

I log out with a sigh. The return to work on Tuesday will be fun – not.

The phone is still in my hand when it starts to vibrate with an incoming call, the number on the display showing as *Mike P – no.66*. My mum's friendly next-door neighbour.

'Mike,' I say. 'How are you?'

'Hello, Helen.' His voice is clipped. 'Good, thanks.'

'Happy New Year, and all that, is everything all right or—'

'Sorry,' he says. 'I know you're away in the Dales so I wasn't sure whether to ring you, if you'd already be aware, or . . .'

I frown into the phone, moving into the hall so I can hear him better. 'It's fine, we just got back this afternoon. Aware of what, Mike?'

'Oh,' he says, apologising again. 'It's just that there's an ambulance outside Peggy's – I mean, outside your mum's house. Been there for the last fifteen minutes.'

11

My mum is on the kitchen floor when I arrive, propped up against the fridge with her legs straight out in front of her, still in the long brown raincoat she wears for going to the shops. A green-uniformed paramedic kneels by her side, his bulky equipment bag open on the lino beside him. He's laid a blanket over her legs, draped another around her shoulders. I had made the ten-minute drive to her house in five, a rising tide of panic as I dialled her number over and over again on the hands-free. Each call going to voicemail until I turned the corner into her road and saw, with a fresh spike of fear, that an ambulance was indeed outside the three-bedroom semi where I'd grown up.

'Mum!' I hurry into the kitchen and kneel on the cold tile floor beside her, put my hand on hers. Her skin is papery and cool to the touch but she's alive, awake, *thank God*. 'What happened? Are you all right?'

Her eyes swivel towards me, glassy and unfocused. She cradles her left wrist in her right hand, dark bruising already beginning to show.

'Just a silly bump,' she says slowly. 'That's all. My daughter will be here soon, get this . . . all sorted out.'

I swallow the lump in my throat. 'It's me, Mum. Helen.'

The paramedic gives me a summary of what seems to have happened, pointing out the eggs, milk, bread and assorted tins that are spilled across the floor beneath the kitchen table. Mum had tripped over a bag of shopping, he thinks, and either sprained or fractured her wrist, maybe her collarbone as well. But he is most worried about a possible concussion. It was lucky, he says, that a charity fundraiser going door to door had spotted her through the side window and called an ambulance.

I move closer to her, catching the faintest floral scent of Chanel No.5. It has always been her favourite.

'We need to go to the hospital, Mum. So the doctors can take a proper look at you.'

She blinks slowly, the hint of a frown as she stares at me.

'No,' she says. Her voice sounds as if it's coming from a long way away. 'Not yet.'

'This nice man—' I indicate the paramedic '—says you need to go to hospital, Mum. I'll follow you in the car, come with you.'

Her eyes sharpen. 'We can't go until your dad gets back. He's not got his key. He'll be locked out.'

In my chest I can feel something tearing, a familiar wound that re-opens again and again every time we have this conversation. A grief kept raw with repetition.

'Mum,' I say gently. 'He's not . . . Dad's not here, remember?'

The paramedic glances a question at me, a slight lowering of his eyebrows. I give a quick shake of my head in reply.

Mum doesn't seem to notice our wordless exchange.

I look up at the picture on the kitchen windowsill, a shot of my parents at their fiftieth wedding anniversary party. It had been taken in a fancy French restaurant, all of us and the kids gathered around a long table, an afternoon of good food and wine and laughter. My dad had made a speech that was funny and heartfelt, clever and kind – he had always been good at that sort of thing – about how lucky he was to have met my mum, how she used to call him her toy boy because he was a year younger than her. About how proud he was to be celebrating their golden wedding anniversary.

Less than a year later he was dead. A massive heart attack while he was pruning roses in the garden, sudden, unstoppable, unsurvivable.

It was only in the weeks after he died that my brother and I came to realise how much he'd been covering for our mum. How hard he'd been working to disguise her symptoms – thinking for her, organising her daily intake of heart pills, driving her to the GP, taking on all of the cooking and cleaning and shopping, in addition to the gardening and looking after the house. Physically, Mum was still in reasonable shape for a woman approaching her eightieth birthday, if rather unsteady on her feet. But mentally, she'd been slipping away into dementia for a while – a process that seemed to accelerate as she struggled with her grief. Even as she denied it, even as she insisted that she could still cope perfectly-well-on-her-own-thank-you, even as she fell victim to a telephone scammer later that year who had persuaded her to transfer almost all of Dad's life insurance payout to an untraceable account. A sophisticated, convincing fraud that had taken almost all of her savings too. The guilt, the impotent anger that we had not stopped it in time still ached like a shard of broken glass buried too deep to heal.

Mum has good days and bad days, but I am shocked by how much she seems to have deteriorated in even the few days since I'd last seen her.

A female paramedic appears, rolling a stretcher into the kitchen. She's older than her colleague, late forties, and chats to Mum in a warm, no-nonsense Yorkshire way that finally convinces her to make the trip to hospital. As they help her onto the stretcher, I go upstairs to pack an overnight bag for her then come back down to tidy the mess under the kitchen table. A quick check around the house reveals that the back door is unlocked, as is the patio door. The fridge is almost empty, all the bins are full, and there is a load of damp washing in the machine that smells mouldy and stale, as if it's been there for days. I put in fresh washing powder and set it going again, making a mental note to come back and do a proper clean-up tomorrow. Trying to ignore the voice in my head that says: *You're a bad daughter.*

Then I hurry to my car as the ambulance pulls out and accelerates away, silent blue lights throwing ghostly shadows up and down the street.

12

Miranda

Miranda stared at the text on the screen of her iPhone, stomach churning as she read it for the third time. Checking over every word, every detail, to make sure it was all correct. It felt awkward, revealing so much that was personal, opening herself up to total strangers.

It didn't necessarily *mean* anything. Not yet. Not unless she decided to take it further. To actually dip her toe in the water and do something about it.

Even so, it still felt like a kind of betrayal.

She pulled up another tab on the browser and read some of the Frequently Asked Questions, going over how it all worked, how soon you could expect to make contact, how it worked from there onwards.

It wouldn't be her first time – but it had been different, before. Much more face-to-face. Now, first introductions were all online, obviously. There were so *many* to choose from, so many options out there, an endless parade of possibilities. In the end, she had just gone for the one she'd heard of, the one that her friend Louisa had recommended. It had turned out pretty well for Lou, after all. Obviously, Miranda hadn't told anyone what she was planning to do. It was better that way. Maybe she would tell Louisa once things had progressed, but not yet.

Miranda put her phone down on the table, rubbed her eyes.

She didn't *want* to do this.

She wasn't a bad person.

But she had to follow her heart.

No one could hold that against her, could they? And it wasn't as if New Year's Eve had changed anything. The money, the arguments, the mad and bad decisions that had followed, all of it had simply confirmed what she already knew: no one listened to her. No one took her seriously.

Her own *husband* didn't even listen to her.

Well, maybe it was time to find someone who *would* listen to her. Who would be there for her, who would put her interests first. Who would make time for her.

Miranda picked up her phone again and scrolled down, the pad of her delicate index finger flicking to the bottom of the screen.

She read the words one last time and clicked *submit*.

13

It's three hours in A & E before we're seen by a doctor, a harried-looking young guy with dark bags under his eyes who doesn't look much older than my eldest son. He checks Mum over in a side room, tries to get her talking without much success before she's sent for X-rays. He then informs us that he wants to keep her in for at least one night, possibly two, for more tests and observation, and a bed is found for her on a small side ward with three other women.

By the time I get home, it's gone nine o'clock. Jason pours me a large glass of white wine and makes me supper as I collapse into one of the stools at the kitchen island, relaying the day's events. He listens as he takes cheese and margarine from the fridge, letting me vent my anxiety and frustration, a routine that's become familiar.

It's only when he slides the plate over to me – Brie-and-cucumber-topped crackers, grapes and nuts and slices of apple – that I realise how hungry I am.

'Did you speak to your brother?'

'Called him while I was driving to the hospital.' I bite into a slice of apple. 'He was tied up with some client issue today but said he'd see Mum tomorrow.'

As I eat my supper and Jason pours more wine, the conversation turns inevitably to a subject we've discussed a dozen times over the past year. If not twenty times. Fifty. *What do we do about Mum?* A question that didn't seem to have an answer. Not that we hadn't tried. We had jumped through the hoops to get home visits from council carers three times a week – despite Mum's objections. And the reality had been a string of well-meaning but completely inexperienced teenagers and twenty-year-olds, fresh out of college, who didn't have the first idea about how to relate to a 79-year-old widow. It had lasted barely a month before Mum put her foot down and refused to let them in the house anymore.

Next, I had taken her to visit her friend, Eileen, who had moved into a care home a few months previously. I had suggested it, had picked Mum up and driven her there, sat with them both in the big overheated lounge in the hope that she'd see the appeal of living somewhere she could be looked after twenty-four hours a day. I hoped we might at least have a conversation about it. But the place had been so depressing, so understaffed and institutional, the air heavy with a stifling cocktail of body odour and bleach and boiled vegetables, that I never even asked the question on the drive back to her house. The next care home I'd visited was little better, and the one after that was worse. They had convinced me that I couldn't put Mum in a place she didn't want to go, somewhere *I* didn't even like when I visited it.

But she clearly wasn't safe alone at home, either. As today had demonstrated.

Not for the first time, I wonder whether we should move her in with us, into the room that Noah had vacated when he moved to London. But Mum had been adamant that she didn't want that either, and besides, she'd be alone here as well on the days when Jason and I were at work and Alfie was at school.

There wasn't a right answer, to any of it. Just a variety of answers that were each wrong in different ways.

This was how the conversation with my husband usually went. It was circular, always bringing us back to where we started. Frustrated. Resigned. Feeling like we were failing Mum in some fundamental way.

But tonight, Jason is more animated than I've seen him in a while.

'This place has got availability.' He taps at his iPad, turns it towards me. The screen shows a glossy homepage of what looks like a high-end hotel or country club. Harcourt Park. 'And it's only four miles away from here. Have a look.'

I scroll down: more images show beautifully decorated apartments, a swimming pool, a library, a gym and a restaurant with a terrace looking out onto low rolling hills. All the images feature smiling, well-dressed pensioners looking as if they're having the time of their lives.

'Very nice,' I say. 'But why have you been checking availability at this place?'

'Purpose-built,' he says, as if he hasn't heard me. 'Privately run, right on the edge of the countryside.'

'And astronomically expensive, I seem to remember. That's why we didn't even bother taking Mum there to have a look.'

The truth is, we'd already burned through most of our savings supporting Noah through university, paying his accommodation and living costs. He'd worked during the holidays, and done part-time bar shifts while he was studying, but there had still been a big hole to fill. And now we'd be trying to do the same for Alfie when he headed off to uni in the autumn. My brother's company was doing well but much of what he made was ploughed back into the business, with most of the rest swallowed up by his daughter's exorbitant school fees and maintenance payments to his ex-wife. There was Mum's house, of course, but how long would it take to sell, even assuming we could persuade her to give it up?

I click a link on the Harcourt Park homepage menu, scroll down again until I find a table of figures.

'Here you go,' I say. 'Fees start at £1,500 per *week*, plus an upfront deposit.' I nudge the iPad back towards him. 'Come on,

Jason. Be serious. There's a reason why we didn't visit this place already. It's way out of our reach.'

He finishes his glass of wine, reaches for the bottle to refill it.

'Not anymore.'

I sigh heavily, rub at my closed eyes. My eyeballs feel like they're coated with grit.

'Let's not have this conversation again today, Jason. I haven't got the mental energy left for it after all those hours at the hospital. My brain feels like mush.'

He tops up my glass as well. 'You've not seen the Signal group, then? The messages this evening?'

'My phone was off in the hospital.' I pull it out of my handbag. I had switched it back on in the car park, but hadn't checked it since then. 'Why, what's happened?'

'Remember Kat took a few of the notes from the backpack with her? Four notes from four different bundles?' He indicates my mobile. 'Have a look.'

I swipe the screen until I find the blue-and-white Signal icon. I only have one chat group on the app with just the six of us as members. Jason has named the group 'The Weekend'. There are new messages from Kat, the first one only a couple of hours ago. As is her style, she has sent a string of one-liners rather than an entire paragraph.

Hey, guys, hope you all had a good trip home, lovely to see you all. x
So anyway I tested the timber like we agreed.
All four bits of it.

'Timber?' I say to Jason, nonplussed. 'She means the money, right?'

He nods. 'Christian said we should use a code word, remember?'

I cast my mind back to the conversation in the Black Swan this lunchtime, the 'ground rules' Christian had insisted upon. After my mum, after the paramedics, the hospital, it already feels like a week ago, even though it's only been a few hours.

I return to the string of messages from Kat.

Checked with both UV light and detector pen.
The UVs in particular are v v good and rated as 99.9% accurate.
And the result is . . .
The timber is definitely genuine.

14

The timber is genuine.

The money is real.

It's no longer an abstract concept, a theoretical possibility that we can ignore. We no longer have the get-out clause, the excuse, that it's not really a question we have to answer because it's not legal tender.

It's real. One point six million pounds.

And it's sitting under the bed right above our heads.

I realise, as I read and reread Kat's words on the encrypted Signal chat, that I had been secretly hoping the UV lights would show it up as counterfeit currency. That the decision would be made for us, that we would no longer have this strange discovery hanging over us and could write off the last thirty-six hours as merely a curious postscript to an enjoyable New Year's break. Something we'd look back on in years to come with wry smiles and fond memories. *Do you remember the year Helen found that backpack in the cave? And at first we thought the money might actually be real?*

That would have made it easy. Clean. Straightforward. But instead, I realise with a sick quickening of my pulse, the reality has just got a whole lot more complicated.

Below Kat's last message there's only one reply so far – from my brother, Christian.

> *Thanks K. Let's get together next week as planned to discuss next steps, gives us all time to do our research – 7 p.m. Friday at mine? With verbal updates on any new info discovered in the meantime.*

Jason indicates the phone.

'So?' he says, a note of expectation in his voice. 'What do you think?'

I look at the messages again, reading each one in turn. Then I finish the last of my wine and glance up at my husband across the kitchen table.

'Honestly?' I say. 'I think I want to go to bed.'

I spend the morning of Bank Holiday Monday at Mum's house, restocking her cupboards with armfuls of shopping from Tesco, then a couple of hours tidying up, sorting out the washing, ironing and whipping around with the Dyson. I text Kat to let her know about Mum and she calls straight back, asking if there's anything she can do, offering to come over to help clean the house. I tell her, thanks, but it's fine, that I've done the worst of it and Mum seems to be recovering well.

We skirt around the other issue. The elephant in the room: the money. I can tell she wants to talk about it, unasked questions hovering in moments of silence on the line. *Where did you hide it? Did you see my messages on the chat group? What do you think?* But I don't have the headspace, not today, not with everything else going on.

'So,' she says finally, 'I'll . . . see you Friday week?'

'Of course,' I say. 'See you then.'

At the hospital, I find Mum in a better mood, chatting with one of the women on her ward, yet slightly indignant that the young doctor wants to keep her in for another night to run more tests.

The events of yesterday seem forgotten already and she is brighter, sharper, almost her old self. Thankfully, her wrist is only sprained and her collarbone is not broken either. She'll need her left arm in a sling for a few weeks and she has a lot of bruising, but it seems like she's got off fairly lightly all the same. At least this time, anyway. I try not to think about her being all alone in that house, a whole new year unfolding in front of us.

Going back to work is the usual nightmare.

It always is after the Christmas break, when the whole team has been off together. Nigel is keen to re-establish his alpha male credentials and to ensure that no one is trying to get away with any post-festive slacking. The flurry of emails he'd sent while we were all on leave turns out to be a fuss over nothing, a potential problem with a client that might – or might not – arise at the very end of the financial year. There was nothing to be gained by flapping about it over the Christmas and New Year break, unless you were an insecure middle-aged middle-manager who liked reminding his 'guys' who was in charge.

By the end of my first week back, I'm scrolling through a recruitment website to see if there are any vacancies offering a better salary. It is my January tradition – dip a toe in the water, see what's out there, maybe even fire off some CVs. Then lose my nerve and decide to stay put for a little while longer. In this particular week I have enough on my plate anyway, taking Mum home from the hospital and getting her settled again.

I shop for her on Saturday and spend a couple of hours cleaning and ironing at her house. On Sunday, Alfie drives over and brings her back to ours for a roast dinner and thankfully the weekend passes without further incident.

And then it's back into the routine, the January grind at work, going through the motions just to get through each day. Thoughts of the money popping into my head while I'm stuck in traffic, stuck in boring meetings, stuck listening to the endless drone of some self-important colleague. All of a sudden I'll find myself thinking of the secret, of thick bundles of money under our bed. Silent. Dormant. Like a pile of presents under the tree on Christmas Eve, waiting to be unwrapped.

On Wednesday, Jason picks me up from work at lunchtime and says he has a surprise.

It's only as we're turning into the long, curving driveway that I see the signs and realise where we're going.

15

Dev

The magistrates' court was one of those old buildings that was unbearably hot in summer and impossible to heat in the winter, but despite the chill, Dev still felt the trickle of sweat beneath his arms. It was always the same with cases like this.

He tried to volunteer at least two days of each month to being here on the bench, even though most of the time it felt like Groundhog Day. He listened as the presiding justice – sitting to his left – read out the sad litany of charges against the latest defendant on today's list, a 22-year-old drug addict. He had pleaded guilty to theft from his employer, as well as stealing from his foster parents. A sum of just under £450, which he had spent on spice, cannabis and ketamine over a two-week period. There was also a charge of criminal damage – a broken window – and a drunk and disorderly to add to the list for good measure.

It was a pitiful start to his young life. But pity was the last thing he needed.

Dev sipped his water and studied the young man in the dock. The defendant seemed entirely uninterested in the proceedings, slumped and glassy-eyed as if he was resigned to whatever punishment was meted out today. Dev glanced down at his notes, scanning through the details again. The defendant had worked in a newsagent's for six months, gaining the owner's trust to the extent that he had been allowed to open up in the mornings on his own, and close up at night. Trust that he had then violated in a deliberate and systematic way by pilfering from the till whenever he was alone in the shop. Five pounds here, ten pounds there. When his theft was discovered and he had been fired from his job, he had stolen from his foster parents to feed his addiction. When they had changed the locks on their house, he had broken a window and stolen from them again.

Dev found his mind wandering, thoughts drifting back to New Year's Eve, to stacks of banknotes piled on a table. A sum that made *this* theft seem like pennies. Like nothing. Should he tell the police? Should he tell them everything, lead them to Helen's door? Do what none of them had been able to do?

He dragged his attention back to the defendant slumped in the dock.

Here was a young man who was unable to resist temptation when it was put in front of him.

A young man who needed to learn an important lesson.

The bench chair turned to Dev, a questioning eyebrow raised, and Dev responded by arguing in no uncertain terms that they impose *the maximum sentence permissible under the guidelines*. Closing with a variation on what he always said: *We are magistrates, not social workers*. The bench chair grunting his usual reply. *Although very often it's hard to tell the difference.*

The defendant had been tempted, he had been tested, and he'd been found wanting. It was as simple as that. Dev knew the age-old story better than most.

He also knew there was only one way to deal with temptation: in the harshest terms possible.

Perhaps that was a lesson his friends would soon be learning too.

16

'Hear me out,' Jason says, as we sweep past manicured lawns on the way up to the elegant, modern reception building. Harcourt Park is styled to look like a five-star hotel, lots of glass and clean white lines. 'It's a fifteen-minute visit, no obligation. Let's just look, OK?'

'Just because we're here,' I say. 'It doesn't mean anything.'

We're greeted at reception by a young woman in a pristine white blouse and navy skirt, her blonde hair pinned carefully back. She asks a few questions about Mum and takes us on a tour of the facility, chatting amiably about the restaurant on site, the ten-thousand-book library, the physio room, about cinema night, visiting speakers, summer coach trips out to Whitby and Filey and Harrogate. About the different levels of care available according to Mum's needs. To my surprise, the place actually *does* look like the pictures on the website. Clean, airy, modern. The contrast with the other care homes I've taken Mum to visit is like night and day.

'Helen?'

We're being shown around the on-site gym when a voice interrupts our guide mid-sentence. I turn to see a bald, broad-shouldered man in his early fifties in a dark, perfectly cut suit with an open-necked white shirt and a smile of delighted surprise on his face. It takes me a second to place him – he's older, more tanned and toned than I remember. But then I haven't seen him – in the flesh at least – for many years.

For a moment, surprise sweeps everything else away.

'Alexander,' I say finally. 'Hi, how are you?'

'I'm really good, thanks.'

He moves towards me and I'm not sure whether he's going for a handshake, a peck on the cheek or something in between – and before I can react he's leaning in for a hug, enveloping me in a cloud of powerfully musky aftershave.

'*So* good to see you.' He continues to beam at me, as if he can't believe his luck. 'You look great! God, it's been too long, hasn't it?'

I feel the heat of a blush rising up my neck. Thinking of his annual New Year texts, his regular birthday wishes, all the times I had given him a perfunctory reply and hoped he'd eventually get the message. Of how many years it's been since I've told Jason that my long-ago ex-boyfriend is still in touch.

'Much too long.' I nod a *hello* to the smartly dressed younger woman by his side, trying and failing to remember his wife's name. 'What a surprise to see you here. Are you visiting family?'

'No, just keeping an eye on things. You're looking for somewhere for your mother?'

'For Mum, yes.'

'And what do you make of Harcourt Park?'

'Very nice. I think she'd love it here.'

'Well, it's our flagship. Our newest. She'd be very welcome.'

'Oh,' I say. 'So . . . you're the manager here?'

'Rebecca's the manager.' He gestures at the efficient-looking woman beside him. 'I'm the owner. This place, and some others.'

'Really? I had no idea.'

He gives me a warm smile. 'Well it's been a while since we caught up, Helen. Must be fifteen years or more.'

Jason continues to stand to one side, a third party to this exchange. Alexander finally turns to look at him, the two men exchanging an awkward handshake and the briefest of greetings.

'Well,' Jason says. 'We should probably get on. Lots to see here.'

Alexander returns his attention to me. 'Of course.' He checks a watch that flashes with diamonds. 'Helen, do let me know when your mum's coming in and I'll make sure she gets the five-star treatment. It's *so* good to see you.' He flashes another bright smile. 'We should catch up properly some time.'

A few minutes later, we thank our guide and take a brochure as we're leaving. Jason gives me a sidelong look as we walk back out to reception.

'Is that who I think it was? Your ex?'

'Yes,' I say. 'Hardly recognised him.'

I could never see the point of reminding Jason that Alexander had stayed in touch. Jason would have told me to ignore him, block him, but that wouldn't feel right – not when Alexander and I had that little piece of shared history. As long as I could keep him at arm's length. I suppose it wouldn't be a bad thing if it meant Mum got a little preferential treatment here, if we could persuade her to try it for herself.

Alexander is still there in the car park as we walk out of the building. He's talking on his phone, standing in the open door of a bright orange sports car that is so low to the ground it barely reaches his waist. He gives me a wave.

'Lamborghini,' Jason says with grudging admiration as he unlocks our Nissan. 'Nice. Did you see his watch, too? Patek Philippe.'

'Was it?'

'I guess someone's doing all right out of the OAP business.'

'I suppose.'

He pulls on his seat belt.

'Why are you being weird?'

'Am I?' I shift in my seat. 'It's just ... weird to see him again after all these years.'

We drive the rest of the way back to my work in silence.

Thursday evening finds me home alone: Alfie is out with friends and Jason heads off straight after tea for his weekly squash game with my brother. I collapse onto the sofa but after flicking between Netflix, Prime and iPlayer for fifteen minutes and failing to find anything that grabs me, I fling the remote down and open my laptop instead. Remembering Christian's ground rules again, I pull up the browser and select 'Private Mode'. My hands hover over the keyboard and I realise I don't *really* know where to start.

Prim strolls in and jumps up silently onto the sofa, flopping down next to me and rolling over so I can stroke her tummy, fluffy black fur with a white stripe down the middle like a feline tuxedo. She purrs softly as I begin to type one-handed queries into the search box.

Missing money Yorkshire
Yorkshire Dales money
Yorkshire £1.6 million
Yorkshire Dales million
Black backpack missing

Each one throws up hundreds of thousands of results – none of which look relevant. I realise the search engine is only as good as the question you ask of it, and I wasn't even sure what I *should* be asking.

I go into the kitchen and find a half-empty bottle of Pinot Grigio in the fridge. I fill a glass and bring it back into the lounge. Prim has moved and is now sprawled comfortably across the laptop as if claiming ownership. I lift her off carefully and lay her on the sofa, then sit down and blow some of her fine black hairs off the keyboard. Maybe I was barking up completely the wrong tree, approaching this the wrong way. Right from the beginning, I'd assumed there was something criminal about the money. My brother had pointed out that we didn't have any actual *evidence* for that, but how else could it have got there? I click back to the search page.

Drug money missing
Drugs Yorkshire millions
Drugs gang cash missing
Bank robbery millions

Bank robbery cash
Bank robbery missing money

Tens of thousands of results for each one. My eyes start to glaze as I click through page after page of results, looking for any kind of connection that might link with the little cave near Scar House Reservoir. *Click, scan, back, click, scan, next page, click.*

An hour later, all I have to show for my research is an empty bottle of Pinot. I'd expected to find *something*, however tenuous, but there seems to be nothing online at all. Which meant one of two things. Either I was using the wrong search words, or . . . there was nothing online to find. And if it was the latter, could the next thing be true as well?

That there was nothing online because no one knew about the money?

The thought gives me a strange feeling of lightness, of safety, of being anonymous and hidden in a crowd. Of being invisible, almost. If the money wasn't public knowledge, if there hadn't been any kind of police search to find it, then perhaps *no one* knew about it apart from the person who had put it there – and us. Surely, there was no way that person could connect it back to us? Could that be true? Maybe it's the wine, I'm not sure, but the house feels *different* somehow. Warmer, as if a draught has been blocked.

There is something else, too. Something more.

If there was no way of tracing it back to us, why *couldn't* we spend some of it? Carefully, slowly, in the right way, for the right reasons. We could take Mum to Harcourt Park and show her around, at least have a conversation about it. She could be happy there – and she'd be safe. Properly looked after by professionals, seven days a week.

I feel its heavy presence above my head. Feel it calling to me, from our bedroom. Not lines of code on a server somewhere, an electronic bank balance floating in the digital ether, but here in our house: solid, tangible, real. I close the laptop and head upstairs.

Maybe there *was* something we had missed in the backpack. I'd been sitting on my sofa scouring through Google, but maybe the answer was waiting under our bed. I'd checked in the cottage but there had been a lot of distractions with all of us there, talking and arguing and drinking.

I pull up the base of the bed, hydraulic struts squeaking as they extend. After pulling on a pair of yellow Marigolds from under the sink, I reach in for the backpack, drag it into the en suite then shut the door and turn the lock. The plastic-wrapped slab of money is even heavier than I remember and I need to grip it with both hands to heave it out with a *slap* onto the tiled floor. I pull the backpack inside out, shining my phone light into each pocket and feeling along the seams.

Nothing.

The money sits beside me in its sealed wrapping, heavy and inert.

At the holiday cottage, there had still been a sense of unreality about it. A sense of being away from home and free of our normal routines, away from everyday life. But here, in our little bathroom, it looks completely authentic and I can't believe I ever thought otherwise.

Without really knowing why, I open the airtight seal and tip it up. Bricks of money come tumbling out, dozens of them.

Sitting cross-legged on the cold bathroom floor I count it carefully, twice, a chill creeping over my skin as the warmth of the central heating fades.

At 9.30 p.m., I hear Jason's car pulling into the drive. I unlock the en suite door and a minute later he appears in the bedroom, tracksuit over his squash kit, giving me a peck on the cheek that smells faintly of his post-game beer with my brother.

'Hey.' He looks down at my feet, where bricks of cash are stacked in piles. 'What's going on with the—'

'I need to talk to you.'

'About your mum?' he says, seeing my expression. 'Is she OK? Hasn't fallen again, has she?'

'No,' I say. 'I mean, yes, she's OK. I spoke to her earlier. Some pain with her wrist but she seems all right. I need to talk to you about this.' I point down at the floor. 'About the money.'

'What about it?' He frowns.

I take a breath, try to calm the drumming in my chest. To think of another explanation, even though there can be only one.

'You counted it on New Year's Eve, right?'

He nods. 'Three times. Exactly one point six million, on the nose.'

'Well I've just counted it again.' I swallow, my throat dry. 'And it's short.'

'What?'

'It's not one point six anymore.'

He stares at me, then down at the money, then back at me.

'But . . . I haven't touched it. Haven't even looked at it. I swear.'

'Well,' I say, 'someone did. That night, before we left the cottage. Someone's helped themselves to more than fifty thousand pounds.'

PART II
THE SPLIT

17

Friday, 13th January

A stunned silence settles across the table in my brother's dining room.

The six of us are seated in high-backed chairs around a long oval table set with white china and gleaming cutlery, two bottles of wine in the centre. Jason and I are on one side, Dev and Kat on the other, while Christian and Miranda sit at either end. The dining room overlooks the garden of my brother's elegant Georgian townhouse in a sought-after suburb north of the city centre. Bigger than our house but he had worked hard for it, was *still* working hard towards the ultimate goal of selling his company and easing into a more relaxed lifestyle in his mid-fifties. Still, he enjoyed the occasional perk of success – like the special set menu delivered from an award-winning local restaurant, appetisers of smoked salmon, beef carpaccio and stuffed olives, expertly plated up and served by Miranda. I had waited until we all had food in front of us, before explaining in a low voice what I had discovered last night.

Christian is the first to break the silence. 'What?' His fork stops, halfway to his mouth. 'What are you talking about, Helen?'

'Some of the money is missing.' I glance at the door, even though there's no one else in the house. 'I counted it again last night.'

'How much are we talking about?'

'Fifty-six thousand.'

He puts his fork back down on the plate with a clatter. 'Jesus. Are you sure?'

Jason leans forward in his seat. 'Helen's right – I checked it too. And I counted it three times when we were at the cottage – twice when we got back from the walk, then again after the poker game. I made a note on my phone of how many stacks of each. There were sixty-five stacks of fifties, now there are sixty-three. Thirty-eight stacks of twenties. Now there are thirty-six.'

I glance around the table, looking from one face to another for any traces of guilt. Any sign that one of my friends knew this was coming. But all I see is shock, confusion, surprise. To tell the truth, I had been dreading this moment all day, sitting at my desk this afternoon trying to think of a way to break the news that would soften the blow. I hated confrontation and tried to avoid it where I could. But a look across the table is enough to tell me that's exactly what's coming, as shock dissolves into anger.

Dev puts his hands on the top of his bald head, like a surrendering prisoner of war. 'So let me get this right,' he says, eyes scanning around the table. 'All that talk of waiting and being careful and trying to find out where the money came from – that was crap, was it? One of you decided to just *help yourself* to a chunk of cash, without telling the rest of us? You just fancied a fifty-grand bonus to start off the New Year?'

Kat puts a hand on her husband's arm. 'Hang on, Dev, let's not start throwing accusations around before we have all the facts.'

'Facts?' He gives her an exaggerated shrug. 'The only *fact* that matters is that someone has broken their word already. Someone has gone rogue. So who was it? Is someone going to own up?'

No one replies.

'Nice new watch, eh?' Dev indicates the heavy Omega on Christian's wrist. 'Bet that cost a few thousand.'

'It was my dad's, actually.' My brother's voice is dangerously calm. 'He left it to me in his will.'

His anger undimmed, Dev turns to the other end of the table.

'Or maybe the necklace your wife's wearing tonight?'

Miranda snorts. 'Don't be ridiculous.'

'Looks fresh out of the box to me. Looks like—'

Kat puts a hand over his, giving it a squeeze. 'That's *enough*, love. You can't just sit here accusing our friends, especially when you've got no idea what's happened.'

'Yeah, but I bloody knew something like *this* would happen. I *knew* it.' He looks absolutely stricken, as if he might be sick. 'We should have left the money in that cave, we should never have brought it home. This is so messed up.'

'Kat's right,' Christian says, his voice still weirdly calm. 'We shouldn't jump to conclusions. So I'm thinking . . . the only time it could have been taken is the early hours of New Year's Day, when the cash was left out on the table in the cottage after we all went to bed. About a six-hour window between perhaps 1 a.m. and 7 a.m. It wasn't repacked until the morning when we were getting ready to leave.'

'No,' Dev says suddenly. 'That's not true. It could have been any time since then too, any time over the last fortnight actually.'

It takes a second before his words sink in; a hot flush of anger clogging my throat.

'What?' I turn to him. 'You're saying *we* took that money while it's been at our house?'

'I'm just saying—'

Jason cuts him off, his voice low and hard. 'That's bullshit, Dev, and you know it. You're way out of line. Why would we come here and *tell* you fifty-six grand was missing if we were the ones who'd taken it? That doesn't make any sense.'

Dev slumps back in his chair, muttering under his breath.

Next to him, Kat holds her hands up like a bouncer trying to mediate between a pair of belligerent drinkers at closing time.

'Guys,' she says. 'Please. No one's accusing anyone of anything, all right? Dev didn't mean that, did you, love? Maybe there's a straightforward explanation, we might have just mislaid it that night? We were all pretty drunk. And then packing everything up on New Year's Day, we were all a bit hungover, I mean maybe it's still at the cottage somewhere. Kicked under a sofa, or something.'

Jason is shaking his head. 'Two stacks of fifties, and two stacks of twenties? Each of them three inches thick? You can't just *lose* that amount.'

Silence falls across the table again, broken only by the soft strains of Beethoven's Ninth Symphony coming from a Bluetooth speaker on the mantelpiece. It's flanked on either side by framed photos of Cressida, Miranda's teenage daughter from her first marriage: holiday snaps, baby pictures and a studio portrait of the three of them together.

Miranda plucks the white wine from its ice bucket, the bottle beaded with moisture, and refills the three glasses nearest to her.

'This . . . discrepancy,' she says slowly. 'You two discovered it twenty-four hours ago but you're only just telling us about it now?'

The skin of my cheeks is unpleasantly warm. 'I thought it would be better face to face. I didn't want to put it on the Signal group chat because I thought everyone would want to discuss it properly, this evening.'

'Just a bit of a surprise, that's all.' Her tone is casual, as if we're discussing some minor school-gate scandal that involves someone else. 'And for it to be such a small amount, as well.'

'I wouldn't call fifty-six thousand pounds a small amount.'

She waves a hand dismissively. 'You know what I mean. In proportion to the whole sum.'

'Look,' Christian says, refilling the remaining glasses with Sauvignon Blanc. 'Let's all calm down a bit, shall we? None of this matters, not really. It doesn't change anything.'

I love my brother but sometimes his devil-may-care attitude is infuriating. Ever since we were children, he's had that confidence, that charismatic certainty that everything would turn out all right. And it had worked for him: he'd done better than all right. His nice house, his company, his upwardly mobile trajectory was evidence enough of that.

'Christian,' I say. 'Of *course* it matters. It matters because we agreed that we wouldn't do anything with the money until we could find out whether anyone was likely to be looking for it.'

'Understood,' he says. 'I totally get where you're coming from. But we are where we are, OK? So let's just park that money discrepancy for a minute and do what we were supposed to be doing this evening.'

Dev snorts. 'Working out which one of us is a thief?'

Christian raises an eyebrow at him but says nothing, as if he's an irritating insect who will fly away soon enough.

'We were going to see if anyone had found anything out about where the money might have come from. We've all done our own quiet research, yes?'

There are various nods and murmurs of agreement around the table. I describe the online searches that I'd done last night, and the absence of any tangible result that seemed to link to the money. Kat, Jason and Miranda have also come up blank. Dev gives the impression of wanting very much to have found a deal-breaking piece of information online, a killer fact that would stop this conversation in its tracks. But when it comes to his turn he simply gives an angry shake of his head.

Christian is the last to speak. And by the way he waits for everyone's attention, I can tell it's something he's been dying to tell us since we arrived.

'I may have found something,' he says, with a small smile. 'And I think it could be good news.'

18

In his usual style, Christian has gone one better than everyone else.

Rather than searching online for information himself, he's made discreet inquiries via a private investigator that he's used in the past for due diligence, corporate intelligence and other work relating to his company. While Miranda bustles in the kitchen, my brother relates the details of a court case his investigator has found: the 2018 armed robbery of a Securitas cash management depot in which just over three million pounds in new and used currency was stolen. All three perpetrators were eventually caught, he says, but most of the money remained unaccounted for when they were sentenced to lengthy jail terms just before the pandemic hit in 2020.

'Hang on.' I hold a hand up. 'What happened to not telling anyone outside us six? Your ground rules for keeping the circle small?'

'Exactly what I was thinking,' Dev mutters into his wine.

'My investigator is completely discreet,' Christian says. 'I've been using her for years, right back to when my divorce was threatening to get messy. She's ex-police, very experienced. Anyway I gave her a deliberately general brief, very broad, to look back over the last ten years at criminal activity where seven-figure cash sums have been involved. Nothing specific.'

'What makes you think it's the same money?'

My brother gives an elaborate shrug. 'Honestly, there's no way to prove it, without knowing more. It's guesswork, a hunch. But the robbery happened in Manchester, which is where these three guys came from. One of them was arrested in the city but the other two were picked up by Northumberland Police in a little seaside town called Amble, way up in the north-east above Newcastle. If you look at a map, the Yorkshire Dales is in between those two places.'

'So it might relate to our money,' Jason says. 'Or it could be a complete coincidence. It might have nothing to do with it at all.'

There is a strange, loaded silence again, as if we're all considering his choice of words.

I half turn towards my husband. 'It's not *our* money, Jason. *The* money. Someone else's money.'

He shrugs. 'You know what I mean, Helen.'

'You're right,' Christian says. 'It's only a theory: that the two of them arrested in Northumberland travelled that way, through the Dales on the run or whatever, and stashed half of the money in the cave to come back for it later. Maybe after a few months, a year, after the police investigation had been scaled back. But instead they got caught and convicted.'

He sounds convincing. My brother always does. But something nags at me about the geography, the route north and east that would have taken them away from the scene of the crime.

'The receipt we found,' I say. 'In the backpack. It was from a hiking shop in Newcastle, as if the backpack had been bought there.'

Across the table, Kat raises a finely contoured eyebrow. 'So?'

'So how does that work? If they were driving from Manchester with all that cash, surely they would have bought the backpack there before they left? Not in Newcastle, after they'd already travelled through the Dales and left Yorkshire behind them?'

She grins. 'Fair point. I always was terrible at geography.'

'Maybe,' Christian says, 'they bought the pack on an earlier trip. A trial run.' He spreads his hands. 'Like I say, it's only a theory at this point. But the main thing is, the three men who took it are all in prison, serving sentences of between eighteen and twenty-six years.' He pauses, letting his words sink in. 'My investigator also established that one of them has since been diagnosed with multiple sclerosis and his comrade had an extra nine years added to his sentence after attacking a prison officer with a razor blade. The third one – the ringleader – won't even be considered for parole for another seven years at least.'

Jason leans towards him, chin resting on his fist. 'So the police got all the guys who did it, they got convictions with hefty sentences. They closed the case.'

'*Exactly*,' Christian says. 'You think the cops have the time, the resources, the motivation to track down money that's probably long gone and absorbed back into the system? Of course they haven't. Not when they're chasing a hundred other equally bad guys who need to be caught.' He looks around the table, at each of us in turn. 'The other important point is that all the money would have been insured anyway. So the banks don't lose out, they claim one hundred per cent of it back. No one loses out. It's a victimless crime.'

Dev jabs a finger at him. 'That's crap, Christian. There's no such thing as a victimless crime. You should join me at the magistrates' court one of these days, you'll see exactly what I mean.'

'What about the staff?' Miranda returns from the kitchen with three steaming plates on a tray. 'The ones at the bank, or wherever it was. If those awful thugs were armed, was anyone hurt?'

'No,' Christian says. 'They were all threatened and a few were bit roughed up, but nothing serious.'

She considers this for a moment as she puts the plates down on the table. 'They were still victims though, darling.'

I take a sip of my own wine, a crisp white Sauvignon chilled so cold it makes my throat ache.

'I don't know, Christian. It all sounds a bit convenient to me.'

'*Convenient?*' Dev says, his voice rising. 'It's the proceeds of crime, for God's sake – even more of a reason to put it back where it came from. We can just drop a pin on Google Maps for the exact location and then report it to the police. In fact, I'll bloody take it back to that cave. Tomorrow.'

Kat puts a hand on his arm. 'With our fingerprints all over it, love? All over the bag and the money?'

'Not mine,' Dev says. 'I wore gloves.'

'My gloves ripped,' Jason says. 'While we were playing poker.'

Miranda pauses on her way back to the kitchen. 'I couldn't wear them either,' she says. 'My contact dermatitis flared up, had to take the gloves off.'

'*Great*,' Dev says, sarcasm drawing out the word. 'Well that's just brilliant, isn't it?'

'Look,' Christian says, 'even if they do check for fingerprints, none of us have got a record, none of us are on any database anywhere. So why does it matter?'

Dev slaps the table with his palm, hard enough to make the cutlery bounce. 'Because it *does*, OK!'

Jason cuts in. 'Guys, listen. Even if they *don't* check for fingerprints, some of the money is missing. How do we explain that?'

'Dunno,' Dev says. 'How *do* you explain it mysteriously vanishing while it's been at your house, Jason?'

My husband's face darkens. 'What's that supposed to mean?'

'You heard me. You've had the best chance to skim a little off the top. You've had the most time to—'

'Screw you,' Jason says, his voice suddenly tight with anger. 'We didn't even want to store the money at our house. So to get accused of nicking it is pretty rich. In fact, you know what? We should split it equally, keep equal shares from now on. So everyone takes responsibility and no one can accuse me of being a bloody thief.'

Christian is nodding. 'Seems fair.'

'No,' Dev says. 'You can't put this on us.'

Jason glares across the table. 'It's *already* on you! It's on all of us, we did it together.'

Miranda returns from the kitchen a second time, bringing three more of the white china plates loaded with food.

'Listen,' Dev says, once she's returned to her seat. 'This is not rocket science. We don't *have* to explain that some of it is missing when we report it, we just have to make an anonymous call.'

The dish cooling in front of me – a beautifully presented monkfish with dauphinoise potatoes and broccoli – smells absolutely irresistible, the sauce a rich blend of creamy herbs. But in the last few minutes my appetite has shrivelled to nothing.

No one else is touching their food either.

'One phone call,' Dev says. 'We don't *have* to explain to anyone why a few packets of cash are missing – we just take it back to the cave and leave it. Then we find a phone box in some little village, somewhere without CCTV, make an anonymous call to give its location. Then it becomes the police's problem. And we forget it ever happened.'

19

Christian is shaking his head.

'A *phone box*?'

'Somewhere remote, yes.'

'And when was the last time you saw one of them? One that actually had a working phone in it, instead of second-hand books or a defibrillator or just a load of broken glass and dried piss? Even if by some miracle you *did* find one that worked it would be in a town, where there'd be cameras to pick you up.'

'Not if I was wearing a hoodie, a baseball cap.'

Christian shrugs. 'They'd have the time and place of your call, they'd spot you, follow you to your car and get the registration. Then it would be game over.'

Dev throws his hands in the air. 'Well, then, I'd use a bloody burner phone instead!'

'Nothing is really anonymous anymore, mate. They'd trace the location or pull an IP address off the Google location pin. They'd find their way to us somehow.'

'Hang on, so *you're* trying to tell *me* about how people get caught? *Christ*.'

'I'm just saying we need to be smarter than the idiots and lowlifes who end up in front of you at the magistrates' court.'

Abruptly, Dev pushes his seat back from the table and stands up.

'This is bollocks,' he says, throwing his napkin down. 'You've all made your minds up already, this bloody money has sent you off the deep end. I want no part of it.'

He stalks off towards the French doors onto the patio, ignoring Kat's calls to him to return to the table. We all watch as he pushes the door open and heads outside, going down the steps and pulling a vape from his pocket. Motion-activated lights flick on as he makes his way down the garden path, illuminating his progress.

'He just needs a minute to calm down,' Kat says. 'Then I'll talk to him. He's been quite wound up about all of this since New Year's Eve.'

Miranda gestures at the food laid out in front of us. 'Please,' she says. 'Dive in, before it gets cold.'

We all begin to eat, the clinking of cutlery on china the only sound. The monkfish is delicious but I'm eating out of politeness rather than hunger, my stomach tight, as if a strap has been pulled taut around my middle.

'Did you mean it?' I turn towards my husband. 'About splitting up the money?'

He nods, chewing a mouthful of broccoli.

Before he can swallow, Kat says: 'It's not fair that you have to hold it all, Helen.'

'What about Dev? He's never going to agree to stash half a million pounds at your place.'

As if on cue, there is a chorus of pings and chirps from phones around the table, all of them receiving a message. I take mine from my handbag and open the Signal app, selecting the chat thread called 'The Weekend'. There is one new notification.

Dev has left the group

Kat glances out of the window towards her husband in the back garden. 'It's OK,' she says quietly. 'He doesn't need to know.'

I raise my eyebrows but she just shrugs, gives me the old *So what?* smile she used to give me at school while she was copying my homework – and I was worrying she'd get caught.

'As long as you're sure.' I turn to my brother. 'But we're still not doing anything with the money yet, right? We're just holding onto it, see what else we can find out about where it might have come from?'

He spears a piece of fish with his fork and puts it into his mouth, chewing thoughtfully. 'I don't see that there's much holding us back now.' He lifts his glass, the white wine shining like liquid gold in the soft lighting. 'I'll be getting the final report from my investigator next week. I've also been doing some of my own work on the financial side. In case we decide to take a positive course of action.'

'Positive?' I say. 'Meaning what?'

'If we choose to . . . grasp this opportunity. What I mean is—' he circles the air with his fork '—if we're smart, there's a way we can keep the money. Safely. All of it.'

My brother lays it out, as the rest of us continue to eat. The financial rules to be circumvented, avoided; how some of the money could be routed through a business to avoid suspicion. How we could all open multiple new accounts with different banks, so it wasn't concentrated in one place. And when paying money into those accounts, the threshold level to stay below so standard banking checks wouldn't be triggered. And so on. His voice is persuasive, commanding, almost hypnotic in its confidence. He knows what he's talking about. He doesn't use the term 'money laundering', but that's what it sounds like to me.

While he talks and answers questions, I scan the other faces at the table, most of them people I've known for years, decades, more than half my life.

There is a dull, formless ache in my chest that has been building all day, threatening to push up into my throat.

One of my friends has lied.

One of us sitting around this table has lied to the rest, lied to our faces, and is still lying now. They have deceived us, have ignored decades of friendship, of trips and house moves, weddings and funerals, christenings and birthdays and a million meals together, have ignored all of our shared history because of a bag full of money.

But who is it? Who took those four packets of cash in the first hours of New Year's Day, and done more than anyone else to bring us to this point? And *why*, when we had agreed to wait?

My eyes find Dev in the back garden. Still vaping, blowing huge angry plumes up into the freezing night air. He has been against this from the start and I am pretty sure I can rule him out.

Miranda leans over and tops up my wine, blonde hair falling perfectly to her shoulders, half a dozen slim silver bracelets jingling on the tanned skin of her wrist. My sister-in-law has that careless way with expensive things, the way well-off people do, as if this exquisite jewellery is nothing special. Of the six of us, I've known her for the shortest time but I can't picture her taking the money either – it doesn't seem to make sense. The same goes for my brother, at the opposite end of the table. He's aiming to sell his company soon, why would he need a trifling fifty thousand? And yet . . . he has been one of the loudest advocates for keeping the contents of the backpack.

Opposite me, Kat is asking him a question, something about banking rules and tax. My oldest friend, my best friend for more than forty years. We have always shared everything and never kept secrets from each other. I can't believe she'd have kept something like this from me either.

And then there is Jason, eating and drinking silently beside me. But I would just *know*, if it was him, I'm sure of it. I know my husband too well, almost better than I know myself.

None of which changes the fact that one of us *is* lying. And I can't see it being Miranda, or Dev – which leaves my brother, my best friend, or my husband. Who do I trust the most? Or the least? Who do I actually *know* the best? One of them has taken that money and accelerated this whole crazy situation, pushed us deeper into it than I had ever planned to go.

One of them is lying.

And I realise, with a chill that touches the base of my spine, that I have no idea which one.

20

We split the money the following day.

Christian comes to our house first, backing his big Audi all the way up the drive until it's only a few feet away from the front door. He emerges from the driver's side dressed in a tracksuit and sunglasses, carrying a navy blue Nike gym bag. On the doorstep, he gives me a grin and a peck on the cheek. His stubble is rough against my skin and he still smells of last night's wine.

'Morning, Helen,' he says. 'Got any coffee on?'

He breezes past me and heads into the kitchen, where I fetch a mug from the cupboard and pour him a cup from the filter machine. As always, I feel a little twinge of awkwardness when he comes to the house. I love my little three-bedroom semi – we had raised the boys here and we liked the neighbourhood, the schools, the community vibe – but it was conspicuously modest compared to the Georgian townhouse in Bootham that Christian and Miranda had moved into a few years ago. Our lives had taken on a different trajectory a long time ago – his angled up towards the stratosphere; mine on a more conventional path.

He would never say anything, never make a big deal out of the disparity. And I knew how hard he'd worked, how many lows and scrapes with bankruptcy there had been along with the highs, how close he was now to achieving his dream of selling the company he'd built and downshifting into semi-retirement while he was still young enough to enjoy it.

'Thanks for last night.' I hand him the coffee. 'The food was lovely.'

'Hmm.' He takes a sip even though it's still scalding hot. 'It was an . . . interesting evening.'

'That's one way of putting it.'

He had sent a link to our Signal group chat by the time we got home, with more information about what his investigator had discovered. It was a news report at the end of a trial held at Newcastle Crown Court dated 11th March 2020, within a week or so of the country heading into its first Covid lockdown. I could see why it might have been overlooked, overshadowed by bigger events.

Christian peers through the kitchen window into our small garden, the edges of the patio still rimed with frost.

'Jason not home?'

'He's taken Alfie to football.'

We talk about Mum for a few minutes, exchanging updates, and I tell him about my visit to Harcourt Park. He leans against the kitchen counter, both hands cupped around his coffee.

'I've been thinking about that too,' he says. 'About Mum, what's best for her. I've wanted to do more, since Dad died. It's just that with the company, the investments and everything else—'

'I know,' I say. 'You don't have to explain. We're both doing the best we can.'

I knew that my brother was doing well on paper, but most of his money was sunk into the company; most of what he made was ploughed back into the business to keep it expanding, moving forward.

'Yeah,' he says gently. 'But now we *can* do something about it, and we don't have to wait. Before she ends up in hospital again. Next time might be a lot worse.'

I refill my mug from the coffee pot. 'You think Mum will finally see sense?'

'It's certainly worth a try.' He looks up, his unshaven face filled with concern. 'She's getting worse, Hels.'

'I know.'

We agree to meet at Harcourt Park tomorrow, so Christian can see it for himself, before we think about next steps.

He finishes his coffee and picks up the empty gym bag at his feet.

'So,' he says. 'Shall we? Let me guess: you've hidden it in the . . . in the master bedroom, under the ottoman.'

I frown. 'How did you know that?'

'You're lovely, Helen.' He flashes me a smile. 'And trusting. And you always put the kids' birthday and Christmas presents under the ottoman.'

'Am I really that predictable?'

He shrugs, as if I've answered my own question, then follows me upstairs with the empty bag hanging loosely in his hand.

When we'd got home last night, Jason had kept his gloves on to count out the money into three equal piles, wrapping each one in a black bin liner and stashing them back into the hiding place under our bed. Christian follows me up the stairs and into the bedroom, then gives me a hand heaving up the heavy bed base.

Jason has left his gloves on top of the dresser. I pick them up and hold them out to my brother.

'Do you want these? You two are about the same size, aren't you?'

He shrugs. 'We're a bit past that now, aren't we?'

'Are you sure?'

'I'm fine without gloves.'

I pass him one of the black bin liners and he reaches into it, pulling out bricks of money, laying them side by side on the bed. Stacks of fifties and twenties in separate rows.

'Jason counted it into equal shares last night,' I say. 'It's all there.'

'Apart from the chunk that went walkabout.'

'Seriously? We had enough of those accusations last—'

'Just pulling your leg, sis.' He grins up at me. 'It's small change compared to the whole amount, anyway.'

I watch him as he resumes counting. My impulsive little brother, who had never been troubled by doubt or indecision, who didn't hesitate once he'd made up his mind. Even from a young age, he had always been the brave one, the impetuous risk-taker who wanted to do everything at a hundred miles an hour. I was the cautious older sibling, the responsible one, who had put plasters on his bloody knees when he fell off his bike and kept an eye on him at the beach to make sure the tide didn't pull him out of his depth.

He had always thrown himself into everything life had to offer, and life had rewarded him for it. Maybe it was time I took a leaf out of his book. I think about what Jason had said too, the day we brought this money back from the Dales and stowed it under the bed.

We could pay off Noah's student loans, pay off the rest of the mortgage, get your mum the help she needs.

We can do some good with it, for people who deserve it.

And the day before that – what Kat had said on New Year's Eve.

It's like buried treasure. Like a chest of gold that we've found on a desert island.

But most of all I think of Mum, sitting awkwardly on her kitchen floor, a hand cradling her bruised wrist. The look of helpless confusion etched into her face.

I come to a decision.

It feels like stepping off a high diving board into open space. It's almost liberating, that moment when you decide to go and you just have to close your eyes, take a deep breath and hope for the best. No more worrying about what choice to make: whatever will be, will be. The relief of taking *action*.

Reaching into the second black bin liner – the one containing our share – I pull out a slab of fifty-pound notes. It's a dense brick of polymer-paper three inches thick, heavy and smooth and perfect, a solid mass of power and potential in the palm of my hand. It feels good to finally be on the front foot, to be *doing* something tangible to help our mum, rather than just reacting and responding each time the situation got a little bit worse. I hold the money out to my brother.

He stops counting. 'What's that for?'

'For Mum,' I say. 'Tomorrow, let's take her with us to Harcourt Park, shall we? Show her round – maybe she'll like the look of it. The point is . . . I don't think we should waste any more time and I want to pay my share.'

'OK.' He places the money off to the side, separate from his own share. 'Just a couple of grand each for now, bring it tomorrow and I'll do the same. We'll try a two-pronged charm offensive, see if we can persuade her.' With a smile, he adds: 'You've changed your tune, thought you were all for handing it in to the police?'

'Seems like we've gone past that stage, without even realising it.'

'Do you want a receipt?'

'Seriously?'

'If you like.'

'No,' I say. 'I trust you.'

The words come out automatically, without any conscious thought, and I wonder if I actually mean them. I'd always trusted him before – we were the same flesh and blood, after all. But there was still the niggling question, the sliver of doubt that had crept in when I'd discovered four packets of money were already missing.

I watch him count for a moment, his hands moving with a quick, practised ease.

'Christian?'

He doesn't look up.

'What?'

'Do you think we should be doing this? Splitting the money?'

'It's the fairest way,' he says with a shrug. 'Rather than you looking after it all. And anyway, it was your husband's idea – he seemed pretty keen for us to slice up the pie into three equal shares. Not that they're equal anymore, of course.'

I hesitate, trying to think of an indirect way to ask a much more important question.

'Who do you think it was?'

'Who do I think *what* was?'

'Who took that fifty-six thousand?' I pause again, my resolve wavering. But I was his *sister*, for God's sake, I should be able to ask him anything. 'Was it you?'

He turns towards me, with exaggerated slowness. His Ray-Bans are propped on top of his head and I see for the first time that his eyes are bloodshot, dark shadows beneath them.

'Jason say that, did he?'

'What? No.'

'But he dropped a few hints that it was me, right?'

'No,' I say again. 'He's not said—'

'It was, wasn't it?' He starts shoving bricks of money into the bin liner more aggressively now, as if he might tear the plastic. 'He's a cracking bloke, your husband. I've always got on well with him. But we've all got our demons, right? Our weaknesses?'

His words hang in the air between us for a long moment. It feels as if the temperature in the bedroom has suddenly dropped a few degrees.

'What are you talking about?'

The packing finished, my brother folds the plastic of the bin liner over itself and shoves it into the gym bag, as if it's no more than a pile of dirty washing.

'Nothing,' he says, zipping the bag shut. 'Forget I said it.'

I put a hand on his arm. 'Come on, what demons? What do you mean?'

He sighs. 'OK. Fine. I don't suppose he's ever mentioned Paris to you, has he?'

'In relation to what, a trip? I mean . . . when?'

'Last few months.'

I search my mind for any conversation we've had about Paris. We were hoping to go to Crete for a week this summer, before Alfie's A-level results. Last year we'd been to Cornwall on holiday, Spain the year before that. It'd been quite a few years since we'd had a holiday in France.

'He's not mentioned it, no.'

He hoists the bag up onto his shoulder with a grunt. 'I thought not.'

'What about Paris? Is he planning a trip?'

'Just ask him.'

'Wait,' I say, as he heads for the landing. 'You can't just drop that on me and then walk out of the door, Christian. What about Paris, what do I need to know?'

'Sorry, got to dash, errands to run before lunch.'

'Christian, wait! At least stay for another coffee?'

But he's already on the stairs.

'Tell Alfie his uncle said hi. I'll see myself out.'

I hastily cover up the remaining money and lower the bed frame, but by the time I get downstairs my brother's Audi is already accelerating back out onto the street.

21

Jason texts me to say to say he's taking Alfie to McDonald's after his football match. I don't need to ask the score because a meal under the Golden Arches only ever means one thing: that his team has suffered a thrashing and he needs cheering up. It has been a tradition of theirs since our youngest son first started playing in goal for the Cavaliers, our local youth team, more than ten years ago.

I don't ask about Paris either. That had to be done face to face.

When they arrive home, Alfie is caked in mud and carrying a half-finished milkshake, his left hand tucked protectively against his stomach. Jason goes straight into the kitchen, empties a tray of ice cubes from the freezer into a plastic sandwich bag and hands it over to him. Alfie takes the bag wordlessly and presses it against the knuckles of his left hand. The third and fourth fingers, I notice, are strapped together with muddy white tape.

'What happened to your hand, Alfie?'

'Went to gather a loose ball.' He shrugs. There is a smear of mud on his cheek, mud in his ear, clods of it drying in his hair. 'It was right on the line and I went down for it, got kicked out of my hands by this absolute nobber from the Tigers.'

'Well I hope he got a red card, love. Show me.'

He reluctantly raises his left hand, the taped fingers swollen and bruised-looking. My son smells of earth and sweat, damp football kit against cold skin.

'Ouch,' I say. 'Looks nasty. Is it painful? I'll get you some paracetamol.'

'It's *fine*,' he says, moving his hand away again. 'Just a bit of a bang, that's all.'

Jason shrugs off his parka, unwinds his scarf. 'It's not fine. He's had a couple of paracetamol already but I'm going to take him to the walk-in centre in a bit, get it checked properly.'

Alfie rolls his eyes, as if this is a conversation he's already had with his dad in the car, an argument he's already lost. He tucks the milkshake into the crook of his elbow and turns toward the stairs.

'I'm going for a shower first. Don't want to sit there for hours in stinking kit.'

Over steaming bowls of vegetable soup and slices of crusty baguette, Jason describes the match, an 8–1 defeat on a sloping pitch that was more brown than green. He gives me an account of our son's injury and the first-aid treatment he'd had pitchside after being subbed off, then launches into a lengthy rant about the opposition player who had done it and the fact that he had not even received a yellow card, never mind a red. Finally, he pushes the kitchen door closed, lowering his voice.

'How did it go with your brother this morning? Did he . . . say anything else about last night?'

I describe Christian's visit, the conversation about Mum's care and our plan to see her tomorrow, take her to the restaurant at Harcourt Park so she could see the facilities there for herself. He nods his agreement, dipping a hunk of bread into his soup.

'Good idea,' he says.

'Christian said something else,' I say. 'Something a bit . . . weird. I asked him if he was the one who took the money.'

Jason doesn't look up from his bowl. 'And?'

'He denied it.'

'Of course he did.' He tears off another piece from the baguette. 'Why is that weird? He's not going to admit it, is he?'

'He asked if it was *you* that was accusing him.'

'*Me*? I'm not accusing him of anything. Sounds like your brother's getting a bit paranoid in his old age.'

I swallow. 'He said something else as well. He said I should ask you about—'

'In fact,' Jason says, gesturing with the crust of bread, 'if I was going to accuse anyone, if I had to put money on it, I'd say it was probably your best mate who fancied a bit of an advance on that cash.'

'Kat?'

'Yup.'

'Why would you say that?'

'Come on, Helen.' He gives me a frowning smile. 'I know you're loyal to her and that's very admirable and lovely, but . . . this is Kat we're talking about, remember? She's always been a bit gung-ho, hasn't she? Always been the one to jump into things feet first and worry about the consequences later. Never seen a rule she didn't want to break. And what about Dev? I'm not sure what's going on there. I mean, he's protesting a bit *too* much about the money, don't you think? A bit *too* loudly? Perfect cover for him, for the both of them.'

'But . . . Kat wouldn't *do* that. She wouldn't lie to us.' I look up at my husband. 'She wouldn't lie to me.'

'So ask her, then. When she comes over this afternoon to pick up her share.'

'What? I'm not going to ask her if she lifted fifty thousand pounds without telling us.'

'Why not? You asked your brother.'

'That's different.'

'Why?'

I shrug. 'Because it's different with your sibling. They're your flesh and blood, they're always going to be there.'

'So am I,' he says. 'So is your best mate.'

'I know that.' I gather up crumbs of baguette from the table, pressing my finger into them and dropping them into my half-finished soup bowl. There is a weight in my chest, a pressure that has been growing since I talked to my brother, my imagination spinning evermore terrible scenarios spawned by a single throwaway comment. 'Christian said something else, too. He said I should . . . ask you about Paris. What does that mean?'

Jason shoves one last piece of bread into his mouth, chewing slowly, eyebrows drawing together in a frown that's even deeper than the last. Finally, he gives a slow shrug, swallowing the mouthful. 'He said that today, did he?'

'This morning.' I try to summon a smile. 'Are you planning a surprise trip for our twenty-seventh anniversary?'

He considers this for a moment. 'Wouldn't be much of a surprise if I told you, would it?'

'He said it as if you'd know what he was talking about.'

'Nope. One of your brother's little jokes, maybe.'

I'm about to ask another question but it's cut short by the sharp *click* of the bathroom lock on the landing, the rapid tread of footsteps descending the stairs. The two of us sit back in our chairs, trying to look natural, normal, as if we're enjoying a regular Saturday lunchtime. Alfie appears in the kitchen in jeans and his favourite purple sweatshirt, his hair still wet from the shower, left hand cradled against his stomach.

'Is there anything else to eat apart from soup?' He opens a cupboard. 'I'm *starving*.'

I push my chair back and take our bowls to the sink. 'I thought you didn't want lunch, Alfie? You literally just had a McDonald's.'

He shrugs. 'Like, an hour ago.'

'Apple? Banana?'

He points at the table. 'How about the rest of that bread?'

I hand him what's left of the baguette and he bites into it, holding it like a foot-long ice cream. Careful not to knock his injured hand, I help him into his coat.

Jason stands up, shrugging his own parka back on. 'We'd better get going,' he says. 'Want to be in and out of that walk-in centre before the first Saturday evening drunks start to arrive.' On his way out of the kitchen, he gives me a peck on the cheek. 'Thanks for the soup, love.'

I try to catch his eye but he won't look at me.

'Let me know how you get on, what the doctor says.'

He waves a goodbye and with that, they're gone, the house falling silent again. I clear the kitchen, stack the dishwasher and flick the kettle on for a cup of peppermint tea. Waiting for it to boil, I check the Signal chat but there are no new messages – the most recent notification is from last night when Dev had angrily left the group halfway through the dinner party.

I switch to my electronic diary instead, pulling up Jason's shared diary alongside it. Had he blocked out our anniversary weekend in June for a trip to Paris? No. Was there some other weekend marked in his diary that would indicate he was planning a surprise, perhaps on my birthday, or his? Also no. Nothing in there for months apart from the unremarkable milestones of everyday life: his regular squash game with my brother, Alfie's football fixtures for the rest of the season, a mate's birthday, a blood donation appointment and a handful of other random entries.

There is nothing in his work diary either to suggest a trip to Paris in the last six months or the next. It was hardly likely – considering he worked in adult social care for the city council – but my brother's throwaway comment has got me chasing shadows. I type my husband's name and the word 'Paris' into Google and get millions of results, none of them relevant. A sportsman and a CEO who share my husband's name top the list.

I close the browser and find that my tea has already gone cold. My phone pings with a message from Jason.

Walk-in centre think prob not broken but have sent us to A & E just to be sure. Min 3 hr wait apparently. See you later.

I type a quick reply, asking if they'd like their favourite takeaway – from Little India around the corner – when they get home tonight. Within seconds, a thumbs-up response comes back. The takeaway menu is buried in a kitchen drawer and I dig it out to remind myself later. There was a time when Alfie had thought it funny because there was a girl in his class at school called India and she had been the tallest in the year, even though—

The memory brings me up short.

India. *Paris.* Maybe I'd jumped to the wrong conclusion. Maybe it wasn't about a place, but a person. A colleague? A friend? An old classmate?

Christian's words come back to me. *We've all got our demons, right? Our weaknesses?*

I realise, for the first time, that I'm actually nervous about what I might find. An unpleasant, creeping sense of dread about what might appear if I keep trying to prise open this particular Pandora's box. But Jason wouldn't have been unfaithful, would he? It was ridiculous, I'd never worried about that before. It had never even crossed my mind in twenty-six years of marriage. Not in a serious way.

Ignoring a needle prick of shame, I pull up Facebook and select my husband's profile. It takes another half an hour to scan through all of his friends there – he's never used it that much and only has a couple of hundred. He only posted once in the whole of last year, something about the FA Cup, and there's no one in his friends list with the name Paris, as a first or last name. Nothing on LinkedIn either. It's an unusual first name so I go back to Google and search using variations of *York Paris woman*, scrolling through more pages of image results. Looking for a face that might ring a bell, anything that might dislodge a memory or at least give a hint that this hasn't been a complete wild goose chase.

But as the freezing drizzle turns to rain outside, I drop my phone onto the table in frustration and rub my aching eyes.

There doesn't seem to be any link to my husband at all.

22

Kat doesn't arrive until mid-afternoon. She had texted me to say she was waiting until Dev was on his way to the Community Stadium before slipping out of the house ten minutes after him. He's been a season ticket holder at York City FC for as long as I've known him and he never misses a home game. This afternoon's match is – apparently – a bottom-of-the-table clash against Aldershot, and he won't be back home until at least half past five.

She pulls me in for a quick hug on the doorstep. A Cath Kidston overnight bag hangs empty in her hand, the white fabric patterned with multicoloured flowers.

'Afternoon, lovely.' She gives me a conspiratorial grin. 'I've come to make a withdrawal.'

I usher her inside, glancing left and right to check none of the neighbours have heard, waiting until the front door is firmly shut before returning her greeting.

'You've recovered from last night, then?' I take her black puffa jacket and hang it on a spare peg. 'Did you tell Dev you were coming over?'

She waves away the question. 'What he doesn't know can't hurt him.'

'You're going to have to tell him eventually though, aren't you?'

'Sooner or later – just not yet. Anyway, let me worry about that.' She glances towards the kitchen. 'Are we having tea, or something stronger?'

I make us both a brew – Yorkshire Tea for her, another peppermint for me – and tell her about the injury that has landed Alfie in A & E. As his godmother, she's always taken a keen interest in his sporting efforts but it's been a few years since he had allowed her to go to one of his games. She'd turned the air blue on the touchline enough times to get a warning from a string of referees.

'So,' she says, shaking the empty overnight bag. 'Shall we?'

I lead her up the stairs and past all of our framed family pictures on the landing. Past holiday pictures of Jason and the boys on a beach, the four of us on a campsite in Devon, family parties, school photos and Christmas dinners. A posed shot taken on our wedding day, Jason and me framed by a church lychgate, a scattering of pastel-coloured confetti at our feet.

At the door to the master bedroom, I turn back.

'Kat?' I feel suddenly awkward. 'Does the name Paris mean anything to you? Has Jason ever mentioned someone with that name?'

She frowns, shakes her head. 'Don't think so, love.'

I describe the conversation with my brother, the way he had dropped the name on me just before he left.

'Jason said he had no idea what I was talking about.'

'Well, that makes two of us.' She puts a hand on my arm. 'I'd take it with a pinch of salt, if I were you. Jason's not the type. And you know your brother, he's always liked to stir the pot. He's been an expert at winding you up since he was five years old.'

Prim is ensconced in her usual place in our bedroom, on Jason's side of the bed next to his pillow. She gives a sleepy squeak of protest when I pick her up and put her carefully on the armchair, stretching and yawning with a delicate slowness. Kat pulls on the strap to lift the bed frame, the top half gaping up like an open mouth, and leans in to survey the tightly packed clothes, bags, shoes and other detritus inside.

'Wow,' she says. 'You could do your very own car boot sale, Hels.'

I turn to look at her.

'You knew,' I say. 'Where it was hidden.'

She shrugs. 'It's your go-to place, where you've always stashed the kids' Christmas presents.' She gestures at the piles of clothes. 'Ever thought about having a declutter session?'

'You think I'm bad,' I say. 'You should see my mum's house.'

She turns to me. 'How is she doing?'

We talk about Mum for a few minutes, about my concerns that her dementia is getting worse, about Harcourt Park and the difficult conversations that lie ahead. Kat has been through this before with her own elderly father, a decade older than mine, who had point-blank refused to leave the family home until a fall down the stairs had put him in the hospital – where he died three weeks later. That had been some years back, but we'd had many conversations since about how we could encourage Mum down a different path.

'The sandwich generation,' she says. 'That's what we are: the generation that's somehow ended up caring both downwards and upwards – for our children and our parents – at the same time. No wonder we're all terminally cash-flow challenged. It's a genuine thing, you know. The sandwich generation. You can look it up, Google it.'

'I'll take your word for it, K.'

'This is your way out though, don't you see?' Her eyes are bright. 'You could quit your job, you've got the financial cushion now, you could quit tomorrow if you like. Tell your idiot boss to shove his job up his arse, like I did. *Very* satisfying, believe me. Don't tell me you've never been tempted.'

'More times than you can imagine, Kat. But I'm still a bit young to retire, don't you think?'

'I don't mean retirement. But how about a three-month break while you focus on getting your mum sorted out? Six months, if you like. Or maybe find something for just a couple of days a week so you can spend some quality time with her while she's still . . . you know. While she's still herself. At least some of the time.' She points at the blanket-covered backpack. '*You* deserve this more than any of us. You were the one who found it.'

'I can't just resign.'

'Why not? Give me one good reason.'

'Well . . . because I can't.'

'There's only one thing stopping you now.' She taps her index finger against her temple. 'This. *You*. You're the only one who's stopping yourself from doing what you want. You've done an amazing job with your boys, but Noah's living his best life down in London now and Alfie will be off to uni soon, then you'll be empty nesting even while you've got your hands full with your mum. Jason's pretty self-sufficient and you've been on about leaving your job for years.' She gestures vaguely into the mass of stuff in the space under our bed. 'This money gives you the breathing space, the freedom – and it's time to put yourself first for once. Take it. Grab it – do what's best for *you*. Now's your chance.'

23

I try to find a flaw in her argument, a problem in the logic of what she's saying. But nothing is forthcoming.

'Come on.' I lean down and pull the blanket off the backpack. 'We might as well get this done.'

I haul it out and drop it onto the floor at our feet. Even with a third of the contents removed, it's still bulky and awkward to lift one-handed. Prim jumps down from the armchair and strolls over to give it a good sniff, her small black nose twitching. Satisfied that it doesn't smell of food, dogs or other cats, she jumps up into the bed frame, picking her way across piles of clothes before curling up on a blanket in the now-empty corner.

I remove one of the two remaining black bin liners from the backpack and hand it to her, explaining that Jason had counted it carefully into three equal piles last night. I expect her to simply stow it inside her flowery Cath Kidston bag and suggest we go downstairs for a cheeky G & T, a celebratory toast and a quick Google search for *Luxury group holidays in the Caribbean*.

Instead, she opens the bin liner and shakes the contents out onto the floor.

Packets of money tumble out onto the cream carpet, like sweets from a selection box. She kneels down and starts to lay the bricks of fifties in a row, counting each one.

The same thing my brother had done.

Why did both of them insist on counting it?

'It's an equal split,' I say, perching on the edge of the armchair. 'A third of what was left. Five hundred and fourteen thousand, six hundred and sixty pounds. We had to break up one of the packets of twenties to make it exactly even.'

'It's all right,' she says. 'I trust you.'

'So why are you counting it?'

She holds one of the packets to her nose, breathing in deeply as if it's a bouquet of flowers or a freshly baked loaf of bread.

'Belt and braces,' she says. 'Don't mind, do you?'

'Where are you going to put it, when you get home?'

She taps the side of her nose. 'Somewhere safe. Where my grumpy husband won't find it.'

She looks down at the money and I can tell she's trying to be serious, trying to count it calmly like a bank teller, but a smile creeps across her face anyway.

'Still can't quite believe our luck,' she says. 'Can you?'

'Can't believe we've got to this point already, no. That we might actually start spending it.'

'Someone already *is* spending it,' she says, putting the first stack into her overnight bag. 'You think they took that fifty grand just to put it on the mantelpiece and look at it? Of course they didn't – they've splashed out on something, or tucked it away in the bank for a rainy day. And you know what? Nothing has happened. The sky hasn't fallen in, Helen. The police haven't kicked down anyone's door. Because no one *knows* about it. No one is looking for it. It's safe.'

As she talks, I watch her scooping up the dense bricks of colourful banknotes into her bag, Jason's words from earlier coming back to me. *If I was going to accuse anyone, if I had to put money on it, I'd say it was probably your best mate.* Even though I've had sleepless nights thinking about the money under our bed, seeing so much of it taken away gives me a strange, loose feeling of unease. I'd thought getting rid of it would make me feel better, lighter somehow. But instead, it feels like we're opening ourselves up to more danger.

'That fifty-six thousand,' I say. 'What would you have spent it on?'

'Me?' She grins. 'You know, all my usual vices: *Take That* tickets, cat-themed jewellery and the finest wines available to humanity.'

'Seriously,' I say. 'Was it you?'

She looks up. 'What if it was?'

'Well, was it?'

'No.'

'Would you tell me if it was?'

She shrugs, goes back to packing her bag. 'Of course. We're besties, aren't we?'

I'd seen her lie before. To traffic wardens and ticket inspectors, to teachers when we'd been at school together. The very first time, we had been walking at the tail end of a cross-country run, chatting about boys, cutting through a farmer's field to avoid half the distance, jogging the last hundred metres to catch up with the rest. My thirteen-year-old self watching in awe as Kat lied with a straight face to our PE teacher, Mr Godfrey, convincing him that we had in fact run the full two miles.

Was she lying now, though?

'I just can't believe *anyone* took it,' I say. 'I thought the six of us were . . . you know.'

'What?'

'Friends. Nice to each other.'

'You think everyone's nice, love. That's always been your problem.'

'But we are, aren't we?'

'Money does strange things to people, Helen. It changes them.'

'It hasn't changed my brother. And he's doing well.'

She zips the bag shut and stands up, brushing cat hair from the knees of her jeans, and I follow her out onto the landing.

'Only one thing worse than being poor,' she says. 'And that's being rich first. Then poor.'

'Not sure Christian will ever have that problem.'

At the top of the stairs, she turns and gives me a strange look. 'Has he . . . talked to you recently, about his business?'

'Only that he's still looking to sell up and do the semi-retirement thing. Why?'

'Nothing.' She gives me a tight smile and starts down the stairs. 'Listen, I'd love to stay for a cheeky G & T but I'd better get off, stash this before Dev gets home.'

I follow her down, a few steps behind.

'You're not going to tell him you've got it in the house?'

'Not yet.'

'Are you sure that's a good idea? What if he finds it?'

She scoops up her car keys from the windowsill.

'He won't.' She turns to give me a one-armed hug, the bag hanging heavy in her other hand. 'You're catastrophising again, love. It'll be fine. Tell your mum I said hello, OK?'

It's only after I've closed the front door to watch her through the little side window that my eye is drawn to the row of hooks on the wall. Above a spot that had originally been taken up by our old landline phone but was now occupied by the Wi-Fi router. All the keys for the house, the garage, the shed, the bike locks. Spare keys to Kat's house for pet-feeding duty when she was away. And to my brother's house, to reset the alarm or water the plants when his cleaner couldn't make it. I'd had those keys for years.

Just like Kat and Christian had had spare keys to *my* house for years. Front and back, so they could come in any time they liked.

Any time over the past week, for example.

When he'd dropped in earlier, my brother had figured out very quickly where the money was hidden. He had known where to find it.

And so had Kat.

24

Kat

It had been almost funny. The way Christian had sat in that pub lecturing them – in the slightly pompous way he had – that they should use the Signal app to talk to each other about the money. Because Signal had all the secrecy features and unbreakable encryption, all that stuff. And Kat had nodded along with the rest of them, making all the right noises, agreeing it was a good idea, saying she would download it when she got back to their home Wi-Fi.

Not letting on that she'd had it downloaded on her *other* phone a few years ago.

She pulled the door of the utility room shut and opened the cupboard next to the washing machine, kneeling down so she could reach in all the way to the back. She hooked her thumb into a gap beneath the chipboard panel, levering it up and away from the frame. Reaching down through the cobwebs and dust, her fingers found the smooth plastic of a Ziploc bag.

She lifted it out and opened it, tipping a small mobile phone into her palm.

Switching it on, she waited for it to come to life, double-checking that it was still set to silent. She kept it hidden down here in the utility room – among the washer and the tumble dryer, the mop and the iron and the bleach – because it was the *last* place Dev would look. She wasn't even sure he knew how to turn the washing machine on. Let alone find a loose panel behind all the bottles stacked in the cupboard.

The little phone was perhaps half the size of a regular mobile. There were no numbers stored in its contacts book and barely any text messages either – those she did send were only ever a few words, short innocuous phrases that didn't mean much unless you knew what they were about. *How's it going? You around today? This afternoon good?* The replies similarly oblique, opaque and never using times, dates, places. Nothing concrete. Everything deniable.

She selected the app and typed a short message on the little phone.

Later today usual place?

She waited, watched, the familiar buzz building in her chest: the thrill, the promise, the warm glow of anticipation.

A reply appeared on the small screen.

K

She smiled, shook her head. The reply was even more cautious than her message – but it was never more than the bare minimum, a few words, a handful of letters. Or a single letter.

The muffled sound of the front door signalled Dev's return, his footsteps, a jingle of keys, the click of the kettle flicked on.

'Kat?'

She powered the little phone off and watched the screen go black.

'In here.'

'Making coffee.' His voice was muffled through the closed door. 'Do you want one, love?'

'Go on then.'

Kat sealed the phone back inside the bag and replaced it in its hiding place. She shut the cupboard and busied herself with the basket of washing, shoving handfuls of clothes into the machine, switching into the autopilot of a task done a thousand times before. Shirts, underwear, towels, trousers. Dev was a bugger for leaving things in his pockets, usually tissues that would dissolve into a thousand sodden fragmentary blobs in a forty-degree wash. She took a pair of his jeans from the basket and did a quick check now.

No tissues this time, but tucked way down in a back pocket there was a receipt of some kind, a ticket, just a small strip of paper . . .

Not a ticket. Something else. A printed logo at the top, a name familiar from the high street, times and dates. She turned it over in her hand, studying numbers and letters. Allowing herself a moment to think before tucking it into the pocket of her own jeans and continuing to load the washing machine.

Perhaps it was nothing. Perhaps she was jumping to conclusions.

Or perhaps she wasn't the only one keeping a secret.

25

Mum's front door is standing open when I arrive on Sunday morning.

Two upstairs windows are open too, all the curtains open and every single light in the house is blazing. At first I assume she's been waiting for me, looking out for my car, standing in the hall in her hat and coat. But she's not there when I push the door open all the way.

'Mum?' I shut the front door behind me, suppressing a shiver. There is a cold breeze blowing through the hallway. 'It's me, Helen. You left the front door open.'

I go through to the kitchen, put a bag of shopping down on the counter. There is a half-drunk cup of tea on the small kitchen table, a single slice of toast on a plate beside it. A kitchen window is pushed all the way open too, cold January air knifing through the house.

'Mum?'

I touch the teacup. A bare vestige of warmth left in the china, the tea dark, almost black. Despite all the lights being on, the house feels vacant, abandoned, empty of any presence except my own. A cold, hard ball of panic starts to grow in my stomach as I check the small utility room by the back door. She's not there. I hurry through to the lounge, then the little dining room that she had turned into her crafting area. No sign of her. I take the stairs at a half-run, calling her name again, checking her bedroom, the spare room – which had been mine, all those years ago – and the little box room that had been Christian's as we were growing up. All the beds are made. All the rooms are neat and tidy. All the lights are on.

But my mother is not here.

The hospital doctor's words come back to me. The quiet conversation we'd had while Mum was being X-rayed after her fall on New Year's Day. *There is a tipping point with dementia*, he'd said. *When the patient tips over from being just about able to cope at home, most of the time, to losing their ability to live a safe, independent life without help.* He had not offered a judgement on where she was on that timescale. But he'd not needed to.

The ball of panic expands, rising up into my chest, pressing against my lungs, my heart. More in hope than anything else, I take out my phone and dial her number on the way back downstairs. My breath catches as the call connects – I can hear it ringing, so she must be close by – before it rings for a second time and I realise why. It trills again as I open the cutlery drawer and it's there, alongside the dessert spoons, *Helen mobile* showing on the display.

I end the call and run out into the back garden, then the garage, the shed and to the neighbours on each side to ask if they've seen her. Not caring that I must look manic, frantic, my coat flapping in the cold January wind. Only Mike at number sixty-six is home – but he's not seen Mum since yesterday. All the while a thought circles high above me, like a bird of prey riding the thermals, a dark, forbidding speck against the blue. *The money. Does this have something to do with it? Mum gone, her house empty? Bad fortune to balance out the good?*

Or worse: *Has someone taken her?* The dark possibilities swarm and multiply. *Maybe Alfie is in danger too. Noah and Jason.*

I shake the thoughts away. First, I have to find my mother.

But where would she go? Her car is on the drive, where it has sat for months, so she is on foot. What is nearby, where has she been a thousand times, where has she gone before and not been able to find her way back?

Maybe that was it.

I pull the front door shut and get back into my car. I reverse hurriedly out of the drive and head for the parade of shops at the end of the road. I dial Christian's number on the hands-free and he answers on the first ring.

'I've got her.' He doesn't bother with pleasantries, his voice calm and steady. 'She's OK. We were just about to come back to the house.'

Relief pulses through me like a balm and a moment later I'm pulling up by the little row of shops that have been here since I was a girl, only a few hundred metres from the house. On a bench across the road, Mum sits with my brother, his hand in hers, his big navy overcoat draped over her shoulders. Her small frame is swamped by it, like a child playing dress-up with an adult's clothes.

Once she's safely in the back of my car, Christian explains that he had been driving past on the way to the house and seen her shivering at the bus stop with a bag of shopping, no coat, no glasses, slippers on her feet, staring down the road.

'No buses stop here on a Sunday,' he says quietly. 'Not since we were kids.'

'Something's got to give,' I say. 'She can't carry on like this.'

He nods, climbing back into his Audi. 'I know.'

Safely back in her kitchen, Christian goes around the house turning off lights and closing windows while I make a fresh pot of tea and unload the shopping.

Slowly, Mum seems to come back to herself.

'I just went up the road to get some milk for the tea and a paper for your dad,' she says finally, her tone slightly aggrieved. 'That was all.'

To my astonishment, Mum takes to Harcourt Park like a duck to water.

After giving us both a scare in the morning, we take her for a three-course lunch in the on-site restaurant – it also helps that the food is excellent – and Christian uses all his powers of persuasion to talk her round to the idea of staying here just for a few days, like a mini-break, to see if she could get used to the idea. I had already established on the phone that they could offer a three-day trial visit, like a stay in a hotel – if we put down a £1,000 deposit today plus the first two weeks' fees of £3,000 as a fully refundable goodwill gesture.

I had done the groundwork in a long phone call, a manager explaining that they would accept a deposit and a certain number of payments in cash. It's not standard practice, he had said, but it was not unheard of either. They liked to be as flexible as possible for their new clients and were aware that some still preferred to keep savings at home, in cash, rather than at the bank. *Stashed in a kitchen drawer or under the bed* is the subtext, although he didn't say that part out loud.

Just like the brick of currency I'd taken from under *our* bed yesterday.

My heart had been racing this morning as I slid out a slim wedge of fifties from the pile – £2,000 in total – which would cover my half of the initial payment. I'd felt almost drunk, giddy with nerves, as I sealed the cash inside a plain white envelope and tucked it into my handbag. Even stacked together, the forty notes were so thin, so insubstantial, that it felt ridiculous that they could have so much power to make things better. To make Mum's life better.

At lunch, I let Christian do most of the talking. As the golden younger sibling, her little prince, she would always listen to him in a way that she didn't to me. Over the years it had morphed into a sibling joke between us, that he was her favourite, the baby boy, the one who could do no wrong.

After a dessert of tiramisu and delicate chocolate wafers, we have another tour of the facilities. This time it's given not by a staff member but by a resident, a smiley seventy-something called Janice who shows Mum around and introduces her to various people along the way. Janice seems to know everyone and it's not long before Mum is chatting away to another couple of ladies in the sunroom as if they've been friends for years. Christian and I loiter by the door, sipping takeout cups of fresh coffee that tastes as if it's come straight from Starbucks. I'm half expecting to see Alexander Sykes again, checking in with one of his managers, but thankfully there is no sign of him. In the grand scheme of things today, another awkward encounter with an ex-boyfriend should be the least of my worries. All the same, I'd prefer it if I *didn't* bump into him again.

'I think it's working,' I say quietly. 'Mum likes it here.'

My brother nods slowly. 'Haven't seen her look like that since Dad died.'

'Like what?'

'Happy.'

It was true. She *did* look happy, or at least engaged, interested, talking with a couple of strangers in a strange place. She would be safe here. It felt like progress.

But a splinter of doubt still remains.

'Except she wouldn't be happy,' I say. 'If she knew how this was being paid for.'

'We're doing a good thing, Helen.' He sips his coffee without looking at me. 'We're using the money for a good purpose. We're bringing something positive out of it.'

I shoot him a glance. 'And what about Paris? Is that a good thing too?'

A pause. 'Not really, no.'

'What, or who, is it? Jason said he didn't know what I was talking about. So are you going to tell me, or what?'

'Just forget it,' he says. 'Forget I said it, sis. It's not important.'

I look across at him, take a good look at him for the first time today. He's made more of an effort than yesterday, in a white shirt and dark grey blazer, but his skin is blotchy and grey and there is a shaving cut under his chin, his eyes shadowed with tiredness.

'What's going on with you, Christian? Is everything OK?' Mum is still chatting to her new-found friends and she turns to give me a little wave. I wave back. 'With the business, I mean?'

'Everything's fine,' he says. 'Why wouldn't it be?'

'It's just that—'

'Is this Jason again? Honestly, I can't work out why he's being such a shit stirrer this week.'

My phone buzzes and I dig it out of my handbag. A text from Kat.

Nice to see you yesterday. Enjoyed the timber too ;-) Coffee Thursday, as usual? X

After the word 'timber' she's added an emoji of a winking face.

Christian mutters something about going to fill out some paperwork at reception, leaving me with Mum in the sunroom.

That night, Jason and I watch a film in the lounge with Alfie. It's our son's turn to choose and he finds something on Netflix called *Adrift*, a thriller-cum-horror about a group of friends sailing the Pacific on a yacht. At an early stage in the movie they all jump off for a swim – before realising they have forgotten to lower the ladder so none of them can climb back onboard, or call for help. It's fairly schlocky and mercifully short but as I'm watching, and the first sharks begin to circle the yacht, my mind keeps drifting to that cave in the Dales, to the backpack, the cottage. The slim stack of fifty-pound notes I had sealed inside an envelope. The money we had already started to spend.

We had jumped off the boat now. And there was no way to climb back up.

26

Jason

She was late.

Jason checked his watch again. Already ten past the hour, ten minutes after the time they had agreed. He checked his phone but there were no new messages, nothing from her to say why she'd been delayed. Or whether she'd changed her mind and wasn't coming at all. He decided to give her ten more minutes.

Street lights glittered a cold, white light onto wet tarmac as he sat in his car, rubbing his hands together against the cold. It was an area of the city he knew all too well, tired sixties housing sagging with neglect on a cluttered street. In the small front garden opposite – it wasn't a garden really, just a slab of cracked concrete – a mouldering brown sofa rotted like the carcass of some long-dead sea creature. In the next garden along, the twisted metal skeletons of a pair of old garden chairs rusted next to an old washing machine, its door hanging open on one hinge.

He turned the key in the ignition. The Nissan's engine coughed quietly into life and he turned the heaters up to maximum, angling the warm air onto the windscreen to keep it from fogging. Onto him as well, to chase the chill from his bones. Just a few minutes of heat while he waited, then he'd switch it off again. How many times had he sat on a street like this, waiting for a girl like her? Sitting in his car with one eye on the mirror and the other on his phone?

Too many.

And how many times would it be before he got caught? Because he would get caught, eventually – he knew enough to realise that. With devastating consequences for all concerned, no matter how careful he was, how secretive, no matter how many precautions he took. No matter what he told Helen. He tried not to think about her on nights like this.

But *until* he got caught, he would continue to roll the dice. To play the odds. What was it that brought him back here, again and again? He'd asked himself that many times but he still wasn't exactly sure. Some sort of compulsion. Frustration, for sure. What was it Christian had said to him that time? That Jason needed to *paint outside the lines* once in a while. And there were dozens of girls like her, hundreds, in every neighbourhood like this. In every town, every city. You could find them everywhere – if you knew where to look.

He killed the engine and the car sank into silence again.

He had booked a room at the usual place. One of his regular haunts. It was discreet, out of the way, the kind of place where you weren't likely to bump into someone you knew. And one of the few left that still accepted cash. He patted his pocket, felt the reassuringly solid shape of the envelope.

He checked his phone again. Still no new messages.

Finally, just as he was about to give up hope, he saw her, turning the corner and hurrying down the street towards him.

Jason got out of the car, locked it, and waited for her to reach him. He walked beside her the last few steps to the big glass double doors, pulling one open and gesturing with his free hand.

'After you.'

With one final glance over his shoulder, he followed her inside.

27

On Monday I go to the bank at lunchtime and pay £900 into my current account.

I use one of the paying-in machines rather than going to the counter and facing an actual member of staff. But even so, my hands shake as I fill out the slip and drop the sealed envelope into the slot, aware of the glass globes of CCTV cameras that dot the inside of the branch. I wear my big coat and a woolly bobble hat pulled down low over my ears, keeping my head down even though I know it's ridiculous, considering I've written my name on the deposit slip.

According to Christian, the threshold for triggering any kind of additional scrutiny from the bank is £1000, but I want to play it safe until I know for sure. There's some kind of annual limit too, but we'll cross that bridge when we come to it, I suppose. When the first deposit clears, I will transfer it into the joint savings account we have for Alfie to go to university.

Next to the bank is a boarded-up greengrocer's shop, a homeless man sitting cross-legged in the doorway on a pile of flattened cardboard. Beside him is a skinny dog sitting at attention, shivering in the cold. I reach in my pocket for some change and then realise I can do better than that. Better than just a few coins. I go across the road to the café, buy a sandwich and a cup of tea, then a box of dry dog food from the Tesco Express next door. The homeless man accepts all of it from me with a disbelieving smile, a flurry of thank-yous as he shakes out a good portion of dog food onto the cardboard and the animal tucks in hungrily. I have two twenty-pound notes remaining in my purse, and hand them both to him. He is still thanking me in a broad Geordie accent – 'Bless you, madam, bless you' – as I walk away.

On Tuesday, I open two more accounts, with two different banks, paying in opening deposits of £925 into the first and £890 into the second. I'll open two more next week and keep on putting the money in a little at a time, different amounts each time, keeping them small and separate from each other for the time being at least.

Jason is doing the same.

After work, I drive over to Harcourt Park to visit Mum. I find her in one of the lounges, playing gin rummy with three other residents.

She smiles when she sees me, excusing herself from the game and getting up slowly from the table to give me a hug. Her left arm is still in the sling, a support on her wrist to protect it while the sprain heals. She seems to have settled in well, even though she's only here for a trial visit, and I'm relieved to discover that today seems to be one of her lucid days.

I fetch cups of tea for both of us and we settle into armchairs by the big picture window, looking out onto a sweeping lawn bounded by paths that meander down to the lake. She seems brighter, livelier than I've seen her in a long time, as if simply being here, surrounded by people instead of alone in her empty house has brought out the best in her. I know the dementia means tomorrow might be a bad day, but it's good to see a flash of her old self. Like having her back, after a long absence. As we sip our tea, she tells me about some of the other residents she's made friends with, about the meals and the book club, the swimming pool and the coach trip to Whitby next weekend.

It's more than I've heard her say in weeks, maybe months. Seeing her here, in this warm, welcoming place, with its professional staff and amazing facilities, I feel for the first time that maybe Jason had been right all along. Maybe we *had* made the right decision. Yes, perhaps our route to this point had started from somewhere bad, out of a bank losing a tiny fraction of its billions. But that money had probably been made from screwing customers anyway, from rinsing them year in, year out with high interest and overdraft fees and penalty clauses and all the financial machinery at their disposal. We had turned it into something good, something positive. We were using it for a good reason, a little bit of wealth redistribution to help someone who deserved it more than most.

Perhaps this is what it feels like, not having to worry about money anymore. It feels *good*. There is a lightness to it, a relief, as if I've finally put down a heavy load I've been carrying all my life. As we talk, I allow myself to daydream about Noah getting himself established in London, giving him the money for a deposit on a little flat. About wiping out the tens of thousands he's carrying in student debt, lifting it off his shoulders, being able to do the same for his brother so he can start his adult life unencumbered too. I allow myself to daydream about the day we're finally free of the mortgage, free of the millstone that's been around our necks for the best part of thirty years.

Mum asks about the boys, about Jason, about our New Year trip to the Dales. I don't tell her about the money.

'I've been thinking,' she says, 'I might like to stay here for a while longer. You know, not permanently, but the people here are so nice and the food's lovely.'

I put a hand over hers, the skin paper-thin beneath my palm.

'That's good, Mum, I'm so pleased you like it. I can bring some more clothes and things from your house tomorrow, what would you like me to fetch?'

She gives me a short list and I take notes on my phone. Clothes, toiletries, a few cosmetics, the slippers she got for Christmas. When I look up, she fixes me with a concerned stare.

'You look tired, Helen. Are you all right, love?'

The daydreams vanish like morning mist.

'I'm fine, Mum.'

'Are you sure? You know you can still talk to me, don't you? Tell me anything.'

I give her what I hope is a reassuring nod – but it was true, I *felt* tired, deep in my bones. I'd been sleeping badly, the nights disturbed by dark visions of police and prison, of being in the dock of a courtroom and sitting on a pile of fifty-pound notes. And when she asks this question – the same way she had asked me when I was an anxious child, a moody teenager, a sleep-deprived new mother – I suddenly find that I'm swallowing back tears, a hard lump in my throat. She's always been able to see straight through me.

'I'm OK.' I look down into my tea. 'It's nothing, just a bit of the January blues.'

'Is that all, love?'

My phone rings and I retrieve it from my handbag to see my boss's name on the display. I reject the call.

'And how's work?' Mum glances at my phone too as it vibrates against the table with the ping of a new voicemail. 'Do I even need to ask?'

'The usual,' I sigh. 'Same rubbish, different day.'

'That boss of yours, is it?' She makes a disapproving noise in her throat. 'Do you want me to talk to him, tell him where to get off? Jumped-up little shit.'

'*Mum.*'

The casual profanity is so unexpected I feel a smile tugging at my lips. Mum shrugs and smiles back and then I'm giggling, we're both giggling like schoolgirls at the back of the class. I still haven't got used to her swearing. She had never done it when Christian and

I were growing up, but her internal filter had crumbled in recent years and now the curse words seemed to pop out frequently, as if she's been saving them up all this time.

The phone rings again and I reject the call again. Another ping signifies another voicemail.

'He *is* though,' she says, looking at her small wristwatch. 'Six thirty in the evening. He can't call you round the clock, love, it's just not right. You're his PA but it doesn't mean he owns you.'

'I know, but that's what he's like. He'll keep calling and calling until I pick up.'

I dial into my voicemail and listen to his messages, establish which document he can't find in the client database, and text him instructions on how to get to it.

'Done,' I say. 'He'll be all right now, he's got what he needs.'

'Stupid useless bastard,' Mum says, even more loudly than before. 'Men like him never learn, love, they think they're bloody wonderful but still need their asses wiped.'

'*Mum?*' I give her a warning look, checking to see if anyone has heard. One of the card-playing ladies at the next table is looking over, eyebrows raised. 'You're being a bit loud.'

'He is though, isn't he? Needs a bloody good clip around the ear. And the rest.'

I smile and nod at the lady on the next table. After a moment, she goes back to her card game.

'You're right,' I say to Mum, quietly. 'And yes, he certainly does.'

My phone vibrates again, a different sound this time, and she puts down her mug of tea decisively on the table.

'Enough is enough,' she says. 'I'm going to talk to him, give him a few home truths.'

But it's not another phone call. It's a notification from our doorbell camera at home, the motion sensor tinkling like a wind chime. Probably Alfie's friends calling round, although I can't remember him saying he had plans for this evening. I bring up the Ring app on my phone just as it gives the sonorous chime of the doorbell, the default sound of three notes rising in sequence. I click on the live feed from the doorbell camera, which points down our drive. The background is familiar, our small garden deep in winter shadow, Jason's car parked on the gravel driveway just off to the side.

In the foreground, two figures on the doorstep are illuminated by the harsh white wash of a motion-activated light. They're too old to be Alfie's friends. In fact, I've never seen them before in my life. Two men, one young, one older. Both in suits and overcoats, both looking cold and tired.

As I watch, my mum leans over to see what I'm looking at. Through the phone's small speaker, I hear the click and scrape of the front door opening, Jason offering a muffled greeting to the strangers.

The older of the two men replies, saying something I can't hear, then reaches into his jacket and pulls out a slim black wallet. Because he's directly in front of the camera, the wallet looms large on my phone screen as he flips it open. It takes a half-second for the lens to focus before I can make out a photo ID and some kind of official crest. Below the photo, four words that send a needle of panic straight through my chest. *Detective Sergeant Andrew Docherty.*

Police.

28

My first thought is: *the money*.

Immediately followed by a flush of shame, of guilt, that my instinctive fear had not been about the boys, not about Alfie or Noah, not that something had happened to one of my sons that was bad enough to bring police to our door. But about myself. My actions. My decision to start spending someone else's money.

I say a quick goodbye to Mum and hurry out to reception. In the car park, I break into a half-run and dial Jason's number as I'm digging for my keys. It rings three times before going to voicemail and I imagine Jason standing there in the hall or the lounge, talking to a couple of police officers as his phone rings, unable to answer as they take turns to fire questions at him. I leave a hurried voicemail telling him I'm on my way home and asking him to call me back before pulling out and accelerating up the long driveway towards the main road.

Held up at a red traffic light a minute later, I hold my phone in my lap and type a quick text to Jason.

Why police there? Are the kids OK? On way home now. x

Surely, *surely*, they couldn't be here because we'd paid some cash into the bank, could they? That was only hours ago. Was it possible it had already triggered some banking alert, some notification that had gone up the chain and been passed on to the police to be investigated? The way Christian had sold it to us, the first alert would go to the HMRC or some banking regulator. Some bureaucrat. Not the police.

So it couldn't be that. Could it? But as I drive, I find myself desperately hoping that it *is* the money, hoping a hundred times over as I consider the alternative scenarios. Remembering with a sick jolt of panic that Alfie had said he was going out after school with his friend Taylor – who had just passed his driving test and had inherited an unwanted Vauxhall Corsa from a grandparent. *Oh, God. Please not that.* My mind flashes on a vision of Alfie and his friend being cut from the wreckage of the car, an ambulance rushing them away, a police visit to notify us that they were in hospital. Or was it Noah, in London? Mugged or stabbed or run down in the street? London was a dangerous place and violent crime there seemed so commonplace that most of it never even got reported in the media. What if—

Stop it. If it was one of the boys, Jason would have called back by now. At the next red traffic light, I check my phone again. My message is unread and he's not replied. I fire off another and stamp on the accelerator as the amber light shows below the red.

Ten minutes later, I'm turning onto our drive, past a dark-coloured Volvo saloon parked on the street in front of our house. All the downstairs windows are lit up but the master bedroom, above, is in darkness. Jason's Nissan is on the drive too, pulled up close to the house.

I find my husband sitting in the lounge, his palms flat on the rounded arms of the chair as if he might launch himself forward at any moment. The two men I'd seen on the Ring doorbell are on the sofa, both of them perched on the edge of the seat, looking faintly uncomfortable in their suits and overcoats, as if they don't plan on staying long.

As I walk in their conversation stops, three pairs of eyes swivelling towards me. The room is thick with tension, the meaty smell of chilli con carne reaching through from the kitchen. The older man – the one who had held his ID up to the doorbell camera – nods a greeting. He's in his mid-forties, with dark greying hair and the jowly good looks of a once-handsome guy on whom years of police work had taken their toll.

'What's going on?' I say, my heart thudding painfully in my chest. 'Is it Alfie, are the boys all right? Jason, you didn't reply to my messages.'

'The boys are both fine, Alfie's upstairs in his room.' He says it slowly, holding my gaze as he speaks, as if he's trying to communicate something with his eyes. 'This is Detective Sergeant Docherty and his colleague . . .' He points at the younger of the two men. 'I'm really sorry, I didn't quite catch your name at the door.'

'DC Roe.' The younger officer is taller, thinner than his colleague, with short gingery-blond hair and a smattering of acne scars across his cheeks. He has a small black notebook open on his knee, a pen in one hand. 'Nice to meet you, Mrs Cooper.'

Docherty shifts slightly on the sofa, turning slightly towards me. 'We were saying earlier to your husband, apologies for dropping in on you like this and interrupting your dinner. We'll try to be as quick as possible, then we'll leave you to your evening.'

'What's going on?' The sharp relief that my children are safe is replaced by something slower, more anonymous. A dark, creeping dread, spreading out like molasses. 'What's happened?'

Jason indicates the older of the two officers.

'The sergeant was just telling me about an investigation.' With a tight smile, he adds: 'Would you mind filling my wife in too, so she knows what you're after?'

'Not at all,' Docherty says, with a slow nod. 'But just to reiterate, this is a highly sensitive point in our investigation and we'd really appreciate your discretion. I can't give you chapter and verse, but what I *can* tell you is still highly confidential.'

'Of course,' I say. 'What is it . . . that you're investigating?'

'Well,' he says. 'As I was saying to your husband, my colleague and I are with the Serious and Organised Crime Unit at Greater Manchester Police. We've been working for some months now on one particular case with a lot of different aspects to it, a lot of moving parts.'

'Oh,' I say. 'Manchester. I assumed you'd be North Yorkshire police.'

'We are liaising with the local lads, yes, and with the Northumbria force too. But we're the taking the lead on this one for reasons which will be obvious if I give you a bit of background. As I said, please don't repeat this to anyone else, Mrs Cooper.'

I take off my coat and sit down on the remaining armchair, glancing across at Jason. He is sitting very still in the other chair, like a mouse that's spotted a cat and doesn't want to draw attention to itself. It gives me a loose, unpleasant feeling in my stomach.

'Sorry.' I drag my eyes back to the two men on the sofa. 'Can I get you anything? Tea? Coffee?'

Docherty shakes his head, indicating a glass of water already on the table beside him.

He and his colleagues, he explains, are investigating an organised crime group that has been operating for some years across the north-west. Calling themselves the Kingsway Crew after a road in south Manchester where they originated, they had become established as one of the major suppliers of cocaine, ecstasy and ketamine in the region.

'Two months ago,' Docherty says, 'they were in contact with another organised crime group based on Tyneside, hence the Northumbria Police connection. Following that there was supposed to be a large transaction for a significant quantity of class A drugs between the two groups. A wholesale deal, in Manchester.'

As he talks, my stomach sinks lower and lower, a watery sensation in my thighs, my knees. I try to maintain a neutral expression, as if I have no idea where this is going to lead. I need to get Jason into the kitchen, have a conversation with him that won't be overheard, but when I try to catch his eye he's looking fixedly at the detective, his expression impassive. Ever the poker player.

'Anyway,' Docherty continues, 'somehow, this deal went wrong. We don't know exactly what happened yet, but we do know that no drugs changed hands and the money disappeared. Two men were shot, one of whom died and the other left in a coma from which he's not expected to recover. Subsequent inquiries led us to believe that evidence may have been hidden somewhere in the North Yorkshire Dales by one of the Tyneside group on his way back up to the north-east.'

I clear my throat. 'What kind of evidence?'

'A holdall,' Roe cuts in. His voice is surprisingly deep, his Manchester accent more pronounced than Docherty's. 'A gym bag of some kind, or maybe a backpack. We have reason to believe that bag contains the weapon that was used in the double shooting as well.'

'A gun?'

'Yes, and other forensic evidence that could link to both the Kingsway Crew and the Tyneside group. Possibly some of the missing money too. In or near a town called Pateley Bridge.'

He stops talking and a heavy, loaded silence settles on the room, broken only by the soft background burble of the TV in the kitchen.

'Sorry,' Jason says, 'I'm not quite following. Still not sure why you've come to be *here*, at our house?'

Both detectives turn towards my husband.

Docherty says: 'Long story short, we believe the original couriers concealed a passive tracking device with the money. Last week a phone belonging to one of them – the one now in a coma – was finally cracked by our forensic people and they were able to analyse it. They found it was connecting to a passive device, but it wasn't where we thought it would be. It wasn't in the Yorkshire

Dales.' He points an index finger down, as if picking out a blemish in the tired living room carpet. 'The device was pinging from this address. Here.'

'A tracker?'

'That's right.'

There is another painful silence. I feel as if someone is pressing down on my chest, squeezing my lungs back against my spine.

Finally, Jason says, 'You know what? I think it must be upstairs.'

I throw another desperate glance at him, trying to catch his eye. Trying to communicate a string of panicked questions with a single look: *What are you doing? Are we just going to hand it over? What do we say about all the money that's missing?*

But Docherty is already getting to his feet, gesturing towards the hall, the stairs.

'Lead the way.'

Jason goes first and the two detectives follow, the staircase creaking as they climb. My legs are leaden as I bring up the rear behind Roe, a faint smell of citrus aftershave following in his wake. It occurs to me that this is what I'd wanted all along, what I'd *said* I wanted. This was what I'd argued for at the cottage – to hand over the money to the police straightaway – while Jason had quietly suggested an alternative course. Somehow, in the weeks since then, we had swapped places.

What had changed since that cold, wet New Year's Eve out on the moors? What was different? The answer, now that I'm forced to consider it, is suddenly obvious.

I had tried the forbidden fruit.

Perhaps I'd already got a taste for it.

Whereas my husband, for his own reasons, had gone in the other direction. Despite all of his persuasive arguments, he'd decided to surrender our windfall without a second thought.

In the master bedroom, Prim is nestled in her usual place on Jason's side of our bed. But when she hears strange voices she jolts awake, leaps to the floor in alarm and scuttles off between our legs towards the landing, ears flattened to her head.

DC Roe pulls out two pairs of white nitrile gloves from his coat pocket, handing one pair to his colleague. They both snap them on with practised ease.

I try one last time to catch Jason's eye, to ask him questions I can't speak out loud. *Are we doing this? Right now? Just handing it over?*

But he ignores me. Instead, he heaves up the bed frame to reveal the storage space beneath, pointing at the backpack in the corner.

'That's it,' he says. 'That's what we found.'

29

Docherty reaches in and lifts the backpack out with a gloved hand. Unzipping the top, he peers inside. But the way he handles it, the ease with which he lifts it, gives me another jolt of shock.

The backpack is empty.

I stand, frozen in place, as the detectives examine it. It feels as if all the air has been sucked out of the room.

Half a million pounds. Gone. Our plans for the money up in smoke. Had we been robbed? Had my brother returned with his key when the house was empty, cleaned us out? Or maybe it was Kat?

But Jason's face is untroubled by shock or surprise.

Abruptly, I realise why. He already *knew* the bag was empty when he brought the detectives up here.

Until a few moments ago, I had assumed that he wanted to come clean, to tell the truth. A change of heart prompting him to tell the police everything, to hand over our share of the cash and call an end to all of it. But he had never intended to tell them. The reversal makes me dizzy, as if I can't trust myself to say the right thing anymore.

Docherty turns the backpack around, examining it from all sides while Roe shakes out a clear plastic bag the size of a bin liner. Docherty lowers the backpack into it, his partner pulling off a seal-strip at the top and filling in a panel headed 'Evidence Bag – Do Not Open' in quick black capitals.

While they're both occupied with bagging and tagging, I move behind them and finally manage to catch Jason's eye, mouthing a single silent word to him.

Where?

He gives me a tiny, almost imperceptible shake of his head. All I know is that our share of the money was there in that bag this morning, and now it's vanished. Without moving his head, Jason raises his eyes to the ceiling – just for a split second, and then it's gone. *The attic.*

'OK,' the older detective says, turning back to us. 'So this is how you found it? Empty?'

'Yeah,' Jason says, without hesitation.

'You didn't remove the contents?' he says. 'You didn't take what was inside?'

'No, there was nothing—'

'Because, obviously, that would be an offence.'

I hold my breath. I want to lean against the wall, to brace myself against something solid, to sit down, to scream into a pillow. But I can't do any of those things.

'Of course.' Jason nods his agreement. 'Actually, it was my wife who found it. Wasn't it, Hels?'

I stare at my husband, trying to keep my face neutral, to digest the implications of what he's just said: a straight-faced lie to a police officer. An abrupt change of direction down a new path, one that I had to follow – unless I contradicted him with my next breath.

In the moment, I realise I don't really have a choice.

'Hmm.' I feel light-headed, as if I've stood up too fast. 'Yes. That's right. I mean, I was actually trying to retrieve my water bottle.'

I describe the moment in the cave as we had taken shelter from the storm outside, a flat fissure in the rock that stretched back into the darkness, my bottle rolling into the gap. The chance discovery of something else pushed way down deep into that dark, claustrophobic space.

Roe is scribbling in his small black notebook again.

'And this was when, exactly?'

'New Year's Eve. Mid-afternoon, maybe around three o'clock.'

He looks up from his notebook. His small, unblinking eyes are a very pale brown, almost hazel.

'And there was nothing at all inside it?'

I shake my head, a little too vigorously.

'No,' I say, absently straightening a pile of books on my bedside table. 'Nothing.'

'And this cave, could there—'

'You know what?' I hold a hand up. 'There was something in there. A receipt, in one of the side pockets, from a shop in Newcastle.' I look around the bedroom, trying to remember what I'd done with the small piece of till roll, before locating it on top of the low bookcase under the window. It curls up from beneath a black ceramic paperweight in the shape of a Siamese cat. 'Here it is. We've already touched it, looked at it, sorry. Is that a problem?'

With a gloved hand, Roe plucks the slim strip of paper from beneath the black cat and drops the receipt into a small plastic evidence bag. Once it's sealed, he peers at the faded black ink, holding it close to his face. Docherty joins him, both of them squinting at the receipt through the plastic.

Too late, I realise what else I've put under the ceramic paperweight for safekeeping: a white envelope. Even from across the room, it seems obvious to me what's inside from the shape, the size, the rectangular uniformity of the contents. Both detectives are within touching distance of a wedge of fifty-pound notes from the backpack – the next payment ready to go to Harcourt Park. I hadn't even sealed it yet. All they had to do was lift the paperweight and the envelope's flap would lift open to reveal what was inside.

A hot flash of panic threatens to buckle my knees.

Docherty's eyes swivel towards me.

'This cave,' he says. 'How big was it? Could there have been anything else hidden down there as well as the bag?'

'Maybe.' I nod, as if I'm giving it serious consideration. 'It stretched back quite a long way. I only had my phone torch and it was really low down, really dark and awkward to see very far.'

'Big enough for a person?'

'That's what I thought it was, at first.' I shiver at the memory. 'When I was reaching out, I thought it was someone's jacket, that someone had crawled in there and got stuck.'

'So it was pretty well hidden? Well out of sight?'

'The thing is,' Jason cuts in before I can answer, 'the backpack looked almost new, and it was good quality, a good brand, so I thought maybe we could use it. At first I was thinking I'd see if there was any ID and I could package it up and send it to whoever it belonged to.' He's talking quickly now, as if he doesn't want to leave any gaps for me to dive into. 'But there wasn't any, so I just thought, there's no point handing it into the police and I thought I'd keep it instead. Sorry. I shouldn't have, really.'

Docherty shrugs. 'No way you could have known,' he says. 'That we'd be interested. We have to assume at this stage that someone found it before you did, before we did. They've taken the contents and left the empty backpack behind – probably because they suspected it might contain a tracking device.'

'Right.' Jason rubs thoughtfully at the stubble along his jawline. 'Makes sense, I suppose.'

As we've been talking, Roe has put away his notebook and is handling the backpack through the plastic evidence bag. He runs his hands around all the seams, around the base, the zips, the padded back. When he gets to the left-side strap he stops, feeling for something between his thumb and forefinger.

'Here,' he says. 'Here it is, boss. Stitched into the lining of the strap.'

He hands the bag to Docherty, who feels the same spot with gloved hands. He nods slowly, gives a grunt of satisfaction and proffers it to me. Through the plastic evidence bag I can just about feel something more rigid inside the black canvas strap, maybe the size of a thumbnail.

'Passive tracker,' he says. 'Sends out a secure Bluetooth signal that will be picked up by any other device within range. That location data is then squirted up to the cloud and shared with whoever is tracking the device.'

I hand the bag back to him, remembering something else from that walk on New Year's Eve.

'Where we found it,' I say. 'There was no signal at all. It was in this little valley in the middle of the Dales, one of those places that's like a dead zone for reception. We were all trying to get a signal on our phones but there was nothing, so . . . how would the tracking thing have worked?'

'When you took the backpack, brought it up out of that cave and into a location where there was signal, or Wi-Fi, that probably enabled the first location ping to be sent.' He starts to peel off one of the white plastic gloves. 'You said, "*We* were all trying to get a signal?" Was it a group of you?'

'Six of us,' I say. 'Our friends were there, too.'

'We'll need to speak to them as well, Mrs Cooper.'

Roe has his notebook in his hand again, scribbling names and addresses for Kat and Dev, Christian and Miranda. He double-checks he has our numbers correct too before sliding it back into his overcoat.

'How much?' Jason says. He tries for a natural tone but to me it sounds forced, too eager. 'If I'm allowed to ask?'

Docherty peels off his other glove with a tight *snap*, pushing it into his coat pocket. 'How much what?'

'What kind of money are we talking about?'

'This was a transaction between two organised crime groups. Let's just say it was a significant sum.'

'Millions?'

The detective considers my husband for a moment. 'A serious sum. These are serious people, as well. And I'll tell your friends the same thing I'll tell you: if you see anything unusual in the next week or so, any cars outside your house that you don't recognise, strangers loitering around, anything at all, get in touch.' He hands Jason a card embossed with a seal. 'Call me straightaway and if you can't reach me, call nine-nine-nine and we'll get uniforms to your address as fast as we possibly can. The levels of violence we've seen these people use . . .' He tails off. 'I don't want to frighten you, but it's quite extreme.'

They will be fast-tracking the backpack to the lab, he says, to see what a full forensic examination and DNA screen might yield. And whatever happens, they will need to find the cave and subject it to a thorough search. In the hall, he thanks us for our time and apologises, again, for interrupting our dinner.

Jason opens the door for them.

'Do we need to . . . do anything else?'

'Like what?'

'I don't know.' He shrugs. 'Like, apart from keeping our eyes peeled, I mean?'

'Not planning to jump on the next plane to Argentina, are you?'

'No. Why?'

Docherty gives him a tired smile. 'I'm joking. Look, we're going to need to locate the cave soon and may ask for your help on that score. We'll be in touch.' He gestures at the business card in Jason's hand. 'If there's anything else you think of or remember in the meantime – anything at all, no matter how insignificant you think it is – just give me a call on this number.'

We watch in silence through the hall window as the two detectives walk to their Volvo. Roe loads the evidence bag into the boot and goes around to the driver's side; Docherty is looking at something on his phone as he gets into the passenger side. After a moment, the car indicates and pulls slowly away.

Only when their car is out of sight do I feel able to turn and look at my husband.

He stares at me, and I stare back.

'What have you done, Jason?' Anger and fear are boiling up my throat. 'What the hell have you done?'

30

Jason crosses his arms.

'I panicked, OK?'

'The bloody police, Jason! Lying to the police! Why did you do that?'

'Wasn't just me, was it?' There is a defiant set to his jaw. 'We both did.'

'But you started it!' I jab an angry finger at him. 'I had no choice but to follow your lead! Unless you wanted me to call you a liar right there in front of them?'

He glances upstairs, then gestures towards the kitchen. I follow him in and shut the door behind us.

'What the hell just happened?' I put my hands on top of my head. 'This is so messed up. What were you thinking?'

'Look,' he says. 'Alfie was hanging around when I answered the door to them, I didn't want to get into the details in front of him. But then he went up to his room and I thought I'd just try to work out how much Docherty knew first, so I could decide how much I had to tell him. Whether I had to tell him all of it, or only some of it.'

'It didn't occur to you just to tell them the truth?'

'What, Helen? That we found one point six million quid and then split the money rather than reporting it? That we've already started spending it?' His voice rises as he hits his stride. 'That your mum has had a lovely week at Harcourt Park, thank you very much, and she quite fancies staying there long-term on the proceeds?'

'Don't try and put this on me!' Heat rises to my face. 'Don't you *dare*! This was your idea, all along.'

'It wasn't my idea to tell them about the others? Why did you do that?'

'Because the detective asked me!'

'He asked you if the backpack was empty when you found it, too.'

We're going round in circles. I lean back against the kitchen counter, massaging my forehead with the fingertips of both hands.

'Why did you even move the money? I thought you were going to hand it over when you took them upstairs. I thought that was it, game over. I nearly had a heart attack.'

'Moved it this afternoon.'

'Why?'

'I had to.' His eyes hold mine. 'After what you did.'

I cross my arms tightly over my chest.

'What? What did I do?'

'You showed them where it was.'

'Who?'

'Your brother,' he says. 'And Kat. They knew where our share of the money was and they've both got a key to our house. Better it was hidden somewhere they didn't know. So I took the money out from under the bed and separated it into five bags, stashed it in different places around the house instead.'

I look at him in disbelief. An angry retort swells under my tongue, but then I remember that I had the exact same thought barely ten minutes ago when I'd first seen the backpack was empty.

'They would never come in and take—'

'Really?' he says. 'You can say that for sure, can you? With one hundred per cent certainty?'

I realise, as I'm about to reply, that I can't. He's right, and he knows it.

'Just can't believe you lied, Jason. To the *police*.'

'Look,' he says. 'It's not as if we were under arrest or anything, was it? We weren't under oath or being recorded or whatever. We *could* still hand the money over, if we want to. We could say that we panicked, wanted to talk to the others first, or maybe get legal advice.'

'There's no *could* about it.' I make a chopping motion with my right hand. 'It's pretty bloody obvious now that we *have* to hand it over. You heard what he said: the people looking for it are violent, dangerous. We should hand it in, say we made a mistake, and there might be some awkward questions but it means we're not putting the kids at risk. Ourselves at risk.'

He leans back, both hands braced on the kitchen worktop.

'You think you can persuade the others to hand their shares over too?'

'It doesn't matter. We hand our share in, let them make their own decision.'

He's shaking his head. 'That won't work. Because if any of the others say no, we'll be dropping them in it with the police.'

'That's their problem!'

'No,' he says calmly. 'It'll be everyone's problem, because we were all there, we're all part of it. Collective responsibility.'

Before I can answer, the kitchen door swings open and Alfie appears.

'What did those police guys want?' He looks at us, on opposite sides of the small space, each of us backed up against the kitchen counter as if we're trying to get as far away as possible from the other. 'Why are you two arguing?'

Jason launches into a retelling of the story we had just told to Docherty and Roe – a sanitised version of the truth in which we haven't done anything wrong. A backpack that had belonged to someone else and might be linked to a cold case they were working on, he says. He doesn't mention gangs, or drugs or a double shooting in Manchester. He doesn't mention the money.

'That bag.' Alfie jerks a thumb over his shoulder. 'Why did they take it away?'

'That was the backpack,' Jason says. 'The one we found, that was empty.'

'But . . .' Alfie's frown makes him look younger than his seventeen years, a confused youth still baffled by adult ways. 'It wasn't empty though, was it, Mum? I took it out of the car, it was well heavy.'

'Told you,' I say. 'It was full of dirty washing.'

'You used someone else's bag for your cowpat clothes and now the police want it?'

'Exactly.'

'OK, that's . . . weird.' Finally, he seems to give up on trying to make sense of his strange parents. He glances at the pan full of chilli con carne that has been cooling and thickening on the hob since the detectives arrived. 'When's dinner? I'm starving.'

'I'll put some rice on now,' I say. 'And reheat the chilli, ten minutes and it'll be ready.'

'OK.' He turns and ambles towards the lounge, pulling his phone from the pocket of his baggy jeans.

As we get our evening meal back on track and Jason sets the small kitchen table, we agree that we won't tell Alfie specifics about what Docherty has told us, or what he'd said about staying vigilant for anything unusual in the neighbourhood. Neither of us wanted to pile more worries on him when he was about to sit his mock A-levels. We would be extra careful and keep a close eye on him instead.

I pull a bottle of red wine from the cupboard and fetch two glasses. Normally, we don't drink midweek but I'm suddenly in need of something to calm my rattling nerves. After pouring us both a glass, I take a first sip, the wine dark and potent on my tongue.

'We need to tell the others,' I say. 'Warn them.'

I pull up the Signal app on my phone, select 'The Weekend' group.

> *Heads up @Christian @Miranda @Kat we just had the police at the house asking about the timber. There was a tracking device in the backpack that they traced to our house.*

Kat is the first to reply. Direct, to the point, no words wasted.

> *Shit what did you tell them?*

I thumb-type another quick message.

> *Said bag was empty, we just took it as looked new and good for hikes etc.*

Within seconds, a reply drops in from Miranda.

> *WTF???*

I can almost hear my sister-in-law's incredulous tone, her voice rising as she stands in the neat kitchen of her lovely house, her perfect features tightening into a scowl.

But Kat replies as if she's not even seen Miranda's three angry capitals.

> *So they don't know we have the timber? How sure are you?*

Beside me, Jason stirs the chilli con carne with one hand and types with the other, a string of replies from him dropping into the chat one after the other.

> *They think someone else got to it before us. Left the bag there. Had to give them your names and addresses as they may want to talk to you too*
> *There's some other stuff you need to know*

Three dancing dots next to Miranda's username indicate she's typing again. A double ping as two messages appear, barely a second apart.

We should burn it.
All of it.

Jason mutters a curse under his breath as he types a reply.

Can you all jump on a group call now? Need to give you more info.

We both stare at our screens, waiting for a reply, Jason's thumb hovering over the *call* icon. There is no response for a few moments, until the three dancing dots appear next to Christian's username for the first time, to show he's about to join the chat.

Too late.

More dots, then a second message from my brother.

They're already here.

31

Wednesday

We meet at lunchtime the next day in Dean's Park. Iron-grey clouds cover York like a shroud, a bleak, persistent cold sending most of the tourists into the coffee shops and museums, leaving the park unusually empty. The Minster looms over us, over everything, a huge gothic edifice of creamy-beige stone bigger than anything else for miles around. The park is in the grounds of the cathedral, central for all of us and just across the road from Christian's office. My work is a bit further out, but I can just about make it here and back during my lunch break. Jason works from home on Wednesdays and Kat's managed to get cover at the shop for an hour.

I glance at my brother, who is looking slightly sheepish.

'Only four of us? Where's Miranda?'

Christian rubs a hand over his face. 'We had a bit of a . . . row last night.' He nods towards Jason. 'After those police officers left. She started going on about that Tarot card reading she did on New Year's Eve, the Tower and the Devil, all that crap, how it was all coming true. She found some lighter fluid in the garage, said she was going to stick our share of the money in the firepit and burn the lot of it.'

'Shit!' Kat says. 'Seriously?'

'She'd had a few drinks as well. She got a bit emotional.'

'How do you know she's not lighting it up as we speak?'

'Because I put it all in the safe.'

'Probably wise.'

We had agreed last night to meet face to face, somewhere out in the open where we wouldn't be overheard. All the benches are still wet from the overnight rain so we stand in a loose semicircle next to one of the memorials, all of us bundled up in coats and scarves and gloves, Jason and I clutching takeaway coffees that he bought on his way into town.

Christian describes the visit of the two detectives last night: Docherty and Roe had spent half an hour at my brother's place going over much the same ground as they'd covered with us. They had also suggested that there might be 'other items of interest' still hidden, within a fairly small radius of where we had found the backpack. As soon as she'd seen the messages on Signal, Kat had driven over to my brother's house on the pretext of being helpful – so they could talk to her at the same time, kill two birds with one stone – and also to ensure that her husband was kept out of the loop.

'How is Dev?' I say. 'Does he suspect anything?'

'God, no.' Kat pulls a face. 'Told him the burglar alarm had tripped at the shop again, and I had to go in to reset it. If he thought the police were involved he'd be going up the wall by now.'

'He hasn't asked to rejoin the Signal group?'

'I've just told him we're all sitting tight, no one's doing anything. No one's spending any of it yet.'

I glance around the group, but none of the others can hold my gaze.

'Is that . . . wise? Keeping him in the dark?'

Christian cuts in before she can answer. 'Dev is a situation we can handle,' he says, breath steaming in the winter air. 'He's a known quantity, he's our friend. I know that it's a bit of a surprise to have Greater Manchester Police turning up on the doorstep – I totally get that – but nothing has really changed. All this sergeant knows is we found an empty backpack, that's it. They don't know we have the money, they have no reason to suspect us, none of us have criminal records and we've been totally cooperative. They've got no grounds to investigate. None.'

I turn on my brother.

'*Nothing has changed*?' I can't keep the edge from my voice. 'Are you serious? Police knocking on the door, evidence bags and drug deals and people getting shot in Manchester? What planet are you on?'

Jason gestures at him with his takeout coffee cup. 'I'm curious, mate,' he says. 'About the story you told us last weekend too, the bank robbery, three guys in prison and the money never recovered. No one getting hurt, a victimless crime and all that? You seemed pretty sure that was where our money came from.'

Christian shrugs. 'It was only ever a best guess, based on the information available. I never said it was *definitely* the same case. But, let's be honest, you all *wanted* to believe it. I did too. My investigator's very thorough and she came up with a highly plausible option of what might have happened.' He stops talking while a young couple walk past with a black Labrador puppy straining at its lead, waiting until they're out of earshot. 'Let's be honest, no one really believed it had been left there by Santa Claus for us to find, did they? No one thought it was a divine gift from on high. I think everyone just needs to take a breath and calm down a bit.'

'Seriously?' Kat says, echoing my tone. 'Because telling people to *calm down* always works, right?'

A sudden gust of biting wind slices through the park, bare tree branches trembling against the grey sky. Litter whips and eddies around our feet as I hunch a little tighter into my coat.

'Christian,' I say, raising my voice against the wind. 'None of us are naive, it's just . . . I didn't realise how bad it might be, how dark. Two people were *shot*, for God's sake.'

'Two drug dealers.' He shrugs. 'Lowlifes. An occupational hazard, I'd imagine.'

Kat says: 'And what if they come looking for us?'

'How could they possibly find us?'

I take a swallow of lukewarm coffee. 'The police already did, they said there was a tracker stitched into the lining of the backpack.'

'Look,' my brother says. 'We all knew there was probably something a bit shady about what we found in that cave, but we took it anyway.'

'*We?*' I say. 'I didn't. Neither did Miranda, nor Dev.'

Christian reaches into his overcoat, pulling out a business card and brandishing it in his leather-gloved hand.

'OK then,' he says. 'We could have another vote, if you like? I've got that copper's card right here. Raise your hand if you want me to call him right now and tell him we'll be dropping off all the remaining money in an hour?'

'Maybe she's right,' I say. 'Miranda, I mean. Maybe it's more trouble than it's worth and we should just burn it.'

Jason holds a hand up. 'Now hang on, no one's suggesting we—'

Christian puts a leather-gloved hand on my arm. 'Let's not be hasty. I was simply asking if anyone wanted to come clean to the police. Tell them the truth. Tell them everything.'

He glances first at Kat, then Jason, then me.

None of us raises a hand.

32

'Didn't think so.' Christian puts Docherty's business card back into his pocket. 'So I take it you've all started making small cash deposits?'

I check over my shoulder but the path behind us is empty.

'Yes,' I say. 'But maybe we should put that on hold, though? Until things have calmed down a bit, until it's . . . safer?'

'Much safer in the bank,' he says, 'than stashed under your double bed. How about you, Kat?'

She gives a reluctant nod. 'Irregular amounts, like you said. No round numbers. I've opened some new accounts too, with different banks. Going to put some through the business, too – keep us on our feet.'

'Post-Christmas blues,' Christian says. 'I know what you mean.'

He steers us back towards a blow-by-blow comparison of what Docherty and Roe had asked, what they'd said to us last night, what they'd revealed. Checking each detail to make sure it was consistent with what they'd told him. His main concern, he said, was that the detective might try to play us off against each other. Try to muddy the waters between us, make one of us suspicious of the rest. To make sure that didn't happen we needed to keep talking, keep lines of communication open, be honest with each other.

He manages to say the word 'honest' with a straight face, not a hint of irony.

I stand among our loose semicircle in the shadow of York Minster, huddling in the biting January wind, Jason on one side of me and Kat on the other. Without Dev or Miranda here I feel cornered, outnumbered, in a minority of one – the only one who had voted to hand the money in on New Year's Eve. It was never easy trying to argue with my brother and his ironclad confidence, even at the best of times. Never mind when my only allies in the conversation had both decided to walk away from the situation. Dev, who was so strait-laced, so buttoned-up, always obsessed with how things *looked* and how they might reflect on him. And my sister-in-law, who has always seemed to operate on a different plane to me: a decade younger and by some margin the poshest person I'd ever met. She'd always seemed to have that cushion of wealth and privilege, surrounding her like bubble wrap so that nothing ever really fazed her.

Even Jason and Kat, both initially sceptical about my brother's insistence that *nothing has changed*, are struggling in the face of his relentless, bulldozing logic.

'But what if they get warrants?' Kat says. 'If they come back and want to search our houses?'

Christian shrugs. 'They have to have reasonable grounds that an offence has been committed, to get a warrant. And that the evidence is on your premises. Evidence they don't have.'

Jason says: 'You sure about that?'

'Positive.' He pulls back a leather glove to check his watch. 'I have to get back to the office but there's one more thing we need to discuss. Docherty was asking where we found the backpack, said he was going to send a forensic team to make a full sweep of the location, check for anything else. Trace evidence or whatever they call it. They need a guide, someone to tell them exactly where it is.' He looks around the group. 'Any volunteers?'

We all look at each other in turn. Kat is the first to speak up.

'I suppose I could go,' she says. 'But Dev's working from home tomorrow and he's home all weekend too, the football's away down south somewhere so he'll be watching it on the telly instead. I can't just tell him I'm going out on some jaunt to the Dales for the best part of a day, he'll get suspicious.'

'I don't think a woman should go on her own in any case.'

She makes a face. 'Sexist, much?'

My brother colours slightly. 'Not at all. Just ... you know. Should probably be one of the guys.'

'Or is it that you don't trust me?'

'Honestly, it's not that either.'

I raise a tentative hand. 'I don't mind doing it,' I say. 'My boss will go ballistic if I call in sick tomorrow, but I could go Saturday or Sunday.'

Kat frowns. 'Couldn't we just give the police a Google map location, a red pin thing? Rather than going all the way back there?'

'Actually,' Christian says, 'I don't mind taking the trip myself – a perk of being my own boss. And I've got a better idea than dropping a Google pin for them.'

'Which is?'

'Well, I've been thinking.' He gives us a wolfish grin. 'We walked past a half-dozen caves in that valley alone.'

'What do you mean?' Jason says. 'You don't know how to find the right one?'

'No, I'm saying would it be *so* bad if I took them to the wrong one?'

A heavy ball of unease begins to settle in my stomach. 'Lying to the police, you mean?'

'We've already lied, sis. All of us.'

'But this would be ...' I turn to drop my empty coffee cup into the nearest bin. 'Obstruction, perverting the course of justice, wouldn't it?'

'I could just say I got *lost*.' He illustrates the last word by making air quotes with his fingers. 'And it means we could guarantee they don't find anything else, any other physical evidence, because they'd be looking in the wrong place. It's a chance to close this whole thing down once and for all. Like I said though, just an idea.'

'A bad idea.' Jason stares at my brother, his jaw set hard. 'We've been riding our luck as it is. No reason to push it any further.'

'Fine,' my brother says with a shrug. 'Understood. I'll let you know how it all goes, anyway.'

Jason catches my eye. We had discussed this last night, when Docherty and Roe were gone. I had been fairly sure my brother – the predictable alpha male – would want to take the lead on this. That he would be the first to volunteer to guide the police back out to the cave – if they asked.

I was also fairly sure that Jason no longer trusted him.

'Better if there's two of us, Christian,' my husband says. 'I'll come with you.'

33

Dev

Dev was miles from his own neighbourhood and had taken the driving school livery off his grey Toyota, but he still felt horribly conspicuous. He slid down a little further in the driver's seat, baseball cap pulled low over his eyes, keeping an eye on the parade of shops opposite. Studying one shop in particular. He would wait until it was almost empty, during the mid-afternoon lull before the worker bees hit it on their way home – there was less chance of being recognised.

As he watched, another customer left, then another. Both of them looking gloomier than when they'd arrived. There were only two left inside now, both staring hopefully at a bank of wall-mounted screens. Dev touched his jacket pocket again, feeling its reassuring weight, its density, the heft and warmth of it like a living, breathing thing. Talking to him, calling to him. Impossible to resist.

He felt the anger again, the frustration rising

It was *their* fault. The others.

They had pushed him into this. If they'd listened to him, if they'd done the right thing, then he wouldn't even be here. He wouldn't have had to come out here to North Clifton, wouldn't be sitting in his car outside this grubby little parade of shops, ready to exorcise his oldest demons one last time. Because this *would* be the last time. He would get it out of his system and walk away – and that would be it, forever. He would show his demons who was the master now. He'd lost count of how many days of his free time he'd given up to sit as a magistrate, marinating in one sad case after another. Now it was time to prove that he had learned the lesson. He was better than that. Better than every defendant that had come before him.

Across the street, another customer emerged from the shop and shuffled miserably away towards the pub on the corner.

It was time.

Dev put on a pair of sunglasses and got out of his car. He locked the Toyota and walked quickly across the street, keeping his eyes forward, head down. Ten metres from the shop, then five, then he was pushing the door open and he could almost feel the—

'Dev?' A familiar voice from over his shoulder. 'Is that you?'

He turned, cursing inwardly, to see Jason coming out of a café next door, a dark-haired young woman following him.

Shit.

He let the door of the shop close again.

'Hi, Jason.'

'How's it going? Didn't know you worked this part of the city.'

'I get around.' Dev felt the heat rising up his neck. 'Busy, busy, you know.'

'Right.' Jason nodded. 'No rest for the wicked?'

Dev forced a smile. 'Something like that. How about you?'

'Same here.'

The woman with Jason – who looked young enough to be his daughter – touched him lightly on the arm.

'Got to shoot off, Jase. Thanks again, you going to call me, yeah?'

She turned on her heel and left, handbag swinging over her shoulder.

Jason shifted uneasily, burying his hands in his pockets. He looked awkward as hell.

'Work,' he said. 'Client. Difficult home situation. So we meet here.'

'Right.'

'Look, Dev . . . I'd really appreciate it if this stayed between us, mate. Confidentiality and all that.'

Dev glanced up at the multicoloured logo above the shop door. A single word in large white letters.

'Of course, Jason.' He lowered his voice. 'In fact, you could do me the same favour. Neither of us were ever here, right?'

Jason nodded. 'Deal.'

Dev pushed the shop door open and went inside.

34

DS Docherty calls back late on Thursday afternoon to make the arrangements.

I offer to drive Jason over to the police station where the two of them would be picked up at 8 a.m. sharp. With a limited amount of daylight, the detective says, and the fifty-mile drive out to the moors, he wanted to make an early start to make full use of the day.

Dev texts me as I'm about to leave work.

It's not on the Signal group – he's still not rejoined it after storming out of the dinner party at my brother's house – but just a regular text message.

Hi, Helen, how are you?

It's a bit strange to get a message from my best friend's husband. I don't think it's happened since Dev was arranging a surprise night out for Kat's fiftieth and it feels a bit surreptitious, a bit sneaky, as if he's going behind her back. In any case, I can guess the real reason he's got in touch.

I send a brief, anodyne reply, and his response drops in almost immediately.

So what's going on with the money?

A shiver skitters over my skin at his choice of words. We had all agreed not even to use the word 'money' on Signal – which was encrypted – and yet here Dev was blithely throwing it out there on a bog-standard text message. I take a screenshot and send it to Kat who replies with a string of exploding-head emojis before a brief text response.

Tell him nothing is happening yet, we're all sitting tight. I'll handle him.

I do as Kat suggests and I'm walking out of the office by the time Dev sends back a simple 'OK' in response. Does he know we're pulling the wool over his eyes? Does he regret cutting himself out of the loop now?

Alfie has gone straight to a friend's house after school, for A-level revision and pizza. The two fingers of his left hand are still strapped together after his football injury but it doesn't seem to bother him – no matter how many times I tell him to be careful while it heals.

Jason has made lasagne when I get home from work and we eat in the kitchen, just the two of us. When Alfie heads off to university in September, it will be like this all the time, I suppose. Just the two of us for much of the year. *The empty nest.* It's an odd feeling, with the house quiet around us, and I'm not looking forward to it. Although at least we know we can afford to pay for his accommodation and living costs now without piling up another decade of debt.

The money is in five separate plastic bags of a hundred thousand each stashed around the house: one at the top of Jason's wardrobe, one in the attic, the others in his bedside drawer, the airing cupboard and an old metal filing cabinet in the box room that we'd converted into a home office.

'In a way,' Jason says. 'It's good to get the police stuff out of the way. Better like this than to have it hanging over us, not knowing when they're going to knock on the door. At least we know how the land lies, we know where the money's from, we know what the police are doing. We're not guessing anymore.'

'My husband, the eternal optimist.' I raise an eyebrow. 'Let's hope you're right.'

'And being out with them tomorrow, we might be able to find out more. Get them chatting.'

'Just be careful what you say. That detective is probably thinking the same thing, I reckon he's sharper than he looks.'

I refill our wine glasses and the conversation moves on to Alfie, who has finally sent in his UCAS application to study architecture. His first choice is University College London, with Kingston as a backup. We have always encouraged him to do what he loves, to follow his dreams, his passion, not to think about the expense and future debt. I suppose our encouragement has played a part in him picking one of the longest courses of study – seven years, all told – in the most expensive city in the country.

His dream has a high price, but it isn't beyond our reach. Not anymore.

We leave at just after 7.30 a.m. on Friday for the short drive to Fulford Road Police Station. It's another dark January morning, a fog of grey half-light beyond the windows as if the night is grimly reluctant to yield anything to the dawn. Heavy cloud covers every inch of the sky. Beside me in the passenger seat, Jason is dressed in his hiking gear, walking boots, jacket, a small backpack in his lap with a packed lunch, water and a torch. Just as if we were heading out on a walk on New Year's Eve again.

'Let me know how you get on,' I say. 'And when you think you'll be back.'

He nods absently, looking at something on his mobile.

'I'll try,' he says. 'Phone signal's a bit hit and miss out there though. The drive is about an hour and twenty each way, plus the walk out to the cave and back, we should probably be back mid- to late-afternoon, depending on how long they want to spend poking around up there.'

We pull up behind a line of traffic waiting to cross a T-junction.

'Jason?' I rest a hand on his knee. 'Keep an eye on my little brother, will you? Make sure he doesn't do anything . . . you know. Foolish.'

'I will.'

'What he was saying yesterday about leading the police to a different cave – sometimes he just gets a bit carried away with his own ideas.'

'I know.' He shoves the phone into a trouser pocket, zips it closed. 'I'll keep him on the straight and narrow.'

'And be careful. Don't let your guard down, even for a minute.'

Christian waves us over when we pull into the big car park outside the police station. It's next door to a council building and the car park is already filling up, but my brother has saved us a space next to the detectives' Volvo. He's standing by his own car's open boot, chatting to the younger detective, both of them holding steaming silver cups from the Thermos I bought him for Christmas. Docherty emerges from the station's main entrance and raises a hand in greeting, paperwork clutched in his other hand. He and Roe have ditched the suits and overcoats they wore on Wednesday and are both in walking gear, heavy boots and thick waterproof coats, like a pair of ramblers out for a winter hike. Jason gives me a peck on the cheek and climbs out to join them. Docherty hands each of them a form on double-sided A4 with a shrug of apology, digging in his pocket for a couple of biros. From what I can catch of the conversation they're release forms, some kind of health and safety thing, which have to be completed and returned to his inspector before they can set off.

Seeing them all together, with their gear and woolly hats and backpacks, makes them look like some kind of outward bound group, a quartet of old friends or a middle-aged stag party embracing wholesome country pursuits rather than simply going to the pub.

My nine o'clock meeting is uneventful. I take the minutes, as usual, typing them up straight afterwards and sending them to Nigel for approval. He won't read them – he rarely does – but always insists they're done within an hour or two. Jason texts me just after ten, to say they've parked up at How Stean Gorge and are about to walk up onto the ridge.

At lunchtime I drive to Harcourt Park, the envelope of money that had so nearly been discovered by the detectives tucked securely into my handbag. I make a payment for another week's stay and find Mum in the TV lounge, dozing in an armchair. I sit with her for fifteen minutes, but she looks so peaceful, so *at home*, that I don't want to disturb her.

On my way back to the office, I take a detour to a local bank branch, another of the new accounts I set up earlier this week.

Christian's words return to me. *Money is safer in the bank than under your bed.*

In my handbag is another paying-in envelope for the bank. The details are already completed in neat capital letters, the cash inside already counted and double-checked, all sealed and ready to deposit in the automatic machine so I could spend as little time in the branch as possible. I had gathered quite a collection of paying-in slips and envelopes from different banks over the past week so I could do all the form-filling at home, and it meant I could be in and out within a minute. No fuss, no undue attention. No delays. I would be on their CCTV but not for long, and barely recognisable bundled up in my scarf and hat and winter coat. I had been doing this for barely a week and I was already learning.

But when I park and walk around the corner to the branch, there is a police car outside.

35

The police car is facing me, pulled up to the kerb on the double yellows right outside the branch. A uniformed officer is leaning against the bonnet, bright in her hi-vis jacket, chatting with a couple of pensioners. The other is in the driver's seat of the car, radio held to his lips.

There is a sick lurch of panic low down in my stomach.

Just keep walking. Go into the bank and make the deposit like you planned. They're nothing to do with you, they have no idea who you are.

And yet...

They're outside the branch. Are they waiting for me? Will there be a tap on my shoulder as I'm standing at the paying-in machine?

The two police officers look relaxed, unruffled, as if they're in between calls. But the envelope in my handbag suddenly feels like an unexploded bomb, ticking loudly enough for everyone around me to hear and I know I can't stop, can't turn on my heel and walk away in the opposite direction without drawing attention to myself. The female officer, I can now see, has a blonde ponytail and is sipping from a takeout cup of coffee as she talks to the two elderly shoppers. There is a Costa next door to the bank branch.

Of course they're not here for me. They've just stopped for a drink and a breather in the middle of a long shift. I'm being ridiculous.

I don't go into the branch.

Instead, angling away from the bank's sliding glass doors, I walk past the two officers and studiously avoid eye contact. Around the block to do a full circuit of the shopping street before returning to my car. Fumbling for my keys, I wonder whether it will always be like this from now on, every time I see the bright yellow of a hi-vis jacket or a blue flashing light, every time I hear the wail of a police siren. A sickening spike of unease that today could be the day.

The afternoon passes with leaden slowness. My boss is out on a client visit and half the team work from home on Fridays so there is a vacant, listless feeling to the office as if everyone who remains is just going through the motions. The envelope of cash remains in my handbag. I'll try again on Monday. Probably.

I send a WhatsApp message to Jason asking how things are going. By my calculation they should already be on their way back, having done what they went out there to do. Docherty had indicated that once they had the location of the place, they would cordon it off so they could stop any other walkers going into the cave and interfering with potential evidence. Take the time to do a proper forensic search and see what else might have been left behind. Even though I don't think there's anything there that would incriminate us, nothing to suggest we had taken the money, the nervous flutter in my stomach returns when I think of white-suited forensic officers going over every inch of the cave.

When he doesn't reply after fifteen minutes I send the same message to my brother. For a moment I think about asking DS Docherty for an update – I've saved his number in my phone – but I don't want to bombard them all with the same request. The business card Docherty left has a landline number on it too. When I call, a female detective answers, saying she'll pass on a message the next time he phones into the office.

I know the phone signal out in the Dales is patchy, but Christian must be on a different network to Jason because after a few minutes the two grey WhatsApp ticks turn blue, to show my message has been read. His reply is short and to the point, as usual.

All fine, on way back now. x

The message I sent to Jason is still showing as not received. I send him a regular text message instead and open the Signal app, but there's nothing new in 'The Weekend' group either, just the back-and-forth of cagey messages from the last few weeks. Christian, Jason and Kat have been on the chat the most; Miranda and I the least, apart from Dev who had left the group entirely. Most of the messages are short, fairly cryptic, but one of them stands out: the link Christian had sent last weekend. His suggestion that *this* was where the money had come from, that the men who hid it in that cave were now in jail. He had been so convincing – until his theory was overturned by DS Docherty. Jason had called him out on it yesterday, at Dean's Park.

I click on the link again and a page loads from the *Daily Mail* news website. *Gang convicted of cash depot robbery.* The date on the article is the middle of March, 2020.

The details are familiar from when I first read them, last weekend. A night-time raid by three men, who had taken the depot manager's wife hostage and forced him to cooperate, letting them into the facility where they had helped themselves to almost five million pounds. Their subsequent arrest, a court case with lengthy sentences handed down to members of the gang. Could there still be a connection with the people Docherty and Roe were investigating? A link that none of us have seen yet?

Scanning for the name of the ringleader, I type 'Tony Dowd robbery' into Google. There are lots of hits for the name, but none that link to news about the robbery or his conviction. I try a few other combinations of words without any luck before switching to one of his accomplices instead. 'Andrew Armstrong robbery'.

More combinations of the same words, all kinds of random pages and links that relate to hundreds, thousands of men out there in the world with that name.

Nothing comes up about a multimillion pound robbery, or a nationwide manhunt to find the perpetrators. Nothing about the subsequent court case.

Maybe that was because of the timing? The trial had concluded right before the first lockdown was imposed on the country, as the pandemic started to take hold – maybe it was overlooked because of Covid? Because every news story in every bulletin was completely, utterly dominated by the frenzy of panic and preparation that led up to it? Perhaps the *Mail* had been the only one to follow the story in those tumultuous weeks.

My phone vibrates and I switch out of the browser hoping to see a new message from Jason giving me his ETA at home. But it's just junk, a spam message about a bogus delivery, urging me to click on a link that will no doubt take me to some dodgy website. I delete it and go back to my Google search, realising abruptly that I've forgotten to follow one of the rules laid down on New Year's Day – I've not been using a private browser. With a twinge of guilt, I go back and delete the search history from the last half an hour. Would that make a difference? Were things ever really deleted? I didn't actually know, but I select *Incognito mode* anyway and open another browser window.

This time I just go to the *Mail* website and type 'Tony Dowd cash' into the search bar. Lots of results about a love-rat footballer who had cheated on his pregnant wife, but none about a robbery. Multiple searches yield the same result: nothing relevant.

I sit back in my chair, rubbing my eyes. Frowning again at the small screen of my phone. It didn't make sense. How could it have disappeared?

Using the link Christian had sent to the group chat on Signal, I pull up the story again. And there it is, a six-year-old news article.

Gang convicted of cash depot robbery. My head feels fogged, fatigued after a long week, as if there is something obvious just beyond my reach and I'm too tired to grasp it. A way to make this all make sense. I read the article again from start to finish, the names and places, then look at the articles around it, the date, the byline.

My brain fog refuses to shift.

Until I tap the address to pull up the whole link in its entirety. A long jumble of letters and numbers, forward slashes and other gobbledygook, preceded by the root *DMailNewsUK/*. Something about it looks odd, almost artificial, so I pull up another browser window and type the name of the newspaper in again. The top link goes to *DailyMail.co.uk/*. Every link I click from that homepage has the same domain name. So where did *DMailNewsUK* come from? Maybe they had two different sites, an old one and a newer one? But surely all the pages on there would be connected?

I send another WhatsApp message to my brother, telling him about the discrepancy.

It's only when a colleague walks past my desk and wishes me a nice weekend that I realise it's gone five o'clock, dusk has darkened the world outside and I'm virtually the last person left in the office. I check my emails one last time in case anything has dropped in from Nigel – he was fond of his 4.55 p.m. messages to check I wasn't slacking off early – power off my computer and head down to the car park.

By the time I get home, I half expect that Jason will have beaten me to it. That I'll find him in the kitchen already preparing dinner with a glass of wine, a story to tell about a day hiking in the Dales with the police and full of apologies that he's been incommunicado.

But the house is in darkness when I pull up on the drive. Only one of the cats is there to greet me, Prim sitting alone in the hall, passing silent judgement on the lateness of her dinner. I flick on light switches, put some cat food down and shout upstairs for Alfie, but there's no reply from him either.

I send Jason another WhatsApp message.

Starting dinner, when do you think you'll be back?

I watch as the two ticks change from grey to blue to show it's been read. As if on cue, the doorbell rings, the familiar three-note chime loud in my silent house. My husband, apparently, could find his way back to some half-hidden valley in the Dales but had forgotten his front door key – so it was a good thing I'd got home before him.

I go to the hall and pull open the front door, the smile of greeting freezing on my face.

A woman and a man stand on the drive, their eyes narrowed in the glare of the security light. Both in their early thirties, grim-faced in dark clothes and dark gloves. The woman is stocky, thick through the waist and shoulders like a rugby player, a fading bruise under her left eye. The man beside her is tall – six foot four at least – with black buzz-cut hair the same length as his beard.

The woman studies me for a second, her mouth set in a hard, flat line. 'Helen Cooper?'

'Yes?'

'Can we have a word?' Her right hand dips into her coat pocket, emerges holding something black. A wallet. The flash of an ID, a picture, a logo too quick for me to take in.

'I'm sorry, what—'

'Police,' the woman says, breath steaming in the frigid evening air. 'Could we come in for a minute?'

36

My first thought is: *Jason. He's hurt. An accident on the way home, a crash in Friday night traffic.*

'What's happened?' I grip the front door, its hard edge digging into my palm, icy night air slipping past me into the house. 'Is Jason OK? He's supposed to be back any time now.'

The woman's neutral expression doesn't change. 'Jason Cooper?'

'Yes,' I say. 'My husband. He went out with your colleagues this morning. They were going to . . .'

I think back to DS Docherty's instructions, wondering how much I was allowed to share with this other police officer. *What I can tell you is still highly confidential, please don't repeat this to anyone else.*

Her eyebrows lower a fraction in the merest hint of a frown. 'They were going to do *what*, Mrs Cooper?'

'He was . . . helping them with something.' I glance behind them to the quiet street, devoid of people and fully dark on this cold January evening. Behind me, my empty house. No husband, no sons, no one but me and two strangers on the doorstep. A sliver of fear worms its way under my ribcage, a sudden awareness of my vulnerability. The door chain, unhooked, hangs straight down alongside the frame. 'So you're not here about Jason?'

She stands very still, unblinking, gloved hands loose by her sides. Her hair is short, shaved at the sides almost to her scalp.

'I don't have any information about that, I'm afraid.'

My phone buzzes in my pocket but I don't want to reach down and take it out if it means taking my eyes off her.

'Then why are you here?'

'Can we come in, Mrs Cooper? It would be easier if we can talk inside.'

'Sorry,' I say, inching the door closer to the frame. 'I didn't catch your . . . where did you say you were from again?'

'North Yorkshire Police,' she says in a flat monotone. 'My name's Detective Constable Michaela Smith and this my colleague, DC Wilf Pritchard. We're from headquarters at Northallerton.'

The man gives me a brief nod and I notice for the first time, almost hidden by the hood of his parka, the edge of a blue pattern on the skin of his neck. The dark ink of a tattoo just visible over his collar. He seems to realise I've seen it but doesn't move to cover it up. He doesn't do anything. He has the eyes of a predator, lying still in the long grass so as not to spook its prey.

In my pocket, my phone buzzes staccato against my leg with another message. The sliver of fear in my chest starts to wrap around my lungs.

'What's this about?'

'We need to talk to you about a serious matter and we can either do it here, or at the local station in town. It's important.'

For the third time, my phone vibrates but this time with the continuous *buzz-buzz-buzz* of a call. My ringtone, the familiar intro to 'Just Can't Get Enough' by Depeche Mode sounds horribly casual and out of place as it cuts across our conversation. I drag the phone out of my pocket, see Jason's name and picture on the display. He doesn't bother with a greeting.

'Listen very carefully.' He sounds breathless. 'You're in danger, Helen. You can't let them in.'

'Jason?' I push the phone closer to my ear. 'Are you OK? What's going—'

'Just do it, *please*. Shut the door now.'

I keep my eyes on Smith. 'It's the police.'

'I can see them on the doorbell camera. Listen to me carefully, OK? Can they hear me too?'

Smith takes a step towards the threshold, lifting her palm as if to brace it against the door and stop me from closing it. At her shoulder, Pritchard moves forward too, his bulk looming over the doorway. I start to close the door with my left hand, pushing it until there is only a gap of a few inches.

'Jason, you're scaring me, what are—'

'Whatever they've told you,' Jason says. 'It's a lie.'

'What are you talking about?'

'They're *not police*. Whatever you do, you can't let them into the house.' His breathing is ragged, desperate. *'Don't let them in.'*

I look up and meet the woman's eyes again, her flat expression starting to curdle into something else. Irritation. Anger. The bearded, tattooed man next to her, his eyes flat like pennies. Both of them strong, fit-looking, twenty years younger than me. Neither of them have shown me any ID that I've actually had a chance to look at. In my ear, Jason repeats the words. *They're not police.*

If they're not, there's only one reason why they're here. A reason that has been hidden in five separate packets, in five different places around the house.

What will they do to me, if I plead ignorance?

Then again, what will they do if I just hand it over? Leave me be, to get on with my Friday evening?

Of course not.

An electric shiver of fear races up my spine.

There is a rustle of leaves and I glance down to see Katniss shouldering her way through the hedge from next door, her black fur shining like oil in the security light, eyes like two bright points of luminous gold. She catches sight of the two visitors at the front door and freezes, ears flattening to her head, teeth bared in a hiss of warning. The woman half turns towards her, distracted for a moment and I use the opportunity to slam the door shut as the cat bolts away down the garden. With a shaking hand, I slide the security chain into place and push the deadbolt across.

'It's done,' I say into my phone. 'I've shut the door on them.'

'Good,' he says, blowing out a heavy sigh of relief. 'That's good. Look, I've got to go but I'll be back soon and then we can sort all of this out, all right?'

The knock on the door is heavy enough to rattle it in its frame. *Bang-bang-bang.*

'Mrs Cooper?' The woman's strident voice is muffled through the wood. 'We'd like to talk to you, please open the door.'

I push the phone closer to my ear. 'Hang on, Jason, where are you?'

But he's already gone: either the signal dropped out or he's cut me off. I try to call him back but it rings and rings with no answer.

Through the frosted glass of the door, I can see shadows shifting in the security light as the two strangers remain at my front door. They're not going anywhere. Without Jason's voice in my ear, I realise how isolated I am here. How easy it would be for them to smash a window and climb through. I'm not safe – more like trapped. I turn all the downstairs lights on in the house and pull all the curtains closed before retreating back into the kitchen, making sure the back door is locked and deadbolted. My eyes fall on the knife block next to the toaster. I pull out the shortest, sharpest blade and slide it into the back pocket of my jeans.

The knocking on the door continues, although it's not quite as heavy.

'I know you're not police,' I shout to them from the hall. 'So I'm calling nine-nine-nine, doing it now.'

'I've got a better idea.' The woman's voice is lower now, more placatory. 'I've called my DCI at Northallerton. You can talk to him, I've got him on now. Let me pass him over to you.'

When I open the lounge curtains, she's at the big bay window, holding her iPhone flat in her palm as if it's on speaker. Her partner is nowhere to be seen. She gestures to the small top window – far too small for an adult to fit through – but I wonder for a moment if this is some sort of trick, a distraction to catch me off guard.

'DCI Mishra,' she says through the glass. 'My boss.'

I open the window and she hands over her phone as a wash of cold air rushes in. The screen shows a WhatsApp video call, half the screen showing my pale face and the other half a middle-aged Asian man in what looks like an office. He has a greying goatee beard and dark bags under his eyes, a white shirt with the top button undone, a tie at half-mast. I can see papers pinned to a noticeboard behind him, the corner of a filing cabinet, something framed on the wall.

We exchange stilted greetings and he's courteous, polite, introducing himself by name and rank. But as he talks, my husband's words form a desperate undercurrent trying to drown him out.

Whatever they've told you, it's a lie.

After a moment, caution wins out. I hand the phone back through the window.

'He could be any random person,' I say to Smith. 'In any office, anywhere.'

She takes the phone from me with a frown and I allow myself a brief flare of hope that she'll give up, walk away, that she'll get in her car and drive off. That she'll leave me alone.

She loiters on the other side of the glass instead for another brief exchange with the middle-aged man before she ends the WhatsApp call.

'OK,' she says, turning back to me. 'So . . . use your own phone. Google the number for the Major Crimes Unit at Northallerton, ask them to put you through to DCI Jag Mishra. I've told him to expect your call. We'll wait.'

I do as she suggests. A receptionist connects me to someone else, who connects me to another detective constable whose name I don't catch. He then transfers the call with another click.

'DCI Mishra.' The voice is the same: polite, calm, educated. 'Mrs Cooper?'

'Yes.'

'Hello again,' he says. 'How about we stop going around in circles and you tell me what's going on?'

I explain, without getting into too much detail, that it seemed strange to have more police turning up to my house when we were already helping officers from another force. He types on a keyboard as I talk, interrupting only to double-check the details.

When he finally speaks again, his voice is heavy with concern.

'These two men who came to your house,' he says. 'Docherty and Roe? There's no record of them working for the serious crime task force at Greater Manchester Police. There's no record of them on the system at all.'

It takes a second for his words to sink in, for the blurry truth to sharpen into focus.

'What . . . are you talking about?'

'I don't know who they are, Mrs Cooper. But they're not police officers.'

PART III
THE MONEY

37

Jason had been sure. He had told me to keep them out. He had told me I was in danger, that they were impostors.

He had been wrong.

And he's still not answering his phone.

Cold tendrils of fear dance at the back of my neck. DCI Mishra's words playing over and over in my head like an earworm I can't unhear. *I don't know who they are, Mrs Cooper. But they're not police officers.* They had no record of any officers called Docherty and Roe, and yet Jason and my brother had been out with them all day. Out in the Dales, in the middle of nowhere. If that *was* even where they had been going. I had to assume that they knew the truth by now.

I slide the chain off the front door and open it, gesturing towards the lounge. DC Smith goes through and settles herself on the sofa, Pritchard following.

Jason's text message arrives as I'm pushing the front door closed.

Get rid of them. SAY NOTHING.

Why was he still convinced they were the danger? I fire a quick message back as the two detectives regard me from across the room.

Docherty is not real police. Be careful. Call me back asap.

Smith and Pritchard sit side by side in the lounge, a disconcerting echo from two days ago when Docherty and Roe had occupied the same space.

'So,' Smith says, after going over brief introductions again. 'Why don't you start by telling us where your husband is, Mrs Cooper?'

My nerves are jangling, my thoughts a tumbling mass of anxiety and confusion.

'Why don't you start by telling me why *you're* here.'

'We're following up lines of inquiry relating to a major ongoing investigation.'

'An investigation of what?'

'I'm not able to go into specifics, at this stage. But as I said, it relates to a large number of very serious offences, with possible links to organised crime.'

'In Manchester?'

'Can't give out that information, I'm afraid.'

'But why here? Why me?'

She exchanges a quick glance with her colleague. 'A combination of phone data, ANPR and . . . other intelligence. We've been talking to lots of people over this past week, knocking on lots of doors.'

DC Pritchard takes a notebook from his jacket and flips through pages until she finds what he's looking for.

'You were booked into Millbrook Cottage near Pateley Bridge from the twenty-ninth of December until the first of January, correct?'

'Yes. There were six of us, plus my younger son. But he came back on New Year's Eve.'

'Anything out of the ordinary happen to you while you were there?' He clicks his ballpoint pen. 'Anything unusual at all?'

The urge to tell them is a rushing, rising tide. The urge to come clean, to put an end to the lying, the hiding, the deception. But there is still an edge of uncertainty, of confusion, too many things happening too fast. I *think* they're police. But can I be one hundred per cent sure? The last message from Jason's phone had arrived only moments ago. *SAY NOTHING.*

I swallow hard on a dry throat.

'No.'

Smith gives a slow nod. 'New Year break, was it? A long weekend?'

'Yes.' I try to make it sound casual, as if this year had been just like any other. 'We've been going for years now, since our kids were small.'

I wait for one of them to say more, but instead Smith fixes me with the same unblinking stare she'd shown me on the doorstep. She's guarded, secretive about the nature of their case and the contrast with Docherty – if that was even his real name – is stark in the extreme. He had been only too happy to spin us a yarn of drugs and gangs and stolen money. He had been *so* open, had given us so much information that it should have been obvious. He had shown us enough of the bait, told us enough of a story, to entice us in. To make us believe: a fisherman showing us the lure. Thinking back, I suppose we should have seen it for what it was. But what now? Where was Jason, and where was my brother?

Smith glances towards the hall, as if she's reading my mind and expecting them to appear at any moment.

'Where's your husband this evening, Mrs Cooper?'

The phone feels heavy in my hand, like a piece of damning evidence ready to condemn me.

'He's out.'

'You said he was with two people who suggested they were police officers.'

My phone dings with another text from Jason, repeating what he sent a few moments ago. I guess he can tell they're still in the house because he's not seen them leave on the doorbell camera.

GET RID OF THEM

'No,' I say. 'I mean, I was confused earlier, a lot going on at the moment and it's all getting on top of me. Sorry, bit of a crossed wire.'

She frowns, as if insulted by my abrupt change of direction.

'All the same, we'd like to talk to him too. Do you mind if we wait?'

'I'd rather you didn't.' I make a show of checking my watch. 'I'm actually about to go out to see my mum at her care home and visiting closes at eight, so I'm going to have to head off.'

We spend another few minutes going back and forth, her repeating the questions and me giving non-committal negative answers. Finally, she stands up and hands me a card. *Detective Constable Michaela Smith, North Yorkshire Police.* A number for her colleague, DC Wilf Pritchard, is written hastily on the back in blue biro.

I show them out and watch them head down the drive to their car before pushing the door firmly shut. I lean forward, with my forehead against the wood, trying to make sense of what's just happened. With numb fingers, I dial Jason's number and put the phone to my ear.

Pick up. Pick up. Pick up.

It rings out.

I try again, leaving a message for him this time when the voicemail kicks in, asking him to call me back straightaway. There are no new WhatsApp messages from him either so I send a reply.

They're gone. Where are you and what's going on? Worried about you. Call me x

The two grey ticks go blue to show that it's been read but he doesn't respond straightaway. I pull up the Signal app and tap out a quick message to 'The Weekend' group.

@Jason @Christian please message or call back asap.
Two detectives just been to the house, DCs Smith and Pritchard.
Probably on their way to yours too @Kat @Miranda
Say they have no record of Docherty and Roe on any police force.

Kat is the first to reply, bare seconds later.

WTF???????

I need to speak to my best friend but also need something to settle my jangling nerves. There's a half-full bottle of red wine on the kitchen counter and I take a glass down from the cupboard, my hand shaking so much that half of the wine splashes onto the kitchen side as I pour it, a slick of dark red like a pool of blood. A picture message arrives on my phone from 'DS Docherty' as I'm wiping up the spillage with kitchen roll. I click on it and the image blows up to fill the screen.

My stomach plunges into freefall.

It's a photo of my husband and my brother, their faces streaked with blood and dirt, eyes wide with fear, zip-tied at the wrists and ankles. They're in a dark-shadowed room with concrete walls and a dirt floor. Three more messages drop in, almost simultaneously.

I want my money back.
All of it.
You have until noon Sunday. Or you'll never see them again.

38

The room spins and loops around me.

I can't bear to look at the image of Jason and my brother but I can't tear my eyes away from it either, my heart thudding painfully in my chest. Both men have dirty grey duct tape covering their mouths, my husband's left eye is swollen almost shut with bruising. Christian's nose looks broken, the tape beneath it a dark mass of blood. They look desperate, beaten, utterly terrified, their eyes telling the grim truth of what's happened since they left with Docherty and Roe this morning. All that time, I had thought they'd been driving out to the Dales to help the police when in fact they were being tied up and brutalised in some anonymous place. Perhaps even tortured, forced to reveal what they knew. A shudder rattles through me. How much had Docherty forced them to reveal?

As if to answer my question more text messages start to drop in from the same number, each one like a bomb landing from a great height.

I know you've split it. Now you can put it all back together.
If you involve police I'll send your husband and your brother back to you in pieces.
And I'll let you choose which one I slice up first.

I feel a sob rising up my throat, my legs weakening beneath me. *Jason.* I've never seen him like that before, never seen his calm, familiar face so wracked with fear. Dragging one of the kitchen stools over I collapse into it, head in hands. *What have we done? How did we end up here?* Scrolling back up the thread of messages I read them all again, trying to tamp down the rising surge of panic, all the while trying to work out how much of the money we had already spent, how much was gone. How much the others might have spent already.

I want my money back. All of it.

All of it.

Noon on Sunday was less than forty-eight hours from now.

My hand hovers over the photo message and I search for the *Forward* icon, selecting Kat and Miranda in the Signal group. But instead of pressing *Send*, I stop. If Docherty had Jason's phone, would he see everything that appeared in 'The Weekend' chat thread? In any case, I couldn't just forward a picture like this to my sister-in-law – it had to be done face to face. I'm about to call her when the rattle of the key in the front door makes me jump. For one hopeful, agonising moment I wonder if it's Jason coming home, if the photo and the texts and the threat are all some kind of giant mistake, some kind of strange joke that could be explained away. The universe playing a trick on me. But before the hope can even fully form, it evaporates.

'Mum?' Alfie's voice reaches me from the hallway. 'Dad?'

I try to reply but find my voice is strangled and hoarse. I clear my throat and try again.

'In here,' I say. 'In the kitchen.'

Sitting up a little straighter on the stool I reach for the glass of wine and take a steadying sip.

'God.' Alfie drops his coat and school backpack onto the kitchen table, going straight to the cupboard and taking out a half-full tube of cheese and onion Pringles. 'You won't believe what happened today, Mum, it was *so* mental. Josh Bowler literally passed out right in front of me, in the middle of our maths mock. He was like, putting his hand up and then *bang*, he falls sideways off his chair and he's down like, literally, face down on the floor in the sports hall. Mrs Whickers almost had a *fit* when she saw him, we all thought she was going to pass out as well, then she asked me and Sam to help walk him down to the nurse's office, and—' He stops mid-flow, studying me for a moment. 'Are you all right, Mum? What's happened?'

'I'm fine.' The concern in his voice is almost too much to take and I swallow down the tears again. *My sweet boy.* Whatever happens now I have to shield him from all of it, keep him safe, insulated from the danger we've brought to the door. From somewhere, I summon a smile. 'I'm just a bit tired. Long week.'

'Are you worried about grandma?' He slides a wedge of Pringles from the tube. 'Is she all right in that new place?'

'She's doing well, she likes it there.' With a pulse of shame, I realise that my mum can no longer stay at Harcourt Park. This place where she had settled so well would now be snatched away, and I would have to break the news to her. 'I might go and see her this weekend.'

'Can I come?'

'Haven't you got football?'

He holds up his splinted fingers. 'Not for another four weeks.'

'Listen.' I strain to keep my voice steady, as if this is just a normal Friday night. 'I've just got to nip out to your uncle's house in a minute but I shouldn't be too long. How about I pick up a Chinese on the way back?'

'Oh.' Through a mouthful of crisps, he says: 'Was going to stay over at Alex's tonight actually, is that all right, Mum? His dad's getting pizzas in.'

'That's fine, love.' I'm actually glad that my son won't be staying here at home, our address known to Docherty and Roe and God knows who else. 'Have fun, don't forget your key.'

'Yeah. Cool. Just going to get my charger and a few bits then I'll be off.' He turns and heads out of the kitchen, taking the tube of crisps with him.

A moment later, he's back, leaning around the door frame.

'Where's Dad?'

'Had to work late,' I say, surprised at how easily the lie comes. 'Then he's gone straight out to a work thing. Did you go to Erik's after school?'

Alfie nods, retrieving his backpack from the kitchen table before disappearing again. His footsteps recede as he climbs the stairs, and I push the kitchen door shut before calling my sister-in-law.

'Hi, Helen.' Miranda sounds out of breath. 'Sorry it's not a good time right now, I'm just finishing up with—'

'Listen to me,' I say. 'I'm coming over to yours. Need to show you something.'

'But Christian is due back any time now and—'

'No,' I say. 'He's not. That's what I need to see you about.'

'What?' Her voice takes on a higher tone. 'What do you mean?'

'I'll be at yours in ten minutes, then I'll explain.'

She starts asking another question but I ring off to call Kat. My friend's phone goes to voicemail and I try to remember whether she's out at her spin class tonight.

Alfie reappears in the kitchen. 'See you tomorrow, Mum.'

He gives me a brief peck on the cheek and I try to fold him into a hug, to hold him close just for a moment. But he's too quick and in too much of a hurry, already slipping away beyond my grasp, out of my reach.

'Take care, Alfie. Love you.'

His reply is swallowed by the opening and closing of the front door. And then he's gone.

I return my attention to the phone. After calling Kat again and getting her voicemail for a second time, I send her a message instead.

Need to see you and Dev NOW. Urgent. Meet me at Christian's house, will explain when I get there.

I grab my coat and keys, before hurrying out to the car. Christian's house is halfway between mine and Kat's, normally a ten-minute drive but Friday evening traffic is heavy and I find myself in a queue snaking slowly around the city centre. Thinking back to my last, fractured conversation with Jason as Smith and Pritchard stood on the doorstep, he had sounded fearful, desperate. Words he must have been forced to say– words that were a mirror image of the truth.

You're in danger. They're not police.

He was the one in danger. And he had only me to rely on now.

At the first red light, I check my phone but there's no response from Kat yet. Scrolling through my other messages, I return to the one that my brother had sent a couple of hours ago – or rather, that had been sent from his phone. Looking at it again, there is a clue that he'd sent it under duress. That something was not right.

All fine. On way back now. x

The clue was there. A single *x*, a single character that revealed the lie. My brother almost never signed off with a kiss, it wasn't his style. Only on my birthday, or very occasionally when he was drunk. As I adjust the phone in its hands-free cradle, my finger brushes the browser button and the screen fills with a familiar headline. *Gang convicted of cash depot robbery.*

The light turns green and the queue of traffic starts to crawl forward again.

The text from my brother was a deliberate deception – but it hadn't been his first, and it's taken the shock of these past few hours to help me see clearly. This time last week he had told us another lie, at the Friday night dinner party when he had 'revealed' what his private investigator had found, convincing us all that the money had come from a big bank and it wouldn't really be missed. That the men who'd taken it were safely locked away for years to come, and there was no way to connect it back to us.

And we had believed him – because it was right there. *Online.* Because there was a link to click, a webpage and a news story and it all looked totally legitimate. It all *looked* real. We spent half our lives on our phones and tablets and laptops and it looked like just any other page, any other story, any other random corner of the internet. But when I'd scratched beneath the surface, when I'd tried to go a little deeper, there had been nothing there. It was just a shell, a film set with nothing behind it. How hard could it be to mock up a webpage with a fake news story that looked real? With the same layout, same formatting, similar web domain? With the resources Christian had at his disposal, not very hard at all.

A shudder makes me grip the steering wheel so hard it feels like my knuckles will burst through the skin. How could we have been so naive? But I already knew the answer: because none of us even considered the idea that Christian – friend, husband, brother – would deliberately mislead us. We had all *wanted* to believe him. Including me.

He had played us.

What did he call it? *A victimless crime.* Except there *were* victims. My brother's deception, his trickery, has taken him down a dark path and pulled my husband into the slipstream behind him.

Both of them set to become victims less than forty-eight hours from now.

39

Miranda dissolves into tears when she sees the picture.

She stares at her husband's bloody face on the screen of my phone, great gulping sobs shaking her shoulders as fat tears run tracks through her mascara. Beside her, by contrast, Kat is frozen with shock. She stares at the image, her mouth set in a grim line, using her fingers to zoom in and out, studying every detail.

Kat had been getting out of her car when I pulled onto the drive and we'd climbed the steps to the front door together. Miranda, in skinny faux-leather black jeans, killer heels and a full face of Friday-night makeup, had greeted us with a worried look but seemed to grasp this was not a conversation we were going to have on the doorstep. She'd ushered us into the snug, a sunken side room, deep sofas arranged on three sides of a square facing the black-mirrored screen of a large TV. One wall of the room is dedicated to framed photographs of Miranda's daughter from her first marriage: Cressida as a bonny baby and a cute toddler, paddling at the beach, on her first day of prep school, as a bridesmaid at Christian and Miranda's wedding.

Kat is shaking her head in disbelief. 'But . . . you saw the two of them off this morning. You dropped them *off at the police station*. You said they filled out health and safety forms, you were *there*.'

I explain what I'd discovered since with a brief web search: that the car park was shared with the council building next door as a cost-saving measure, plus another couple of offices too. That it was used by staff at all of them, and by visitors. Docherty had probably just waited in the police station reception area and come striding out when he'd seen us arrive. The office number he'd given me, with the helpful female 'detective' who had taken a message, now goes through to a robotic voice that says, *This number has not been recognised.*

'Oh God,' my sister-in-law says now, wiping tears in a messy black smear across her cheek. 'Oh God, *oh God*. Look what they've done to my poor Christian. What are we going to do?'

I had never seen Miranda cry before, never seen her visibly upset, not even at my father's funeral. Of the six of us, she was the one we'd known for the shortest time – a decade younger and the newest entrant to our tight little group, Christian's second wife after the implosion of his first marriage. For the first few months of their relationship, Kat had referred to her on texts to me as BTW – *Blonde Trophy Wife* – rather than by her name. *Will BTW be joining us for the barbecue?* or *If BTW bangs on about mindful yoga again I'm going straight onto the double gins :-)* I'd tick her off for being mean, even as I was smiling at a message. But when it became clear that Christian was serious about her, we had got to know Miranda a little better and realised she wasn't too bad, in small doses. It can't have been easy for her, joining a social circle in which most of us had known each other since our teens, or twenties. Christian seemed genuinely smitten and eventually the acronym had been filed away and forgotten.

Kat answers Miranda's question with a single whispered obscenity.

'How long ago did you get this?'

'Half an hour.' I pick up my phone and send the picture to the two of them on a newly created Signal group chat that has just the three of us as members. 'Where's Dev? We need him too.'

'Went out for a drink after work, not answering his phone.' She swears again. 'I think he's still pissed off with me after last weekend, to be honest. With all of us. He's been pretty frosty this week.'

'How much does he know?'

'Nothing that's happened since the dinner party last weekend. Every time I try to talk to him about it he cuts me off, says he doesn't want to know anything else like he'll be *infected* by the information or something.'

'Well, we need him,' I say. 'We need all the help we can get. Can you try him again?'

She digs her phone out of her handbag and dials his number, holds it to her ear. When it goes to voicemail, she leaves another message.

'Like I said.' She scrolls the screen for a moment before dropping it back into her handbag. 'He's still pissed off with me, probably screening my calls.'

From the front of the house comes the sound of the heavy front door slamming shut.

I turn to peer out into the hallway. 'Is Cressida here, Miranda?'

'No.' Her voice is distracted, as if she's still in shock. 'She's at her dad's, not back until Sunday night. Dario was here, finishing up some prep for tomorrow night. We're supposed to have my parents over for dinner.' She takes a deep breath, then another, shaking out her fingers as if she's trying to shake off the emotion. 'I just can't believe this is happening. It's an *actual* nightmare. I can't . . . I can't deal. I knew it was a mistake to bring that money back, the Tarot told us everything we needed to know. And I just *knew* it.'

'Hey,' I say. 'Come on.' I pull her into a hug, enveloped in her expensive perfume. She's skinny and slight, everything toned and minimised from long hours at the gym. 'We're going to get them back, OK? Both of them.'

She sniffs. 'We have to do the right thing now.'

I pat her back as if comforting a child, her shoulder blade angular beneath my palm.

'Whatever we need to do.'

'Yes,' she says. 'You're right.'

Detaching herself from the hug, Miranda slides her own phone from the back pocket of her skintight trousers, taps the screen and holds it to her ear.

Kat's head swivels towards her. 'Christian's not going to answer,' she says. 'They've got his phone, remember?'

Miranda turns away, keeping the mobile pressed to her ear.

'Miranda?' Tension prickles at the back of my neck. 'Who are you calling?'

'The police.'

'*What?*'

My sister-in-law opens her mouth to reply but Kat is already on her, closing the distance between them in two quick strides, grabbing the other woman's wrist in one hand and her iPhone in the other. Miranda is fit but Kat is taller, longer limbed, and she's never been one to shy away from a physical confrontation. Something about growing up with three older brothers, probably. She was the one who had faced down a bully who was making my life miserable at school, waiting for him outside the PE block one afternoon. All I knew was that he turned up the next day with a black eye – and never said another word to me. Nor had he told anyone else, too embarrassed to admit he'd been given a shiner by a lanky thirteen-year-old girl. Kat had never mentioned it to me either.

Miranda's iPhone drops to the floor, the operator's tinny voice still asking which of the emergency services we need. Kat hooks it towards her with a shoe, holding the other woman at arm's length as she scoops it up and taps the red icon to end the call.

Miranda screams in frustration. 'Give it to me!' She lunges towards Kat. 'Who cares if we have to tell the police about the money? Who cares if we get in a bit of trouble for it? Who cares if it helps to get the boys back?'

Kat circles away from her, shoving the phone into her jeans pocket. 'Not until you calm down.'

'Give me my phone!' Miranda says again, her voice cracking.

'Stop!' I stand between them, holding a palm up to each. 'Stop it, both of you!'

The mobile rings in Kat's pocket, the ringtone some pop song I don't recognise. She plucks it out and answers, smoothly telling the emergency operator that *No*, we didn't need help and *Yes*, the call was a pocket-dial and *Yes*, she was very sorry to have wasted their time. She ends the call.

'Look,' I say. 'We took that money. Like it or not, we did. I know you were against it, Miranda; so was I, if you remember?' I throw a pointed look at Kat, who gives me a small shrug. 'But it was a group decision and it's done now. We can't change it, we can't go back. We *can* bring Jason and Christian home without involving the police, without making everything that much worse. But only if we work together, if we all agree.'

Kat nods. 'Right.'

Miranda slumps back onto one of the sofas, sinking into the thick cushions. 'Agree? Like we *agreed* at the cottage on New Year's Eve?' My sister-in-law's cut-glass boarding school accent becomes sharper, clearer, *posher*, the angrier she gets, almost as if she tones it down in normal conversation but the fury makes her forget herself. She turns her flashing eyes on Kat again. 'Do you even remember the Tarot reading I gave you that night? Did you think it was *all just a bit of fun, stringing silly Miranda along with her silly deck of cards*? Because I remember it. The Tower, the harbinger of distress, misery, ruinous change. The Fool's journey. Any of this ringing bells? Then the Devil to round things off with all his negative, violent energy and seduction by the material world. It was *all* there. All of it. Everything that's happened in the past three weeks, it was right there in the cards. Staring us in the face. And what about the date last Friday, the last time the six of us were all together?'

'What about it?'

'Friday the thirteenth?'

Kat snorts. 'Seriously?'

'It's another sign!'

'It's a sign of *something*, all right.' She turns towards me, as if tired of the conversation with the younger woman. 'Did you reply to Docherty's message yet?'

'Not yet,' I say. 'Thought we should discuss first.'

Miranda pulls a tissue from the box on a side table. 'What's to discuss? We give this horrible man what he wants, we get the boys back and we never, ever speak about this again.'

'And no police?'

She gives her nose a delicate blow. 'No police.'

'So we're agreed?' I say. 'We're going to give the money back, right? In exchange for Jason and Christian?'

Miranda is nodding. 'Right.'

'It's not as if we have any other cards to play at this point.' I sit down on the middle sofa, my limbs feeling suddenly weak and watery as the adrenaline begins to drain away. I retrieve my phone from the pocket of my coat. 'OK, let's send a reply.'

Kat sits down on the third sofa, so that we occupy three sides of this square of expensive soft furnishings, the two of them facing each other with me in the middle. She fixes me with a stare.

'There is another alternative, you know. A third option.'

'Which is what?'

'We don't pay, and we don't involve the police either.'

Miranda looks up sharply. 'What?'

'We find them instead.' She gives her trademark shrug, as if she's stating the obvious. 'And we get them out of there.'

40

The room is silent for a moment, the whole house silent around us, no sounds of the outside world reaching us through the double-glazed glass. Miranda stares at Kat, a furrow lining her Botox-smooth forehead, her mouth hanging slightly open.

'Have you gone *completely* mad?'

'It means we get to keep most of the money, too.'

I sit forward. 'And how exactly do we do find them, Kat?'

'We use the cash' she says. 'We have more than enough to pay for the resources we need, the information we need, the help we need, and still have plenty left over. You know Dev's always been good with computers, tracking and tracing and all that location-based stuff. We've got options, rather than just rolling over and giving up – which is what they want us to do.'

Miranda stabs a manicured index finger at her. 'That's easy for you to say! It's not *your* husband tied up like an animal in a bloody basement! It's not your husband whose life is hanging by a thread!'

'My thoughts exactly,' I say. 'Seriously, Kat? Even if we could find them, you've seen what they've done to Jason and Christian. We can't go up against these people, we can't risk it. We just *can't*.'

She's shaking her head. 'Docherty's cover story about drug dealers and people getting shot, everything he told us is complete moonshine intended to frighten us. But it's completely fake – just like he was.'

I pull up the photo he'd sent me, pointing to the blood, the bruises.

'You think *this* is fake? I mean, seriously Kat, even if we did manage to find them and spirit them away somehow, do you want to spend the rest of your life looking over your shoulder? Waiting for Docherty to knock on our door again? Do any of us? He knows where we live, remember?'

Kat holds her hands up. 'Look, I'm just saying it's worth considering all the options. Before we hand them our money.'

Miranda slaps her palm into a cushion with a dull *whump*. 'Screw the money! Who cares about the money?'

'Agreed,' I say. 'I'm with Miranda on this one. We do what they want, pool all of the cash from the backpack and take it to them on Sunday.'

'OK,' Kat says finally in a defeated tone. 'I understand, I'm outvoted. Sorry for suggesting it, all right? I want to get the boys back just as much as you do.'

I pull up the last message from Docherty and type out a reply.

OK. We will do what you say but gathering all the money together is going to take a little time. Please don't hurt them anymore. Let me know where to deliver money.

We all stare at the phone as if expecting an instant reply. The message shows that it's been read at the other end, but there is no immediate response.

'Here's what we're going to do,' I say. 'We have to work together, pool all the money again. I put some into different bank accounts which I can draw out tomorrow morning and we've spent a bit on Mum's care home, but we should be able to make up the shortfall if we clean out our other savings, make some withdrawals on the credit cards.'

Kat frowns. 'So we're going to end up *worse* off, more in debt, than when this all started?'

'I honestly don't care at this point.' I push my hair back from my face, a wave of exhaustion flowing over me. 'We just need to do what they say. What about you two? You've still got most of it left, right?'

Miranda shrugs. 'All of it, I think. Christian liked to have his rainy day fund. He always talked about having a cushion to fall back on.'

'And he made you a director of his company, right? A silent partner, or whatever they call it? So you can pull some money out of the company if we need to fill any gaps.'

My sister-in-law nods, and I turn to Kat.

'What about your share? I take it Dev hasn't touched it?'

She snorts. 'He doesn't even know where I've hidden it. If he did, he probably would have burned the lot by now.'

A shiver goes through me as I imagine Dev standing in their small back garden at this very moment, feeding stacks of banknotes into his chiminea. Grey smoke rising into the dark night sky as he burns our only chance of getting my husband and my brother back.

'Where did you say he was again, tonight?'

'Out with a mate.' Seeing my worried face, she puts a hand on my knee. 'Don't sweat it, Hels. He has no idea where it is.'

'You're sure?'

'Yup.'

She holds my gaze with her usual confidence but there *is* something there, something I can't quite put my finger on. A ripple in her normal certainty, but it's only there for a moment before it vanishes.

'All right then.' I shake the feeling away. 'Here's what we're going to do. Miranda, my brother still has that safe upstairs in the master bedroom, right? Although I think he's under the impression that you don't know the combination.'

Miranda snorts. 'Welcome to my world, Helen. Constantly underestimated by everyone, including my own husband. If you must know, the combination is—'

I hold a hand up. 'I don't want to know. Just want to make sure you can get into it.'

'I can.'

'Good. Me and Kat will go home now, gather up all of our bundles and bring them back here to put in the safe so no one can get to them before noon on Sunday. Before we do that, we count it to see how much is missing, see how much we'll need to find to make it back up to the full amount.' I turn to Miranda. 'And no calls to the police while we're gone, agreed?'

She gives a single nod. 'Agreed.'

Kat stands up, loops the strap of her handbag over her shoulder. 'Sounds like a plan,' she says. 'See you back here in an hour.'

41

Miranda

Miranda mixed herself a large gin and tonic at the kitchen island, drinking half of it before she put the glass down. She exhaled as the alcohol hit her bloodstream and began to work its magic, easing the tension in her shoulders, the twist of anxiety at the base of her spine.

She *could* call the police. She could. It was the smart thing to do, the logical thing. God knows, it was about time someone did the smart thing. If they'd done that in the first place, Christian would be safe, home with her now, no doubt telling one of his interminable stories about the business, or a new client, a new competitor, a new deal. All his stories merged into one, after a while. But all the same: *poor Christian*. She had surprised herself at her own reaction to the picture of him battered and bruised, at how much of it had been real. How much had been genuine.

It was a surprise, to realise she still had feelings for her husband.

She still cared for him, but perhaps more like a sibling now, a friend, than anything more. Was that enough? For now, today, tomorrow? Yes. It would have to be, until he was safe. But as for next month, next year, the next ten? That was the question she'd been asking herself for so long, turning it over in her mind until she thought she'd reached a decision. *A Boxing Day epiphany.* Christian drinking more and more, until he'd passed out on the sofa, her daughter miserable and lonely away from her oldest friends, the house a mess, the kitchen a disaster zone, a realisation that it was no longer enough. That the life she had with him was no longer enough.

And then New Year had happened. *This* had happened.

She had to focus her mind on the here and now.

She wouldn't call the police. Not yet. There *was* someone else she wanted to call, but not tonight. There would be time for that afterwards. She had taken the first step already, made the first approach, sent the first email in what had already grown into a lengthy correspondence over the last fortnight.

After all, everyone had secrets. She was no different.

Her secret just happened to be a family law specialist with twenty years' experience in high-net-worth divorce cases.

Her wrist still ached where Kat had twisted the phone from her grasp. That bloody woman was *so* patronising. She thought she kept it hidden but Miranda knew, she knew Kat had always looked down on her like she was some kind of bimbo gold-digger. She'd been the last one to warm up to her, to accept her as a new arrival in their little clique after the wedding.

Miranda refilled the glass with another healthy splash of gin and took it up the sweeping staircase, across the high-ceilinged landing and into the master bedroom, motion-activated lights glowing into life as her feet sank into the carpet. On the wall by the en suite, there was a watercolour portrait. A painting of Miranda in a long white dress and wide-brimmed sunhat, commissioned by Christian for their first wedding anniversary. She had never been keen on it, but he had insisted. And so here it was.

She gripped the frame of the painting on both sides and lifted it up and off the mount, revealing the blue steel door of a safe built into the wall behind. She put her drink on the bookshelf and typed the code into the keypad, holding her breath as she pressed the last digit. He wasn't aware that she knew it. But had he changed it? Had he got more paranoid since their return from the Dales on New Year's Day?

There was a whir and a click from the mechanism as the lock disengaged and the door huffed open a few millimetres. The code was unchanged. Good old predictable Christian.

She pulled the heavy steel door open all the way. The safe was compact, maybe the size of a microwave oven or a little bigger. Miranda had only looked inside it a handful of times – not that the safe was any kind of big secret, just that there wasn't normally anything very interesting in it. There were some envelopes on the left, some document folders, a small box which she knew contained his dad's old cufflinks. A few other bits and pieces that had more sentimental value than anything else.

The cash was on the right. Pushed up tight to the back wall of the safe, it was in two stacks, one that reached almost to the top and another that was only half as high. All the notes were loose, freed from the paper binders that had kept them bundled together, and one stack was slightly shorter, narrower: the smaller stack was the purple twenty-pound notes, the bigger one fuchsia-pink fifties.

She eased out the lower stack, taking half of it in each hand and laying the notes on the floor at her feet. Then did the same with the stack of fifties, reaching in for two handfuls, then two more, until it was all arrayed in front of her on the deep cream carpet. It was weird that Christian had unbundled the money so it was all loose – he was normally pretty gung-ho about things like that, preferring the simplicity of large round numbers, the ease of knowing its value had been calculated by someone else. But it looked like her husband had wanted to count and check every single note, one by one.

She began to do the same.

Sitting cross-legged on the floor, she counted the twenties into piles of five, putting ten piles together to make a thousand. When she finished with them she started on the fifties, counting these twenty to a stack like a casino cashier doling out winnings. Before long, notes began to surround her like a Roman mosaic of coloured tiles on the floor.

It was pretty, in its own way. But she would be glad when this money was out of the house.

And she would be glad when Christian was back.

Yes, that too. Of course she would. Whatever had happened since New Year's Eve, he didn't deserve this.

She took another swig of gin and tonic before resuming her work, touching each pile as she mouthed the number, trying to pick up the thread from where she'd left off. She'd lost count of the money; she started again. It wasn't until her last year of school that she'd been diagnosed with dyscalculia, described as 'maths dyslexia' by the expensive specialist summoned to the house – although by that point it had been too late to salvage much in academic terms. *It's a good thing you're the prettiest girl at Roedean*, her father had said at the time. *At least you should be able to find yourself a nice chap to settle down with.* Even twenty years later, she could still feel the sting of his words, the tone of disappointment in his youngest child compared to her two clever brothers.

None of their friends knew she struggled with numbers, only Christian. Miranda had spent her whole life covering it up, disguising it, hiding it like an embarrassing teenage tattoo that could never be erased. And it was easier still if you had money, if you could just wave your phone at a waiter or a barman or a shop assistant, let Apple Pay take care of it.

Fifteen minutes later, the floor around her was a mass of banknotes, radiating out from her in a half circle like the dials on a clock. It *seemed* like there was a bit less than five hundred thousand there, but she couldn't quite be sure. She'd lost count several times and ended up just trying to do a rough calculation in her head, the numbers bouncing and jumbling as she tried to put them in order. It didn't really matter though. Whatever was missing, there was plenty in the company, plenty saved elsewhere to pay what they had to pay and bring this whole pitiful saga to an end. Christian undoubtedly had enough in one of his many personal bank accounts to take care of it.

But without him here, it would be easier to access company funds. He had made her a director when they got married – not that she actually did anything. It was more to do with tax stuff and dividends and financial details she didn't really understand. Twice a year – in April and October – a nice dividend arrived in her bank account and Christian insisted she keep it just for *her*, not to spend on house things or holidays or Cressy's school trips or any of those everyday costs, but just for Miranda to spend on herself. The next one wasn't due for a few months but she knew just how to bring things forward a little to take care of this situation.

She didn't have access to the company's accounts but she had the next best thing: she just had to speak to Tony.

It was Friday night, but she knew he'd take her calls. They had . . . history, of a sort. Which is to say, her husband's accountant had a history of trying to chat her up at company events when Christian's back was turned, and Miranda had never told her husband because she liked having that little bit of leverage. As repellent as he was – and Tony was one of those men whose supreme confidence was inversely related to his physical appearance – it was still useful to keep him onside.

She went to the en suite, reapplied her mascara and a slash of dark red lipstick as she worked out what she would say to him. The truth was too messy, too complicated. Something simple would be better. In her dressing room, the MacBook was open on a table so she woke it up and went to FaceTime, selecting his number. He answered after half a dozen rings and his florid face filled the screen, cheeks already rouged with a red wine blush.

'Miranda.' He smiled. 'It's been too long. To what do I owe the pleasure?'

She gave him a couple of minutes of small talk, asking about his two sons and his long-suffering wife. It looked as if he was in the back garden of his big house, up the road in Clifton, cigar smoke curling around him.

'Listen,' she said, leaning closer to the screen. 'I need a favour, Tony. And I need to ask for your absolute discretion too.'

'Of course,' he said, raising an eyebrow. 'My lips . . . are sealed.'

'I'm planning something special for Christian's birthday and I've found this amazing villa just outside Cannes. It's absolutely *perfect* but the owner says he can only hold it for me for twenty-four hours, so I need to pay up front to secure it. I'd be *super* grateful if you could pull my April dividend forward so I can get it booked this weekend.'

As she talked, he raised a thick cigar to his lips and took a long drag, exhaling plumes of dense grey smoke that almost shroud him from view.

'I see.'

'Or a director's loan, or whatever they're called, if that's easier?' She gave him her best damsel-in-distress smile. In her experience, men like Tony couldn't help themselves when she really turned it on. 'Sorry, I'm terrible with all the financial terminology.'

'Christian's out tonight, is he?'

'Yah,' she said. 'It's just me and you, Tony. So I wonder if we could say . . . fifty thousand?'

He pulled on the cigar again.

'Fifty K?'

'That should do it.'

'You see, the thing is, Miranda . . .' He exhaled grey smoke. 'I'm sorry to be the one who has to tell you. But I'm afraid that's not going to be possible.'

42

Kat

Kat spent the short drive back to her house deciding how much to tell her husband.

As far as Dev knew, all of them were still sitting on the money, deciding what to do next. Whenever she'd tried to talk to him about it recently he'd just cut her off – as if refusing to discuss it would make the problem go away. As if the bundles of cash were radioactive, poisonous. The only thing he wanted to know was that their share was stored away from the house, whether that meant a safety deposit box, a train station locker, a hole in the ground – he didn't care. As long as it was away from their home address, away from *him*.

The shock of this evening was still raw, the grim photo of Jason and Christian still vivid in her mind.

She *had* to talk to Dev now, to warn him, whether he wanted to hear it or not. However many times he said *I told you so*, insisted he had been right all along.

Stopping at a red light before she could turn into her road, Kat glanced at her phone again but there was still no reply from him. She wondered if he's been at home this whole time, watching the snooker with a beer and deliberately ignoring her texts. Still playing the martyr card. Although – thank God – his self-righteous bullshit had saved him from what the other two men were going through today.

The house was in darkness when she got back. Dev's little electric car was not in the drive, either. She opened the front door and reached around to the switches, bathing the hall and stairs in light.

'Dev?' She listened for a moment, but the house gave her nothing back. 'It's me.'

She went through to the kitchen-diner, the small sitting room, turning on more lights as she went. Dev must still be in the pub with his mate. Satisfied that she was alone, she went upstairs to the little spare room, which used to be Georgia's bedroom and was barely used now since their daughter had moved to Brighton with her job, settled down with her girlfriend. Kat had pulled up the old carpet to sand down the bare boards beneath as a summer project some years ago, laying a collection of rugs in its place. She went to the corner of the room now next to the bookcase still full of Georgia's favourites – Suzanne Collins, John Green, JK Rowling and a hundred others – knelt down and rolled back the corner of the rug to reveal one of the wooden boards beneath. This one was cut shorter because of the skirting, with a coin-sized knothole at one end. She slid her thumb into the knothole and eased it forward, the wood sliding smoothly away from her until there was a gap of a few centimetres. Putting her hand into the opening, she gripped the end of the board and pulled it up, then towards her, the whole board coming away in her hand.

The money was stacked in its neat bundles in the space beneath, just as she'd left it.

Yes, she'd lied to her husband about taking it out of the house. But it was actually safer here, where she knew about it, rather than in some locker out *there* where anyone might discover it. Her other hiding place – in the utility room, where she kept the little burner phone – was much too small to accommodate the money. She took it all out, laid the bundles side by side. Held one of them to her nose, riffled the notes with her thumb and inhaled the faint, musky, indefinable scent of money. God, they should bottle it, that smell. They'd make a fortune. *Haha*. There had to be a way to keep it. There *had* to be. Or even some of it. To have this good fortune land in their laps and then surrender it without a whimper, it was just . . . crazy. It made no sense.

The count was what she'd expected. About twenty-five thousand of their share was gone already, a chunk of it through the tills at the shop to help Angela, the owner, keep her head above water. More of it to pay down a handful of credit cards and loans.

And then there was Tate: her other little secret. A chunk had gone to him, and the goods from that transaction were in the narrow space beneath the loose floorboards, in a black drawstring bag. She took the bag out and pulled the opening wide, feeling the familiar buzz of anticipation as she reached inside and laid the contents on the wooden floor. Separate packets of powder, pills and weed along with a few prescription drugs, Xanax, benzos to help her sleep. Enough to keep her going for a few months.

Out on the street there was the dull slam of a car door, the idling of an engine. Dev's car, or maybe an Uber? She froze, straining to hear footsteps, the sound of his key in the lock, the front door opening. Her eyes fell on the array of drugs and cash spread out on the floor in front of her, one hand reaching for the floorboard, ready to shove it all back into its hiding place. A bus lumbered by in a huff of diesel, and then there was nothing. No more engine noise, no one outside. Silence.

She exhaled a shaky breath, heart juddering in her chest. *Get a grip, Kat. You're jumping at shadows.* Tonight was looking like it might be a long night and she needed to stay sharp, stay on it, stay focused. Using the little spoon she had a quick toot from the bag of white powder, exhaling with pleasure and chasing it straightaway with one of the small pink pills, just to smooth out the edges and keep her steady.

Just to smooth out the edges.

That was how she'd been introduced to it, her and a colleague happily drunk in the ladies' room of some swanky London hotel, late in the evening at a team-building event. The two of them reapplying their lipstick side by side, laughing, swaying, comparing notes on which of the directors was going to make the biggest fool of himself. Her colleague tapping out a line onto her makeup compact, snorting it right there. *Ever tried this? You don't know what you're missing.*

It had started as a one-off. Then became a little pick-me-up every now and then to get her through long days at work, keep her energy levels up. And slowly it had gone from every-once-in-a-while to every week, and then to several times a week. It gave her that extra zip for a big presentation, a board meeting, a client event; the energy that had come naturally in her twenties but needed a little help by her mid-forties. She'd been managing it, staying on top of it, giving all the outward signs of a confident, capable senior manager moving towards a higher branch of the corporate tree. And how was it so different to the copious free alcohol the company dished out to staff at events and away days? She'd always pushed things, skirted the edge, always enjoyed taking risks and beating the odds, from driving without a licence when she was a teenager to telling a few white lies on her CV, skirting the rules at work, to a little bump of cocaine to help her shine in the boardroom.

She'd always got away with it, *always*. She'd never been caught.

Until the day she was.

She'd just never imagined she'd be tripped up by the colourless drones in corporate HR, of all people. It had started with a junior member of staff, caught smoking a Friday afternoon joint in the car park. Sacking him wasn't enough, the ultra-conservative American owners of the company wanted to *send a message* to the rest of the workforce. And so they brought in a programme of drug testing: three per cent of staff, randomly selected every fortnight to provide hair and urine samples.

It was only a couple of dozen employees at a time, but Kat's name had come up in that very first sweep.

Which was the *real* reason why she'd left her high-powered corporate job.

They had offered her a payout to go quietly after signing an NDA, rather than risk having it blow up into something public and unpleasant. She had access to lots of sensitive customer data, lots of strategic intelligence that would make their biggest clients very nervous if they knew the truth. The company didn't need another scandal. The last thing they needed was a high-profile sacking, a tribunal or maybe even a court case. So they'd paid her off and she'd told everyone she was just jumping off the corporate ladder for a change of pace, that she was having a mid-life career shift to get some balance back, starting with three months of gardening leave to find her feet.

Everything derailed, wrecked. Everything she'd worked for, ruined by one stupid mistake that dumped her back out onto the job market at the age of fifty-two with one of those three-line references that said nothing and everything at the same time. Two years ago, and she still hadn't told her best friend. Helen, bless her, had never even thought to question the decision – had told Kat she was brave to do something new, to find her own path like it was one of those naive self-esteem mantras you'd see on Instagram.

She hadn't told Dev either. Although things between them had been ... difficult. For a while. Since Georgia left, really. Their daughter's departure from the nest had left the house unbalanced somehow, as if she had been the glue holding her parents together. The one main thing they still had in common.

Kat felt the drugs start to kick in properly now, the warm rush expanding outwards from her core as if she was caught in a beautiful slipstream of energy. *This* was how she had coped after losing two-thirds of her salary overnight, how she would help get her best friend's husband back too. This would help her get through anything. The New Year cash had allowed her to make a bulk buy to keep her going for a while, rather than have Tate coming to the shop every week or two. He'd given her a volume discount as well. She thought of the small black burner phone nestled in its hiding place in the utility room.

A muffled noise reached her from downstairs. *A knock on the door?* No, nothing as definitive as that. Maybe the click of the letterbox, junk mail landing on the doormat.

She stood still, listened. Was Dev back?

The noise came again. *Tap. Tap.* Like a tentative, half-hearted knock at the door.

She went across to the main bedroom, pulling the curtain aside at the front window, but the pitch of the roof made it impossible to see right down to the front door. The only unbroken porch light threw a weak glow on the edge of *something*, a bag or maybe a package, but the angle was too tight to be sure. On the way to the stairs she passed by the open door to the spare room, where piles of money were laid out on the wooden boards next to her black drawstring bag. Rather than put it all back in the hiding place, she simply pulled the door closed and went downstairs.

She was reaching for the front door when her brain served up a flashback of the picture of Jason and Christian, all blood and black eyes and bruises. She paused, looked around the hallway for anything to hand, picked up Dev's golf umbrella from the stand. But it felt flimsy, insubstantial. She dropped it back in with the rest and fetched the rolling pin from the kitchen drawer instead, gripping its solid heft in her right hand as she opened the front door with her left.

Something had been dumped on the doorstep, an old coat and some other bits and pieces. *What the hell?* A scan of the street left and right revealed no one, no cars, no figures running away. As her eyes returned to the clothes and adjusted to the gloom, they took in something shining wet in the moonlight, the faintest shudder of movement from beneath the old coat. Kat pulled the door open wide and stepped forward, the rolling pin held low down against her leg.

She reached back inside to flick on the light switch, heart barrelling up into her throat as she recognised the sensible boots, the dark canvas jacket, the bald head.

Dev.

'Oh, God!' She knelt down to him, touched him gently on the shoulder. 'Dev!'

His face was a mass of blood, his eyes swollen shut, lips puffy, mouth sagging open in unconsciousness.

'Dev!' she said again, cradling his cheek. 'Can you hear me?'

Her husband gave no reply.

43

I can't get the image of Jason's battered face out of my head.

Adrenaline has been pushing me along for the last hour but now, back home in our bedroom, I slump onto the bed and risk looking at the picture again. In twenty-six years of marriage I've never seen him so scared, so beaten down, his eyes like a cornered animal. Here in our home, surrounded by all that is familiar and normal from our life together – the half-read thriller on his bedside table, his broken-backed slippers waiting by the door, his Pink Floyd T-shirt hung over the chair – it all comes rushing in. The enormity of our situation, the spiralling danger, the catastrophe hanging over my family.

Then the tears come, and I don't try to stop them.

Three weeks ago today we had been at the cottage, the day before New Year's Eve, oblivious to what was waiting out there on the moors. Just living our normal lives, with our normal problems and worries, happy in our ignorance. I would give anything to go back to that day now. Anything. Kat's words still ring in my ears too, her parting shot as we'd left my brother's house barely fifteen minutes ago. Said in her usual spirit of brutal honesty regardless of the impact her words might have.

I hate to be the one to say it, Hels, but we've got no guarantees they'll do what they say. We hand over the money, we're just taking it on trust that they'll keep their side of the bargain. That they'll release Jason and Christian.

She was right, of course, but it had still sent a sick pulse of fear corkscrewing through my stomach. We just had to hope Docherty kept his side of the bargain. And what choice did we have, really? In truth, there was only one choice: to give back something that had never been ours in the first place.

After a minute or two, I grab a tissue from the box on the bedside table and wipe my eyes, pulling in deep breaths to dispel the sobs. There was no time for this. The clock was already ticking and we needed to get busy. I had the outline of a plan, at least: gather all the money together again, work out how much we're short, scrape together what we can from other savings and credit cards, then pull a bit more out of Christian's company to make up the difference. Deliver the money on Sunday, get the men back and then we put all of this behind us. Agree that we would never, ever speak about it again.

It occurs to me that we'll also discover who took the extra money on New Year's Day – who had helped themselves to extra bundles of the cash without telling the rest of us. Unless they've spent it already.

Jason had hidden the money before Docherty's visit, redistributing it all over the house in smaller amounts. He told me where they are and I find four of the five bundles quickly, but the fifth – in the attic – is in a part of the house that has always been Jason's domain. I extend the pull-down ladder and climb up into the dusty space, reaching for the pull cord to switch on the bare forty-watt bulb hanging from a wire. It's full of *stuff*, cobwebbed old suitcases, empty cardboard boxes that Jason insisted we could reuse one day, stacks of exercise books from when the boys were at primary school, Alfie's old pushchair, carpet offcuts and old dumb-bells, an airbed that was surely full of holes.

It takes fifteen minutes of searching before I find the bag tucked inside a box of his parents' old photo albums, curled and yellowing with age, which he'd not had the heart to throw away.

I take it back down to the bedroom and put it with all the rest, brushing cobwebs out of my hair. After unwrapping all the packets, I separate the bundled notes according to value. By the time the six of us had split the money, each share had amounted to just over £514,000. We had spent around £4,000 on Mum's care, and paid in around £5,000 each to our various bank accounts. So there should be around an even half-million spread out on the bed in front of me.

The total comes to just under £493,000.

I must have miscounted. Not a surprise really, considering how today has unfolded, how strung out I've been since the police knocked on our door. I check it all again.

But it's not a mistake: there is around £7,000 missing and unaccounted for. I guess Jason must have hidden the rest somewhere else in the house, for some reason known only to him? I check back under our bed, just in case, but the space previously occupied by the backpack is still empty save for a scattering of black cat hair left behind from one of Prim's visits. His working-from-home desk in the little box room is the usual mess of papers and files, three drawers similarly stuffed with old bills, receipts, bank statements, stacks of old magazines. In normal circumstances I'd never poke around in here – he had his stuff, and I had mine – but tonight I just scoop everything out of the drawers in turn, spreading it all across the floor.

I don't find any missing money.

But I discover something else instead.

Buried in the bottom drawer is a black A4 binder that looks newer than everything else. No label on the spine to indicate what's inside. It's light, only a few pages tucked neatly inside.

The first thing clipped into the binder is smaller than the rest, a printed leaflet in blue and pink pastel colours for somewhere called The Camberley Clinic. Some sort of healthcare provider. I snap open the binder and pull it out, flipping open the first page.

Confusion gives way to the first stirrings of nausea.

It's an abortion clinic.

Why would Jason need *this*? Why would he hide it from me, tucked away somewhere he knows I would never look? My first thought is the boys. Noah, our eldest, in London. Had he got a girlfriend pregnant? Had Jason been keeping it from me, trying to shield me? Instinct tells me that's what he would do: he would try to handle it himself if the boys couldn't face telling me. I flip through the leaflet, pictures and words blurring in front of my eyes. An address finally swimming into focus. *York*.

Not Noah, then. Alfie.

Not even eighteen, still my baby, still at school. Is this because of him? For a girl in his year, a girl he's met at a party? I swallow down the ache in my throat and flip to the next page clipped into the folder. It's a handwritten sheet of names, a number in brackets next to each one.

Summer F (3)

Chantelle O (1)

Paris A (2)

So there it is. There *she* is. Paris. I hear my brother's words again, a none-too-subtle hint that he knew something was going on.

I don't suppose he's ever mentioned Paris to you, has he?

I force myself to look at the rest of the page. Beside each name is a local address, also written in my husband's confident hand. More numbers and acronyms I don't understand. *AH. RR. SAI.*

I flip to the next page, the breath freezing in my throat.

A hotel receipt.

So is the next page, and the next. One night here, a couple of nights there. Different places, some in the centre of York, some nearer to us – none of them hotels where I have ever stayed. Because what would *I* need with a hotel room so close to home?

What would my *husband* need?

One of the hotels is barely half a mile from our house, near the boys' secondary school. I've probably driven past it a thousand times, never for a second imagining that my husband might be in one of the rooms above, sharing an hour or two with Summer or Paris or Chantelle.

Sitting on the floor of Jason's home office, I flip over another handwritten page of numbers and letters, sums and acronyms and crossings-out. How much had he spent on this? No wonder he had been so keen to keep the money on New Year's Eve. The leaden realisation that it was not our sons paying for hotels. Not our sons with a list of women's names and information about a local abortion clinic.

Jason, what have you done?
Why have you done this to us? To me?
All our years together, tossed away like they were nothing.

I slam the folder shut and throw it across the room with an exasperated shout.

It spins off the filing cabinet, sheets of paper fluttering to the floor like autumn leaves.

44

Miranda has lost some of her usual poise when she opens the front door to me for the second time this evening.

She gives me an odd smile and ushers me into the big entrance hall but it feels like something has shifted, sharpened, as if a layer of her usual self has slid away to reveal the unvarnished original underneath. She's barefoot and has an ice-filled tumbler in one hand, cheeks flushed, mascara smudged under her eyes. Pushing the front door shut with the heel of her foot, she wanders off towards the kitchen without another word and I follow, throwing my coat over the banister as we pass.

I had spent the drive back to her house composing myself, trying to push down the starburst of pain inside my chest, the tears and the rage and the million angry questions I have for my husband. Trying to *compartmentalise*, as my brother would put it. And at the same time, trying to think of an innocent explanation for the contents of the black folder Jason had hidden somewhere I should never have found it.

On the outside, I'm just about calm again by the time I arrive back at my brother's house.

Barefoot, Miranda is even more petite than usual, her delicate tread almost silent on the heated stone floor as she leads me to the kitchen. Does she know about Jason's secret? Had my brother told her? The two men had sometimes been close over the years, and it was Christian who'd first mentioned the name Paris to me. Perhaps my husband had made some kind of confession on New Year's Eve? I think back to the two of them in the cottage, well past midnight, deep into a whisky-fuelled conversation by the fire. By that point, Dev had stormed out and Miranda had already passed out on the sofa. Perhaps they *all* knew about Jason's secret, Kat and Dev too, all of them except me. *Poor, trusting Helen*, always the last one to find out. None of them with the heart to break it to me.

But surely Kat would have found a way to tell me, if she knew?

It doesn't matter who knows. All that matters is getting the two of them back, safe, and then I'll confront him. Ask him point-blank and try to deal with whatever comes next. First, we have to give Docherty what he wants. The financial hole we're in is deeper than I'd thought it would be, but it's a problem that will soon be solved once we make up the shortfall.

On the kitchen island is a collection of bottles, chopping boards, half-cut fruit, an ice tray and a silver flask for mixing cocktails. An empty family-sized bag of crisps and a white bowl half filled with peanuts, more of them strewn across the counter. It looks like Miranda has been busy in here since I left. *Sky News* plays silently on a huge wall-mounted TV, a reporter standing in front of The White House as the headline ticker scrolls across his waist. 'Pure Shores' by All Saints plays softly from speakers mounted in the ceiling.

Miranda picks up the silver mixing flask, pours a last dribble of dark fluid into her glass and downs it in one, ice cubes rattling against her front teeth.

She puts the empty glass down, hard, onto the counter.

'Will you have a drink with me, Helen?'

'Thanks, Miranda.' I jingle the car keys, still in my hand. 'But I'd better not.'

'Oh, come on. Just one.' There is a brittle, jagged tone in her voice that I've never heard before. 'Just one can't hurt, can it?'

'Really, I'm fine. Have you heard from Kat?'

She ignores my question with a theatrical sigh.

'It *is* Friday night, Helen. And if you can't have a drink with your sister-in-law on a Friday night, when can you?'

'Well, I suppose a Diet Coke would be fine, if you've got—'

'Have a fucking drink, for fuck's sake!'

We stare at each other for a moment, the air suddenly crackling with an electric charge. There's never been a single swear word between us before; never even a raised voice, not in the ten years we've known each other. Her cheeks are flushed a deep crimson, her small fists clenched tight on the black marble of the kitchen island.

'OK,' I say finally, slipping the car keys into my handbag. 'Why not. I could actually use a drink, right now.'

'Good,' she says loudly, slapping a palm onto the marble. 'One Dark and Stormy coming up for my sensible sister-in-law.'

She busies herself mixing dark rum and ginger ale in the silver flask, slices of lime and a hefty dash of something else before sealing the lid and giving it a perfunctory shake. She prepares two ice-filled tumblers and pours the mixture in, filling both with the dark golden cocktail before sliding one across the counter towards me.

She raises her glass, as if the fiery exchange of a few moments ago never happened.

'Cheers.'

I do likewise and take a sip, the alcohol hitting the back of my throat like pure spiced-sugar fire. It tastes like it's *mostly* rum with barely any mixers to dilute it.

'What's going on, Miranda?' I put my glass down. 'Did you find all the money? All of your share?'

'It's in the study.' She waves over her shoulder in the general direction of the hallway.

'How much?'

She shrugs, takes another sip of her cocktail. 'Might need another count.'

On the silent TV behind her, *Sky News* switches to show a gaggle of people with placards standing in front of the High Court in London. It occurs to me that I haven't told anyone yet about my suspicions from earlier this evening.

'Remember Christian's story about the robbery?'

She frowns. 'Robbery?'

'The one he told us last week at your dinner party – the gang, the cash depot down south, that link to the news story? There's something weird about it.'

'Uh-huh.'

'I think ... I don't think it actually happened at all. The story wasn't anywhere else on the internet. I think it was fabricated to make us think it was safe to go ahead. He made it up.'

She stares at me for a moment, eyes narrowing, then gives a short bark of laughter. 'Ha! Sounds just like my dear husband.'

'So you knew?'

'No.' She snorts. 'But let's just say it doesn't surprise me. *Fake news.*' She says it in an American drawl, almost to herself. 'Come on, there's someone you need to talk to.'

She leads me across the hallway and into Christian's study, which looks out onto the drive. It has dark walls and framed abstract prints, and is dominated by a black desk holding four monitors, one pair mounted above the other. It looks like the workstation of some city bond trader except all the screens are black, inert, like the rest of the room. Stacks of money are lined up in front of the keyboard.

Miranda drops into the black leather swivel chair and moves the mouse to wake the four monitors up, all of them flickering into life with an identical screensaver of Cressida in immaculate riding gear atop a horse.

'So,' she says, half over her shoulder. 'Tony Barnes-Johnson is my husband's accountant, handles all of his personal and business stuff as well. I spoke to him earlier. You need to—'

She's interrupted by the first bars of Depeche Mode's 'Just Can't Get Enough' blasting from my phone and when I pull it from my handbag, I see Kat's name on the display.

'Dev's hurt,' she blurts before I can even say hello. 'Someone attacked him, Helen.'

'What? What do you mean, what's happened?'

There are voices in the background at her end of the line, the beep of a vehicle reversing.

'I'm with him now.' Her voice is high, taut, and I can tell she's been crying. She hardly *ever* cries and the sound alone makes me want to reach out through the phone line to give her a hug. 'We're at A & E, he's still being treated.'

'Wait a second, Kat, just going to put you on speaker.' I tap the phone's screen and lay it flat on the desk. 'Dev's hurt? Are you OK?'

Haltingly, she describes how her husband had staggered back to their house before collapsing on the doorstep, beaten and bloody. An ambulance had been quick to arrive and the doctors had assessed him in the emergency department of York Hospital, establishing that he had a dislocated jaw, a fractured wrist, two broken ribs and possible concussion, as well as extensive cuts and bruises. They want to keep him in for at least a few days for more tests and observation, she said. I shudder as she hangs up.

Miranda looks at the phone, then at me.

'Poor thing,' she says, swilling the ice cubes in her glass. 'Never heard her sound so upset. Still, at least Dev is in the right place, I suppose.'

'Those men know where I live.' I look up at the window, a black mirror in the darkness. 'We should probably assume they have this address too. Are all your doors locked?'

She nods. 'Think so.'

I see my own fear reflected in her eyes, can tell she's thinking the same as me: that Dev being attacked is no coincidence. That it *must* be somehow to do with the money.

'It's like a nightmare we can't wake up from, Miranda. I keep wishing I could go back to New Year's Eve, back to that cave, and I would never have pulled the rucksack out of that gap. Would never have opened it, never looked inside. Then the six of us would have come home and carried on with our normal lives.'

'Just the two of us now.' She sips her drink. 'The two who never wanted to take that bloody money in the first place. And now we're the ones left holding the baby. Typical, isn't it?'

'Three,' I say. 'Kat says she'll join us in a bit, as soon as Dev is settled on the ward. She's going to go by her house, pick up her share of the money.' I indicate the piles of fifties and twenties Miranda has stacked haphazardly on the desk below the monitors, hers and Christian's share. 'The finance person you mentioned earlier – my brother's accountant?'

'The delightful Tony.'

'Can we speak to him? Now? The sooner we get the ball rolling, the sooner we can pay Docherty back.'

She gives me a strange, blank look, as if the previous conversation has already slipped her mind.

'Of course.' She shrugs. 'Why not. I'll ring him now.'

She grips the mouse, clicking the FaceTime icon on one of the monitors and selecting the last person dialled in the call list.

After a few rings, the screen switches to camera view and a man's face appears. He's in his fifties, with a fleshy face and dark, hooded eyes, dressed in a cardigan over a checked shirt. From the framed certificates on the wall behind him, he appears to be in a study of some kind. Miranda greets him with an icy familiarity and introduces me, without wasting any time on small talk. He starts to ask her a question but she holds a hand up, silencing him.

'Tony?' Her tone is sharper than before, full of head-girl energy. 'I'd like you to tell Helen what you told me.'

He gives her a quizzical look, caterpillar eyebrows drawing closer together.

'What we . . . discussed earlier, about ArcticAir?'
'Yes.'
'You're sure, Miranda? Do you perhaps want to bring Christian into the call, he could dial in?'

She sighs with impatience. 'He's not available at the moment. And as a director of my husband's company I'm *quite* sure, thank you.'

And so Tony tells me, in his drawling public school accent. A long and rambling monologue about market volatility and supply chain issues, invoice defaults and tariffs, lost clients and debt recovery and a bold move to diversify that had spectacularly backfired.

I don't understand all of it, but I get the gist.

And the gist is: my brother's company cannot help us to make up the shortfall. My brother cannot help anyone, least of all himself.

Because my brother is almost bankrupt.

45

My brother's company is clinging on by its fingertips. Debtors, lawyers, insolvency specialists are circling ArcticAir Ltd like vultures scenting fresh carrion. His house is mortgaged to the hilt and has been put up as a surety against other loans which are long overdue. His car is days away from being repossessed. My brother's fortune, his success – the safety net we'd all been relying on – is nothing but a mirage. It's gone. The bedrock of wealth is nothing more than sand that has already run through his fingers.

Miranda sits in stony silence as Tony explains all of this, drinking her way steadily through the hefty cocktail she made after I arrived. When hers is finished, she indicates mine with a raised eyebrow and I hand it over. I've only had a couple of sips, and it's clear that her need is greater than mine right now.

I stare at the grainy FaceTime image of the accountant, feeling as if a void has just opened up beneath my feet.

'But . . . how has he gone bankrupt?'

'The usual way,' he says. 'Gradually. And then all of a sudden.'

'But there must be something we can do? A way of holding things up, I mean, this can't be it for his company, can it? ArcticAir has been his life for the last twenty years, he's poured everything into it.'

Tony puffs on a cigar, the end glowing cherry red.

'There has been an influx of cash these last few weeks.' He blows smoke to the side. 'I didn't ask too many questions about where it was from, and Christian didn't deign to share that information with me in any case. But it wasn't enough. Not *nearly* enough.'

'There must be a way to turn things around, though? To save his company?'

He studies me for a moment, his small dark eyes holding mine.

'You've seen *Titanic*, I take it?'

'Hasn't everyone?'

'There's a point in the film – after Rose and what's-his-name get together – that the sinking becomes inevitable, like gravity. It's no longer a question of *if* the ship goes down, it becomes a mathematical certainty that it *will* go down. No matter what anyone does. And that's where we are with Arctic, I'm afraid. The only thing to do now is man the lifeboats.'

His words sting like a flurry of hailstones. When he's finished, I can't even think of another question to ask.

'Shit.'

'Indeed.'

'I had no idea.'

'Your brother has always been very good at keeping secrets.'

He asks again to speak to Christian this weekend, as a matter of urgency, and Miranda says she'll pass on the message. After she ends the call, we both sit in stunned silence for a moment.

'So,' she says quietly. 'Now you know.'

'What about your family accounts, personal savings?'

Miranda shakes her head. 'Almost all of that's gone too.'

'I'm so sorry, Miranda.'

'I never really kept tabs on our joint accounts day to day, Christian handled all of the financial stuff and there were always monthly transfers into my accounts, for clothes and shopping and food, for Cressy's allowance, her schooling and everything else. But he's raided all of it. I have a few thousand in some personal accounts but that won't even last to the end of the month.' She puts a hand over her mouth. 'Oh God, I'm going to have to pull Cressy out of St Peter's too, find her another school. She'll be devastated.'

It occurs to me that I didn't ask the accountant if it was possible to claw back any of the cash Christian had funnelled into the company over the last fortnight, or whether it was gone forever. From the way he'd talked, we had to assume the latter.

Miranda holds the ice-filled tumbler against her cheek. She stares at the wall beside my head, as if she hasn't taken it in yet.

'We're going to lose the house.' She says it quietly, as if it's only just sunk in. 'We're going to lose it, aren't we?'

'Miranda, I know this is a horrible shock but we have to focus on the here and now, just for a couple of days. We have to think about how we're going to—'

'My beautiful house!' Her eyes flash. 'Where are we going to live? All my beautiful things, gone!'

The words come out before I can stop them.

'And you're going to lose your husband too, if we can't figure this out! My brother!'

She recoils as if I've slapped her, eyes wide. Her next words catch on a sob. 'Wh-what are we going to do?'

Her shoulders sag and she starts to cry. I pull her in for a hug, her petite frame almost childlike, her head resting on my shoulder as if we are real sisters instead of only sisters-in-law. She smells of expensive perfume and expensive alcohol, the two of them mingling and merging as she sobs for her husband, her daughter, her house, her life. Perhaps for herself, too.

'It's hopeless,' she says, pulling in a shaky breath. 'It's all gone.'

'We need to make a new plan,' I say. 'Work out where we stand.'

When her crying subsides, I go back out to my car and open the boot. Pulling up the floor layer, I retrieve the plastic-wrapped packets tucked in and around the spare tyre, stacking them into the crook of my arm and bringing them into the study.

'Listen, Miranda.' I dump the packets of cash on the low coffee table. 'We're in a hole, no two ways about it. First thing we need to do is find out how deep.'

Kat arrives just before midnight.

She looks wired, almost manic, ringing the doorbell three times and knocking as well by the time I pull it open, as if it's the middle of the day instead of almost twelve.

We hug on the doorstep and she launches into a hundred-mile-an-hour recounting of the hospital, the doctors and Dev's injuries. Her husband would be spending at least a couple of nights on a ward, she said, possibly longer, while they kept him under observation for the concussion. The staff had told her to go home and get some sleep.

Instead, she had driven straight here.

'Poor Dev,' I say, leading her into the study. 'Must have been terrifying for him. Does he remember anything?'

'They've got his jaw wired, he can't really speak. And they had him on some pretty hefty pain meds, so he was in and out of consciousness.'

She has not – yet – reported the incident to the police because of the ongoing danger to Jason and Christian, and the risk of alerting detectives to our role in what had led up to it. I notice, as she's recounting her story, that Kat's own pupils are huge dilated circles against the bright sky blue of her eyeballs. Perhaps she is still in shock. I look from one to the other, Miranda slow and sloppy with booze, Kat wide-eyed and half manic, and wonder if I'm the only clear-thinking person left in the room.

'Kat?' I put a hand on her arm. 'Are you OK? Like, *really* OK? Do you want a coffee or something else?'

'I could murder a cold can of Diet Coke, actually.'

Miranda rattles ice cubes in the bottom of her empty glass, standing up with a slight wobble.

'I'll get it.'

'Kat,' I say quietly, when Miranda has left the room. 'Are you drunk, too?'

She gives a single, solid shake of her head. 'Nope.'

'Because Miranda's been hitting the gin and cocktails and God knows what else since she saw that picture of Christian, and I need you straight for this.'

'I'm as straight as a die, love.'

She holds my gaze, her pupils still huge black discs as if they're trying to suck up all the light in the room. The lighting is soft and subtle in the study, but it's not *that* soft. I tell her about Christian's company, her face clouding as she takes in the news that he's facing bankruptcy, that our safety net is gone.

'Jesus,' she says. 'Well . . . that changes things.'

'How much of your share have you got left?'

She blows out a heavy breath, explains that she was halfway through counting it when she realised that Dev was lying, injured, on the doorstep. I clear a space for her on the coffee table so she can lay it out and count it properly. Miranda reappears with a tall glass filled with Coke and ice for Kat and some other concoction for herself, sipping it while I count her share. She had been vague about the total and she's in no fit state to do it now. It doesn't help that the bundles have been split up for some reason, so all the notes are loose.

When I've finished counting, I write her total on an A4 pad lying open on the desk. Below that, I write the amount we have left, a cold dread spreading across my skin as I add the numbers once, twice, three times, to make sure I've not made a mistake.

Kat looks up. 'OK,' she says. 'I think I've got it.'

'How much left in your share?'

'Five hundred and four thousand,' she says. 'And change.'

I write the number on my pad, before pulling out my phone and tapping the calculator app. It is only a matter of adding three six-figure sums together and working out what was still missing, but I don't trust my mental arithmetic anymore. And certainly not with an amount like this.

My phone displays the answer to the calculation. I stare at it for a moment, black digits on a white screen, my knees turning to water. The figure is multiples of my annual salary, of Jason's salary, considerably more than both of them put together. There is a little bit I can withdraw from the bank tomorrow, the amount of cash that I'd paid into my newly opened accounts. But it's only five thousand, maybe six, not enough to put much of a dent in the number in front of me.

I clear the screen, add the numbers up again. Maybe I'd made a mistake in my haste. I add each of the amounts together again, going carefully this time, checking each digit and double-checking against the notes I've written on the A4 page.

But there is no mistake. Instead, there is the swooping, weightless feeling like the vertical drop on a roller coaster, stomach rising up into my throat as we plummet towards the ground. The chilling clarity of Docherty's text returns to me, pinballing around inside my head. He had been very specific. No room for error or misunderstanding.

I want my money back.

All of it.

Kat inclines her head towards me.

'Well? How much are we short?'

I clear my throat, trying to find the words. Trying to grasp the full meaning of the number on the screen, to articulate it in a way that makes sense. To describe what we have to do, to meet the demands of a man who was holding a gun to the head of my husband, my brother, who said he would kill them both unless his ultimatum was met, in full.

'Just over ninety-five thousand pounds.' The room spins around me. 'That's how much we have to find between now and noon on Sunday.'

46

Kat stands up, walks across the room with her hands on top of her head, a single obscenity repeated over and over, louder and louder, until the one-syllable word is bouncing and echoing off the walls of the sparsely decorated study. It's almost as if she's forgotten we're here in the same room with her, all three of us trying to process the same news. Finally, she stops in the middle of the room and turns to us, hands dropping to her hips.

'So what the hell are we supposed to do?' Her eyes are wild. 'Rob a bank? Buy a lottery ticket and hope for the best? Look for the pot of gold at the end of the bloody rainbow?'

Anger radiates off her like the heat from an open fire – as if this is somehow, someone else's fault – even though I know it's just her natural frustration boiling over. I just feel sick, nausea heavy in my stomach as if I'm on the deck of a ship pitching and rolling in rough seas. Alone on the sofa, Miranda takes another hefty sip of her drink, sets the glass down on the coffee table and starts to cry again.

'You're sure?' She cuffs a tear away with the sleeve of her cardigan. 'About the numbers?'

I swallow down my nausea. 'I've double-checked everything but you're welcome to go over it again if you like.'

She waves my offer away as if she can't bear to look at the money, never mind going through the thankless task of counting it again.

'It's crazy ... thirty-six hours to find ninety-five thousand pounds.' She shakes her head. 'How do they expect us to do that? It's just impossible.'

'You're absolutely sure there's no other family accounts that might have some money left? In the safe upstairs?' I shrug. 'Or ... maybe offshore? *Anywhere?*'

'Not according to Tony. Christian stripped all of it to the bone, it's all gone. There's no way.'

'Then we have to *find* a way.'

Miranda sniffs. 'We still don't even know who took that missing fifty thousand on New Year's Eve, before we'd even agreed it. We never found out. Maybe we should—'

'That's *done*,' Kat cuts her off. 'It's old news, it's gone. We can't get hung up on it now.'

Eventually, she stops pacing and drops heavily onto the couch with an exasperated sigh. I look at them for a moment, my best friend and my sister-in-law at opposite ends of the deep leather sofa, wondering again how it had come to this. How we had ended up here, our husbands kidnapped or hospitalised, the three of us left staring down the barrel of an impossible situation.

Our group of six, who had been reduced to five when Dev walked away. Then four, at the gathering in Dean's Park.

Now only three of us remained.

'Can't believe this,' Kat says. 'I cannot bloody *believe* it. Why the hell did Christian and Jason just blindly go off with those guys anyway? How can they have been so—'

Miranda slams her glass down on the table so hard I fear it might shatter.

'Don't you dare!' Don't you dare blame someone else!' She gestures at me. 'We never wanted this, me and Helen. Any of it! *You* wanted to keep the money all along!'

Kat points a finger. 'We agreed, all of us.'

'I never wanted—'

'It was a joint decision so—'

Then they are both shouting, gesticulating, each hurling accusations at the other about who is most to blame for our situation and who should admit it was their fault.

'Hey.' But my single word is too quiet and the two of them continue to rant at each other until I fill my lungs and shout it as loudly as I can. 'HEY!' Their heads swivel towards me. 'That's enough! It's on *us* to fix this. No one else. Us. Arguing about whose fault it is doesn't help bring them back. Argue next week, if you must, but right now we need to make a new plan to find that money. Whether we have to beg, borrow or steal it.'

They both decline coffee but I make it anyway, even though it takes a few false starts to figure out the gleaming chrome barista-level coffee machine on the worktop. I get them both sat down at the kitchen island, a rectangular slab of black marble as big as one of those huge snooker tables, pushing mugs of steaming coffee towards them. Kat and Miranda face each other on opposite sides, with me in the middle.

It's a few minutes before one o'clock in the morning. I've made the coffee a lot stronger than I intended and the first sip from my own cup is like rocket fuel, a jolt of caffeine straight to my eyeballs.

'At the risk of sounding like my idiot boss,' I say. 'We need to think outside the box. There are no bad ideas for the time being and everything is worth considering, OK?'

Half an hour later, the sheet of A4 in front of me is filled with ideas, thoughts, possibilities, with lots of looping arrows and crossed-out words. A list of different options marked with a tick, a cross or a question mark.

There is close to three thousand pounds set aside in the separate account for Alfie's living costs at university. My only credit card has a limit around the same amount that I could draw against. A bank loan might net us a few thousand more but it would take far too long for the paperwork to come through. Cashing in my modest pension presented the same problem: it would take time that we didn't have. Unless we could get an extension from Docherty, property also was a non-starter. And what property would we sell? My mum's house? Then she would have nowhere to go, once we stopped paying the fees at Harcourt Park. If there was more time, we could remortgage our own house to raise some funds. But time is the one thing we don't have.

The next most valuable thing I own is our car, but it's a ten-year-old family estate with seventy thousand miles on the clock. A cursory search on a couple of car-buying websites values it at around four thousand pounds; Kat's Volkswagen isn't worth much more. Miranda has some nice pieces of jewellery worth a few thousand, a Cartier watch and some handbags that might fetch a couple of thousand more in a short-notice sale on eBay. She draws the line at selling her wedding or engagement rings, which unfortunately are the most valuable items she owns. I put a question mark next to them on my sheet of paper.

It still won't put a serious dent in the amount we have to find. All of it – scraped together – will net us less than twenty thousand pounds, and that's assuming we can spend the whole weekend glued to eBay and whatever other online selling platforms are available to actually sell stuff on. Even if we did, it would still leave us miles adrift of where we need to be.

It's not enough. Not even close. But perhaps I can buy us a little more time.

I take out my phone to send a text to Docherty.

We will get all of your money back to you, I promise. But we're going to need a little more time.

Docherty replies a few minutes later, a chill prickling across my skin as I read his words.

No problem at all re: extra time.
But each extra day will cost a finger.
Let me know whether you want me to start the cutting with your brother or your husband.

47

With a shaking hand, I show my phone to the other two. There is an ache in my throat, hard and hollow, that makes me want to cry. Instead, I send another reply, asking Docherty whether we can give him everything we have today, as soon as it gets light, and gather the rest over the next week.

'Maybe if we give him what we have now,' Miranda says. 'He'll release one of the men as a gesture of goodwill.'

We exchange a look and I know what she's thinking: *Christian, rather than Jason.*

Kat pulls a bowl of peanuts towards her across the island and begins feeding them into her mouth, one at a time.

'What about one of those payday loans?'

I indicate my pad. 'Already crossed that off, it'll take too long. And no bank will lend us enough.'

She chews thoughtfully.

'Wasn't thinking about a bank, actually. There's someone I know, he might know one or two people who have contacts. Guys who can offer . . . you know. *Community* banking services.'

'Who?'

'Just some guys.'

'You mean loan sharks.'

'They don't really call them that anymore, Hels. More like unofficial moneylenders.'

'And when we can't make the crazy interest repayments, they come around and break our kneecaps? Could they even get us that amount of money?'

'Probably fifteen or twenty grand,' she says. 'It would be a contribution, at least.'

I raise an eyebrow at her but add it to the bottom of my list anyway. Miranda slides off her high stool and makes more coffee, refilling all of our cups before going to a cupboard and filling a couple of bowls with M&S crisps that look – and smell – like potpourri.

It's only when I glance up to the kitchen windows that I realise snow is falling, fat flakes caught in the soft glow of the garden lights, drifting slowly down and already blanketing the world outside in a shroud of white. Was Jason suffering the cold on this freezing mid-January night? From the picture of him and my brother, it looked as if they were being held in a cellar, a barn, an outbuilding of some kind. How would the two of them keep warm? Would they feel hope slipping away into the dark?

I tear off the sheet of A4 from my pad and start on a new page.

'What else?' I say. 'We need to keep going.'

Kat raises an index finger as if she wants to make a point. 'OK,' she says. 'I've got another idea. But you're not going to like it.'

Miranda leans forward, resting her elbows on the marble countertop. 'Try us.'

The idea, Kat says, could net us all the money we need very quickly and with a minimum of fuss. It would be totally legal. And we could do it tonight. She gestures to the stacks of cash on the table.

'We have the tools right here. We use what we have to get what we need. Simple as that.'

'Right,' I say, trying to keep the scepticism from my voice. 'But how?'

'We drive to Leeds or maybe Manchester, find the biggest casino we can, sit down at the roulette table. And stick fifty grand on red.'

Kat looks at me, then at Miranda, then back to me. 'You see?' Her eyes shine with the possibility. 'Then we take the fifty grand we've made, and do the same again at the next casino. Problem solved.'

'You were right,' I say. 'I don't like your idea. At all.'

Miranda frowns. 'But what if the first spin of the roulette wheel comes up black?'

'Then we double up,' Kat says. 'Put down a hundred grand on the next bet to recoup the loss. Eventually, by the law of averages we're going to get a win, we just have to hold our nerve.'

'Or lose even more,' I say. 'Chasing your losses is the absolute *worst* strategy, Kat, it's why punters go bankrupt every day but casinos hardly ever do.'

'Obviously we'd all have to play, to spread the money out. Maybe even go to two or three casinos. But it's perfectly doable, all we'd need is a little good luck and this could all be sorted out by tomorrow morning. Done and dusted, our boys home in time for tea.'

'Even if I thought it was a viable idea – which I don't – would a casino even let us bet that kind of money?'

Kat sits back with an elaborate shrug. 'I thought you said there were "no bad ideas for the time being"?'

'I did. But we still have to look at things from all the angles.'

'Have you got a better idea?'

Miranda is on her second cup of coffee and seems to have come back to herself, recovering some of her composure. Slowly, as if she's figuring it out as she tells us, she pitches another idea into the mix. A few hours ago, she says, we had been thinking we could pull some money out of Christian's company to make good what we'd spent, but we hadn't considered two similar options. Namely: the company *I* work for. And the shop where Kat is deputy manager.

I have to admit, it's an intriguing idea. As PA to the managing director I have access to most of the financial tools that he uses day to day; from approving bill payments on his behalf to using the company Amex for purchases, and authorising staff expenses.

With fifteen years' service, I've been there longer than he has and it was me who had set up many of those systems in the first place. I did a lot of it for him already when he was travelling abroad or out visiting clients – or when he simply couldn't be bothered. I had keys to the office, to my boss's office, to his filing cabinets, I had the usernames, passwords and secure keys to all of our online banking platforms. Nigel had insisted on it, years ago. Because most of the time he was just *far too busy* to bother with day-to-day financial stuff. He just gave the orders.

Except this time all of the expenditure would be unauthorised and even if I was able to delay the inevitable for a few days, a week, sooner or later it would come out that there were holes in the balance sheet. The finger of blame would focus on just a handful of individuals, with me among them. The thought of being caught stealing from work brings another sick roll to my stomach, but what would it matter if Jason was home? Who cared, as long as Christian was safe, back with his family? And maybe there was a way of covering my tracks, shifting suspicion?

I write a new paragraph on my pad of paper.

Kat has fewer scruples about the idea of stealing from her employer, but that is not the issue, she says. They did still take cash at the shop and a few of her older customers still preferred it, but there was rarely more than a few thousand pounds on the premises at any one time.

'Don't get me wrong,' she says. 'I'm willing to give it a go.'

'You're willing to get fired?'

'Or,' she says with a grim smile, 'the two of you could get a couple of balaclavas and "hold me up" at closing time?'

'For a few grand?' I shake my head. 'Not worth it anyway.'

Miranda fixes me with a slow-blinking gaze, sounding more sober than she has for hours.

'We're supposed to be coming up with ideas but you're just shooting everything down without even giving it a chance.'

Kat slides off her stool, clutching her handbag.

'Has anyone tried googling it? Or asking Chat TCP, or whatever it's called?' She heads for the annexe, where there is a downstairs bathroom. 'I'm going for a wee.'

Miranda clams up, hunching over her phone. I follow suit, typing, scrolling, trying a series of increasingly desperate Google searches for *Make money quickly* or *Get cash quickly* or *Get money fast*. When they yield nothing useful, I ask the latest fashionable AI engine to come up with ideas in the same vein. Surely this amazing, world-changing technology would be able to solve our problem in the blink of an eye? This multi-trillion-dollar behemoth that had gorged on so much knowledge, on hundreds of years of human learning, trained by thousands of the smartest people out there, pampered and fed and fattened on millions of stolen books and research papers, images and songs? Surely AI could offer us a solution?

No. Apparently, it couldn't.

48

Most of the AI-generated results contain predictably bland side hustles: *To make money quickly, consider dog-walking, babysitting, gardening or selling unwanted clothes and electronics. Filling in online surveys or testing apps.* It seems that even the most powerful AI engine in the world is completely and utterly hopeless in solving this very human, very real-world problem. I drop my phone onto the counter, rubbing my eyes. Fatigue is fast catching up with me and we don't seem to be any further forward.

Miranda's voice cuts through the silence, low and urgent. 'Do you think we can trust her?'

It takes me a moment to realise who my sister-in-law is talking about. 'Kat?'

She leans towards me across the black marble counter. 'Casinos and loan sharks and balaclavas, I mean, is she even taking this seriously? And she was the only one of us who wanted to keep the money right from the start, remember? She's not got a flesh-and-blood stake in this, not like me and you have to get our husbands back. She's not *family*.'

'She's like family to me,' I say. 'We've been friends since we were kids.'

The obvious subtext – *a lot longer than I've known you, Miranda* – seems to go over her head. She lowers her voice to a hoarse, insistent stage whisper.

'And she's obviously *on* something tonight, all that nervous energy, did you see her eyes earlier? She looked like she'd—'

Kat returns to the kitchen and starts bustling with renewed energy around the toaster, the bread bin, taking out a plate and rooting around among the shelves in the fridge. 'I'm absolutely *starving*,' she says with a grin. To Miranda, she adds: 'Don't mind if I make some toast, do you? Only just realised I missed dinner. Anyone else want something?'

We both decline but I keep watching her out of the corner of my eye as she pulls jam, marmalade and lemon curd out of the big Smeg fridge and lines them up on the kitchen island. She turns her back to me, dropping four slices of bread into a shining chrome toaster, going back to the fridge for a large slab of butter on a covered dish.

On the wall beside the fridge is a framed family photograph of Christian and Miranda beaming on their wedding day, Cressida a cherubic three-year-old bridesmaid between them. The trio are flanked on either side by an older couple, a tall, severe-looking sixty-something man with a salt-and-pepper moustache and a beautiful, elegantly dressed woman whose resemblance to Miranda is striking. Behind them is what looks like a castle, or a grand country house.

'What about your parents?' I say to her, studying the photo. It's one of three, flanked either side by a shot of Miranda plus her five bridesmaids, and Christian with his best man.

'What about them?'

'Your dad, isn't he a . . . viscount, or something?' I had only met him twice. Once at the wedding and once, briefly, at a garden party Miranda had organised for Christian's fiftieth birthday party a couple of years ago. He and his immaculate wife had arrived late, hovered on the edge of proceedings, talking mostly to their daughter and not really engaging with anyone else before slipping away early. 'Or a lord, is it?'

She considers me over the rim of her coffee cup. 'A baronet.' With the air of someone who has answered this question many times before, she adds: 'Above a bog-standard knight of the realm but below a baron. Not a member of the peerage so he doesn't sit in the House of Lords.'

It hits me then, all at once, and I feel foolish for not thinking of it sooner. How could we have overlooked this? A solution might only be a phone call away.

'But he's rich, right?' I gesture at the wedding photo. 'Would he give you a loan? You could keep it vague, say it's a short-term thing for his son-in-law's company, cash-flow problems, something like that?'

For the first time in several hours, Miranda seems to find something amusing. A mirthless snort of laughter erupts from her and she turns her face to the ceiling with a sigh.

'No,' she says simply, her laughter dying away. 'Out of the question, I'm afraid.'

'Why not?' I say. 'Why is that funny?'

'Because Daddy can't *stand* Christian. He's never liked him and they've never seen eye to eye. Grubby new money and all that. *Such a cliché, my dear old dad.* They're both as stubborn as each other, didn't help that your brother was already divorced, either.'

'But . . . so were you.'

'True.' She shrugs. 'But I'm his daughter.' Seeing my reaction, she adds: 'You didn't know, did you? He never told you that Daddy doesn't like him?'

I shake my head. '*Everyone* likes Christian.'

'Not everyone.'

The toaster pops with a metallic *shunk* and Kat drops all four slices onto a plate, blowing on her fingers to cool them.

'Here's a radical idea,' she says, stabbing a knife into the slab of butter. 'What if we told your dad the truth – or at least some of it? That his son-in-law's been kidnapped and his life is in danger?'

Miranda shrugs. 'Daddy would probably feel vindicated. That Christian must have ripped someone off in business and it served him right. In any event, he's very set in his ways – he'd want to go to the police, let them handle it.'

Which is what you tried to do a few hours ago. I think it, but don't say it. Instead, I feel my frustration starting to rise, that what might be our only viable option was just beyond our reach.

'Worth a try though, isn't it?'

We go back and forth like this for the next few minutes. When I suggest we have nothing to lose, my sister-in-law explains that not only would her father not pay for Christian's release, he would also insist on taking charge because *a situation like this needed the leadership of a man*, because women *lacked the killer instinct* and having three women in charge of anything was *a recipe for lots of chat and not much action*. And he would *definitely* involve the police – careless of the risks to which Christian and Jason would be exposed to as a result.

Finally, Miranda stands and puts her palms down on the counter, as if this conversation is at an end.

'I'm starting to see double, I'm so tired.' She yawns delicately, covering her mouth with the back of her hand. 'Going to put my jim-jams on then we'll have a nightcap, shall we? The two of you are welcome to stay here tonight, if you like. Both spare rooms are made up.'

She turns and heads out into the hall, towards the broad staircase.

Standing at the counter beside me, Kat takes a hungry bite of her jam on toast. 'Can't work your sister-in-law out tonight.' She chews thoughtfully. 'One minute she's crying, then she's laughing. She's worried sick, but then in the next breath she's buggering off to put her Liberty pyjamas on. She's pissed off when her ideas get shot down, then what does she do when you come up with something that might actually work? Shoots it down before it can even get off the ground.' She takes another bite of toast. 'Something's off about her tonight.'

'It's not often you discover your husband has bankrupted the family, I suppose.'

'Not going to be sleeping in the gutter though, is she? With parents like that? Even if her dad is a tightwad.'

I glance at the clock on the wall, the hands creeping around towards 2 a.m. 'No one's sleeping yet,' I say. 'Not until we decide what we're going to do.'

My phone buzzes against the solid black marble of the kitchen island. It's Docherty's reponse to my last text, my request for a little more time to gather the outstanding money – if we give him all the cash we *do* have right away.

No deals. No part payments.
You send one more delaying text like this I'll start on your husband's thumbs with a bolt cropper RIGHT NOW.
When I run out of thumbs and fingers I will take his eyes. GET ME MY MONEY.

Bile floods up my throat, a vision swimming into my head of Jason bloodied, mutilated, maimed and in agonising pain. My husband begging for his life, begging for mercy, trying to staunch the flow of blood as he slides into darkness. Believing I'd failed him, given up on him.

I show the message to Kat.

'We'll get them out.' She puts a hand on my arm. 'I promise.'

I pick up my coffee, try to swallow down half a mouthful. I want to tell her about what I found in Jason's study, the black folder, the women, the hotels. But my head is too full at the moment, overloaded with everything that's going on, with the bleakness of the options facing us. All of them bad. None good.

'Who's this?'

Kat is holding up my phone, the Messenger app open. Alexander Sykes is still near the top of the list of messages.

'No one. Just . . . one of those old Facebook connections.'

'Wait,' she says, clicking on his profile picture. 'This isn't *Alex* Sykes, is it? From school? Your ex, from back in the day?'

I sigh. 'Yes. He messages me every once in a while. It's kind of awkward because I don't want to block him but I don't want to encourage him either. Just want to keep him at arm's length, so he doesn't get the wrong idea.'

'God.' She scrolls further back up the list of messages. 'He's *very* persistent, isn't he? Very keen. Can't believe he's still in touch with you after all these years. You never told me.'

'It's just a bit . . . weird. Bumped into him the other week at Mum's retirement village and it was even more awkward, because Jason was there too and I've never really talked to him about Alexander.' I think back to that moment at Harcourt Park, the stilted conversation at reception, the way he had gone in for a hug when we met. 'Jason said I was being weird about it afterwards but I know he got a strange vibe from Alexander too.'

'One of those touchy-feely, a little bit creepy guys, is he? A bit too keen to put his hands on you?'

'Maybe,' I say. 'A bit like that.' How foolish it all feels now, though. How naive was I, to worry what Jason would think? After what I've discovered about my husband just a few hours ago. 'I mean . . . he wasn't like that when we were together, but it was a long time ago, I suppose. People change.'

Kat is still scrolling messages. 'Looks like handsy Alexander might want to rekindle an old flame.'

I swirl the last inch of coffee in the bottom of my cup.

'It's funny, what Miranda was saying earlier, about her dad not approving of Christian when they got married. My dad was the same with Jason, at least at first. He always preferred Alexander. Said I should have married him.'

She puts down my phone and picks up her own. 'I wonder what he does now?'

'He owns it,' I say.

'Owns what?'

'The retirement village. And a load of others all across Yorkshire and Lincolnshire.'

'Seriously?'

More memories float up from that brief meeting. Alexander's exquisitely tailored suit. The Patek Philippe watch hanging heavy on his wrist.

The orange Lamborghini.

'Oh . . .'

Kat looks up from her mobile. 'What is it?'

I pick up my own phone again, pull up Google and type in a quick question.

'Maybe the answer has been staring me in the face all night.'

'What are you thinking, Hels?'

I show her the figure on the screen of my iPhone.

'Maybe an old ex-boyfriend is the answer. Maybe he can help us. All of us.'

She gives me a sceptical look. 'In return for what, though?'

'I don't know.' I switch back to Messenger. 'But I have to try. He might be our only hope.'

PART IV
THE PLAN

49

Saturday

I nearly change my mind twice on the way to meet him.

Alexander has suggested a Michelin-starred restaurant in a little courtyard off Duncombe Place, in between the river and the Minster. The streets are already filling with weekend tourists as I park my car and walk across the bridge, the Ouse flowing fast and high beneath me. I'm twenty minutes early, so I cross the street with my double espresso and find a bench beside the war memorial.

I'm too nervous to feel tired, wound too tight to let the exhaustion creep in. It had been 3 a.m. by the time I returned to my empty house and fallen into a fitful, dream-filled sleep. Barely five hours later, I was woken by Prim jumping up onto the bed and pacing circles on Jason's empty side of the duvet, purring and patting the side of my head with a soft paw.

It had been almost too easy to arrange a meeting. I take my phone out and look back at the latest thread on Messenger.

Hey Alexander, it was good to see you at Harcourt Park the other week, I was thinking it would be nice to catch up. You free for coffee tomorrow? X

His reply had dropped in while I slept, just after 6 a.m.

Wonderful to hear from you too Helen. I was just thinking about you! A catch-up would be lovely – I have the perfect place in mind. Midday? Look forward to it. xx

It had taken me the best part of an hour just to decide what to wear. A first outfit discarded because it was too casual, another because it wasn't casual enough. A third which felt like it was trying a bit too hard, too dressed-up for a Saturday lunchtime. What do you wear to ask your ex for ninety-five thousand pounds? I had no idea. In the end I settle for my best jeans and a pale cream merino jumper, with my belted winter coat and boots. Enough makeup to hide the tired shadows beneath my eyes, a little lipstick and blush. Not too much.

Sitting on the bench across from the restaurant, I feel exposed. Vulnerable. Kat has offered to hang around in a café nearby, ready to step in if she was needed. But I had insisted I'd be OK – it was a public place and I knew Alexander. At least, I *had* known him. If I needed a reason to extract myself from the situation, I was to text her with the codeword *GO* and she would call straight back with a fictitious emergency that meant I had to leave right away. It's a last resort that I won't use unless I absolutely have to – Kat will be busy with a task of her own today and I don't want to disturb her. The same goes for Miranda.

Kat had done the same Google search as me while we sat in my sister-in-law's kitchen last night.

'Bloody hell,' she'd said. 'According to the *Yorkshire Post*, Alexander Sykes is worth millions. A bunch of those retirement villages, property, farming and investments. Ninety-five grand is loose change to him.'

At ten minutes before midday, I cross the street and turn into the courtyard, pulling open the tall glass door of The Ledbury. Downstairs is already busy with early lunchtime customers but when I tell the maître d' who I'm meeting, he leads me up a flight of wood-panelled stairs to a private lounge area with deep sofas and a quiet, calm ambience of unhurried luxury. A member of staff takes my coat, gesturing towards a pair of velvet-covered armchairs in the corner, while another appears with a bottle of champagne and two glasses. He shows me the label of the bottle – Dom Perignon 2015 – proceeding to uncork it and pour a generous measure into one of the glasses. He places the bottle in an ice bucket, the glass on a side table beside my chair, and disappears.

I guess we're not drinking coffee, then.

It's early – still not quite noon – but I take a nerve-steadying sip from my glass anyway. The champagne is crisp and smooth, perfectly balanced, delicate bubbles dancing on my tongue. It feels surreal to be sitting here in such expensive surroundings, drinking premium champagne while my husband languishes in a dark room somewhere, beaten and bound, a prisoner. A month ago I would have been nervous about meeting like this, in public, where someone could just walk in and spot me having lunchtime bubbly with an ex. But it occurs to me, as I settle back into the armchair, that the thought of being recognised here has not even crossed my mind.

My nerves are jangling for a different reason. I run through the different options I've been thinking about since last night, the various stories I might spin for Alexander to persuade him to help us. Overseas treatment for a cancer diagnosis? A short-term loan to help out my mum, my brother? Trouble at work, or with my children? Perhaps I'll just tell him the truth. Or is that the worst possible option?

I check my phone for any messages. Just one, from Kat.

You OK, all good?

I send her a thumbs-up in reply, then fire off a quick message to my mum, asking her how she's doing today. She probably won't even have her phone switched on, or with her, but I want to check in anyway. The thought of her reminds me that I need to go and see her to break the bad news that she will have to return home soon. Just as she was starting to settle in at Harcourt Park, I will have to pull this rug from beneath her—

'Helen. Hi.'

I look up to see Alexander standing there, shrugging off a cashmere overcoat and handing it to a staff member. He's dressed in another perfectly tailored blazer with immaculate dark blue jeans and a crisp white open-necked shirt, that same heavy wristwatch that glints in the light.

'Hi, Alexander.' I rise from my seat and he moves closer to kiss me on both cheeks, expensive aftershave enveloping us both. 'It's so nice to see you again.'

'You too.' He gives me a bright white smile, appraising me, his hands still on my forearms. '*Really* great to see you. If I'm honest, I'm a little bit surprised. Wasn't sure if you'd stand me up.'

'You look well.'

It's true. I hadn't really registered it when we bumped into each other at Harcourt Park, but he *does* look good. A deep, even tan that speaks of winter sun somewhere near the equator, toned and fit in a way that suggests a personal trainer. He's broader than I remember, filled out from the slender 22-year-old I had once known. The sandy hair is all gone, his bald head as tanned and taut as his face.

His brown eyes are darker than I remember them. So dark they're almost black.

We sit and chat for a while, sipping our expensive champagne, and I'm surprised at how easily it comes, reminiscing about old school friends, jobs and families, the pubs and clubs and places we used to go when we were together. He had been the smartest person in our year at school, maybe the smartest person I've ever met, before or since. Always Alexander, never Alex. But he'd had sharp edges back then, a spiky side that sometimes came out when he didn't get what he wanted. A hard-headed, forceful streak that always unnerved me and had been part of the reason for our split. But three decades of success seem to have smoothed those edges down, or at least polished them to a high shine. He's divorced now, he tells me, with a grown-up daughter who spends most of her time with her mother in London.

Neither of us mention the day I broke his heart. Two years of a long-distance relationship at university – him in Cambridge, me in Glasgow – and another year after we'd graduated before I decided it wasn't what I wanted. That *he* wasn't what I wanted.

It was the first time I'd ever seen a grown man cry.

I wonder, as we talk, what my life would have been like if I'd made a different decision back then. If we'd stayed together, taken the road not travelled. How much had he changed in the years since? What had it done to him, all the striving and struggling to build his business empire, all the wealth and success that had followed? I try to gauge how much life has changed him and whether anything was left of the young man who had begged me to take him back all those years ago.

It was my turn to beg now.

After half an hour of reminiscing, with both our champagne flutes refilled by a solicitous waiter who hovers just out of earshot, Alexander puts his glass down and considers me, his dark eyes boring steadily into mine.

'Helly,' he says, the old familiar version of my name he'd used when we were together. 'It's absolutely wonderful to see you, I mean that. And I hope you don't mind me asking. But is everything OK?'

I swallow. This is it.

'Alexander . . .' I search for the right words. 'It's lovely to catch up. But there is something else I wanted to talk to you about.'

He leans forward. Puts his warm hand over mine. 'It's OK.' He smiles. 'I know what you're going through.'

A first shimmer of fear flutters in my stomach. Was it possible that he *knew*, somehow? That he knew about the disaster hanging over our heads?

'You do?'

'Yes. I've been there myself. I know how hard it can be.'

I open my mouth. Close it again. *Did* he know? 'It's ... complicated.'

The weight of his fingers curl around mine, gently squeezing.

'I know, I get it.' He lowers his voice. 'So why don't you tell me the reason you wanted to meet today, Helly? The *real* reason.'

50

I stare at the bubbles rising up my tall glass of champagne.

'It's hard to explain,' I say. 'But you're the only one I can talk to about it.'

'It's OK.' He gives my hand another gentle squeeze. 'I've been there, I know what it's like.'

I look up at his tanned face, the knowing confidence in his look. How *could* he know? Had one of the others talked to him? Or . . . was he somehow connected to all of this? To the money? To Docherty? No, that was crazy. Wasn't it?

'Do you?'

'I think so, yes. I knew you pretty well when we were together, I think I still do. You always did wear your heart on your sleeve.' He pauses for a moment, then adds: 'It's Jason, isn't it?'

I nod. 'Yes.'

'And all your friends are too close to it to be objective, aren't they? Everyone's in each other's pockets, you've all known each other for years. You're looking for a friendly face, a shoulder to cry on.' He leans in, lowering his voice a little further. 'I've never been a superstitious man but when we bumped into each other at Harcourt Park, it felt like fate bringing us together again. That's when I noticed it, if I'm honest.'

'Noticed what?'

'The tension,' he says. 'The strain, the friction between the two of you. Put me in mind of me and my ex-wife, towards the end when things were getting really bad. I take it Jason doesn't know you're here with me, today?'

'No,' I say slowly. 'He doesn't know. But I think you've got the wrong end of the—'

'Probably for the best, at least for the time being. At least until you work out what you want to do next. Presumably you've tried counselling already, have you? Pretty pointless, in my opinion.'

'Wait, Alexander.' I disentangle my hand from beneath his clammy palm. 'That's not it. Me and Jason are OK, we have our ups and downs but we're all right. It's not what . . . this is about.'

He frowns, a deep furrow appearing between his eyebrows. There is a subtle shift in his body language too as he moves back in his chair, crossing one leg over the other.

'So what *is* this about?'

I sit up straighter, trying to gather myself, to arrange my thoughts into some kind of order. All the persuasive lies and clever stories I came up with earlier seem to have vanished from my brain like leaves scattering in the wind.

'I . . . I need your help.'

'With your mother?'

'No. Not exactly. Although I don't think she'll be able to stay at Harcourt Park much longer.'

'Then, what kind of "help" are we talking about?'

'Jason is in—'

The maître d' comes over with a couple of menus, offering a little bow towards Alexander before telling him his usual table is ready and launching into an elaborate description of today's specials. Alexander cuts the man off with a wave of his hand and he beats a rapid retreat.

'You were saying, Helen?'

'Jason's in a lot of trouble. My brother too. Christian, do you remember him?'

'What kind of trouble?'

'The worst kind.'

He sips his champagne. 'I'm sorry to hear that. And you think I can help you somehow?'

'That's what I'm hoping, yes. I think you might be the only one who *can* help me, help us. I can't tell you why, or exactly what's happened, because it will put Jason and my brother in even more danger.'

He seems to consider this for a moment. 'I have a very good legal team I can put at your disposal. How soon are we talking? Monday?' Seeing my expression, he adds: 'Sooner than that? Today?'

'It's not really a matter of law. I mean, it is, but not in the way you might think.'

'The police and crime commissioner for the county is a good friend of mine, I could make a call and ask him to—'

'No police,' I say. 'They can't be involved.'

'Why not?'

'It's complicated, like I said.'

'If you don't want legal assistance or help from law enforcement, what exactly *do* you want?' He sits fully back into his armchair, his expression darkening as he realises where this is going before I even have a chance to say it.

'Alexander—'

'It's money, isn't it? You want money.' A statement, not a question. 'I see.'

'Not for me. For my family, and I can pay you back. Not straight-away, but over time. I promise.'

'You're quite desperate, aren't you?'

I nod. 'I wouldn't be here unless I was desperate.'

As soon as the words have left my mouth, I realise it was the wrong thing to say.

'That's the real reason why you asked to meet? Not because you wanted to catch up?'

There doesn't seem to be any point in lying anymore.

'Yes. I'm sorry, I should have been honest with you from the start.'

I look up, meeting his eyes, trying to read his expression. Where there had been warmth before, while we chatted about old times, now there is only cool calculation. A hardness too, as if shutters have come down. As if he's reverting to type: a very successful man negotiating a deal, nothing more, nothing less.

'How much?'

'Ninety-five thousand.'

His expression doesn't flicker. 'Pounds?'

'Yes.'

'Jason and your brother really *are* in rather a lot of trouble then, aren't they?'

'Trust me, I hate having to ask you, to beg. But I *will* beg, if you want me to. And I promise I will pay back every penny.'

A couple appear at the top of the stairs, a red-faced man in his late fifties and a beautiful dark-haired woman who is younger – much younger – than him. She doesn't even look twenty-five. They're guided by the maître d' over to a deep sofa in another corner of the room, where a bottle is already chilling in a silver ice bucket.

Alexander picks up his glass of champagne and finishes it in one gulp, refilling both our glasses from the bottle. He's silent for a long moment, not even looking at me, looking past me to the street outside. I can't work out whether he's angry and offended, or surprised and disappointed. All these things, perhaps. The silence between us spools out for so long that I start to wonder whether he's just going to stand up and walk away.

'Perhaps,' he says finally. 'I might be able to help.'

I feel a rush of relief, a first release of the tension that has gripped me ever since I realised Jason and Christian had been kidnapped.

'Thank you so much, Alexander, you have no idea how—'

'Not here though. Somewhere more . . . discreet. You'll have to come to my house, I keep a certain amount of currency in a safe there. For emergencies.'

'Of course,' I say. 'Is it nearby?'

'Fellstone Hall. On the edge of the moors.'

I try to place it, in my head. The name is vaguely familiar, somewhere I might have seen on road signs on one of our New Year trips. A name on an Ordnance Survey map. As far as I can remember, Fellstone is a tiny village, miles from anywhere.

'I assumed you'd have a place here, in York.'

'I do. But Fellstone is my main house. My weekend place, only about an hour from here.' He stares at me, not even the slightest flicker in his dark eyes. 'And we can discuss this properly there. Over dinner.'

'Dinner?'

'I can show you the house. Then we can talk about the details of this little *arrangement* and how it will work.'

'Like I said, I'll pay back every—'

'No, Helly. That's not what I meant.'

The feeling of relief starts to recede, to shrivel back into itself. He had shifted so fast from an old friend, someone I had a shared history with, to this cool detachment. This man who made deals and set the terms. *Somewhere more discreet.* What did it *mean*, exactly? What did it mean in reality?

'Can we not go to Fellstone now?' The antique clock on the wall says it's almost quarter to one. Less than twenty-four hours remained before Docherty's deadline expired. 'I mean, if that's OK? I don't have much time to get what I need.'

'Tonight,' he says again, more firmly this time. 'Dinner. Perhaps you might even like to stay the night. It's a long way out, rather remote. And of course the weather can be rather unpredictable this time of year.'

I stare at him, and he stares back.

So there it is.

He hadn't said it, but at the same time, he had. If he helped me, there would be strings attached. Quid pro quo. *We can talk about the details of this little arrangement and how it will work.*

I pick up my glass and take a large sip, the champagne bitter in my mouth. Could I do this? Could I really step over this line? For my husband, with his little black folder of women's names? For my brother, who had done more than anyone else to get us into this situation in the first place?

Or was there another way?

I feel hot and cold, as if I'm sick with a fever. I had never wanted to keep the bloody money in the first place. Why was I even still here, talking to this semi-stranger from my past? I think of Kat and Miranda, of all we had talked about last night. All of our other ideas to gather enough money to bring this nightmare to an end. None of us had considered *this*. None of us should have to stoop this low, because everything tells me this situation is wrong. There had to be another way. There *had* to be.

'Goodbye, Alexander.'

I stand up and walk away.

51

Miranda

It was strange, Miranda thought, to creep like a burglar through the house you'd grown up in, where you'd spent the first eighteen years of your life. Even though there was no one home, even though she had waited to see her father's big green Range Rover heading out towards the main road before turning into the drive herself. Her mother would be having her usual Saturday brunch with friends in the village, and none of the staff – cleaner, gardener, cook – worked weekends.

Despite all that, Miranda still felt like an intruder.

Last night this had seemed like such a good idea. An easy win. Even on the way here she had told herself that it was forgivable, understandable, as she had made the forty-minute drive to Great Kirkby with a pounding hangover and a travel cup full of black coffee. But now, standing in the high-ceilinged entrance hall of her family home, she felt her confidence waver. Was she *really* going to do this? She took out her phone, brought up the picture of Christian that Docherty had sent, her husband beaten and bloodied, to remind herself why she was here. Whatever she was about to do, it was nothing compared to what he was going through.

Miranda had even suggested – half as a joke, deep into the small hours of last night – that they could fake a kidnapping of their own. That Helen and Kat could pretend to take her hostage, send her father an anonymous demand for money. But none of them had the first idea how to go about it in a way that would be convincing, in a way they wouldn't be caught. None of them were *criminals*.

Not yet.

Kat had been enthusiastic for the fake kidnapping, perhaps a little *too* enthusiastic. Miranda had always been a little intimidated by her sister-in-law's best friend, not that she would ever admit it. But Kat could be fierce at times, with a sense of superiority, as if she was sitting in judgement. Miranda knew what Kat said behind her back – that she was some kind of bimbo – as if she was trying to keep Helen all to herself, to keep everyone else at arm's length. And any attempt to push back would push Helen away too.

Miranda kicked her boots onto the metal shoe rack. It wouldn't do to leave muddy evidence on the pristine stair carpet.

'Mother?' She raised her voice. 'Daddy? Anyone home?'

An echo of her own voice was the only reply. *Good*. She did a quick tour of the downstairs anyway, checking the kitchen, the drawing room, the front room. All empty, as she'd hoped they would be. She climbed the big sweeping staircase, passed a series of studio portraits on the left-hand wall: her older brothers and their families, then shots of her and Cressida nearer the top. Her heart clenched at the thought of Cressida, just turned thirteen, already into that phase of school life when she was made utterly miserable on a regular basis by her peers, her classmates, the ones who were supposed to be her friends. Not that they would be her classmates very much longer – with Christian bankrupt there was no way to pay the school fees anymore. Unless her father chose to step in.

She was pierced with another shaft of guilt at what she was about to do.

Ignore it. She had to just get this done, and get out of here.

She padded into the master bedroom, through a doorway into her mother's walk-in dressing room with its floor-to-ceiling racks of shoes, mirrored wardrobes and makeup table. She slid open the left-hand wardrobe and pushed aside some dry-cleaning, still in its plastic wrapping, to reveal a shelf with a small brushed-steel safe. The six-digit combination was easy to remember: Granny's birthday. She supposed it made sense, since most of what was inside the safe had originally belonged to Granny anyway.

The door of the safe opened with a soft beep and Miranda peered inside at the neatly stacked jewellery boxes, a rack of earrings, and a handful of bracelets loose on one side. At the back, standing up against the rear of the safe, was a rectangular box bearing a gold embossed insignia beneath a single word in old-fashioned script: *Cartier*.

She reached for the box, undid the clasp and opened it up. Nestled inside on a bed of crushed velvet was a silver necklace, a pattern of sapphires inlaid around a large, exquisite diamond. It was too flashy, too gaudy for her mother's tastes and Miranda couldn't remember her wearing it even once since inheriting it from Granny. She could remember the insurance valuation though, seeing the listing on her father's desk a few years ago. *Thirty thousand pounds*. Enough to cover a good portion of what they needed to get Christian and Jason back.

She removed it carefully from the bed of velvet, slipped it into the pocket of her quilted jacket and replaced the box in its place in the safe. It might be months – years, even – before her mother even realised the box was empty. Perhaps there would be a chance to put things right before that happened. She pushed the door shut, hearing the lock click into place.

It was easy as that.

Three weeks ago, the extent of her law-breaking had been three points on her driving licence for doing thirty-six miles an hour in a thirty-zone. And now she was a thief. Although ... was it even stealing, if it was from your own house – or at least the house you'd grown up in? Could it be called stealing if you were due to inherit it anyway, somewhere down the line?

A crunch of gravel on the drive outside sent a pulse of fear skittering up her spine. *Who the hell was that?* Through a side window on the landing she saw her father's sage-green Range Rover pulled up behind her car, blocking it into the narrow end of the driveway between the house and the stables.

Shit. What was he doing back so soon?

She began to descend the staircase in her stockinged feet, heart galloping in her chest. She tapped her pockets for her phone, her car keys, before remembering she'd left both in her handbag, on the little side table in the entrance hall. From below, she heard the big front door swing open and close again, the stamp of boots on the mat.

Her father stood in her path, with the big front door at his back. He was dressed in his usual brown wax jacket and flat cap; his Alsatian, Maximilian, sat at attention by his side.

'Daddy,' she said. 'I didn't realise you'd be back so—'

'Hello, Miranda.' Her father's voice is calm, almost resigned. 'Are you going to tell us what you're doing here?'

She shrugged. 'Just thought I'd drop in. Say hello.'

'When you thought we'd both be out? Come on, darling. Give us some credit.'

From behind her came the sound of the kitchen door opening, closing. The click of footsteps. She turned to see her mother walking through the doorway into the hall, fists clenched at her sides.

Miranda stopped halfway down the stairs, one hand gripping the polished wooden banister.

'You're . . . both here?'

Her mother stared up, her face white with fury.

'Evidently.' She held up her iPhone. 'Did you forget, darling? I get one of those little alerts every time my bedroom safe is opened. Don't tell me – you went for the Cartier, didn't you? So predictable.' She narrowed her eyes at her only daughter. 'You look absolutely terrible, by the way. Although I suppose that's to be expected considering the circumstances.'

Miranda glanced around for her handbag, with her phone, her purse and car keys. But it was gone; the little side table was empty.

'I need to go,' she said. 'I can explain later.'

'No,' her mother said, steel in her voice. 'You can explain *now*. How about you start with our son-in-law's business being on the verge of bankruptcy? And how he's persuaded you to steal for him. *From your own family.*'

'Please, Daddy, I really have to go.'

He turned, slid the front door's deadbolt into place with a heavy iron *shunk*. 'You're not going anywhere, young lady. Not today. And not until we've had the truth.'

52

I make cash withdrawals from five banks, one after the other.

The accounts at four of them are new, only started last week with initial deposits of money from the backpack. I hit the banks in sequence according to their Saturday closing times and draw all of it out in twenties and tens, a helpful teller at each branch sliding the notes into an envelope until I have thousands tucked into my handbag, each packet nestled side by side. This small portion of the whole amount that now had to be returned. It is a strange feeling, a confusing mix of resentment and relief. It had started to *feel* like it was mine – for a short time at least it had been in *my* account, under *my* name. And yet it would be a relief to be rid of it, too. A relief to return to normal worries about normal things, without the constant fear that a hand might clamp down on my shoulder at any moment.

Alexander's words run on a loop in my head all the while.

We can discuss this properly there, over dinner.

I can show you the house. Then we can talk about the details of this little arrangement and how it will work.

Perhaps you might even like to stay the night.

I'm at bank number five watching as a £960 withdrawal is counted out in front of me, when my phone buzzes in my handbag. I'm half expecting it to be Alexander, either apologising for a *misunderstanding* or – more likely – repeating his offer. Digging the phone out from among the envelopes of cash, I see that it's Miranda's number showing on the screen. Hopefully she'll be on her way back from her parents by now, with good news.

But it's not Miranda. A man's voice instead: a hard, clipped baritone.

'This is Roger Neville,' he says. His voice is headmasterly and precise, sharpened to a keen edge. 'Miranda's father. Am I speaking to Helen Cooper?'

'Yes.' I clear my throat, try to imagine why he might be using his daughter's phone. 'Hello, Roger. Is Miranda OK? Has something—'

'I need to speak to you about a rather sensitive matter. Is now a good time?' It's framed as a question but his tone makes it quite clear that it's not. 'Are you at home?'

In the ten years I've known Miranda, I've spoken to her father only a handful of times and never much more than a few sentences; he had never seemed particularly bothered about anyone who was not a blood relative. From what I could remember he was in his early seventies but still tall and physically imposing, with an iron-grey moustache and cheeks criss-crossed with broken blood vessels. I recall him as one of those people who tended to stand a little too close; the smell of dogs and horses and pipe tobacco heavy on his jacket.

'No,' I say. 'I'm out at the moment. What's happened?'

'I need to speak to my son-in-law and it's a matter of extreme urgency, I'm afraid. Do you understand?'

He says the words 'son-in-law' as if uttering an obscenity.

The teller finishes counting the notes and slots them into a plain white envelope, sliding it under the clear plastic barrier towards me. I mouth *thank you* and hurry towards the exit, shoving the packet of money into my handbag.

'I could give you his number?'

'No,' he says curtly. 'Tried that. He's not answering and no one's picking up at his office either. Do you have another mobile telephone number for him? Thought he might perhaps have one that he reserves just for family or personal matters or what have you? A second phone?'

The main door of the bank slides open with a blast of cold wind and I hurry out into the street.

'He just has the one number as far as I know. The iPhone.' I listen as he reads out the digits of my brother's number, then confirm it's the right one, and that no, he's not changed numbers recently. 'Is everything all right, Roger? Is Miranda OK?'

'Miranda is fine. She will be staying at home with us for a few days, away from your brother's unfortunate influence. Tell me, does he often go completely incommunicado like this?'

'He's . . . away this weekend.' I hurry to cross a road as the little green man flicks to red. 'Abroad. It was a business thing and he said he was going to be crazy busy, I think?'

'Abroad, you say? Where?'

I scramble to think of a good answer, should I say the US or the Far East? Which time zone was ahead of us and which one behind? *Shit.* West or east? Where was it the middle of the night now?

'San Diego,' I say. 'I think, or nearby.'

'And when is he due back home?'

'Monday.'

I hope.

Roger fires more questions at me about the last time I saw my brother. He seems to be pausing after each answer, as if he's writing notes.

'I see,' he says finally. 'Well, if you hear from him, tell him I need to speak to him without delay. Do you understand?'

Midway through my reply, he rings off.

I'm at my front door, digging for my house keys among the cash-filled envelopes in my handbag, when footsteps crunch up the path behind me. I whirl around to see two figures in heavy jackets, bundled up against the cold.

Detective Constables Smith and Pritchard approach, hands in pockets, and we exchange perfunctory greetings.

'Apologies,' DC Smith says, 'for disturbing your Saturday. But something has come up in relation to the matter we discussed with you before, and we'd like to ask you some more questions.'

I make a show of looking at my watch.

'I'm afraid it's not really convenient at the moment, I've got a million things to do and the house is a tip. How about Monday?'

She gives me a weary look. 'It needs to be today. Now.'

'I could give you ten minutes but I then I really need to head off to visit my mum.'

Neither of them move.

'Not here, Mrs Cooper. At the station.'

I blink. 'Are you arresting me?'

'Only if I have to. Or, we can all just be reasonable about it.' She gestures towards a grey Ford Focus parked at the kerb. 'My colleague will drive.'

53

Jason

It was an outhouse of some kind. A barn with rough breeze-block walls, the ingrained stink of engine oil and manure. No traffic noise, no vehicles, only the light patter of rain on the corrugated iron roof. An isolated farm, Jason thought, at the end of a rutted track. Maybe an abandoned property.

They hadn't even made it to the cave where they'd discovered the backpack on New Year's Eve. Not even close. Instead, they'd stopped in a lay-by halfway there, some distance from the main road – where Docherty had produced a gun from his jacket. He'd levelled it at them while Roe tied their hands and blindfolded both him and Christian before taking their phones and bundling them into the boot of the Volvo. Another ten minutes driving and they had stopped, been dragged from the car and shoved through a metal door into this cold, echoing place.

They had beaten Christian first.

Each of them took a turn while Jason could only listen, shouting at them to stop, flinching at the wet smack of punches and his brother-in-law's grunts of pain before he collapsed to the floor with a heavy thud. Then they had switched their attention to Jason, the first punches landing like hammer blows while his blindfold was still in place, unable even to defend himself with his hands still secured behind his back. The worst of it was that neither Docherty nor Roe said a word while they were administering the beating, each wordless attack arriving as if they had agreed this little demonstration of violence in advance. As if it was all prearranged.

Then a photograph as he and Christian lay gasping, retching, bleeding, on the cold concrete floor. The two of them forced to unlock their phones to give Docherty access.

The night had been even worse, the two of them huddled on a stinking pile of old hessian sacks in the corner with only a single blanket to keep out the freezing cold. A bare bulb hanging from the ceiling was left on all night, bathing them in its sickly glow, a face appearing at the window every few hours to check they were still there. Jason spent the night – between fitful snatches of sleep – trying to figure out an escape plan. Because he was *not* going to spend another night in this place.

Now, they sat shoulder to shoulder, bleary-eyed and exhausted, in a corner of the barn.

'Listen,' Jason said quietly. 'I think I know how we can get out.'

Christian raised his head, licking his cracked lips. 'What?'

'My hands are almost free.' Jason had spent an hour rubbing the twine binding his hands against the steel edge of an old cattle trough in the corner, eventually cutting through one strand of the restraints after another. 'See? Then I can undo yours.'

'But . . . the door's padlocked from the outside.'

'We don't go through the door.' Jason nodded towards a small window set above their heads in the wall. 'But look, up there. The frame's rotten, it's virtually crumbling away. I can give you a leg up, it'll be a tight fit but you can make it.'

Christian looked sceptical. 'It's too risky. Must be five miles or more to the nearest village.'

'Look, we came down a track to get here. Just follow it back to the road, find the next farm or flag down the first car you see. Get help.'

Somewhere off in the distance, a cockerel crowed.

'You should go,' Jason said. 'You're younger, fitter as well.'

His fellow prisoner grunted. 'Flattery will get you nowhere.'

'I don't think they're awake yet, it's still early. You can be gone before they even realise anything's happened.'

'I'm not leaving you behind. They'll take it out on you.'

'I don't care,' Jason said. 'Let's at least give it a go, before they—'

Christian's eyes widened in alarm.

Jason turned to see what he was looking at: Roe pulling open the steel door and advancing across the barn, his eyes bright with malice.

'I know what you're doing,' he said. 'I know what you're thinking.'

Jason shook his head. 'We're not doing anything, we—'

'Shut up.' Roe reached under his jacket and pulled out a pistol, brandishing it in his bony right hand like a toy. 'I don't think you're taking this seriously. I don't think you're taking *me* seriously.'

He extended his arm and put the muzzle of the gun to Jason's forehead, the ring of cold steel pressed hard into his skin.

Jason froze. *Don't look at him, don't make eye contact, don't antagonise him.* Instead, he kept his eyes down on the dirty straw at his feet. His breath came in short hitches, his heart pushing its way up his throat as if it would burst. He could hear Christian's voice, as if it was coming from a long way away.

'Please! You'll get your money, you'll get all of—'

'SHUT UP!'

The gun pushed against Jason's forehead again, harder this time, and he felt a sharp jab of pain as the steel bit into his skin, a dark line of blood running down into his left eye. He blinked it away, looking up just for a second. This close, the gun looked huge, an ugly tool of machined metal with only one purpose. In that instant, Jason could see everything. Scuff marks on the barrel of the gun. A fresh scab on Roe's knuckles. His nails, bitten raw and bloody, right down to the quick. Christian's face, just a few feet away, etched deep with pure terror.

Roe thumbed back the hammer of the gun with an ominous *click-clack*. His finger curled around the trigger.

'Any last words?'

Jason closed his eyes.

I'm sorry, Helen. I love you and I'm sorry. For everything. I wish I could—

Roe jerked the trigger.

A solid metallic *snap* sent Jason flinching backwards. After a few seconds, he opened his eyes again.

Roe was laughing, crazed exhilaration dancing in his eyes.

'Next time,' he said. 'It'll be loaded.'

54

Walking through the corridors at Fulford Road Police Station, buzzed through security doors, past rows of small offices, feels like walking a tightrope. As if any moment, any wrong word or phrase or gesture will send me tumbling into the abyss. Any kind of slip-up at all. I'd just about managed to send a quick text message to Kat while Smith and Pritchard drove me to the station, holding the phone low between my knees in the back seat.

Police taking me to station for questioning. Not said why yet.

I slip it back into the bag without waiting for a reply.

Interview room number four is stark white and smells of fresh paint. It's bright and well-lit and not at all what I had expected – not that I've ever set foot in a police station before. Smith gestures for me to sit down at a small table attached to the wall, while she pulls out a plastic chair on the other side. Pritchard appears a moment later and hands me a plastic cup of water before folding his big frame into the chair next to his partner.

'Apologies again,' Smith says. 'For disturbing your day.'

I feel a sudden spasm of anger at this woman, at her assumptions, the look on her face that says, *I know you're guilty of something, I'm just not sure what.* It seemed that was the purpose in bringing me here, rather than sitting down in my living room to question me again. Because that was my home turf, familiar, safe. This was *their* turf, and everything about it – the cameras, the security doors, the atmosphere of sterile control – was intended to intimidate. To squeeze the truth out of you.

'So am I under arrest?' I gesture at the surroundings. 'I mean, are you going to arrest me?'

'No. Just want to ask some questions.'

'But shouldn't I have a solicitor, or someone to advise me? Whatever the normal thing is?'

'If you like.' She spreads her broad hands. 'It's entirely up to you and we can arrange that if you like – we should be able to get a duty solicitor here within a couple of hours. But we're not accusing you of anything, this is just us having a chat.' She points up to the spherical eye of a camera, high on the wall opposite. 'That thing's not on and there's no audio either. To be clear – you're here voluntarily. You can leave any time you like.'

I glance at my watch. A couple of hours waiting for a duty solicitor is time I don't really have. I shift in my seat, the hard plastic already digging into my thighs.

'So why *am* I here?'

She goes through the same spiel she had given me last night in my lounge: a major investigation into some very serious offences, with possible links to organised crime. A task force of officers from eight different police forces across the north of England, Smith and Pritchard part of the contingent from North Yorkshire police. But where last night she had been evasive and vague, today she is much more forthcoming. I listen as she lays out more of the details of their operation to smash a weapons-smuggling ring bringing guns into the UK, via shipping coming into Newcastle. Culminating in a sting operation in December which had been an almost complete success – without a shot being fired.

'There's been a media blackout,' she says. 'Which will be in place until the trial starts later this year. But the headlines are that we arrested most of the main players within minutes of the deal going down, scooped up almost everyone else in the following days. We seized all of the weapons too, including more than two hundred assault rifles believed to come from the black market in Eastern Europe, which was a major result. Enough ammunition to start a small war. Or a large one. No doubt about it, these people are all going to go down for a *long* time. Top brass very happy with the outcome all round. There was only one fly in the ointment.' She sits back in her chair, waiting for me to ask the question.

'And what was that?'

'The money, Mrs Cooper.'

Outside it's only a degree or two above freezing, but the heating in here is cranked up so high that it's stifling. Sweat has started to gather at the base of my neck, under my arms.

'OK.' I try to keep my voice neutral, flat, only half interested. 'Although I'm still not really sure why you're telling me all this.'

'We've got the suspects safely under lock and key, same with the guns. The one thing that slipped through the net was the money being used to make the purchase. It was strictly a cash transaction, for obvious reasons. But when we finally picked up the last of the main players the week before Christmas, he didn't have the money either. He'd jumped in his car and done a runner when all his friends got arrested, gone to stay with his sister in Manchester. Didn't want to get caught with the money so he stashed it en route.'

My hands clasp painfully together in my lap beneath the table. Smith is talking as if they've arrested everyone involved, but had she linked that to Docherty and Roe as well? Was she even aware that other members of the gang were still out there?

'Where did he leave it?'

'He hasn't told us yet, been playing hard to get. But he will.'

'And it was . . . a lot, was it?'

She stares at me, an expression passing across her face that I can't identify.

'If our man is to be believed, one point six million in fifties and twenties.'

I hold her gaze, the ball of panic in my abdomen growing, expanding, pushing up against my heart, my lungs. *Breathe. Don't react. Don't give her anything.* It is a physical effort to keep my eyes from dropping to the handbag at my feet, where thousands of pounds in laundered cash is tucked into unsealed envelopes. Instead, I think back to the different versions of this story I've already heard. The story Christian had told us about, the cash depot robbery, which now seemed almost certain to be a fabrication. The version that Docherty had told us about a drug deal gone sour. Also fake.

And now, finally, the truth. The real story of where this money had come from.

I swallow hard, my throat as dry as dust.

'No one normal uses cash these days, do they?'

She ignores my question.

'Sooner or later he'll tell us where it is, because he knows it will get a few years knocked off his sentence.' She gives me a meaningful look. 'Assuming someone else doesn't stumble across it in the meantime. And decide to take it for themselves.'

55

I take a sip of water from the plastic cup. It's warm and tastes slightly metallic.

DC Smith continues to talk, continues to study me across the table.

'Actually,' she says. 'My colleague Wilf here bet me a fiver that's exactly what *would* happen, that some randomer would come across it and think Christmas had come early.'

'Presumably it's marked in some way?' I try to keep my voice level, try not to think of the money I had already spent. 'So you'd know if that happens?'

'Marked? What makes you say that?'

I shrug. 'I just assumed it would be ... like they do in films? So it could be traced when it goes back into circulation?'

She cocks her head slightly to the side, eyes narrowing.

'This is currency that's come out of the criminal economy, Mrs Cooper. So no, it's not marked.' She gestures to her partner, who is writing in a notepad with a pencil that looks comically small in his big hand. 'And how do you think we know that?'

'I have no idea.'

'Because in the first week of January, our uniformed colleagues over at Acomb Road were doing some routine stop and searches and they arrested a couple of local scumbags known for unlicensed lending activity.'

'Sorry, I don't know what that is either.'

'Loan sharks, Mrs Cooper. A much bigger problem in our fine city than most people admit and it's got a lot worse over the last few years. Anyway, one of the two individuals arrested was in possession of a zombie knife, as it turned out, the other with a taser and four thousand pounds in cash tucked inside the lining of his coat. The charges get logged and three days ago they're flagged to the task force for a routine follow-up. To us.' She indicates herself and Pritchard again, who is still scribbling notes. 'So eventually, the scumbag's mate decides he wants to come clean because he knows they're in deep shit. Wants to tell us who his latest repayment came from. Can you guess who it was, who gave him that money?'

'No.' I swallow, my throat dry again. 'Not a clue.'

'In his words, the cash came from "some do-gooder who works for the council".'

I shrug. 'And?'

'It was your husband, Mrs Cooper.'

Which was why Smith and Pritchard had come to our house last night. Looking for Jason.

'They're lying,' I say. 'That's ridiculous.'

'Why would your husband be paying money back to a loan shark? And why would he be paying in fifties and twenties? Where would he have got that money from, Mrs Cooper?'

Somewhere in the back of my mind, away from all of this, away from this room and these police officers and their questions, a new fact slots into place like a key sliding into a lock. The answer to a question that has been hanging over me. *The first week of January.* The men she's talking about had been arrested only a few days after we'd returned from the Dales. Before we'd agreed to start spending the money. Before I'd discovered that some of it was missing. Which meant—

Jason had lied.

He had helped himself to thousands of pounds, and then he had lied to me about it. Lied to my face, to all of us. We've been married for twenty-six years but I suddenly feel as if I don't know him at all. As if he's a total stranger.

Smith is still talking to me, asking another question.

'Mrs Cooper?' She puts her meaty forearms on the table between us, one on top of the other. 'Does your husband have debts? Have you noticed his spending behaviour changing in recent weeks?'

'No. Not that I was aware.'

'Our assumption was that he'd used conventional credit first but that option had been exhausted.' She taps a cardboard folder on the table. 'Although, we've pulled some of his credit history which doesn't appear to back that up.'

'Because you've got this wrong.'

'Look.' She leans forward across the table, closing the distance between us. 'We'd really like to speak to your husband, Mrs Cooper. We believe he might be in danger. Where is he?'

'He's away this weekend.'

'Where?'

'The Lake District, with my brother. He'll be . . . back on Monday.'

Another lie. They were coming thick and fast now and I felt them gathering pace, as if I was sliding towards a cliff edge. If I didn't slow down, I was going to go over the side.

'Can you give him a call?'

I take my regular phone from my bag and make a show of calling up his name from my list of last calls, dialling the number and putting it on speaker. It rings a few times and then – as I knew it would – it clicks into voicemail. *Hey, this is Jason, leave a message.* I end the call.

'Where they're walking, it's quite remote. The signal isn't great.'

Smith frowns slightly as if she's disappointed in me. 'If I got a warrant to search your house today, Helen, what would I find?'

'Nothing.'

That, at least, was true. Most of the money was in the safe at my brother's house.

'I'll be honest with you,' she says. 'I'm seriously worried about your husband's wellbeing, considering the people he's got himself involved with. Why don't you tell us where he really is?'

The instruction from Docherty returns to me, like an echo from a long way away. *If you involve police I'll send your husband and your brother back to you in pieces. And I'll let you choose which one I slice up first.* My heart rattles a ragged beat against my ribcage.

'I think I'd like to go now.'

My chair scrapes noisily against the concrete floor as I stand up.

Smith, however, stays in her seat. 'Why are you covering for him? You're putting him in more danger.'

'I'll let you know when I hear from him.'

Pritchard gets to his feet and crosses the small room in a few long strides. For a moment I think he's going to lock the door, bar my exit, but instead he pulls it all the way open like a doorman at a posh hotel.

I move to follow him out into the corridor, and Smith's voice follows us both.

'We can help you,' she says from behind me, her voice rising. 'But you have to help us, Helen. Before it's too late.'

56

'Bloody hell,' Kat says. 'Bloody *hell*. Seriously?'
'Yeah.'
'Guns?'
'Apparently.'
She's shaking her head.
'And then Alexander Sykes ... what can I say? Wow. He really said that stuff?'
'He said we could *discuss the terms of our arrangement*, yes.'
'Like some kind of indecent proposal?' She shakes her head. 'Jesus. I never would have thought it, from him. He was all right, back in the day, wasn't he? I remember him being a bit intense, a bit full on. But not ... like that.'
'He was a nice guy, in a lot of ways. That's why it lasted a couple of years.'
'And what's he like now? I mean, apart from being a complete sleazebag?'
'He's ... rich, I suppose. Very rich.'
We're sitting in a café on Stonegate, a narrow bustling street in the heart of the old city. Throngs of sightseers and shoppers pass by the big front windows, with the occasional stag and hen group mixed in. I've updated Kat on my conversation with the police and my strange call with Miranda's father, but she's more interested to hear about the meeting with Alexander Sykes at

The Ledbury. Particularly the part about what he'd said before I walked out.

'You're not going to do it though, are you? Go to his big house on the moors?'

'I walked out when he suggested it.'

She gives me the latest update on Dev, who is still being monitored for signs of concussion and any other complications from his head injuries and the bruising to his kidneys. The doctors are optimistic, she says, and tell her it's mostly being done as a precautionary measure in case there are symptoms that develop over the next twenty-four to forty-eight hours.

Neither of us have heard from Miranda since she left to go to her parents' house this morning. Initially, her phone was ringing before cutting over to voicemail. But now it's going straight to voicemail – which presumably means it's been switched off.

Kat drops her phone on the table between us. 'It's like she's fallen off the face of the earth.'

Aside from our worries about Miranda's wellbeing, there is another issue. What remains of the original haul – just over one point five million pounds in cash – is still locked away in the safe at Miranda and Christian's house.

'I've got a key to their place,' I say. 'What I *haven't* got is the combination to the safe. We'll just have to keep messaging her, see if she responds. In the meantime, I've had another idea about how to raise some of the ninety-five thousand.'

Kat smiles. 'Me too.'

'Is your idea risky?'

'Only a bit. The higher the risk, the higher the reward, right?'

'I don't like the sound of that.'

'Is *yours* risky?'

'Not in the short term.' I sip my coffee. 'Medium term, I don't know.'

Her smile fades, her face taking on a more serious expression. Her eyes drop to the table, as if she can't bring herself to look at me.

'There's something I need to tell you, Helen.'

'Don't tell me – you're starting to have second thoughts about us taking that backpack from the cave?'

'Hey, lame jokes are my department.' But she doesn't smile back. 'What I want to say is, I'm sorry.'

'It's not your fault Alexander Sykes is a weirdo.'

'Not that,' Kat says quietly. 'What I mean is, it's my fault. On New Year's Eve . . . it was me.'

'What was?'

'I took some of the money, after everyone else had gone to bed. I needed it. I'm sorry.'

I look at her, see the genuine regret on her face. It had become increasingly obvious over the past thirty-six hours that I had been wrong about the stacks of cash that had gone missing at the start of all this. I had been wrong to think one person was to blame, one person was the cause of it all.

Because it had been all three of them.

My best friend, my husband, my brother.

All three had dipped into it – and then all three had lied.

57

'How much?' I say to Kat. 'How much did you take?'

She looks down into her coffee. 'Eight thousand – just one of the bundles of twenties. I feel terrible because that was the real starting point, wasn't it? That was the trigger for what came after, splitting it up and starting to spend it. Honestly, I feel awful about it.'

'You weren't the only one,' I say. 'Jason took some too, to pay off a debt to a loan shark. And my brother was using the rest to try and dig his company out of a hole, according to his accountant. Look, it's water under the bridge now, nothing we can do about it. All we can do is try to put things right.'

She nods slowly, chokes out another apology.

'Stop it,' I say. 'Stop saying sorry.'

'I don't know why I did it. I mean, I do know, but . . .' She shakes her head. 'I thought it was all going to get handed in to the police, one way or another, and I wanted to keep just a little piece of it. A little piece of that good fortune.'

I snort. '*Good fortune?* Hasn't exactly turned out that way, has it?'

'I'm sorry,' she says again. 'But I'm going to fix it. Never would have thought Jason would have taken some too.'

'He's been going to hotels, with different women.'

She looks up, genuinely astonished. 'Oh God, I'm sorry, Hels. Are you sure?'

I tell her about the hidden folder, names and addresses, hotel bills. The abortion clinic. I wonder, again, at how naive I had been about the six of us in that cottage on New Year's Eve. At how I had jumped to all the wrong conclusions, assuming that only one of our group had stolen from the rest of us, sneaking back to the kitchen in the small hours of the night to pilfer a little extra for themselves.

How quickly the money had brought out the worst in us.

'It was Dev too.' Kat tells me about finding the gambling receipts when she'd gone through the pockets of his jeans before putting them in the washing machine. 'One of the bundles of fifties, I think.'

'After everything he said.' I shake my head in disbelief. 'All his protests.'

'He didn't want to be anywhere near it,' she says. 'He knew temptation would get the better of him, that it would stir up his old demons, his old addiction. And it did. I think it was flashing the cash around the wrong people, other hardcore gambling people, that got him beaten up and robbed. He only just made it home.'

'So what are you going to do now? Is there someone you can borrow from?'

'I had an idea,' Kat says. 'This morning. I know someone who can help, someone who's got money. Cash.'

'Who?'

'I . . . can't tell you that. It's better if you don't know. I need an hour, two hours tops.'

'And he'll just give you money, will he? No conditions?'

She gives me a half-smile. 'I didn't say he'd be *giving* it. I said he's got it.'

'Sounds sketchy as anything. Dangerous.'

'I can look after myself. We're going to finish this – me and you against the rest of the world, Helen. Just like cross-country when we were back at school, right?'

We hug tightly and I feel tears spring to my eyes.

'Christ,' she says. 'Don't do that, you'll set me off too.' She stands up, cuffing a tear away with her sleeve.

I do the same.

'OK,' I say, a hard lump in my throat. 'Let's meet back here at 5 p.m. Don't be late. And good luck.'

58

I find my mother in the conservatory at Harcourt Park, bathed in a shaft of sunlight. She's dozing in a deep armchair, her head resting against its upholstered wing, a magazine open in her lap. A few other residents are there too, napping, reading, a couple playing draughts. A blue-uniformed member of staff clearing away the cups and saucers of afternoon tea. My stomach churns with anxiety that I might bump into Alexander Sykes again, but thankfully he's nowhere to be seen.

Mum looks so peaceful, so settled, that I almost don't want to disturb her. Breaking the bad news to her can wait a few minutes longer, I suppose. I pull up an armchair next to her and settle back into its deep cushions, watching her sleep, the rise and fall of her chest. She's had her hair done at the on-site hairdressers, a set and blow-dry, and it looks good. Her nails have a fresh coat of pale pink varnish too, the colour she'd always worn when I was growing up. Maybe it's the warmth of the room, the stress of the day or how little sleep I got last night, but after a few minutes I feel my own eyelids growing heavy. The world recedes, images dancing in my head of Jason and Christian, the two of them bound and beaten in a cellar somewhere. I try to reach them but when I open the door they're gone and there is nothing left but—

'Hello, stranger.'

I jerk awake and find my mum looking at me, a small smile creasing the papery skin of her face.

'Mum.' I put a hand over hers, leaning in to kiss her on the cheek. 'Thought I'd wait, didn't want to wake you.'

'Looks like you're the one who needs a catnap, love.'

I rub my eyes. 'Sorry I've not been to visit you for a few days. Things have been a bit . . . hectic.'

The desire to confide in her, to tell her everything, is almost overwhelming. To tell her what's happened, share my problems and talk it through with her, mother and daughter. To listen while she tells me what I should do next.

But of course, I can't do that.

Instead, I search her face for clues to whether she's having a good day – a lucid day – or not. She seems rested, engaged, and her pale blue eyes see me instead of looking through me. All of which seem to be good signs. We exchange small talk for a few minutes and she tells me about Susan, a new neighbour who's just moved into the room next to hers. A member of staff brings cups of tea and I drink mine quickly, grateful for the caffeine. Eventually, I decide that I can't put it off any longer.

'Mum.' I put a hand on her arm. The bones of her wrist feel birdlike, fragile, as if they might snap under the slightest pressure. 'I'm afraid I've got some bad news. I know you've been enjoying it here, you've settled in this past week and made some new friends. But I'm afraid you can't stay here anymore. You're going to have to move back home, Mum. I'm sorry. We just don't have the money. I'm going to see about getting some new carers in, good ones this time, to help you out.'

She gives me a perplexed look. 'I rather like it here.'

'I know, Mum, but—'

'Christian's paying the fees, isn't he? Like he always has? Just tell him.' She waves her small hand in a dismissive gesture, as if batting away a fly. 'Tell him to sort it out with the bean counters in the front office.'

'He can't, Mum.' I pick up my teacup, see it's empty, put it back down again. 'Not at the moment. He's having some . . . problems with his company and he can't—'

'What *problems*? He's never given me a problem in his life, that boy. My *lovely* boy. Never put a foot wrong.'

'All the same,' I say. 'We can't afford the fees here anymore, Mum. So I'm going to bring you home in a day or two, OK?'

She seems to lose her thread, her train of thought, shrinking back into her chair. After a moment she turns to me again, as if seeing me for the first time.

'You look tired, love. How've you been?'

I wonder once again what it would be like to be completely honest and tell her everything. To get all of it off my chest. To get her unvarnished, unfiltered opinion on what's happened over the past few days and weeks. To see what she would have done; and what she'd do now. But the temptation vanishes, like a sunset dipping below the horizon.

'I'm fine,' I say. 'There's been a lot going on recently at home but we're getting through it.'

'Don't give me that nonsense, love.' She shuffles in her chair as if to get a closer look at me. 'You look as if you've got the weight of the world on your shoulders.'

I smile and change the subject, bringing it around again after a few minutes to what we've already discussed: that she has to go home soon. Back to her quiet, empty house.

'Home.' She says it like a foreign word, unfamiliar on her tongue. 'Home.'

Just like before, just like every time, I feel my heart breaking a little more to see her struggle like this.

'That's right, Mum.'

She braces a hand on each arm of the chair and starts to struggle to her feet. 'Going now, are we?'

I put a hand over hers. 'No. Not just yet. But I wanted to let you know.'

'Might as well do it now if we have to.'

'You're all right until Monday, Mum. I'll talk to the front desk and make the arrangements.'

She slumps back into her chair. I sit with her for a while longer until she drifts off to sleep again, her eyes drooping shut. I get to my feet, leaning down to give her a gentle kiss on the temple.

Then I steal silently away, feeling like a thief leaving the scene of a crime.

59

Kat

Kat didn't know much about him.

She knew his current number but then he changed phones all the time, for obvious reasons. She didn't know if he had family, brothers or sisters, whether York was his hometown or he'd settled here from somewhere else. She didn't know how old he was – thirtyish? – or how long he'd been doing what he did. She'd been a customer for quite a few years now but still didn't even know whether Tate was his first name, surname or a nickname.

But she *did* know where he lived.

She'd found out quite by chance a few months earlier, driving through the new estate in Knapton in search of an address where she was due to pick up a set of kitchen chairs she'd bought on Facebook Marketplace. She had turned a corner and seen him there, this bearded hipster washing a black sports car on the driveway of a smart detached house, one of those weird moments when you see someone out of context, out of their usual environment, and you think – *oh* – where do I know *you* from? It was a new-build estate, bright-brick houses nestled close together, with lots of six-foot fences and spindly saplings staked to the ground. The last place you'd expect to find someone like him. Which was precisely why he was here.

He was good at blending in, at being the grey man, the average-looking guy that no one would remember. He would brush off enquiries about how he made a living with vague comments about cryptocurrency and day trading on the stock market. She also knew he was perennially single, distrustful of others, a lone wolf. Which also made sense considering his line of work.

She normally met him at the gym, or at the shop where she worked. And always by arrangement only. He was very particular about that. She had asked to meet him today, had watched his car leave and knew he'd be gone for at least forty minutes before he realised she wasn't going to show up. She would text him an excuse, an apology, but by then she'd be long gone.

He wouldn't suspect her – she had been one of his best, most consistent clients, and she was old enough to be his mother. He also wouldn't call the police, which was the other reason she was here.

Kat had slotted her Mini into a line of parked cars from where she could observe Tate's house. She tugged the baseball cap a little lower over her eyes, sliding down in the seat to make her a little less conspicuous, never an easy task for someone who was five foot ten. She sat behind the wheel of her car, the fingers of one hand drumming the steering wheel, praying the neighbours were not the observant type. A flicker of movement across the street caught her eye, the twitch of a net curtain in the house opposite. She squinted, trying to make out if there was someone looking back at her behind the gauzy material.

Her thoughts turned to Dev again, of what kind of night he'd had in hospital, whether he'd been able to get any sleep on the ward. Kat *hated* hospitals. She always had, from when she was a little girl. And every time she had to visit it underlined her dislike, reminded her, just like last night in the overflowing A & E department full of tearful drunks, aggressive drunks, falling-down drunks. Visiting hours at the hospital today didn't start until two but she had already exchanged a few texts with her husband. At least he would be safe on the ward.

But there was still guilt that came with knowing on some deep level that the beating was linked back to the money. The money that she had lobbied for, argued for.

It was all spinning out of control.

She felt herself sinking, falling into a hole again, sliding down into the black.

It's all my fault.

He didn't deserve this.

I'm sorry, Dev. But I'm going to make it right.

They were not so different, her and her husband. People sometimes said they were one of those yin and yang couples, the introvert and the extrovert, the rule-follower and the risk-taker. But in reality they were much more similar, and *that* was the real reason they got on, the reason they'd been together so long. It was just that Dev managed to hide it most of the time, to suppress it, to pretend he was some model citizen.

Except when temptation was put right under his nose. Into his hands.

As it had been on New Year's Eve.

Temptation that had sent him tumbling back through a door he thought he'd shut forever. A past he'd sworn to leave behind. A part of him that he'd held at bay for years, decades, as he constructed a life as the ultimate rule-follower: a driving instructor, a city councillor, a magistrate.

All of it blown apart by a single stack of fifty-pound notes.

Kat had known, as soon as she found that betting slip in the pocket of his jeans. And more evidence in the days that followed: cash receipts from the Grosvenor Casino in town, thousands in chips for roulette, blackjack, poker, all since the start of the New Year. The credit card bill with payments to one of those ubiquitous betting apps that was constantly advertising on TV, online, everywhere else, with ads telling credulous punters to *stop when the fun stops* and *only ever bet as much as you can afford to lose.*

Dev's demons had caught up with him.

Just like they had caught up with Kat, the day she lost her high-flying job to a random drug test.

But now she was going to do the *right* thing. To help her friends.

She just needed a little sharpener first.

She felt the hunger for it building, expanding, the need pulling at her like a riptide drawing her out to sea, no way to fight against it. Better to just go with the flow. Without even making a conscious decision, she leaned over to the glove compartment of her car and took out a box of paracetamol. Inside the box, tucked in between two blister packs of pills, was a small plastic Ziploc bag not much bigger than a postage stamp. With a quick glance up and down the street, Kat eased the bag open and tapped out two little piles of the white powder onto the back of her left fist.

Not too much. Just enough to keep her sharp. A quick snort – *one, two* – that tiny, beautiful lag of a few seconds and then it was like an electrical charge hitting the back of her skull, fatigue vanishing, veins and capillaries swelling and pulsing with it, details of this suburban street just that little bit sharper, clearer, *prettier* on this bright January morning. It was going to work out. It was *all* going to work out today, she felt sure of it. She sniffed twice, checked herself in the rear-view mirror and wiped away a little stray powder beneath her nose.

She put on sunglasses and gloves, pulled her scarf up so it covered the lower half of her face. She was fairly confident there wouldn't be an alarm – Tate wouldn't want to draw attention to his house in any way that might end up with the police – but he would probably have some kind of security cameras up around the place, and it wouldn't do for her to be recognised.

She climbed out of her car and walked quickly to Tate's house, ringing the doorbell first – just to be sure – before going down the little alley at the side of the house. The garden was a small nondescript square of grass. No furniture, no plants.

The upper half of the back door was frosted glass. Kat took the hammer from her backpack and swung it hard, punching a hole in the glass with two quick blows. She reached in with a gloved hand and turned the key in the door, opening it and stepping inside.

With the hammer still in hand, she moved through the small utility room into the kitchen, blood thrumming with the thrill of the chase. She had already given this some thought. Tate would hide his valuables in plain sight, she had guessed. Just like *he* was doing, living here in this inconspicuous neighbourhood. He would keep it all together, in one place where he could grab it quickly in case he had to leave in a hurry. On the first floor, not the ground floor – near to where he worked or slept. She ignored the kitchen and the lounge and climbed the stairs instead, passing a trio of neatly framed watercolours that were so generic they looked as if they'd been taken from a show home.

There were four doors off the small landing. A bathroom and three bedrooms, she assumed. The first bedroom was completely empty, vacant, a single bare bulb hanging from the ceiling. As if filling the room would serve no purpose. The second bedroom had been converted into a study of some kind, with a chair, a low bookcase and three MacBook laptops arrayed across the desk. A piney, air-freshener smell in the air. She checked the desk drawers quickly. Two were empty, the third contained a bundle of charging cables and large hunting knife in a black leather sheath. No money. She swallowed hard and pushed the drawer shut again.

The last door was the master bedroom, a double bed.

There was a gym bag at the bottom of his wardrobe. No – there were *three* gym bags. Identical black Nike holdalls, side by side. The first one contained gym kit, trainers, a towel, deodorant. The second a dozen or so identical boxes still wrapped in plastic – cheap-looking mobiles from a Chinese company she didn't recognise. Burner phones, presumably. Beside them, another big knife, this one more like a machete. It looked *hideously* dangerous. She unzipped the third bag and found more gym kit. A black tracksuit top and another towel, more of the...

Wait. There was something else, a solid shape beneath the thin fabric. She pulled out the clothes to reveal a rectangular Tupperware box, incongruous among all of the fitness gear covering it up. Beside the box was another, and another. She snapped open the blue lid of the first one, her lips curving into a broad smile when she saw what was inside.

Bingo.

The plastic box was filled with two stacks of ten-pound notes, each wrapped with two elastic bands and at least three inches thick. There must be *thousands* here. The next box was filled with two bundles of five-pound notes. The last one with a single stack of twenties. Breathing fast, she unzipped her own small rucksack and shoved the bundled notes inside before replacing the empty Tupperware boxes into the gym bag and putting everything back into the wardrobe.

She felt a twinge of guilt as she swung the little rucksack back onto her shoulder. Tate had always helped her out, always got her what she needed. But then again, he *was* a drug dealer. This sort of thing happened to drug dealers from time to time, didn't it? Some of this was her money anyway. At least, some of her share from New Year's Eve.

And they needed it, more than he did. They were desperate. Helen was desperate and Kat had promised to do everything she could to help her best friend. They would use this money for a *good* purpose – which meant it was the right thing to do.

Nerves tingling, she went downstairs and out through the back door again, crunching over broken glass as she pulled it closed behind her. She hurried back down the narrow alley at the side of his house and turned into the street, checked back over her shoulder that Tate's car hadn't returned, broke into a jog—

And ran straight into the hi-vis jacket of a uniformed police officer.

60

It's already getting dark by the time I reach my office, beneath a leaden sky heavy with the promise of sleet and snow. I'm still turning everything over in my mind, still trying to grasp how Alexander had switched so quickly from friendly reminiscing to a cold businesslike proposal. And at how close I'd come to accepting his offer. *Perhaps you might even like to stay the night.* Did he really mean that? I don't see what else it *could* mean.

The office car park is empty but it's covered by CCTV so I leave my car on the next street and walk around instead, approaching the rear of the building so I'm not caught on camera. The loading dock at the back also has a camera but it's been broken since last year and Nigel has not yet got around to approving the repair cost. At the back door, I take out the spare security pass I keep in the glove compartment of my car and tap it against the reader, pulling the door all the way open when the LED goes green. Every entry is logged in the system but my spare pass is a blank – given to contractors and clients spending time on site – so it won't register as me.

In the corridor, I stop and listen to the silence of a dormant office on a Saturday afternoon. All the lights are off, all the doors closed that should be closed. I had been working here fourteen years and in all that time have come in on a Saturday only once. Nigel had been at the airport, about to fly out to a client meeting in Paris and flapping about some crucial paperwork he'd forgotten – half pleading and half demanding that I drive to the office, pick up the documents and drive them over to him before he got on his plane.

I had done it, of course.

There are cameras on reception, in the lift and in the break room, so the length of staff coffee breaks could be monitored. But there are no cameras on the stairs. I take the staircase up to the second floor, pausing and listening again for any sign that I'm not alone. The silence is disturbed only by the low hum of a couple of computers that have been left on over the weekend. The main open-plan office area is unlit and deep in the shadows of approaching dusk, but I'm so familiar with the layout that I could move around with my eyes closed. I don't want to turn any of the main lights on in case one of our security contractors happens to drive past. I could make up some fairly plausible story about why I was here – catching up on work or picking up a document for Nigel – but I don't want anyone to know that I've been here on site. Not with what I'm about to do.

This had not been a part of the plan we'd come up with last night. It was improvised after my meeting with Alexander Sykes went off the rails. But then . . . what was that thing my brother was fond of saying? *A plan that can't be changed is probably a bad plan.* I would do this, and Kat and Miranda would do what they had to do. All of us thieves, in one way or another, stealing to pay back a debt we should never have incurred. All of us criminals.

Nigel's glass-walled office is at the far end of the floor, with my smaller space next to it. I push through the glass door and go to my desk, unlocking the top drawer and reaching all the way to the back, for a lockbox that used to be used for petty cash. Now, it contains something much more valuable. Lists of passwords, banking credentials, usernames, corporate accounts and sort codes. And my boss's corporate payment cards. Working for an old-school managing director who claimed to be inept at anything involving technology – as well as being fundamentally lazy – meant I had to do a range of technical tasks for him and over the years I had gathered all of his logins for the online services we used as a company.

I take the box and go through into Nigel's office, then sit at his desk and power on his computer. First of all, I use his username and password to log into the security system and take the reception CCTV camera offline, then go back and delete the footage that's been recorded since midday. Next, I pull up a private browser window and select a secure connection to the bank, typing in his first-stage username and passwords. A coiling of fear tightens in my throat as the screen goes through the preliminary security steps onto our corporate banking platform.

Was I really doing this? Apparently I was.

To my surprise, Docherty had not objected to receiving some of the missing money by bank transfer, texting me back with an account number and sort code within half an hour. My plan was to divert money from a number of the company accounts into one that only my boss used for corporate entertaining, then transfer it all out from there to Docherty's account. My boss always relied on me to handle this account and I could move money around elsewhere to cover my tracks for at least a few days, by which time Jason and Christian would be safely back. When the losses were discovered, the transfers would have Nigel's fingerprints all over them. He would deny it, of course, and try to bluster his way out of it with talk of hackers and scammers who had got inside our security, while I kept my head down and hoped for the best.

It's not much of a plan. But it's the best I've got.

I log into the banking platform and scan the list of accounts, making a series of four-figure transfers. I keep them all under ten thousand pounds, avoiding round numbers and adding pence to make them look like contract payments. They're all effectively internal so there are no additional security checks to be passed. Not yet.

The soft glow of Nigel's monitor is the only light in the gathering gloom.

When I've moved just over fifty thousand, I select *Pay a Supplier*, typing in Docherty's bank details. More password boxes appear for authorisation and I fill them in too. *Here we go. No turning back now.* I take a deep breath, say a silent prayer and press *Continue* to make the transfer out to his account.

The screen freezes for what feels like an eternity before a red box appears in the centre.

Error – contact administrator

It's a message I've never seen before. I check all of the details and go through the whole process again, re-entering the digits and double-checking them before clicking to proceed.

The message appears again.

Error – contact administrator

I log out, heart thudding painfully against my ribcage, then open a new browser window and log back in again. I'm entering all of the bank details for a third time when my phone starts to ring and I flinch as the music of my ringtone cuts through the silence of the empty office, the phone screen showing my boss's name. *Not now.* I press the red button to end the call, and a few seconds later it starts ringing again. He'll keep doing this until I either turn my phone off – which I only do at night – or answer his call.

I answer the call.

'Helen?'

'Hi, Nigel, how are—'

'Listen, I'm getting some weird messages on my phone about the business banking account? Are you getting those too? Only I was wondering if you could possibly ring the banking people and get to the bottom of it, obviously I'd do it myself but I'm out at the moment with some Rotary Club pals and it's all rather irritating with my phone going off every two seconds.'

'Messages?' I try to keep my voice even. 'What kind of messages are you getting?'

'Hang on.' There is a rustling sound from his end of the line. 'It says . . . suspicious activity warning, a possible hacking attempt? The bank launched some new bloody security protocols on the first of January, apparently.'

'Right,' I say. 'I'll call them.'

'Sorry to bother you on a Saturday, and all that. Not interrupting anything, am I? Where are you?'

I glance around his darkening office.

'Just . . . at home.'

'I've flagged it with the security company too, they're supposed to get a response vehicle on site within ten minutes. Sweep the building, check everything is locked down tight and no one's got into the premises.'

'Is that necessary?' A pulse of fear propels me to the window and I half expect to see a Bulldog Security van pulling through the gates. But the car park is reassuringly empty – for now. 'Surely hackers would be doing it remotely, from . . . Russia or somewhere?'

'Can't be too careful these days, Helen. And it's what we bloody pay Bulldog an extortionate annual fee for, isn't it?' He snorts with disdain. 'Unless you want to nip round and see if someone left the front door open last night?'

'To the office?'

'Obviously, yes to the office.'

'I'm a bit tied up at the moment. With my mum.'

'Oh.' He gives a grunt of disappointment. 'Well, in that case, let me know what the bank people say. Got to dash, I'll leave you to it.'

He rings off before I can even say goodbye.

I sit down heavily in his chair again, feeling as if the world is falling away beneath my feet. This had been my last hope. My last chance.

I close down his computer and hurry out of the office.

61

I'm late for the meeting with Kat. By the time I've parked up again and hurried to the White Rabbit café it's almost ten past five. It's busy with shoppers and I manage to grab the last table right at the back, sweat beading the back of my neck as I slide into the seat.

There's no sign of her at any of the other tables. We've not missed each other; she's just not here yet. I call her, but it rings out and goes to voicemail. I leave a message then try again, with the same result. I send a quick text and put the phone face up on the table in front of me, willing it to ring, to buzz, to do *something*.

Alfie has asked whether his friends Isaac and Ed can come over tonight to watch football on the TV. It's a relief, to be honest, that someone will be with him if I'm going to be running around the city looking for a way out of this mess. I tell my son that his friends are welcome to stay over as well. He replies with another question.

Is everything OK Mum?

Swallowing back tears, I type a quick reply.

Yes all fine, see you later. x

Miranda's phone rings out, as it has done all afternoon. She's been out of contact since she left this morning to drive to her parents' house in Great Kirby. It's another worry not to know how she is, what's happened, but a worry that has simply become one of many.

My hands are still shaking after my rapid escape, empty-handed, from the office.

The only messages I have are from Nigel, my boss, asking what I've heard from the corporate banking people after they alerted him to *suspicious activity* in the company accounts. His first message says, *What's latest re: bank/scam alert?* The next, ten minutes later, *Update pls???* A third has no words, just a long line of passive-aggressive question marks.

I ignore all three messages, keeping an eye on the door of the café, the comings and goings of people. Waiting to see the familiar face of my oldest friend, my best friend, willing her to breeze in off the street with an apologetic smile and a story to tell.

Talk to me, Kat. Tell me you're running late but it's all OK, you've got what we need, somehow you've found the money to make up the shortfall and it's all going to be all right.

The café door opens and shuts as strangers come and go.

But by twenty past the hour, there is still no sign of her. The screen of my mobile stays inert, blank and silent. She was the only person – apart from Jason and my boys – with whom I shared my phone location. I tap *Find My* and wait for the icon to zoom into her location, hoping it would show her minutes away, on her way here.

Instead, it shows her phone's location as a building on Fulford Road.

So she's not coming to meet me here. Because she's at—

—a police station.

Oh, God.

I say a silent prayer that she's OK. A fleeting thought following straight after: *Had she decided to come clean after all? To admit to the catastrophe we had created and ask for their help?*

No. Not Kat. She'd be the last of us to go to the police voluntarily.

But perhaps that's *exactly* where I should be. I could go and tell Smith and Pritchard everything, lay it all out for them, from start to finish. No more lies. Just the simple, unvarnished truth. It's tempting for a moment before I discard the idea. There is too much at stake to take such a risk. Two lives on the line. We are too far into this now, too deeply involved in every way to hope that the police could simply unstitch it all and let us walk away. What we've done cannot be undone. The only way out is through, right through the looking glass, all the way through to the other side.

Even so, I feel stranded, strung out and totally, utterly alone. As if I've missed the last boat home and all I can do is stand on the shore and watch it shrink towards the horizon.

There is nothing left.

I feel a grim determination settle on my shoulders. Of our original six, there is no one left but me, no one else to finish what had been started three weeks ago in that cave in the Dales.

I was the one who had found the money. Now I was the one who would rid us of it. For good.

And I only have one card left to play.

At half past five, I pick up my phone again and select the Messenger app. The exchange of messages with Alexander Sykes is still at the top of the screen. I'd not heard from him since walking out of the restaurant earlier today.

I take a deep breath and begin to type a new message.

62

A black Mercedes saloon pulls up outside my house at eight o'clock on the dot.

The driver, a solid forty-ish man in a dark grey suit and black tie, emerges as I walk down the drive. He stands by the car's rear passenger door, hands clasped in front of him, and gives a curt nod as I approach.

'Good evening, Mrs Cooper.'

He opens the rear door of the Mercedes for me, waiting until I've climbed into the deep leather back seat before closing it and returning to the driver's side. He pulls smoothly away, the door locks engaging with a soft metallic *thunk*.

The interior of the car is dark, luxuriously comfortable, and almost silent.

I smooth down my dress with a shaking hand. Our double bed had been piled high with clothes by the time I had decided what to wear, mounds of dresses and trousers, blouses and skirts and jackets discarded in mounting frustration as I considered each in turn and then discounted them, just like this morning. Striking the right balance felt like an impossible task.

I *had* to have that money. But I wasn't going to beg.

Unless there was no other option.

In the end I had opted for a plain black cocktail dress with a pale grey jacket and a scarf, as much makeup as I might wear on a night out with the girls. Nothing more.

Watching the streets slide silently by, I try not to think about how weird, how inappropriate, how *wrong* all of this is. To be making this journey alone, on a Saturday night, is so far beyond acceptable that I can't even bear to think about it. Out of the heavily tinted window I see teenagers at a bus stop, smokers chatting outside a pub, a couple sitting in the warm glow of a restaurant, their heads close together. People spending a normal weekend evening as if they haven't got a care in the world. *That's me*, I think. *That's who I really am, one of them. A normal person.* I'm seized by a sudden, piercing sense that I'm missing something, that I've overlooked something important. An obvious alternative to what I'm about to do. But it remains elusive, just beyond my reach like a blurred shape in the distance I can't quite make out. The voice in my head says: *I can't do this. This is not who I am. I have no idea what to do or say to him tonight, I've been happily married for twenty-six years and never wanted to do anything like this. I was never even tempted. I love my husband and my sons, I like Abba and Pilates and a gin and tonic on a Friday night, I'm PA to the chief executive of a logistics firm. This is insane. What am I doing here? In this car?*

I love my husband.

That's why I'm here.

It's only when I see a road sign for Thirsk that I realise we're going in the wrong direction.

Fellstone is west – but we've been heading *north* for the last ten minutes. A flutter of fear stirs in my stomach, the sense of being adrift and out of control. I wait for another couple of minutes, peering through the tinted glass for another road sign to confirm my suspicions. The Mercedes glides through a junction that says we're on the A19 heading for Shipton. As a family, we had driven out to the Dales countless times over the years, so often the route was like second nature. I had googled Fellstone Hall earlier, and it was in broadly the same direction – which meant we should be heading west to Harrogate and then up towards Nidderdale.

The driver was going the wrong way.

Either that, or we weren't going to Fellstone Hall at all.

I lean forward and tap a fingernail on the privacy glass separating me from the driver.

'Hello?'

He ignores me.

I rap a bit louder on the glass.

'Excuse me?'

The privacy barrier buzzes down a couple of inches.

'Sorry, but where are you actually taking me?'

'Just another couple of minutes now, madam.'

The glass buzzes up again and the big car powers smoothly onwards into the dark.

It occurs to me that the driver – I don't even know his name – could be taking me anywhere. To any of Alexander's properties. Or somewhere else – a hotel? If he even worked for Alexander? Oh God, could he even be something to do with Docherty and Roe, working with them? I take my phone from my handbag, bringing up my contacts. But a call to Detective Constable Smith would put Jason at greater risk, and there's no one else left to help.

We're beyond the edge of the city now, passing through a small village. The Mercedes slows and indicates onto a smaller road, past a scattering of farm buildings. There is no other traffic here at all, either behind or in front. No street lights, no signs, nothing but the thin strip of black tarmac unfolding in front of us.

I try the door handle. It's locked. The other side too. Another knock on the privacy glass yields no response, the driver making another turn, a sign flashing past on the left but the back windows are tinted so dark that I can't read it. The fluttering of fear beneath my ribcage threatens to bloom into panic.

The driver lifts a mobile phone to his ear, speaking a few words that I can't hear through the glass divider. He ends the call and drives on, headlights illuminating nothing but ploughed fields on one side of the road, tarmac on the other.

Finally, we pull to a stop with a large building on our left, like some kind of warehouse or barn. The driver gets out, walks around to my side and when he opens the door, I finally see why we've stopped here.

A sleek black helicopter sits on the tarmac, its rotor blades spinning slowly in the chilly night air.

63

From the air, Fellstone Hall is visible from a long way away. It's lit up like a beacon of a thousand lights, a sprawling Victorian mansion of turrets and chimneys in pale sandstone. The helicopter makes a long slow circle around the grounds, over the main house and the courtyard, ornamental gardens stretching away from the back of the property, a stable block, tennis court and indoor pool. All of it illuminated with soft lighting that gives the estate an ethereal glow as we approach the landing pad.

The house is set well back from the road at the end of a long drive, hidden from the world behind a thick screen of trees. As the helicopter slows, sinking towards the ground, I realise we're only a handful of miles away from the cottage where we'd stayed at New Year. From Scar House Reservoir and the cave where all this madness had started, three long weeks ago.

It feels almost like returning to the scene of the crime.

We touch down gently and the helicopter seems to settle itself back to earth, the whine of the rotor blades lowering in pitch as they start to slow. The co-pilot jumps down to open my door, escorting me up a gravel path to the double staircase at the back of the house. A dark-suited man greets me on the bottom step and introduces himself as Crowther, the house manager, before showing me up the curving stone stairs and opening the door for me at the top. He doesn't try to engage me in conversation, simply guides me through echoing corridors until we reach the library.

Alexander turns as we enter. He's dressed in a crisp black shirt and black jeans, some kind of tall cocktail in his hand. He smiles and kisses me on both cheeks, a hand on my elbow in a cloud of his aftershave, as if we're old friends and that's how we *always* greet each other. There's no hint of animosity, no suggestion that he's offended I walked out on him earlier, almost as if he knew I'd end up here sooner or later.

'You look incredible,' he says. 'As always. Thank you for coming, Helen.'

'Thank you for inviting me.' I gesture at the room, filled with bookshelves from floor to ceiling on three sides. 'Your house is amazing.'

If *he* can pretend this is an entirely normal evening, not at all weird or surreal or borderline creepy, then maybe I can pretend too. It's not as if I have a choice – I'm here now. Even if being here is already a betrayal. I try to imagine that he's the affectionate, studious 20-year-old I had first gone out with, rather than the intense, supremely confident multimillionaire who was now the master of all he surveyed.

He takes a white wine glass from a silver tray and hands it to me. 'Sauvignon spritzer with ice and soda, not lemonade? Am I right?'

'How did you know that?'

He shrugs. 'Social media. You'd be amazed what you can learn.'

I take the glass from him, force a smile. 'But you never post anything yourself, Alexander?'

'I'm more of an observer. It's funny, isn't it? All those years of keeping in touch and now finally, *wonderfully*, here you are.' He gestures towards a pair of armchairs in front of the fire. 'Dinner will be ready in about fifteen minutes. Shall we get comfortable?'

The meal is exquisite.

I've never eaten at a Michelin-starred restaurant but I imagine this is what it's like: one beautifully prepared course after another, each paired with a different wine, a pair of waiters bustling in and out as they serve and clear for the chef in the kitchen.

Not that I'm really able to enjoy the food, my stomach shrivelling with mounting unease.

Not after Alexander tells me *I* was the reason for his divorce.

How I had broken his young heart.

How he had never really got over me, how his ex-wife had sensed it and how it had eventually driven them apart.

'You know,' he says, 'I have a certain reputation as a businessman, Helly. For being tough enough to get what I want. Maybe ruthless, sometimes. But I've never stopped being an old romantic.' He points a finger at me, with the hand holding his wine glass. 'I've never stopped being that boy who fell in love with you.'

Mechanically, I cut another slice of bluefin tuna and put it in my mouth. Chew. Swallow. Repeat. I can barely taste it.

'You've done incredibly well, Alexander. You should be proud of what you've achieved.'

'But it was always you, Helen. *You* were always the one.' He leans forward, hands clasped in front of him as if in prayer. 'I made so many plans over the years, so you'd know how I felt. So you'd know my feelings hadn't changed. So many different ways to impress you, to win you back.'

'I'm married, Alexander.'

He smiles and gestures at the food, the dining room, the grand house around us.

'And yet here you are.'

Earlier, at the restaurant in York, I had thought he was just flattered to hear from an old girlfriend. Excited to catch up. But here, in his house on the moors in the middle of nowhere, I'm seeing that it goes deeper than that. Much deeper. It wasn't just excitement. It felt like *obsession*. And I had walked into the lion's den.

My phone pings with a message on the table beside me, once, twice.

Alexander raises an eyebrow. 'Are you going to see who that is?'

It's from Docherty.

Just a reminder: if you involve police, or miss the money deadline tomorrow, I'll let you choose which one I shoot first. Unless you want to choose now? Your brother or your husband?

The image that comes next almost stops my heart. It's a picture of Christian, his head bowed, eyes closed, streaks of dried blood reaching down from his hairline. His face is blanched white with terror.

The barrel of a gun is pressed hard to his temple.

I type a quick reply with shaking fingers.

I understand. You'll have your money, please don't hurt them.

Alexander cocks his head to one side. 'Is everything all right?'

I nod, excuse myself and find a downstairs bathroom that looks like it's come out of a five-star hotel in the West End. I lock the door and lean back against the marble sink, blowing out a heavy breath.

This already feels like the biggest mistake of my life.

I pull out my phone to double-check, but there are no other texts, nothing from Kat or Miranda. I'm about to put the phone back into my handbag when I see there's a missed call from earlier. Presumably from when I was on the helicopter. I dial into my voicemail and Kat's voice fills my ear.

'Helen? I don't know where you are but I just . . .' Her voice cracks and she breaks off for a moment. 'I'm sorry. I'm so sorry, love. I tried to help, to get that money we needed, but it went wrong. I . . . Some bloody curtain-twitching nosy neighbour called the police and I got arrested. They're going to hold me overnight, they said I could make one phone call so I wanted to let you know.

I let you down.' She apologises again, choking back more sobs. 'I hope you're OK. Good luck.'

The call ends with a click, a robotic voice asking whether I'd like to listen to it again. Closing my eyes, I push back the tears, curling my fingernails into my palms. Kat's message is final confirmation, if it was needed, that I am well and truly on my own. I check my makeup in the mirror but can't bear to look at myself for more than a few seconds. I put a hand to the back of my neck, the tendons as taut as piano wire. My skin is burning up.

The phone rings in my handbag a moment later.

'Mum?' Alfie's voice fills my ear. 'Where are you?'

'I'm out,' I say, fighting to keep a sob from rising up my throat. 'With an old friend. Are you OK, what are you up to?'

'Sounds really echoey where you are.'

'I'm just in the ladies'.'

'Is it all right if Isaac and Ed stay over at ours tonight?'

He says something else about another friend who might come over, a film they might watch on Netflix. My boy's deep teenage voice untroubled by anything beyond social arrangements for a Saturday night.

'Sure.' I cut him off. 'That's fine, Alfie. There are pizzas in the freezer, and don't forget to give the cats their supper, OK?'

He seems about to ring off when another thought occurs to him.

'When's Dad back?'

Tears spring to my eyes.

'He's out with your uncle Christian tonight.' I swallow. 'Back tomorrow.'

'Right,' he says. 'Cool. See you later, Mum.'

This time he does ring off, just as I'm telling him that I love him. With his voice gone, I feel more alone than ever. I wipe my eyes with a tissue, taking deep breaths to calm my galloping heart.

On the way back to the dining room, I glance out of the window. Snow has started to fall in a thick, swirling mass, the first flakes already settling across the lawn. Dessert has been served by the time I sit down again, some kind of elaborate concoction of tropical fruit, cream and spiced rum. I can't even face a single bite.

Alexander is sitting back in his chair at the other end of the long table, regarding me over his glass of wine.

'So are you going to tell me?'

'Tell you what?'

'What the money is for. Or *who* it's for?'

I pick up my own glass, take a sip.

'I can't tell you.'

'Can't or won't?'

'I wish I could tell you, but—'

'It's a ransom, isn't it?'

'What?'

'It's just the amount. Ninety-five thousand, there's a certain . . . raw cunning to it. A sum that's high enough to be worthwhile, but low enough that the victim might well just decide to pay, and be done with it. Low enough that it was feasible, for someone with means, at least, to put one's hands on such an amount at short notice. Low enough that one might just wish for the whole sordid business to be done with quickly, quietly, and without attracting undue attention that might make one a target for further crimes of a similar nature.'

'I can't tell you who it is. Only that I need it more than I've ever needed anything in my life.'

He finishes his wine, pours more into his glass.

'If I give you this money, I'd want something in return. There will be certain strings attached. Do you understand what I'm saying, Helly?'

I look up at him, this man in black at the other end of the table, offering me an impossible deal. A deal that I could not accept. That I *had* to accept.

'I understand.'

'Good. I've sent the staff home for the night, had them lock up on the way out. So it's just the two of us now.' He stands up, gestures with his wine glass towards the entrance hall and the grand winding staircase. 'Shall we?'

With my heart beating hard in the base of my throat, I stand up as if on autopilot, following Alexander out of the dining room into the high-ceilinged hall, up the wide arc of the stairs. At the top, he turns left across a wide landing lit by a huge chandelier, pushing open the wooden double doors of the master bedroom.

The lighting is low, almost as if he has anticipated this moment.

In the centre of the room he stops and turns to me, holds out his hand.

And even though I'm here, and he's here, and we're standing at the foot of his four-poster bed, I still can't quite believe that it's come to this.

There will be certain strings attached.

Can I be with him for one night? To save Jason's life?

I can.

I *have* to.

PART V
THE TRUTH

64

Sunday

Snow is piled high beside the road, freshly ploughed into the verge after a heavy fall overnight. More flakes drift down to pat against the windscreen of the big Mercedes, batted effortlessly away by the windscreen wipers as we head east and south towards York. The weather is still bad enough to keep the helicopter grounded this morning.

The digital display below the car's rear-view mirror reads: 8.58 a.m.

Sleep had eventually come in jagged fragments last night after what felt like hours of lying awake in a strange bed, staring at shadows on the ceiling of an unfamiliar bedroom. When I did finally manage to sleep, my dreams were full of running, flailing, falling, of having to escape through a maze of dark corridors and huge, whirling chandeliers. And always, around every corner, there had been Alexander Sykes. Grown to an impossible height, with long arms to reach out and grab me, to pull me back into the maze just as I thought I was safe.

The money is beside me on the seat, zipped inside a small blue holdall.

Five thick packets of currency, each one sealed tight inside waterproof wrapping, with a quick-tear tab for ease of opening. The wrapping is semi-opaque, milky-white like frosted glass, but Turing's portrait on the top note is still visible. Across each opening tab is a wax Bank of England seal, a circular image of Britannia with her shield and spear. An unbroken seal, Alexander had explained, verified the correct amount of money was inside.

Four hundred fifty-pound notes to each packet. Each packet about three inches thick and worth twenty thousand pounds.

Five packets. One hundred thousand pounds in total.

I don't want to touch it. I don't even want to look at it. I just want this to be over.

But I had done what had to be done.

Traffic is light as the Mercedes rolls onwards, past fields and farmhouses blanketed pure white with snow. It feels as if everyone I see, every driver passing by, knows what happened at Fellstone Hall last night. They know what's in the bag next to me and how it got there.

I'd had no appetite for breakfast in the big dining room this morning, but somehow I still feel sick. It had been Jason's second night as a captive, and I wonder if he and Christian have eaten since they were taken, whether he is freezing; whether the pain and the cold and the hunger will keep him from sleep. I wonder how I will ever be able to tell him about last night. One day, when all of this is over, I will try to make him understand. That I did it for him. For his sons, his family. To save his life. My brother's life too.

My phone buzzes with a text from Docherty.

He's bringing the exchange forward, he says. Not noon, but 11 a.m. – less than two hours from now. *Corner of Coney Street, on St Helen's Square. Further instructions to follow.* I didn't need to look at a map to know where he meant: it was in the heart of the old city, the kind of place that would be busy with people even on a Sunday. Tourists on the ghost walk, hen and stag groups, students, day trippers, buskers – it was in a part of York that was almost always thronged with people. A good place to get lost in the crowd, I guessed. To hide in plain sight.

I reply to confirm that I'll be there, alone, with the money.

Miranda has still not got in touch. And there have been no more messages from Kat, either.

The Mercedes deposits me outside my house and here, too, everything is covered with a layer of snow, the road messy with slush from morning traffic. I'm acutely aware of walking up the drive in the same clothes I had left in last night, a dead giveaway if any of my neighbours happens to look out of the window.

The walk of shame.

That's exactly what it is.

I fumble my key into the lock and push the front door open, a tiny measure of relief when I can shut the door behind me and hear the lock click into place. I lean back against it for a moment, allowing my eyes to close as I breathe in the familiar smells of my house, my home, my normal life. The sanctuary of my family.

A noise reaches me from the kitchen. The soft, furtive scrape of a shoe on the tile floor.

I freeze, my eyes snapping open.

Someone is in the house.

Alfie? But it's far too early for him to be up on a Sunday. The thought pierces me with cold clarity: Docherty knows where I live. Perhaps he'd decided to bring the deadline forward again.

Slowly, noiselessly, I lift my car keys from the hook by the door and slip them into my pocket. I take out my phone and tap in three nines on the keypad, ready to press the dial button. In my other hand I clutch the holdall with the money. It isn't much, but it has a bit of weight to it if I can swing it hard enough.

The noise from the kitchen comes again, a chair scraping on the stone floor, cupboards opening and closing. Whoever is here, they're looking for something. Should I run? Go to a neighbour, call the police from there? I remember Docherty's instruction again. *No police.* Instead, I edge slowly along the hall, my thumb poised over the dial button of my phone. Ready to bolt back out of the front door, to my car or back out onto the street, across to a neighbour's house.

I edge nearer to the sound, peering around the door frame into the kitchen.

A figure stands with its back to me, both hands leaning on the counter. Tall, slump-shouldered, ragged. Slowly, the figure turns to face me.

A man, his face streaked with blood and dirt.

Jason.

65

Jason's eyes are shadowed with fatigue, his face thick with dark stubble, hair matted flat. His lips are cracked, bruises yellowing along his jaw and under his left eye. He looks shell-shocked, exhausted, shattered. But he gathers me into a hug as if he'll never let me go, each of us clinging to the other in an ecstasy of relief. My flawed, complicated, reckless husband, who had come back from the dark. Back from the brink.

We had lost our way. But now we've found each other again.

I try not to think about last night, about Alexander. Try to force it to the corners of my mind. It was too much, in this moment, to hold in my head. Too much to explain.

I was just relieved beyond measure that I had got my husband back. Everything else would have to wait.

'You're OK,' I say into his neck, not quite believing it. Bathing in the reality of it, that he's here, he's home. 'You're all right.'

He says nothing for a moment, only a deep exhalation of relief before he loosens the hug to look at me properly.

'Are you OK?'

'Me?' I breathe out. 'I'm fine. I am now. How did you get away?'

He shows me the palms of his hands, covered in scrapes and cuts.

'Hauled myself out through a window.'

I take his hands gently in mine.

'But how did you . . . even get back into the house?'

'Back door key under the flowerpot.'

Despite everything, I smile. The key we had always left for the boys, when they first started going out with their friends and would forget their keys every so often. We stand for a minute, holding each other. Him in torn, muddy clothes, with two days' worth of stubble; me in the black cocktail dress I had worn to Alexander's last night. I kiss him again, feeling him flinch as I brush the bruises on his face.

'Alfie's upstairs,' he says. 'Two of his mates slept over as well. They're all fast asleep.'

'Where's Christian?' I ease back from the embrace. 'Where's my brother?'

He tries to say something, his jaw clenching.

'He's . . . still there. I'm sorry, Helen. I couldn't get him out. We couldn't both . . .'

'Sit down,' I say. 'Tell me everything.'

I fill a pint glass with water from the tap and hand it to him. He drinks deeply as I fetch the red first-aid kit down from the cupboard and set about cleaning the wounds on his face, the back of his head, dabbing antiseptic and finding plasters for cuts on his hands and arms. He grits his teeth against the pain.

I lean back to get a better look at him as I work.

'When did you get back? What's happened to my brother?'

'Christian volunteered,' he says quietly. 'To stay behind.'

'Volunteered?'

'He told me to go. The barn where we were being held, there was a small window but it was high up, only within reach if one of us gave the other a leg-up. I told him I would give him a boost up to it, that I would stay while he made a run for it, but he volunteered to stay.' He looks away, his voice choked with emotion. 'He told me I should go, that you needed me. Said he'd never forgive himself if something happened to me. And neither would you.'

I cover my face with both hands, feeling the tears rise.

'Oh God. Christian.'

'When I climbed out of the window – that's how my hands got all cut up – I dropped down and ran around to the door but it was padlocked. I couldn't get him out. Then I saw movement in the main house and I knew that if I didn't go, I'd be caught. There was an old pushbike leaning up against the barn so I grabbed it and set off as fast as I could. I'm sorry. First few miles I thought they were going to drive up behind me, grab me again. So I just kept going and going, even when I was so tired I thought I couldn't carry on. Took me four hours to get back here.'

'What will they do to Christian now?'

'I don't know. They still want their money, I guess. They need him, to make the trade.'

Slowly, as if seeing me for the first time, he seems to register that I'm dressed up as if I'm going for a night out at an expensive restaurant.

'You weren't here.' He puts down the glass of water, almost empty. 'When I got back this morning. Where have you been? What's in the bag?'

Busying myself with the first aid kit, I explain to him about Docherty's demand for all of the money, the shortfall in what we had already spent. Heat creeps up my neck, into my cheeks.

How did we get here, Jason? How did it come to this?

'I got it,' I say. 'I got what we need.'

'Where from?'

'A friend.' I look away. 'I don't have time to explain it now. Not while my brother is still out there.'

His face darkens. 'Just tell me.'

'I can't. Not until Christian is safe.'

'We can't have secrets from each other, Helen. Not anymore, not after this.'

A hot flare of indignation spreads through my chest. 'You want to talk about secrets? How about yours?'

'What do you mean?'

'I know about Paris. And Chantelle, and Summer. Your little folder of women, of hotels. How many are there? How many have there been?'

He stares at me in disbelief, as if searching for the right thing to say.

'No,' he says finally. 'It's not . . . that.'

'An abortion clinic, Jason. I mean . . . I don't even know what to say.'

He puts a hand on my shoulder. 'You've got this all wrong. I would never do that.'

'Then *tell* me. Tell me about Paris, and all the others.'

He gestures at the blue holdall at my feet. 'I will,' he says. 'As soon as you tell me how you got *that*.'

We stare at each other for a long moment in the silence of our kitchen, a stand-off, neither willing to give ground or advance any further. Off in the distance, I can just about hear the faint peal of church bells from St Peter's, ringing in the Sunday morning service.

I look at my watch. Ten o'clock.

'It doesn't matter now,' I say. 'Because we only have an hour until we're supposed to make the exchange with Docherty and all the rest of the money is locked up at Christian's house. We don't have the combination to the safe.'

'Yes, we do,' he says. 'He made me memorise it last night, before I got out.'

'Really?'

'I'll go.' He tries to stand up, wincing with the effort.

'The state you're in? No way. You need to eat something, get a change of clothes. I'll drive over there and get it myself. Then we'll both head into town for the exchange.'

'You're sure?'

'Positive.'

He writes the combination to the safe on the back of an envelope and hands it to me.

I lay my palm on his cheek, thick with salt-and-pepper stubble. We had so much to talk about, to hear from each other, to admit, perhaps to forgive. But there was no time for any of it now.

'Stay here,' I say. 'I'll be as quick as I can.'

66

Miranda and Christian's house is just as we'd left it on Friday night.

I bypass the mess in the kitchen and go straight up the stairs, up to the first floor, wondering whether this will be the last time I ever set foot in this house. My brother's pride and joy. If his financial troubles were as bad as they'd been described, perhaps it would be snatched out from under him in a matter of weeks. I had no idea how long these things took.

In the master bedroom, I take down the watercolour painting of Miranda from the wall to reveal the steel face of the safe. Checking the code Jason had written on the back of the envelope, I tap in the combination and feel a pulse of relief when the lock duly clicks and the door opens. One half of the safe is full of money, stacked from bottom to top, a solid square mass of tightly packed notes like some huge book with thousands of pages.

My phone buzzes with a pair of texts from Docherty.

Change of plan re the money.
New venue.

For a second I think he's changed his mind, decided he wants more money, my stomach twisting with panic. Then the phone starts to ring, his name showing on the screen.

'Have you got it?' He doesn't bother with a greeting. 'All of it?'

'Yes. I'm looking at it now. Can I speak to my brother?'

'All in good time. But we need to change things up a little bit.'

I wonder if he's been spooked by Jason's escape.

'The place in town?'

'No,' he says. 'Let's get it over with. Thirty minutes from now.'

I check my watch. Thirty minutes was barely enough time to get the money from Miranda's house and get to the meeting point in the middle of town. I start to explain this to him but he cuts me off.

'Here's how it's going to work,' he says. 'We're going to come to your house to collect the money. Once we've counted it – if it's all there – we release your brother. And then you never see us again and everyone gets on with their lives. Happily ever after. Do you understand?'

'We've got your money, I swear, every single–'

'*Do you understand?*'

Nausea rises, but I push it down.

'Yes.'

'Good. And is there anyone else at your house right now? Anyone who might cause a complication or ask the wrong question?'

'My son is there,' I say it quietly. 'With two of his friends. They're only eighteen. I'll go anywhere, but please . . . anywhere but there.'

He curses under his breath, irritation curdling into impatience. 'OK. Then where?'

I clutch desperately for an idea, but the only place I can think of is mum's house. I give Docherty her address, telling him the house will be empty apart from me.

More silence, before he replies. 'If there's anyone else there waiting for us, if I even get a sniff of the police, I will cut your brother's throat. That's a promise.'

The line goes dead.

With trembling hands, I text Jason the change of plan, telling him I'll pick him up on the way to my mum's house.

It only occurs to me then that I've forgotten to bring something rather important.

Stupid. I don't have time for this. My head is so full, my brain so exhausted and yet still trying to run at a hundred miles an hour, that I can't think more than ten minutes ahead. I pull open wardrobes in search of a suitable bag. Off the master bedroom is Miranda's dressing room, with mirrored doors on two sides and racks of shoes reaching to shoulder height. I find one wardrobe full of wheeled suitcases of different sizes, half of them plain black, half in a variety of different pastel shades. I choose a medium-sized black case and cram all the money inside. When I'm finished, it only just shuts and I have to put my knee on the casing to pull the zip all the way around.

Back at the car, I heave the case onto the back seat and drive home as fast as I dare. Jason is waiting for me on the pavement, with the blue holdall full of Alexander's money. He's put on clean clothes but still looks haggard, as if he's hanging on by a thread.

We arrive at my mum's house with five minutes to spare, wheeling the case into the kitchen.

'Jason,' I say. 'You shouldn't be here, they might get angry if they see you. I've told them it's just me. You could go upstairs, wait up there.'

But he's shaking his head. 'I'm not letting you face them alone. Not anymore.'

'But what if they—'

'I don't care.' He takes my hand. 'We're in this together.'

I'm too tired to argue with him. My other hand, holding my phone, is shaking. I put it down on the counter and make a fist, the skin showing white over my knuckles.

This was it.

The moment of truth.

Soon, this nightmare would be over. Christian would come home. We would pick up our normal lives again.

The house is silent, everything solid and still, frozen in time like a museum, like a—

I stop. Listen. Not *quite* silent.

The sound comes again. A soft creak of upholstery. A shuffle of clothes. Downstairs.

There is someone else here. Has Docherty got here before me? Straining my ears, I walk quietly into the little front room that Mum uses as a dining room. Empty. The only other door is ajar. I push it open, ready to confront whoever is here, to get rid of them if I have to before—

My mother is sitting in the lounge.

She's perched on the end of the sofa, still with her coat and scarf on, handbag beside her. As if she's waiting for something. She looks up when I walk in, but doesn't speak. Closed curtains have left the room in semi-darkness.

'Mum?' I sit down next to her, put a hand on her knee. 'What are you doing here?'

She looks at me, her eyes wandering to the mantelpiece, the armchair, a framed picture on the wall before her gaze returns to me. She holds up the front door key, still in her gloved hand.

'I live here, love.'

'But . . . you're supposed to be staying at Harcourt Park until tomorrow. I was going to come and pick you up.'

'Thought I'd save you the bother, you've been so busy lately. Nice young man on reception said he'd call a taxi for me. They even paid for it.'

'Where are all your things, Mum? Your clothes?'

She looks at me blankly for a few seconds, then gestures vaguely towards the hallway.

'How . . . long have you been sitting here, Mum?'

'Where?' Her voice is flat. 'Oh. Only twenty minutes. Or an hour? Not long, love.'

The old wooden clock on the wall says it's only a couple of minutes before the hour. Docherty would be here any moment. There was no time to take Mum to my house, or anywhere else. Not even really anyone I can call. On a different day I would have called my brother, or my husband, or Kat to come over and drive her back to my house, somewhere safe.

But today, there is no one.

I pull open the curtains at the window in time to see a grey Volvo pulling up. Three figures inside, one in the front, two in the back.

It is too late.

They are here.

67

My brother looks almost as bad as Jason. His face is puffy and bruised, his eyes bloodshot, skin rubbed raw around his wrists. He had limped as he was pushed in at gunpoint, stumbling into me as if his legs could barely hold him up.

But he's here. He's alive. He's back. We exchanged a few brief words when he first walked in, but since then he's been mostly silent, just watching everything unfold. He stands on one side of me, Jason on the other, all three of us backed up against the counter in my mother's kitchen. Roe holds a pistol on us, at waist height, almost casually, a glint of pure distilled malice in his eyes as if he'd like nothing better than to shoot us all one after the other. I didn't want my mum to get mixed up in this – or see what was going on – so I'd told her to wait in the lounge for ten minutes. Not to open the door until I went back in.

Docherty is counting the money.

He's unloaded the contents of the suitcase onto my mother's kitchen table and is busy checking it with meticulous care, stacking it back inside as he goes. A short-bladed knife is tucked into the waistband of his jeans.

After a few minutes of counting, he holds up one of the sealed packets that Alexander had given me.

'What's this all about, then?' He examines it, turning it over in his hands. 'Why are these fifties wrapped and the rest aren't?'

His dark eyes lock onto me.

'There was a shortfall, we'd spent some of it already. I had to make up what was missing.' I swallow. 'I was able to get it from somewhere else.'

'From who?'

'You've got your money, why does it matter?'

'*Who?*'

I keep my eyes on the floor. 'A friend.'

'You must have *very* rich friends.'

Jason shifts beside me.

'No.' His voice is taut. 'We don't.'

Docherty gestures at me with one of the packets. 'Sounds like *she* does, though.'

'Helen?' Jason half turns towards me. 'How did you do this? Who did you—'

Roe raises the gun and points it at Jason's forehead.

'That's enough from you.' He closes one eye, sighting down the barrel of the black pistol. 'You're already in my bad books for being a sneaky bastard and running off on us when we asked you *very nicely* to stay in the barn. I should shoot you just for that. You'd better wind your neck in, mate, or I *will* shoot you now. And your wife too.'

I take Jason's hand, clasping it in mine.

'You need to know something.' I turn towards him. 'About last night.'

He stiffens, won't look at me. 'Whatever happened, it doesn't—'

'Nothing happened,' I say. '*Nothing.* We had dinner, we talked. We went upstairs to the safe, and he gave me the money. All he wanted from me was that I told him the truth. And then he said he was glad to be able to help, because I was his oldest friend.'

When Alexander had said there were *strings attached* if he was to give me money, it meant he had wanted the full story. To know what was really going on, and why I was so desperate. But there was still shame in the knowledge that I had been mentally *prepared* to do it. I had resigned myself to it. I had been willing to go through with it as I climbed that big staircase at his house.

Jason gives a reluctant nod. 'That was it? You didn't spend the night in his bed?'

'No. Nothing like that.'

Roe gives a grunt of disgust. I ignore him.

'Alexander was kind of shocked, to be honest, that I thought that was what he meant. So now you know. I'm sorry I didn't tell you earlier but I was angry about your . . . about the folder. The names of those women.'

Jason exhales hard, almost a laugh. 'God no, Helen.'

'Paris,' I say quietly. 'Are you sleeping with her?'

'No, love. I'm not sleeping with her. I'm *helping* her. I've been helping all of them.'

'Who?'

'There's only so much I can do in my day job, with all the budget cuts. We've been hit in social services just as hard as everyone else, and there are so many of these young people – young women, a lot of the time, young single mums – who end up falling through the cracks. I've just been trying to help people who desperately need it, off the books if I have to. Hotels to get them away from abusive partners, a bit of money to help them get set up somewhere else so they can start again, healthcare if they need it. Paying off bad debts to bad people. When I saw that cash on New Year's Eve I knew I could do some *good* with it. Genuine good. And that's what I've been doing.'

I remember Kat's face when I'd told her about the folder of names in Jason's neat handwriting. She had not believed it, not for a second.

I shouldn't have believed it either.

'I'm sorry,' I say. 'I should have believed you. Should have asked you.'

'Listen,' his voice cracks. 'You've got absolutely *nothing* to apologise for. I should have been honest with you from—'

Docherty claps his hands abruptly. 'Right!' he says. 'Good news and bad news, Christian. Which one do you want first?'

My brother, who has barely spoken since he arrived and still seems a bit shell-shocked, blinks up at his captor.

'What?'

'It's not complicated, boss. Good news, or bad news. Which one do you want to hear first?'

'Well, good news, I suppose.'

'Fair enough. The good news is that the money's all here. I mean, I haven't opened these dinky little packets that your sister got from her *friend*.' He indicates the five wrapped packets from Alexander, still in the blue holdall. 'But they look legit to me. So, happy days.'

'Happy days,' Roe repeats.

Docherty lets the silence spool out for a few seconds. 'Well,' he says. 'We can't leave everyone in suspense. Aren't you going to ask about the bad news?'

'You've got your money.' Christian shifts uneasily beside me. 'You've got what you wanted. Now leave us in peace.'

Docherty shakes his head. 'Not before the bad news, I'm afraid.' He crosses his arms, staring directly at my brother. 'The bad news is, Christian, I've decided to renegotiate our little deal.'

'I don't—'

'To be specific, my fee. Because I don't think ten per cent is going to be enough anymore.' He grins. 'I think fifty-fifty is a much fairer split, don't you?'

68

I turn towards my brother.

'What deal?' I say. 'Christian, what's he talking about?'

My brother has his hands half-up, palms showing. 'Honestly,' he says. 'I've no idea what he means.'

Docherty swings the case off the table and stands it upright by the door.

'I'm trying to be reasonable, boss. But if that's the way you want to play it, my fee's going to go up again.'

'Christian?' I put a hand on his arm. He's shaking. 'Talk to us.'

'This is mad,' he mutters. 'He's just trying to mess with you.'

But his neck is colouring, filling with a deep red blush. 'He's lying, I would never—'

Jason cuts him off. 'You knew where we were,' he says. 'Yesterday in the barn, when I was telling you to make a run for it. You said it *was five miles to the nearest village.* Then Roe burst in with the gun and I thought I was about to die. But later on, I remembered, couldn't work out how you knew it was five miles.'

Christian is talking across him now, his voice rising, but I tune him out. My mind flashes on all of the moments since the day we found the backpack in that cave, all of the arguments and comments and persuasive tactics Christian had used.

My brother, who had wanted to keep the money, right from the start.

My brother, who had paid someone to fabricate a story online about bank robbers rotting in jail, to convince us this was a *victimless crime*.

My brother, who had more to lose than all of us.

My brother.

Something else comes to me, a throwaway remark Kat had made when she'd come to pick up her share of the money. *Only one thing worse than being poor. And that's being rich first. Then poor.* And Docherty, who had been willing to come here, to accept a change of venue at short notice rather than dictating all the terms himself – which is what a ruthless, pitiless kidnapper would surely do. Docherty, instead, was just someone who was doing what he was told.

There is a surging, rushing noise in my ears like the ocean crashing over my head, and suddenly I can't breathe, can't bear to be in this room with him a moment longer. Thinking of everything he has put us through in the last forty-eight hours.

I look at my brother again, at the cuts and bruises on his face. Were they even real?

'Christian?' My voice cracks. 'What did you do?'

'This is bullshit,' he says.

'Jason?' I grab my husband's hand. 'Talk to me.'

He's shaking his head. 'And that's why he wanted to stay in that barn, instead of making a run for it. He knew there was no danger in staying. He knew there was no risk. And once I was gone they could relax, give up the whole charade. It was all a lot easier, a lot more comfortable for him.'

Suddenly it all seems horribly clear. I stare at my brother, but he won't look at me.

'You paid them to do it, didn't you, Christian? You staged it. So that you could have all the money for yourself and we'd be none the wiser. You set the whole thing up, didn't you? So you could keep all of it, keep your bloody company afloat? Docherty's cut was going to be ten per cent, was it? But you picked the wrong people, and now they've double-crossed you.'

'Look,' Docherty says. 'I can see this is a family thing. Complicated. I *get* it. We're just going to leave now, OK? Let you good people sort it out among yourselves. I'll leave your share where we agreed, Christian.'

He grabs the blue holdall from the table and turns to the kitchen door.

But Roe stays where he is.

He turns the gun towards Jason.

'Hang on,' he says over his shoulder. 'We still haven't given this one his punishment for running off.' He raises the pistol, holding it inches from my husband's head. 'Told you, didn't I? Next time it would be loaded. It's loaded now. So have you got any last requests?'

I hold a tentative hand up. 'Please. Tie us up, lock the doors, do whatever you want. Take all the money, just leave. *Please*, I'm begging you.'

Roe ignores me.

'Any last words, Jason? For your wife?'

'Just let my wife go. Let her leave, now.'

Jason squeezes my hand. I squeeze back.

Roe holds the gun on him, as steady as a rock. 'I don't think so.'

His finger tightens around the trigger.

Jason closes his eyes.

At the last moment, Roe pivots and turns in one fluid movement.

He fires a single shot into the side of Docherty's head.

The explosion of sound is horrifically loud and everyone flinches backwards in the same moment.

Docherty crashes back against the kitchen table, a spray of blood up the wall.

Jason grabs me. Christian shouts an obscenity, over and over again.

Roe looks down at his partner, dying on the floor, with something like fascination.

'Now *that's* what I call a renegotiation.' He turns the gun towards Christian. 'I think I'll go for *one hundred* per cent now. And zero witnesses.'

'No,' Christian says, putting his hand up. 'Please.'

Roe picks up one of the sealed packs of notes from the blue holdall and tosses it to my brother.

'But first, you can get rid of that wrapping. You must think I'm thick, I'm not having any tracking devices attached to my money.'

Christian turns the pack over in his hands, reaching for the red tab, pulling it open as if he was unwrapping a parcel. The plastic strip pulls all the way around, cutting through the Bank of England logo, revealing a pristine stack of fifty-pound notes inside.

Roe gestures with the gun. 'And the rest.'

Christian puts the unwrapped money back into the blue holdall, taking out another of the packages to repeat the process.

Three things happen then, so close together as to be almost simultaneous.

The sealed packet that Christian is tearing open explodes with a concussive *whump*, blasts of blood-red paint and stinging white smoke spraying out in every direction, the room suddenly filled with a kaleidoscope of sticky dye and acrid gas and shouting, screaming people.

Christian lunges for the gun.

And a fraction of a second later – almost as if it is an unconscious reflex – Roe jerks the trigger.

THREE DAYS LATER

69

The four of us sit in the lounge, watching the end of *News at Ten*. Mum is in between Alfie and me on the sofa, Jason in the armchair with Prim curled in his lap, purring. She's been very possessive of him since he's returned, constantly following him around the house and meowing for attention. On the TV, the newsreader gives another brief update on the case: a mysterious double shooting on a quiet street in York, a police investigation still in its early stages. For a couple of days, the media couldn't get enough of it: a story of kidnapping, money and murder. A normal family caught in the middle of a gangland feud. But as the dust has started to settle, it's already dropping down the running order.

Christian had almost died on our mother's kitchen floor.

The bullet had missed his heart by half an inch.

I'd been convinced he *was* going to die. Convinced I was watching my brother take his last breath. Feeling it was somehow my fault, that it had ended like this. He'd been rushed to hospital for six hours of emergency surgery. It's still early days, but it looks like he's going to pull through, against all the odds. I've been to see him every day since it happened, sitting with Miranda, talking to Christian and holding his hand. Just like the way I'd held his hand in that moment of stunned silence after the blast in my mother's kitchen, as Jason was calling 999, pulling off his jumper and using it to put pressure on the wound, our ears still ringing, eyes streaming from the tear gas. I had told my brother to hold on, even as his grip started to slacken.

He'd been shot in the split second after the dye pack had exploded in his hands, throwing red paint and tear gas in all directions. I'd heard afterwards from a police officer that they had been used by banks for decades as an anti-robbery measure, to mark stolen currency so it was rendered useless – and mark the perpetrator too. Of the five sealed packets of money Alexander had given me, three were actually explosive dye packs.

That was also what he'd meant, I've learned since, by *strings attached*.

That he wanted to help me, to help catch the people threatening my family.

Docherty had already paid the ultimate price. But with a record of offending and jail time going back twenty years, he's not attracted much public sympathy. His young partner, Roe, has vanished without trace. His DNA, his fingerprints, did not appear on any criminal database, and the police don't seem to have any good leads on tracking him down.

The £1.6m is gone too. Presumably, Roe is off somewhere with a new name, a new identity, a new passport and plenty of money left over to enjoy. I don't really care. I just want my life back as it was, a return to normality. I hope, wherever Roe is, he's enjoying it. That he thinks it was worth it.

The truth is more complicated than the police know. But all of us six from that weekend, who actually *know* the truth, have a lot to lose by revealing it. A man was dead, and all of us were complicit in one way or another. We had all played a part in the events that brought him to the kitchen of my mother's house, one Sunday morning in late January.

I try not to think too much about it.

I don't know what I'll say to my brother when the doctors wake him from the induced coma. The only words I have for him right now are still full of anger and disbelief. I'll sit down with him at some point in the future, I suppose. But not yet. From what I've heard, his mother-in-law has stepped in to throw him a financial lifeline and the house, at least, will be saved. She evidently couldn't bear the thought – the embarrassment – of her daughter being made homeless.

Miranda, for her part, has opted to stay with Christian for the time being. At least while he is convalescing, until he's back on his feet. After that, who knows? She had been planning to leave him for months before the events that started on New Year's Eve, had started the ball rolling by emailing a family law firm in the first week of January. I guess time will tell whether she finally decides to go through with it.

Kat has been released on bail; it seems the police are not really sure what to charge her with. She's got her hands full looking after Dev, since his release from hospital.

I've exchanged a few messages with Alexander, and we've agreed to meet up soon for lunch. The three of us, Jason included.

Mum has been staying with us since Sunday, wearing mostly my clothes since her sudden departure from her own house. Her place is a crime scene, crawled over and examined in minute detail by white-suited forensic officers. She had become quite upset at all the strangers in her house that day, distressed and tearful and unable to understand what was going on amid the chaos and shouting and running, first the police and paramedics, then the detectives and forensics people, all of them clomping through her little house. So Alfie had come over in an Uber to pick her up and take her back to ours and since that day she's been installed in the spare room, in my elder son's room. I'm not sure what we'll do when he comes home from London next, I guess he'll have to share with his brother again just like they did when they were little.

Alfie sits next to her on the sofa, holding her hand. She likes to sit with him, sometimes turning her head to study his profile.

Of the two boys he's the one who looks most like my dad did when he was young, he has the same nose, the same chin, same dimples. Looking at pictures of Dad as a young man, the resemblance is really quite striking.

After the national news, the regional bulletin comes on and there is a short item on *BBC Look North* about the case. But it's just a rehash of the national story, the shock of such violence and more bemused neighbours reflecting once again that *You don't expect that kind of thing to happen around here.* As the newsreader speaks, the screen switches to footage of my mum's house as it had looked a few days ago, with white-clad scenes-of-crime people buzzing in and out.

Mum is suddenly indignant. 'When am I going to get my house back? That's what I'd like to know. All my own things, my lovely kitchen?'

'The police said they could release it back to us next week, Mum. Probably. Some of your things maybe a little longer. But you can stay here as long as you like. I was thinking actually whether you might want to move in properly, live with us, it'd be nice to—'

'They stole them all, you know? All my clothes.'

Alfie turns to her. 'Who did, Grandma?'

'Those people.' She gestures vaguely with her hand. 'You know.'

'The police officers?'

'No.' She tuts with impatience. 'Those people at . . . thingy park. The place where I went the other week. Took them all. *Disgraceful.*'

'I don't think they did, Grandma.'

But she continues in this vein as the weather comes on, a stream of rambling, confused discontent about the police, the cost of buses, the weatherman's tie, the disgraceful theft of her clothes by the staff at Harcourt Park. Jason catches my eye, raises an eyebrow. It was no good. You couldn't really talk to her when she got a bee in her bonnet now. Sometimes the only way to convince her was to actually *show* her.

I get off the sofa and climb wearily upstairs. Since Christian was shot it's been a horrible, agonising, all-consuming three days, praying that he will pull through. Everything else has had to wait. In the spare room, I pull up the valance hanging down over the edge of her bed. *There*. Just as I'd thought. Mum's case lies underneath, just where she always put it when she came to stay. Out of the way so no one tripped over it. The clothes she *supposed* had been stolen by staff at the retirement village. With an effort, I heave it out from under the bed. It's full, another load for the washing machine, no doubt. I find the zip and pull it all the way around, flipping the top of the case open.

It *is* full—

—of money.

Familiar stacks of notes, bundled together.

Dizziness clouds my vision.

I flash on an image of my mum at her house on Sunday, emerging from the lounge into the midst of the chaos and confusion, amid the shouting and running and panic, the desperate ambulance call for my brother fighting for his life with a corpse beside him, tear gas and red dye mingled with Docherty's blood sprayed up the wall.

Roe had grabbed the wrong case in the confusion.

A black wheelie case by the kitchen door, similar to the one I'd brought from Miranda's house.

Alfie had come over later in an Uber to bring Mum home. My son had simply taken the case that remained, assuming it was hers.

I stare at the money for a long minute, at the packs of fifties and twenties jammed together in a great solid mass, muffled sounds of the TV drifting up from below.

Then I zip the case shut and ease it back under the bed.

I stand up, switch off the light, and pull the door closed behind me.

Acknowledgements

This book is a real milestone for me, as it's my tenth published novel.

To have reached double figures feels magical, unbelievable – particularly as it doesn't seem very long since my first book came out. Before finding a publisher, I spent about a decade writing, re-writing, trying to learn the craft, a period which included the creation of a novel that has still never seen the light of day. At the time, all I hoped for was to get a single novel out there with my name on it – the idea of reaching *ten* was so far over the horizon I couldn't even imagine it.

I first signed on the dotted line with my publisher, Bonnier, in April 2016 and I feel very lucky to have been with them since the start of my publishing journey. I'm extremely grateful to my editor, Sophie Orme, and to her colleagues Sarah Benton, Holly Milnes, Eleanor Stammeijer, Rachel Johnson, Georgia Marshall, Chelsea Graham, Alice Dovey and Beth Whitelaw.

While I was working on this story, I also reached another milestone: that my books have sold more than three million copies in the UK across all formats. It means so much to know that my books are read and enjoyed by so many people, even though *three million* is an almost unimaginable number of copies. Suffice to say it's far beyond even the wildest dreams I had when my debut, *Lies*, first hit the shelves in 2017. So huge thanks to *you*, for picking up this book and being part of the journey.

I was a reader long before I was a writer, and one of the first books that really switched me on to thrillers was *A Simple Plan* by Scott Smith. It's one of my favourite books and was my gateway, in a sense, to the stories I love to write now. As the story of a moral dilemma involving a large amount of dubious cash, it was also part of the inspiration for *The Weekend*.

Many thanks to the author and finance expert Adam Oyebanji, who gave an excellent online talk on money laundering which I found very useful; and likewise to the Crime Writers' Association for facilitating the event. Also to family friend Jennie Hullis for guidance on the due diligence required of banks and other financial institutions in this area. *The Secret Magistrate*, published by Hawksmoor Publishing, gave me a useful insight into the world of the magistrates' courts. Any errors or omissions in areas of law and finance are, of course, mine.

Thanks as ever to my excellent agent Camilla Bolton and the team at Darley Anderson Literary Agency including Jade Kavanagh, Francesca Edwards, Georgia Schindler, Georgia Fuller, Ilaria Albani, Sarah Brooks, Helen Dudley, Rosanna Bellingham and Janice Tedder. Also to Sheila David for her work to bring my books to the screen.

The character of DC Wilf Pritchard was named at the request of Nicola Wood, who won a charity auction at an event to raise money for the Broxtowe Women's Project. The Project does great work to help women experiencing domestic abuse in this part of Nottinghamshire, and I was glad to be able to help.

Thanks as always to my family, for putting up with me. For my brilliant wife Sally, and our wonderful children, Sophie and Tom.

This book is dedicated to some family friends with whom we have shared many holidays and short breaks in some beautiful parts of the UK. Those trips also inspired the opening of this story, and so the book is dedicated to four families. To the Coffeys – Paul, Jo, Grace and Ella – and the Lloyds – Charlotte, Gary, Georgia and Hugh – who came with us on many New Year trips to the North Yorkshire Dales. And to Paul and Jude Harmer, Tracy and Andy Cruickshank, with whom we have shared trips to the Derbyshire Peak District which involved some poker games (and a water bottle that almost got lost).

Finally, for the record, I'd just like to say that *all* of us would do the right thing if we ever found a bag full of money in a cave.

Probably.

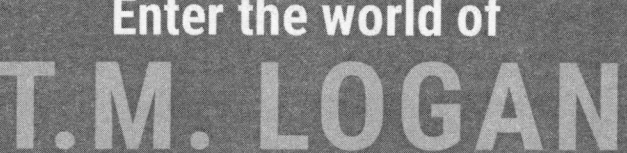

Hello,

I'm often asked if I have a favourite book, or a favourite thriller. It's a difficult question to answer, but a place in my top five would definitely go to *A Simple Plan* by Scott Smith. Along with a few others – including *Tell No One* by Harlan Coben – it was my gateway into thrillers and one of the novels that really inspired me to try writing my own books.

Like all great books it really puts you there in the shoes of the protagonist – in the case of *A Simple Plan*, it's a man grappling with a moral dilemma involving money from a dubious source. The first time I read it, I was completely hooked by the deadly progression of the story, of the spiral of choices one after another that lead him down a very dark path. Without giving away any spoilers, he starts to justify all kinds of things to himself – until he's gone so far he can't turn back.

Like many of the best tales, it made me ask yourself *What would I do in that situation? What choices would I make? How far would I go?* It's one of those moral questions that has always fascinated me and I wanted to explore it with my own story. That was where *The Weekend* started.

My next thriller will be coming out in early 2027 and if you'd like to be the first to hear more about it, you can join my free Readers' Club at www.tmlogan.com. Just click on the yellow 'Sign up' button, it only takes a moment and I promise I won't spam you with too many emails.

All your information will be kept private and confidential by my publisher Bonnier Zaffre, and it will never be passed on to a third party. I'll get in touch every so often with news about my books, giveaways, cover reveals, events and more. When I have news, members of my Readers' Club are always the first to know – so sign up for free if you'd like to become a member (you can unsubscribe at any time).

And lastly, a quick favour ... if you have a minute, please do rate and review *The Weekend* on Amazon, Goodreads or any other e-store, on your blog or social media accounts, talk about it with friends, family or reading groups. Sharing your thoughts and views helps other readers, and I always enjoy hearing what people think about my books.

Thank you again for reading *The Weekend*, I really appreciate it.

Best wishes,
Tim

Read more from
THE MASTER OF THE UP-ALL-NIGHT THRILLER
T.M. LOGAN

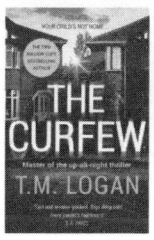    

Can't get enough?
Sign up to T.M. Logan's newsletter for exclusive content and regular updates.
https://geni.us/TMLoganNewsletter

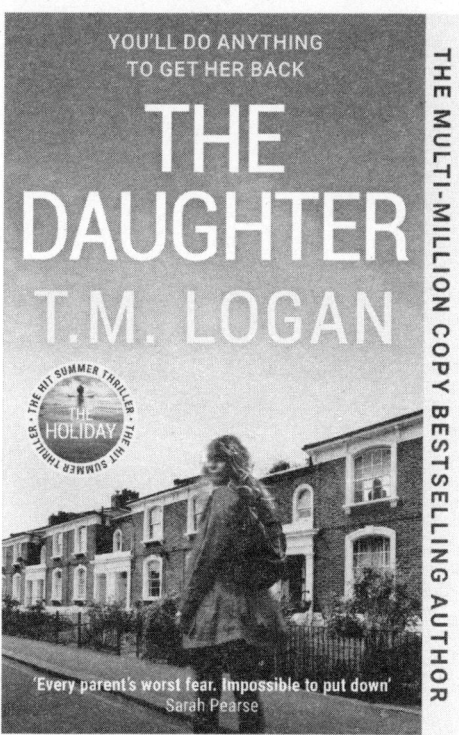

"Clear your schedule because you won't want to put this down!"

Lauren can't wait to see her daughter again, to pick her up from university at the end of her first term. But when she arrives at her hall and knocks on the door to her room, a stranger opens it.

At first, Lauren thinks she must have the wrong room, or the wrong floor. Maybe even the wrong building.

But she soon realises the truth: Evie's not there. She hasn't been there for weeks. So where is she?

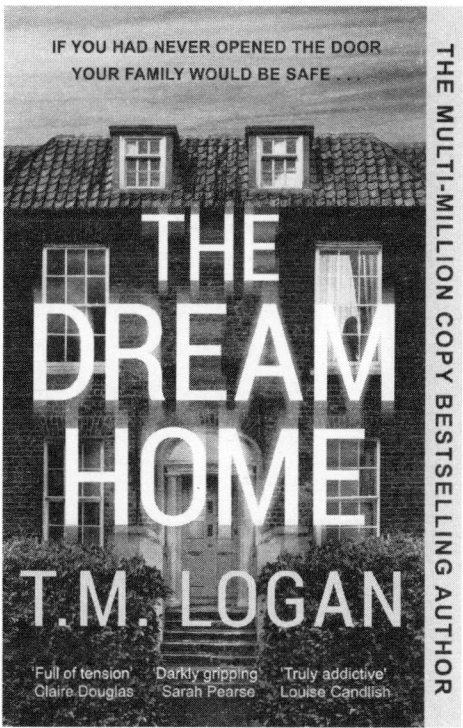

> "Everything you'd want from a thriller ...
> I really can't fault it"

Adam and Jess, along with their three children, move into a beautiful new home: a rambling Victorian house in a nice neighbourhood, right at the top of their price range. Then Adam discovers a door hidden behind a fitted wardrobe, concealing a secret room.

But like the house, Adam has his secrets too. And soon he will find himself setting in motion a series of events that will place his family in terrible danger . . .